W9-AUY-386

THE
SMOKE

THE
SMOKE

A Creeping Narrative

TONY
BROADBENT

THOMAS DUNNE BOOKS
St. Martin's Minotaur
New York

THOMAS DUNNE BOOKS.
An imprint of St. Martin's Press.

www.minotaurbooks.com

ISBN 0-312-29027-6

First Edition: September 2002

10 9 8 7 6 5 4 3 2 1

For my mum and dad.

And for Chris's mum and dad.

And for the men of the Fourth Service.

"Heroes, all."

Acknowledgements

As any writer will tell you, writing is a solitary business, but the truth is, if you're fortunate, you never ever really work alone or unaided.

Thanks to Diana Condell and Philip Dutton of the Imperial War Museum in London for their help, and to the museum for their permanent exhibit remembering the Merchant Navy in World War II. Thanks also to Philip Mansfield for being my guide backstage at the London Palladium.

I'd also like to acknowledge Robert Murphy's gem of a book, *Smash and Grab: Gangsters in the London Underworld*. Faber & Faber Ltd., 1993. Thanks, Bob, for 'filling me in on the business.'

Special thanks to family and friends for their untold help and support. Especially to my wife, Christine; my brother, Seth, and his wife, Helen; Barry and Mary Tomalin; Curt and Linda Fischer; Kirk Russell; Steve Rustad; and, of course, the indomitable, irrepressible Chris Haigh.

Thanks to the wonderful Bill and Elaine Petrocelli, and everyone at the Book Passage Mystery Writers Conference, particularly, the ever delightful Marilyn Wallace, Judy Greber, and Penny Warner.

Thanks to my marvelous agent, Jill Grosjean, for her tenacity and unwavering belief in Seth and Jethro, and me. And to my editor, Pete Wolverton. 'Well met, indeed, my friend.'

And thanks, always and forever, to 'the Angel in the Hawaiian shirt.'

Glossary of London Underworld Slang

Apples and pears: stairs
Bang to rights: caught red-handed
Beak: magistrate
Bent: crooked
Berk: idiot, or worse (Berkeley Hunt)
Blitz: the Blitz. Period of Nazi bombing of London in WWII
Blow: blowing a safe open with explosives
Blower: telephone
Bones: form of skeleton key
Brass: a prostitute, or money
Butchers: to look (butcher's hook)
Case: to survey, or check out premises prior to burglary
Century: one hundred; £100
China: close friend; mate (an old china plate)
Chiv: a knife or razor for cutting and slashing, not for stabbing
Claret: blood

Climb/er: usually refers to the act of cat-burgling; or a cat burglar
Cobblers: a lot of nonsense (cobbler's awls = balls)
Copper: a policeman
Cosh: a club made of lead, iron, wood, or hardened leather
Crack: to open a safe
Creep: entering a dwelling by night, quietly
Creeper: cat burglar
Dabs: fingerprints
Daisy roots: boots
Dip/Dipper: refers to a pickpocket
Doddle: anything easy to achieve
Dog and bone: a telephone
Drum: someone's house or flat
Face: known and reputable villain
Fence: receiver of and/or trader in stolen property
Fiver: five pounds sterling; £5

Flim: five pounds sterling; £5

Grass: an informer; to inform

Guv'nor: gang boss or senior policeman

Half-a-bar/-sheet: ten shillings

Jargoons: artificial stones

Larruping: beating about the bush,
talking too much

Linens: newspapers (linen drapers)

Loiding: 'loid/celluloid; opening a
door catch with a piece of flat celluloid plastic

Manor: the territory of a particular
policeman or criminal

Minder: bodyguard, trouble-shooter

Monkey: five hundred pounds sterling; £500

Nancy: homosexual

Nark: an informer

Nosh: food

Oncers: one-pound notes

Old Bill: the police

Petercane: small crowbar

Peterman: safe-breaker

Ponce: pimp

Pony: twenty-five quid; £25

Quid: one pound sterling; £1

Rabbit: talk (rabbit and pork)

Rosy Lee: tea

Screwsman: burglar or safe-breaker

Skels: form of skeleton key

Smoke: London ('the Smoke')

Snout: informer; or cigarette

Spieler: gambling club

Strength: information; facts

Strides: a pair of trousers

Stripe: to cut someone's face

Stumm: to stay silent

Swallow: to accept a situation without protest

Tart: prostitute

Tealeaf: thief

Team: a gang of people that regularly
work together

Tearaway: small-time criminal, known
to be reckless and violent

Tod: on own; alone (Tod Sloane)

Tom: jewellery; also prostitute

Tomfoolery: jewellery

Ton: a hundred

Tooled up: equipped with weapons

Top: to kill

Tosser: a dubious character

Trouble and strife: wife

Turned over: any premises raided by
the police

Turtledoves, turtles: gloves

Twirl: key, skeleton key

Villain: a crook of some standing

Wilkie bards: playing cards

Workman: a person employed in a
drinking club or spieler

But First, A Word or Two in Your Shell-Like Ear

The War had ended. But the peace that followed was far worse than anyone could've ever expected. Rationing was in full force, we all had to carry identity cards, crime was on the rise, and there was masses of unrest. Bread went on ration in the summer of '46 and was kept on for over two years, and they'd never had to do that once during all the fighting. Then they cut the meat allowance in half, and tried to make up for it by bringing in horse meat, whale steaks, and something called 'snoek'—don't ask me what the hell that was when it was at home, because it came in a tin and tasted bloody awful. But that was just about par for the course for anything you could officially get your hands on, as anything half-way decent went straightaway for export. You had to put up with it though, because there was nothing else. Nothing. And round London's East End, or what was left of it after the Blitz, a good few people started eyeing their cats and dogs in a different light, I can tell you. Make do and mend, it was called.

And just to rub it all in, it was the cruellest winter in living memory. The River Thames froze over and snow blanketed the streets. And as if that wasn't bad enough, the idiots had gone and nationalised the coal mines. And when the Smithfield Market porters went on strike, they had to send the Army in to keep the meat moving. There would have been rioting in the streets otherwise, and that was something the powers that be could never let happen. And in those first bone-chilling months of 1947, it looked as if Clement Attlee's Labour Government had done what even Adolf Hitler hadn't managed to do; bring the country to its knees.

There was no heat, no light, and no water; factories were at a complete standstill, and so were the roads and the railways. Big Ben froze solid. And for a while, it seemed to many of us as if time itself had stood still or started going backwards, because millions of men found themselves thrown out of work again. And deep down inside everyone feared another depression and the mass unemployment that went along with it. It was the friggin' nightmare of the Thirties come back to haunt us. No jobs meant no wages and that meant the dole or the means test, and no one who'd lived through it all before could ever forget it. And neither could their kids. It marked you for life. The Blitz had nothing on it. If a Jerry bomb got you, at least you went quick.

The only way to survive was to bend the rules. There was no other choice, everything was on ration: eggs, bacon, tea, margarine, cornflakes, tinned milk, tinned apricots, tinned sardines, coats, skirts, trousers, socks, shoes, underpants. And to add insult to injury you had to queue for anything worth having, whatever it was. People only had to see a queue and they'd go and stand in it, even if they didn't know what the hell it was for. And if you didn't want whatever it was, you took it anyway and traded it for something else later.

Even with only half a brain you could see the Black Market was one of the few things in the country that was working properly—or at all. So, everyone was on the fiddle in one way or another. And I do mean everyone. High-born or low, it made no difference. Nobs, toffs, men of the cloth; the whole lot of them. The ladies, too, whether they came from Mayfair or Hackney Wick. And if you ever tried pushing your way in front of them, you'd be lucky if you got away in one piece, let alone with your skin still on your back. They could strip a 'spiv'—that's Cockney back slang for 'VIPs' or 'very important persons'—of whatever he'd got in his suitcase in minutes, whether it was nylons, lipstick, perfume, whisky, or a tin of peaches. Horrible to watch, it was.

But you couldn't blame them for it. You've always got to look out for yourself, haven't you? It's how we're made. And unless you're prepared to push and shove with the rest of them, you and your own just end up going without. And who in their right mind ever wants that to happen? I know it was a right carry-on, but it was the only way most people could carry on during those hard times.

Britain can take it? Yes, and they did, too. And with both hands. Because the honest truth is, there's a little bit of larcenous villainy in each and every one of us. But none of us ever need be ashamed of it, all it takes is the worst of circumstances to bring it out into the open. Then you just watch as polite society starts to crumble around you.

Take me. When I was a kid we had nothing. No money. No property of our own. Nothing. Not even a good name to keep up, only the tradition of surviving. And any silver spoons we had in our house had all been nicked from somewhere else, and even then, they always ended up down the pawnshop. So very early on, like everyone else round our way, I had to learn how to survive. And I did. But even I had to be a bit nimble to get me and my own through those grim years of austerity that followed the War. And just like everyone else I bent the rules. Only I bent them until they broke and then kept on going. But I reckon that'd be just about par for the course, for a hard-working London cat burglar. Wouldn't you?

Chapter 1

FOREIGN CLIMBS

So there I was lying on the roof, seeing through my ears and taking in the sounds of the night, my face pressed against the damp soot-covered tiles, yellowy-grey wisps of fog folding about me like cast-off mortuary shrouds. And me, all kitted out for business, in my black screwing clothes; woollen balaclava, wind-cheater, cavalry twill trousers, web belt, and rubber-soled, canvas plimsolls: And, of course, my turtles; my lovely, hand-tailored, black leather gloves. Not, I admit, everyone's idea of the glamorous world of the cat burglar and jewel thief, but much more practical than a dinner jacket and cricket whites, or a striped jersey and a bag of loot marked 'swag.'

I was well hidden behind the balustrade that ran along the front of the house, and I couldn't be seen from the pavement below or from the windows across the street. And if some nosy bugger had happened to stumble upon me up there in all the misty darkness, I'd have simply helped him fall five storeys onto the iron railings below. No, I'm only kidding; I'd have coshed him senseless.

Stillness has got to be learned, it takes years to get the proper hang of it, and however good you were at thieving, there were always times when the waiting could get you down. But, you had no choice, you just had to lie there and do your level best to fade into the shadowy world of

London's not always deserted rooftops. So even when all my senses were on full alert, I took to losing myself in thought so as to keep myself relaxed. Time ceased to matter then, and in that respect, it was a bit like the feeling I got when I was doing a creep inside someone's house; everything in and around me seemed to slow right down. I swear there were times when whole hours went by between each tick of the clock.

The craft of burglary as I was taught it was essentially non-violent, the art was always making sure it remained so, which is why I never carried a shooter when I was creeping. In fact, the only piece in my burglary kit that remotely resembled a weapon was an old army knife that I kept in a long leather sheath strapped across my back. It was perfectly balanced and incredibly strong, and the ideal tool for a whole variety of jobs. And it was a pure coincidence that those two British Army Captains, Fairbairn and Sykes, had originally designed it as a close-combat knife. The story was they'd dreamed it up while serving with the police out in Shanghai. It seems only appropriate then if I tell you I got it from an ex–Royal Marine sergeant down Limehouse way. It cost me a fair bit—six bottles of black-market Irish whiskey, if you must know—but it was well worth it.

So, apart from the knife, all I had with me was a set of skeleton keys, a small jemmy, two lengths of black silk rope, with fold-out grappling hooks, a small pair of needle-nosed pliers, a glim—that's a torch to you—and one or two other little bits and pieces hardly worth mentioning. I had nothing else, nothing, not even the home-made device I used for dealing with rows of coiled barbed wire. I don't even remember me carrying a rabbit's foot or a four-leaf clover. So you really must believe me when I say I never went looking for violence, and I really did try and avoid bother whenever I could, honest. And the bloke who died that night was definitely not my fault, it was his; he should never have used a gun, and he should definitely have had a better head for heights.

The house was in the heart of Belgravia, part of a beautiful Georgian terrace built for the aristocracy by Thomas Cubitt, one of London's very first property developers. And just like every one of the neighbouring houses, terraces, and adjoining squares, it was leased from the Grosvenor Estate; the richest of the rich, of course, being the only acceptable landlords for England's moneyed and powerful. The area became fashionable after a young Queen Victoria rented No. 36 Belgrave Square for her mother to live in, since when of course the place has never looked back. All of which I knew, because I'd gone and looked it up at the public library on the Marylebone Road. I'm not just a pretty face, you know; I've had help.

Old Cubitt built with quality in mind, and even after a hundred years all of his houses still had that unmistakable air of richness, class, and respectability; the doors were solid, the windows wide, and the locks very impressive looking. All the things, of course, that drew me and so many others to the area like ducks to a pond. The linens all referred to the place as an 'El Dorado' for cat burglars, and who was I to disagree?

The truth was, few families could afford to lease an entire house to themselves anymore, let alone staff one of them, and so a lot of the houses got split up into apartments. However, with Belgravia being one of London's better addresses, a lot of buildings got taken over by well-to-do clubs and societies and wealthy American companies. Mostly, though, it was foreign embassies and legations. And my destination that night just happened to be a fourth-floor corridor in one of those embassies, where in two of the master bedrooms I knew I'd find a couple of wall safes brimming over with top-class jewellery.

Now the odd thing about wall safes was that most people with jewellery worth stealing hardly ever used them, and they were saved for special occasions. And that was the only reason I had to be up on that particular roof on that particular night. You see, even though most jewellery that got stolen was covered by insurance, most of what was replaced was promptly stolen again. All of which tended to get very monotonous for everybody except the jewel thief. So, the smarter ladies about town started wearing imitation sets around the house and started keeping their finest pieces of jewellery in bank vaults and safe-deposit boxes. Then on the day of this glittering first night or that gala charity ball, they would send some minion off to the bank to collect whatever precious pieces they'd decided to wear that evening. Then after the lovely things had flashed their adorable selves in front of all the right people, they'd only have to spend one night slumming it at home before they could be safely returned to the bank the following morning.

It was the frequency of those fancy occasions that limited the opportunities for burglary, as those were the only times that all the best jewellery was ever guaranteed to be safe inside someone's wall safe, safe inside someone's house. Those were the nights you waited months for, those were the nights you prayed and prepared for. And just like the rest of London society, the criminal fraternity called it the Season, and as with any shooting party, success depended on how well you knew the habits of your intended quarry. Which was why all the better creepers always took all the better newspapers, studied the social and gossip columns, and read court circulars and society magazines such the *Tatler* from cover to cover, and from top to bottom. In fact, it was in one of their photo-spreads that I first saw the diamonds I was intent on nicking that night. The pictures showed the ambassador's wife and daughter at a banquet looking double luscious in their long ball gowns. And the jewels didn't look too bad, either. I spied them again on a couple of other occasions. Once, larger than life, in a newsreel at the pictures—which I sat through three times just to make certain—and another time, when I acted as a waiter at a posh do the ladies were attending in the West End. It always paid to get a close look if you could manage it, but when I saw them in the flesh, I could tell in an instant the lovely things were one hundred per cent kosher.

It was the windows, oddly enough, that had given me most pause. The main floors looked to be newly glazed, even at the rear, which probably meant new window locks as well. Not overly troublesome, I admit, but I didn't want the added bother, as they might have also been newly alarmed. So, I'd decided to go in through the skylights, which of course, meant me going up the outside of the house. Now, you learned at a very early age to only put your trust in soil-pipes, because they were the ones fixed to walls with two-and-a-half-inch masonry nails. Standard-size drainpipes on the other hand, secured with nails no bigger than drawing pins, had a very nasty tendency to bend under a man's weight, so they were the very last things you ever wanted to find yourself hanging from sixty feet above the ground. The great thing about skylights was that even in the poshest of houses, the skylights were always the very last things people ever re-membered to remember. It's an odd thing about human nature, people generally look out or down, yet hardly anyone ever remembers to look up. Funny that.

The little line of cottages in the mews at the back of a terrace of grand houses was originally accommodation and stable yard for the grooms, horses, and carriages. But over the years, in all the better parts of London, they'd become a terrific little leg-up for many of the better carriage-trade creeping jobs. So, needless to say, I climbed up with no trouble at all and keeping to the shadows I moved quickly across the shallow incline of the cottage roofs to where they abutted the back of the terrace. I went hand over hand up the main fall-pipe to the fourth floor, reached over to a branch pipe that angled up towards one of the bathrooms on the next level and got a foot up onto it. Then I groped my way upright, all the while feeling for the crevices between the bricks with my fingertips and whispering a silent prayer of thanks that it was only the street-facing walls that Cubitt had ever thought to stucco.

The noise from down in the street ended my train of thought and it disappeared back into the tunnel of night in a puff of invisible smoke. I'd seen the ambassador, his wife, his debutante daughter, and some poncey-looking bloke leave earlier in the evening for some posh do at the Guild-hall to welcome the new Yank ambassador, Lewis Douglas, to London. The newspapers had been full of it for days, though why any of the editors thought that anyone who worked for a living would have any interest in the proceedings beats me.

Anyway, ever since the ambassador and his party had gone out on the town, I'd been waiting on tenterhooks for a certain someone to leave the Embassy. I'd seen him a number of times, and familiarity had bred nothing but uneasiness. He was a thickset bald-headed geezer with big bushy eyebrows that looked like two furry caterpillars queuing for a bus. And you could tell by the way he carried himself that he thought he was someone to be reckoned with. He had policeman stamped all over him; a scowling face, a humourless mouth, and sharp, beady little eyes that even in daylight looked like two piss-holes in the snow.

I'd first set eyes on him a couple of months earlier when I'd borrowed an Harrods van and uniform and tried to deliver some packages to the Embassy. He was in one of the side rooms, and moments before the door got closed in my face, I heard him barking at a pretty woman with glasses, a secretary probably. I remember thinking at the time that the look on the woman's face didn't appear very dutiful, it looked more like pure, naked fear. I'm almost certain I heard a slap and a cry of pain afterwards, but as I was being shouted at by some low-grade nerk, and was myself busily mumbling sert-like, 'so-sorry-to-have-bothered-you-sirs,' I couldn't be sure.

I rolled onto my side and sneaked a peek through a gap in the balustrade with my little periscope. It's a handy bit of creeping kit that's really nothing more than a narrow, collapsible cardboard box with two tiny mirrors set at an angle at each end. And sure enough, reflected and framed in the mirror, was Baldy himself just about to get into the back of a long black car; the light from the street lamps reflecting dully on the polished skin of his big square head. I stopped breathing for fear that the slightest tremble of the reflecting mirror might flash the secret of my hiding place. And at that very moment he stopped and looked up and down the street, taking in all the dimly lit porches, and the rows upon rows of heavy-draped windows and dark, empty rooms. And as he turned his head slowly from side to side the watery lamplight seemed to eat at his features like acid, turning his face into a grotesque lump of granite. He looked scary, like Boris Karloff getting ready to tear your head off, and before I could help myself, I began swallowing hard. "You could knock yourself senseless trying to head-butt that," I thought. And then in a blink of an eye both Baldy and the car were gone into the fog and the night.

I let out a long, deep breath and found I was shivering, but I swear it was only from the cold. And I warmed myself knowing that if he kept to his usual routine, he'd be gone until the early hours of the morning, which gave me all the time I needed. I couldn't get on with the job proper, though, until the ladies of the house returned with their jewels hidden beneath their mink coats. But with Baldy now safely out of the way I had work to do. The skylight I'd planned on going in through had been wired and alarmed, but even a kid on his first creep wouldn't have had too much trouble with it. Diamond cuts through glass like a knife through flesh, dead easy, and a rubber suction cup on the end of a piece of string was always a very handy little item for stopping glass from falling inside and shattering its own alarm.

Anyway, I did the necessary with the hidden wires, and pleasingly, no alarm bells started peeling out into the night. I used my glim—my torch—to peek down inside and gauge the length of rope I'd need to reach the landing below. Then after gently closing the skylight I settled down to wait for the Embassy's old Rolls-Royce to arrive. For once the ladies were safely home, then the lovely sparklers were as safe as houses and as good as mine.

I almost missed the Roller as it purred up out of the mist. I tell you, those posh motors could be a right nuisance sometimes, they were so bleedin' quiet. But you couldn't miss the cut-glass tinkling of the women's laughter as whole villages of serfs rushed to open up the doors for them. By the sound of it, the ladies had had quite a night. It was a happy little band, and I remember hearing the ambassador laugh long and hard at something the young bloke had said. Not an earth-shattering event in itself, true, but for some reason or other it struck me as odd. I knew from my time in the Merch—Merchant Navy—that it was far more usual for a junior officer to laugh at his captain's jokes. I mean, that's just the way things are in the world, aren't they? Anyway, as you do with silly things like that, I just filed it away somewhere in the back of my head and forgot about it.

The entire Embassy came alive to receive them with, I imagine, all the proper tugging of forelocks and proffering of warm nightcaps and bedpans. Meanwhile, I was friggin' freezing and I had to try and keep myself warm so I didn't stiffen up, but there's only so much arm flapping you can do on top of someone else's roof before you bring the entire house down. So, I just settled to the task of tying double overhand knots, every eighteen inches or so, into the two lengths of black silk rope I'd brought with me.

I pulled back the edge of my turtle—turtledoves, gloves—and looked at the luminous hands of my watch as they pointed to eleven o'clock exactly. I'd given the house an hour to settle down to sleep, and given myself another full hour to complete the creep. I'd planned on taking no more than twenty or thirty minutes to get in and out, but I'd allowed the extra time in case I needed the cushion to fall back on.

I'd observed the house and its day- and night-time habits a dozen times over the previous weeks and months. And as well as a few casual walks-by and the one fake parcel delivery, I'd spent time sketching around the area, changing my style of drawing and my disguise on each occasion. Well, you can't be too careful, can you? The way you draw and paint is as distinctive as your handwriting, and people remember the oddest things.

Spend a lunch-time walking round the National Gallery if you don't believe me. Even if you don't know the first thing about art, just follow your nose and before long you'll be able to tell the artists apart even if you don't have the foggiest idea who they are. What's more, the memory of some of those paintings you stop and look at, will stay with you for life.

Now, if you could do it, so could any nosy copper with half a brain, which is why it always paid to take the necessary precautions. But I never minded working out in the open; it was all part of the challenge. 'Hiding in plain sight,' my old mate, Ray—a lot more about him later—called it. Anyway, you'd be surprised, how much people will leave you alone if they see you working away at a little painting easel or drawing board. And whether capturing the acres of purple willow herbs that covered the bomb ruins around London Wall or standing in a busy street off Sloane Square made no difference. Kids, of course, would come up and ask to see what I was doing, and occasionally, a thin-lipped, tweedy-looking matron up in town for the day would poke her long, pointed, heavily powdered nose in. But British phlegm being what it is, the rest of the populace usually kept a respectful distance.

There was nothing better for scoping out a place properly, and afterwards, when doing the actual creep, I usually found I was never more than a few feet out in my reckoning of distance or dimensions. And as odd as it may seem, there was many a time my mind worked out exactly how to pull off a job while I was busy, lost in my sketching. It was my good luck, I suppose, that I was born with the knack; but I learned to imitate different drawing and painting styles in the same way I learned to imitate different types of people, by looking and trying very hard to see what I was looking at. In the end I got three or four good pen-and-ink studies and a nice couple of watercolours of the square, the terrace, and the mews at the back. None of them, admittedly, as expressive as John Piper's pictures of buildings or worthy of the Royal Academy, but they all earned a place on the walls of my memory, I can tell you.

I looked at my watch again. It was only ten minutes past; and it wasn't at all like me to be so fidgety. I'd planned the job for months and prepared as fully as ever I'd done, and I'd always been successful. I even asked myself whether it was a sign I should abandon the creep or not. And in the end, to quieten my chattering mind, I decided to wait until the chimes of midnight to see what materialised. So I gave myself up again to London, and just let my mind wander up and out and over the dark rooftops to become one with 'the Smoke.'

As I imagined the city spread out beneath me, it struck me that London was like a huge stage-set being managed by the night. I smiled and whispered, "All the world's a stage." The exits and the entrances; the noises-off, real or imaginary; the acts about to be enacted; the many parts yet to be played. It all rang so true. It did then, it still does, and I think it always will. Old Bill Shakespeare really did know a thing or two about life, didn't he? How he came to know so much, though, I don't know, and neither do I care, I'm just very glad he put it all down for us to see and enjoy. Ray used to tell me of the fisticuffs they got up to at times down the British Museum tea-rooms arguing about whether it was William Shakespeare, or Marlowe, or Edward de Vere, the Earl of Oxford, who wrote all the plays. They even used to divide themselves up into teams, Stratfordians versus Oxfordians, the silly sods. All I know is, it was Londoners that loved him first, and we should all just be bloody grateful the plays got written as they did. One mind or many, there's a single truth that runs through them all.

Then I heard the chimes ring out, and with tools in hand, midnight stole upon me like a thief. And that decided it. And for good or ill, I committed myself to the creep.

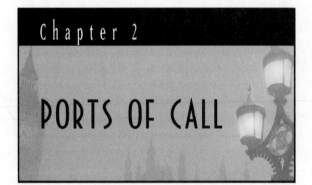

Chapter 2

PORTS OF CALL

I looked down through the skylight to the floor below, looked away, blinked twice, and looked down again. It's always best to check you're not expected when you drop in unannounced. I pulled the skylight open, uncoiled the knotted silk rope, waited a full minute, and then began to ease my way head first down through the tiny gap. That may seem an arse-about-face way of doing it, but I've found that the sooner I get my eyes accustomed to the netherworld the better. And unless you find yourself in a windowless room, there's always a little bit of light quietly tiptoeing about somewhere to help you see, but at the start of any job your eyes have got to work overtime.

I counted to ten, took a deep breath and pulled my body through the gap, swinging my legs down in a perfect arc, all the while taking care not to tangle them in the lengthy adjustments I'd made to the alarm-circuit wire. "Good enough for the Henger's Circus," I said to myself. I hooked my ankles around the rope, then reached up and closed the skylight behind me, leaving a tiny boxwood wedge to hold it clear of the rope and open for my return. Then I climbed down.

You feel houses. Some creepers even like to think of them as women; I don't, though, it'd be much too distracting. But in a way love does come into it. Love, joy, and warmth do something to a house, all the feelings get absorbed into the walls and floors, and settle into the carpets and furniture. I tell you, when you break into a house like that, one that feels warm, it's as if the whole house is unsettled by the invasion and everything in it tries to put you off your stroke and raise the alarm. I suppose it's the difference between a house and a home, sounds corny I know, but a house that's empty of love is indifferent to your creeping. Even a hotel room, so often misused, holds some vestige of loving behind its striped wallpaper, however tired or torn, and will try and gather its secrets around itself like an old dowager in a threadbare dressing gown. But that night in the Embassy, I felt nothing but cold, it was a building that people merely spent time in. They arrived, did whatever work was required of them and went away again. Whole regiments of people must've passed through its big front door in its time, without one of them ever leaving anything of themselves behind. No wonder the house felt as it did.

Hanging in mid-air, gently swinging to and fro in the darkness, I took stock of my situation. To my left was the wooden banister at the top of the back stairwell, and below, a short corridor, more a half-landing really, that led on the right to a door of a tiny attic or a box-room. A lot of Georgian houses had little apartments built into the attic or on top of the roof as rooms for servants. But other than what was behind the door on the landing, there were no additional structures to the house that I could see, just the original, twin-hipped, grey-slated roofs with sloped ends. All of which meant there were no handy dormer windows at the front or the back for me to climb through. However, the two runs of skylights set into the two roof slopes facing away from the street was more than good enough for me to be getting on with.

My toes gingerly kissed the floor, and I was down onto the balls of my feet and ready to jump back up and out again at the slightest noise. My eyes and ears strained themselves probing the dark, searching out the immediate area, while the tiny hairs on the back of my neck waved backwards and forwards feeling for things in the air that clever people will tell you can't be felt.

I stood for a moment like a stag nosing the wind. Then I took a deep breath and once again felt that old, black-magic feeling of time slowing down and billowing out all around me like a cloak. I can't explain it, it's as if I become part of the darkness itself and move within its shadows as one of them. I'm here at the same time as I'm over there, and I think I become invisible, because I'm not what people ever expect to see. When I move in the dark, I sometimes feel that my toes and feet have developed some peculiar set of senses, and over the years it's a marvel what they've not stepped in, if you get my meaning. The trick was to time your movements to the natural sounds of the house. Placing one foot down with the tick from the long-case clock, moving the other in time with the settling of the hot-water pipes or the wind pushing against the windowpanes.

I crept over towards the wooden railing, testing each foot before putting my full weight down onto the floorboards, and I felt rather than saw a worn carpet runner that stretched off into the darkness at the top of the stairs. It meant there was regular foot traffic, so I edged my cardboard periscope over the wooden banister for a look down into the stairwell. There was a faint light coming up from below, but one or two night staff were a normal feature of most legations and embassies, so that didn't worry me. And they usually spent most of their time with their heads buried in a book or guarding the front door to make sure no one got in or out. And the very last thing they wanted to do was disturb the very important people upstairs all tucked up in their beds fast asleep.

I folded the scope flat, slipped it back into the black canvas satchel strapped across my chest, and with my crêpe-rubber-soled plimsolls not making a sound, I padded back to the door of the box-room. I could tell by touch alone it wasn't what Thomas Cubitt originally had in mind, as it was made of steel. I listened, my ear pressed against the door, and ever so slowly turned the handle. There were no sounds of sleeping, no dream-laden grunts, only the tinny silence of emptiness. I chanced the glim again, and in its pencil-thin beam I saw a short stairway of about five or six steps that led up into a long, low, windowless room that'd been squeezed in under the roof line. I shone the torch up the walls and across the low ceiling. And it wasn't a box-room at all, it was a bedroom of some sort, yet one as bleak and as spare as any abandoned barracks room in some far-flung and forgotten outpost of empire.

There was a single foldaway cot with a stained, striped mattress, a thin blanket and a pillow, and it all looked like it could've done with a good dusting of bug powder. Other than that, there was a washstand with a jug and basin, a chamber pot, and a tiny lamp on a tiny table. I could feel a slight draft coming from somewhere inside the room, so I knew there had to be ventilation of some kind. It was more like a prison cell than a bedroom, and unashamed of its purpose it blankly returned my stare, quite indifferent to my thoughts on the matter.

I stepped back and ran the glim over the door. There were two big bolts, both well oiled, one at the top and one at the bottom, and a lock without a key. "Who in hell do they stick inside here?" I said to myself. I closed the door, turned, and crossed the landing. Then keeping close to the wall, I slipped down the short flight of stairs to the floor below. The corridor that opened up to my right led to ten or twelve small bedrooms, but as there were no strips of light visible under any of the doors, I took it that the occupants were all sound asleep. Under normal circumstances, those upper rooms, being so near the roof, would've drawn me like a magnet; easy in and easy out. But that night I only had time for the floor below, where I knew I'd find the master bedrooms and the mistress's jewels. And I crept down those stairs as silently as a dark thought steals into a lonely spinster's worst imaginings.

I came to the main bedroom corridor and stopped dead, and with my feet firmly planted in the thickening stillness, I took a moment to nose the air again. There was no shaded electric light ready to throw its shadows at an unwary night creeper, no night-light candle waiting to point a flickering finger from behind its smoke-blackened glass, but there was light of sorts. Only the very faintest inkling, but enough for me to tell one thing from another. I was always told that the best way to see in the dark was never to look at anything directly, but my eyes just seemed to absorb whatever light there was anyway. 'Cat's eyes,' my dad used to call it. And as I moved my head slowly from side to side, the source of the additional light became clear.

A thin sliver of light showed underneath the door of the nearest guest-room. I hadn't intended on doing that particular room on the creep, but now, with that light on, any second thoughts I might've had about turning it over quickly exited stage-left. Light shed in the wrong place and at the wrong time tends to have that effect on me. In fact, it's the only thing creepers fear. If there's a shared bathroom at the end of a bedroom corridor, a strip of light like that is just like waiting for the pin to drop out of a hand grenade. But as I knew there were four main bedrooms on that floor, each with its own separate dressing room and bathroom, I wasn't too concerned about being caught short.

I blessed again the powerful Afrikakorps binoculars I'd acquired down Bermondsey Market soon after VE Day. Thanks to them I'd managed to pick out many a secret from the vast expanse of London's rooftop desert, especially in the dead of night when every light shone with the promise of an unknown oasis. Hardly anyone used blackout curtains anymore, too many memories of the Blitz, I suppose, so the unconfined glow of an electric light bulb was one of the few ways many people could display their new-won freedom.

That's how I knew there were two master-bedroom suites at the front, one for the ambassador and his wife, and one for their daughter, and four large bedrooms at the back that were reserved for important visitors. The guest rooms had been empty for most of the time I'd been keeping tabs on the house, or at least no light had ever shown in the windows. The regular night-time pattern had changed, however, when the Flash Harry that'd I'd seen hobnobbing around town with the ambassador's wife and daughter had first taken up residence that September. Sometime between the open season on partridges, and the one for shooting pheasants.

Now, even though I was making for the bedrooms at the front, it had crossed my mind that anyone important enough to be a guest on that floor, would very likely have one or two very expensive knickknacks lying around his room. Solid-gold lighter and cigarette case, monogrammed cuff-links, nice wristwatch, that sort of thing. But as I was so dead set on lifting the ladies' jewellery and slipping in and out as quickly as I could, I decided I really didn't need the bother of any further distraction. The other thing was, the light underneath the guest-room door couldn't have been on for very long, no more than five minutes at the most. I was certain of that, because I'd made one last final check down the front and back of the house with my periscope just before I'd started the creep. Everything had looked clear then, by which I mean everything had been nice and dark, and as quiet as the grave.

I drifted over towards Flash Harry's door, but there was no sound coming from inside, no gentle cough or clearing of the throat, no sipping of water, no pouring of whisky, no crackling fire, or crackle of pages being turned. I breathed in, my nostrils flaring, but felt nothing, nothing at all, no threat, nothing. Perhaps he was frightened of the dark and needed to sleep with the lights on. Perhaps he'd fallen asleep, reading. Yes, and perhaps I needed my head examining.

I blinked sleepily, but not because I was tired, it's just one of the things that happens to me during a creep when everything around me seems to slow down like a clock losing time. And holding the unbroken stillness of Flash Harry's room in my mind, I turned and crossed the corridor as no more than a fleeting shadow, and began to sense the room opposite. I can see inside a room just by touching the door to it, and it's the same with picking locks. I just imagine them in my mind, and through my fingertips they become as real and as solid for me as if I was standing inside the room itself or I had the lock in question standing on a work-bench in front of me. I can't honestly explain how it works, it just does. It's a gift, I suppose, and one I'm very grateful for. Time and again it's meant the difference between success and failure, and I know very well I'd have ended up in the clink without it. Call it a sixth sense if you like. I do. Most people take their natural abilities for granted and are truly amazed when other people have difficulty doing what they themselves do so very easily. Me? I kiss the ground I creep on, and say, "Thanks, ever so much."

And so with my sixth sense going ten to the dozen, I stood cloaked in darkness caressing the door to the bedroom suite of the ambassador and his wife, and with my turtles tingling their readiness, I was about to make my first port of call for the night.

Chapter 3

THE WRONG RAFFLES

I love expensive champagne; its contribution to burglary just can't be overestimated. I opened the outer door and was met by what passes for the music of the spheres to most creepers. I couldn't see them, but I could hear them. They were both snoring gently and obviously sound, sound asleep. I closed the door behind me and began to move around their outer dressing room in time with the ebb and flow of their breathing. Their muffled snores gently edged round the inner door of their bedroom, and as the sounds tickled my ears I felt as connected to the ambassador and ambassadress as if a length of silver wire was stretched between us.

The outer room was larger than I'd imagined; more a comfortable-sized drawing room than a dressing room. The style was mock Regency from the furniture and lamps, all the way to the striped wallpaper and the painted-in-the-style-of pictures. It was tasteful in a tasteless sort of way, but I reckoned the Prince Regent still wouldn't have approved. Even in the dark, the furniture seemed too heavy and out of proportion; small, spindly legs, and mean bodies much too big in the bottom. It all seemed more like a middle-class hotel than a better class home, which in a way is what I suppose it was. I took quiet comfort in the carpets though; at least they weren't threadbare.

We all live in hope in our business, but it really was too easy. It was

an instant creeping classic. The key to the wall safe was in her ladyship's—
What, I wonder, is the proper way to address an ambassador's wife? Her
Ambassadress? Her Excellency? Anyway, God's honest truth, the key to
the wall safe was in the top right-hand drawer of her dressing table. With
a chest of drawers you normally started at the bottom and worked up, so
that you didn't waste time closing one drawer to get to the next. But a
lady's fancy dresser was always the one exception to the rule, and you
always tried the little, top right-hand drawer before you tried anything
else. I tell you, you wouldn't believe how many smart women always embraced the obvious before retiring for the night. That was why I liked key
safes; there was nearly always a little key for it somewhere close by. And
having the key in my hands meant I didn't have to spend valuable time
delicately probing with skeleton keys or dialling numbers on a combination lock listening patiently for all the tumblers to click soundly into place.
The key was the key to the creep, and my spirits lifted at the sight of it,
because in terms of time and success it definitely weighted the scales well
in my favour. And my black leather turtles kissed the little key in gratitude
and it took my hand, and we waltzed together across the room.

Paintings and mirrors of a certain size are the first places you look;
only then do you search out the false drawer fronts or the runs of bogus
book spines. So, chancing a quick sweep of my glim, I narrowed my eyes
and followed the thin finger of illumination past the bathroom door, and
lying on the carpet below the heavy, gold-leaf picture frame on the far
wall, I saw a delicately patterned silk handkerchief. It was an odd place
to drop something; the picture wasn't that good, and not really worth that
close a look before bedtime, unless, unless . . .

Always go with the flow. So, buoyed by the tiny silken flag I floated
over and reached up and gently pulled the picture away from the wall. It
moved back soundlessly on its hidden hinges, and then the key was in
and turned in a single, fluid motion, the sequence of infinitesimal resis-
tances giving way to a satisfying sequence of clicks. Then taking hold of
the squat, little handle on the front of the safe, an early Peterson Series
100 by the look of it, and gently turned and pulled. A dark square hole
appeared in the wall and for the briefest of moments I again thumbed my
glim. Oh rapture, leather jewellery cases; and by the weight of them, all
full. There was also a red file, full of top secret papers no doubt, and a

small, black leather-covered book that I took to be a ledger of some sort, but I paid them no heed.

Opening the jewel cases faster than the bloke that shucks the oysters down at Wheeler's, I unclipped the contents and carefully slid each item into its separate pocket in a special chamois leather bag, then rolled it all up and slipped it back into my black canvas satchel. As well as the matched set of necklace and earrings I'd first seen in the magazine photos, there were two other diamond suites; one with rubies, the other with emeralds. And personally, I thought she'd made the right choice going with the plain diamonds, as they always make a woman's eyes shine so beautifully. There were also two antique diamond clips and a half-inch diamond bracelet, all Russian. Two other diamond bracelets, single and double strand, a number of rings with nothing less than two carats, one flawless gem of a piece of at least seven or eight carats, and a fabulous pair of pavé-diamond drop earrings. All very tasty, Marc perhaps, Cartier certainly, and I think I even detected the delicate artistry of the house of Boucheron. But it was of no matter, because now they were all mine and going back to my house. I stared at them. Even in the darkness, diamonds somehow manage to absorb all the available light and continue to twinkle with a depth that's impossible to fathom. They're like so much liquid fire. I love the sight of them.

My fingers repeatedly rippling their delight, almost as if they were tinkling phantom ivories, I closed the wall safe, returned the picture to its harbour, the key to its berth, and set sail again for uncharted waters. I swam silently across the room, pausing only to rescue a gentleman's solid gold Rolex wristwatch from atop a bureau. Next to it was a heavy silver frame with a photo of the ambassador dressed in an admiral's uniform. It must've been him in the war. My eyes slid across the face in the picture and asked, "So, whose side are you on now, old cock?"

Everything seemed to be changing again out there in the world; onetime allies were turning into enemies, and old enemies, friends. It was hard to keep up with it all sometimes. But there was no answer in the picture, only eyes shaded from a sun long since set, staring back at me, unseeing and uncaring, from under a peaked cap. I turned away, and still breathing in rhythm with my two not-so-silent sleeping partners, I unfastened the silvery rope that joined us and floated out the door and out of the room.

The corridor seemed darker than before, but everything in it was so finely etched it was as if the very darkness itself had been polished. When a creep's going beautifully you can't help but feel lighter inside, but that night I knew the luminescence came from the brilliants that were already so very close to my heart. I drifted further along the corridor to my second port of call. The door loomed up out of the mist. 'All the nice girls love a sailor . . .' Breathing deeply, I caressed the door panels and reached down for the knob. 'All the nice girls love a tar.'

The door gave way easily to the touch, and then I heard sounds that suggested the ambassador's daughter was doing the same. The sounds were muffled, but my ears were attuned enough to know they were definitely the cries of a woman caught in the very throes of ecstasy. But the deep grunting sounds Mr. Flash Harry was making, for that of course was who it had to be, suggested that he was having to work hard to keep up with her. It must be all that horse riding she did three times a week down Rotten Row—or *Route du Roi* to those of us in the know—in Hyde Park.

It was lucky for them the layout of the master bedrooms mirrored one another; it meant that the adjoining walls were between the bathrooms and not the actual bedrooms themselves. Otherwise, Papa, his ears burning and his eyes red with rage, might've already taken things into his own hands with a shotgun and unwittingly put paid to my creep, as well as the creep who at that moment was deflowering his very obliging daughter.

Every room has its own special interpretation of darkness and the daughter's bedroom was no exception, but even in those first moments as my eyes readjusted, I sensed it was as unique a place of entrapment as anything I'd ever seen. It was like something out of a Hollywood film; a palace of silks and satins and lace that enveloped you like a perfume with its promise of delights yet to be revealed.

But I had a decision to make, and I had to make it quickly. I could stiffen my resolve and wait for the two of them to ride themselves on into contented sleep. Or I could grasp the moment and go about my business while they were still happily going about theirs. The door into the bedroom wasn't completely closed, so I knew that whatever I did then I had to be very careful about how I moved. In the end, temptation beckoned her little diamond-encrusted finger at me, and as if in a trance of my own, I moved deeper into the room and became one with the rhythmic sounds of the lovemaking, which had me caught somewhere between a waltz and a tango.

Salomé had nothing on this one. Her clothes trailed enticingly across the floor; her satin evening gown and gloves, silk stockings and black underwear all lying in seductive, overlapping curves like the discarded skins of some exotic creature of the night. There was enough lace there to keep the London Palladium's entire chorus line happy and very, very grateful for a show's entire run. It's all right for some, I thought. It was too, for that's when I saw her jewellery lying carelessly abandoned on top of her dressing table. The lovely girl had been so impatient for the pleasures yet to come, she hadn't even bothered to kiss them good night and tuck them all up safely in bed.

They curled round my turtles like a lover's embrace, a beautifully matched set of diamond earrings, necklace, and bracelet, and this time all of it most definitely by Boucheron of Paris. They were classic brilliants, simple and elegant, and even though they flashed a haughty disdain at my unabashed lust for them, they slithered and slid obediently into the empty pockets of my chamois leather bag like so many silk stockings released from their overly stretched suspenders. I smiled, a satisfied smile, and continued on in time with the sound of the movements from the bedroom, and was through the door and out into the quiet calm of the corridor before the next cresting wave of cries could break over me. And I was quietly making for the back stairs when the strip of light under the guest-room door again tripped into my mind. I knew the occupant was otherwise engaged and probably would be for some time. So I did what I would normally never, ever do, I opened the door to the unknown. And my mouth suddenly dry as a bone, I found myself swallowing hard even though I knew the room was empty.

And then I was inside. The light must've been subdued, but it was quite shocking nevertheless, and it took a few moments for my eyes to readjust. I turned away, blinked a few times, then slowly turned back and stole a look. There were two sources of light; a small brass lamp on top of a tall set of dresser drawers in the ante-room; and in the bedroom, a small lamp on a side-table next to the bed. I peeked in. The bed was rumpled, but didn't look like it had been slept in. Beside it, the ashtray was full and the whisky glass empty. The Turkish tobacco almost obscured the expensive, masculine smells that still lingered in the air, but not quite. So, it seemed I hadn't been the only one waiting for the house to fall asleep. I looked around. At least he'd had the courtesy to remove his overcoat, silk scarf, dinner jacket and bow-tie before he'd gone to pay his respects. His shoes, I noticed, were lying on their sides with the laces still tied up. At any other time, I'd have quite liked to have been in them, if you know what I mean.

Conquest carries its own clock. I looked at my watch; I was ahead of schedule and there seemed ample time to skim the room. In the pool of light from the brass lamp, the brightness now a little easier to deal with, a big gold chronograph glowed, sullenly, face down. There was an inscription of some sort on the back, but as it wasn't in English I didn't bother to try reading it. I turned it over to see the face; it was another Rolex, and a very rare and expensive one by the look of it. Lovely. To make it a clean sweep, I also scooped up a solid gold Cartier lighter, as well as the sharp little crocodile wallet basking in the light next to it. Even beneath my turtles the feel of the highly polished skin said there was more than a fold of fivers inside. And very nice, too, thank you.

A set of solid-silver monogrammed hairbrushes flashed and caught my eye, but I resisted, as they'd be much too bulky to carry. I nearly weakened at the sight of an exquisite, little porcelain figurine of a shepherdess, Meissen, by the look of it, but in the end I resisted and bid adieu with a smile. On impulse I tried the top drawer. "You're doing everything arse-about-face, tonight, Jethro," I whispered to myself. I quickly rifled through the drawer; shirts, shirts and more shirts. I shook my head. "Do it right, sunshine. Just start at the bottom and work up." I quickly knelt down, and was reaching for the bottom drawer when my fingers brushed against a leather attaché case sticking out from underneath the dresser. I hadn't seen it before, as it had been hidden in shadow. I pulled it out, placed it on top of the tallboy, and pushed my thumbs to the catches. It was locked. It would be. Otherwise, he'd have left it out for everyone to see, wouldn't he?

I breathed in deeply, then slowly breathed out and sent my senses flying through the house. I waited in the stillness, and heard nothing that might disturb all the little comrades from their sleep. Good. All quiet on the eastern front. Just as it should be. Even I can't stand noise when I'm trying to get some kip. But always measure twice. So I breathed in, paused, and sent my senses out again, and apart from 'little miss insatiable' and her rider still galloping on strongly in her room, everything else seemed as quiet as the grave.

I swallowed, found my mouth was no longer dry, and got down to business. From under a small flap in the front of my satchel there appeared a long, slim pick. In an in-breath I'd released one of the locks from its pins, and on the out-breath I'd undone the other. I thumbed the case open. It was like a Pandora's box inside. The light reflected like satin on the blackened steel of a Walther P38 pistol lying on a bed of chamois leather. "Deadly as a pair of black lace knickers," I almost said out loud. Alongside the gun there was a silencer, an ammunition clip, and a small black leather case about the size of a woman's travelling manicure set, all zipped up and ready for inspection. The case had a crest tooled into the front of it that looked a bit like two letter S's in reverse. "Now that's interesting," I murmured. And as my fingers gently tapped up and down on the crest, I let my eyes slide across the other contents of the attaché case. There were two black leather address books; one with solid gold corner pieces, obviously very expensive, and the other, the sort of thing you'd find in Woolworth's. There was also a textbook of some kind. I picked it up and saw that it wasn't a technical manual at all, but a novel without its paper cover. On the spine it read *Oliver Twist* by Charles Dickens. I opened the book and scanned the pages. No mystery there, it was Oliver and Fagin all the way through. And my eyebrows rose at that; it was a childhood favourite of mine, and an odd choice for Flash Harry, wouldn't you say? "More please sir, I want some more." Then again, maybe not.

More interested than ever now, I unzipped the little leather case and got quite a shock. And even the little hairs on the back of my hands stood on end to get a better look. If what I was seeing actually belonged to him, then just who in hell was Flash Harry when he was at home? And more importantly, who the friggin' hell did he think he was? Raffles? E. W.

Hornung's fabled gentleman cricketer, cracksman, and cat burglar? I hoped not, that was my role in life.

Inside the small zippered case was the best collection of twirls, rakes, picks, skels, spreaders, probes, and bones I'd ever seen in my life. A set of skeleton keys and tools as beautiful in their way as any of the finest pieces of jewellery ever displayed by Tiffany's, Garrard's, or Asprey's. I stood mesmerised. I hardly breathed, but I could still tell I was alive, because for the very briefest of instants my breath dulled the dark blue oily sheen of the lovely blued-steel instruments. I slid one of the twirls out from its pocket, and then did the same with one of the probes. They were perfectly balanced, and as matchless as any set of Purdeys. I also noticed that some of the tools were diamond-tipped. Strength, as well as beauty. The work of a master craftsman, and custom-made for nothing less than a master thief.

I slowly zipped up the case and stroked it, my turtles softly purring, "Very glad to see you, my dears, oh so very glad. Aren't we, boys?"

I came out of my reverie and realised the best thing I could do at that moment was leave. I mean there was no point in me overstaying my welcome, was there? After first pocketing my splendid new set of twirls, I checked the Walther's safety catch, then thumbing the magazine release, I removed the loaded clip from inside the handle-grip. I very gently determined that our friend hadn't also kept a round ready and waiting up the chamber, and then quickly emptied both clips of all eight bullets. Counting them out to myself as I did so, just to make sure.

I left the rounds lying on the chamois leather, but tucked the empty ammunition clips safely away inside my satchel. They were now nothing but harmless bits of metal, or at least they would be as soon as I could get a chance to throw the friggin' things away. The 9mm, Parabellum ammunition was another matter; it was just too dangerous for me to carry around anywhere on the streets of London. And to be honest, I didn't much fancy anyone else within a mile of me carrying it about with them, either. I mean, people could get themselves killed if ever that stuff started flying around.

Chapter 4

SLIDE COMES BEFORE A FALL

The sound of a click raced up the stairs behind me, and it would've stopped my heart dead if it had moved any faster. If you've got the ears, you can easily pick out the sound of someone trying to open and close a spring-lock door without making a noise. It's the tension spring that gives the game away. In the dead of night it can sound as loud as a pistol crack as it pushes to unwind. It's a tricky little bugger for such a simple mechanism and just turning a doorknob a fraction isn't always enough to make it behave. And he should have known better. He should have 'loided it by using a small square piece of plastic to hold the latch-bolt back, or failing that pushed a little piece of felt into the door jamb so as to pad the lock into silence. But I ask you, who's always got a handy bit of celluloid or a roll of felt in their pockets? Not too many people, that's for sure, and not Flash Harry Raffles calling on a lady friend, because the click in the darkness told me he was on his way back to his room, his duty done for the night. I took the stairs three at a time and prayed I didn't slip on the carpet runner, lose my footing, or lose my head.

And I could have easily done that because thoughts were coming at me from out of the dark, thick and fast and furious. What did he want with the matched set of picks and twirls? All right, all right, burglary. But if his real business was creeping, what the hell was he doing in the Embassy, and what was he really after? Gold? Diamonds? Stock certificates? Cash? I know we can all do with an extra bob or two, now and then, but somehow I got the feeling it wasn't simply a question of money. He looked too polished, too educated, and like he'd never ever wanted for anything. It's all in the breeding, of course, a sort of superior attitude people are born with that's recognised the world over; the unmistakable stamp of wealth. It's easy enough to spot, shop assistants in the better stores in London, Paris, and Rome have been doing it for years. And the ones I'd seen in the stores along New York's Park Avenue, before the war, were so good at it they would've probably been able to tell you the exact size of someone's bank balance as well.

The questions kept on running round and around inside my head. Who was he? What was he doing here? What did he do in the war? Something cushy, I bet, and very likely away from all the fighting. Spain, was it? Switzerland? Argentina? And then, of course, there was the little question of him being so high up in the Embassy's pecking order. That didn't fit with him being a creeper, now did it? But what did? Bugger if I knew.

I'd only ever seen him from a distance, and I couldn't tell you what his voice sounded like, or the colour of his eyes, but I knew I'd be able to pick him out of a crowd. Then it came to me in a flash; he'd been in the pictures in the magazine photo-spread of the ladies. He'd been in the newsreel, too, and at the ball where I'd acted as a bloody waiter. "Bloody hell," I said to myself, "I must be going blind." He'd always been in the background, always dashing, always debonair, all polished smiles and brushed-back, brilliantined hair, and looking for all the world like a South American polo player; Flash Harry, the perfect ladies' man and escort. I cursed myself for a fool; my mind had been so focussed on all the jewellery I'd never given him a second's thought. But his set of diamond-tipped twirls had changed all that; now I couldn't think of anything else. And then the penny dropped. "You clever bugger," I said, shaking my head, "you and me, we're not so very different." As Ray had so often told me, 'Hide in plain sight, and they can't see you for looking.' So it was Flash Harry Pimpernel, was it? Seek him here and seek him there, was it? "Well, damn you, whoever you are," I shouted somewhere in the back of my mind, "you can just friggin' well go to hell."

What really burned me, was that he'd not only stolen onto my manor, but I'd missed him slipping in and out of the Embassy all the nights I'd been watching the place. I mean, I was supposed to be good to this game, one of the best, and yet I hadn't caught sight or sound of him. What's more, I hadn't even got a whiff or a whisper about there being a new, high-class burglar on the loose in the Smoke. And the answer I kept getting back didn't exactly cheer me up. If he was that good, then he wasn't just another flash creeper, he was Harry Houdini Pimpernel friggin' Raffles himself. Don't get me wrong, I never minded a bit of creeping competition now and then, it helped keep us all on our toes. But there was something very dodgy about Mr. Flash Harry Raffles, and deep down in my water I knew I didn't like the idea of him creeping about London one little bit.

I know your thoughts can run away with you sometimes, but while the ones I'd been having had been running like mad through my head, I'd been charging up the Embassy stairs like a hungry dog after a rabbit. And I don't know who got there first, me or my conclusions, but I know I made the landing at the top of the stairs at about the same time Harry Raffles made it back to his room. 'Jack be nimble, Jack be quick. And while you're at it why don't you nick the friggin' candlestick, you berk.' I love those old creeping sayings, but I tell you they used to pop into my head at the oddest of times.

The rope hung there in the dark of the landing like a dotted line with the word 'escape' written along it. I went up it like a rat up a fucking drain-pipe, the rope whipping from side to side behind me like a giant black tail. As I reached the skylight and pushed it open, I could hear a voice shout and a door slam somewhere way below me. It meant that Harry Raffles had decided to raise the alarm and wake the house, and not try and come after me all by himself. What a pity, because there was a part of me that would've loved to have taken him on then and there, up on the roof. I abandoned all subtlety after that and simply launched myself up and through the skylight opening, only pausing for a moment to pull the knotted rope up behind me.

In my rush to get away I didn't notice my foot get caught in the wire loop I'd fashioned earlier to bridge the alarm. I felt something snake across the top of my plimsoll, but thought it was nothing more than a coil of the rope. It was just a little mistake, but that was usually all it took for a caper to start going downhill. As I dropped the skylight and stepped away, my foot pulled the wire and broke the circuit. And the first I knew of it was when the Embassy's alarm bells started clamouring into the night. "Not at all like you, Jethro, my old son," I said. "You must really be slipping."

I quickly gathered what wits I had about me, and made for the edge of the roof. I peered over and saw lights coming on willy-nilly in the bedrooms at the back of the house. I reckoned that despite all the shouting that was going on, people would be running around like headless chickens for the first few minutes. I knew that soon, though, there'd be a full-blooded hue and cry sent after me, and my only consolation was knowing that Baldy was good and gone for the night. I'd have really hated having that fat slug chasing me.

I unravelled the long silk rope I'd left coiled and ready next to the parapet, and looped it securely around a stone cap, testing my weight against it as I backed towards the edge. Then, out of the corner of my eye, I saw torch beams throwing jagged shadows up through each of the skylights in turn, and for one crazy moment it seemed as if the fingers of light themselves were reaching out to grab me. It was definitely time to exit downstage, extreme right—and I didn't need any prompting. I took a firm grip on the knotted silk rope, lowered myself over the side of the building, and began my descent. And though it may seem odd, that was when I deliberately slowed down. I tell you, it's the only thing to do if you really need to speed things up. After all, whether you're going up or down in the world, the very last thing you need to do is get too far ahead of yourself.

Then out of nowhere all the skylights and top-floor windows blazed with more light than could've been generated by Battersea Power Station, and I had to avert my eyes or I'd have gone blind. "Fucking hell, that's all I needed," I screamed. My only hope was they'd forgotten where they'd put their friggin' roof ladders.

Someone inside had definitely come to their senses and was establishing order, and suddenly even all the shouting seemed much better orchestrated. I fancy I also heard one or two very loud shrieks in the background, so I took it that the jewels had probably just been missed, as well. Then to my horror all the lights inside began to be switched on in sequence, and storey by storey they lit my descent as effectively as a bank of theatre stage-lights. I gasped for air and slid down the dangling rope like a gibbering, half-crazed monkey.

The rule is, don't ever look down, but there are times you shouldn't look up, either, because it can give you the shits either way. Way up above me I caught a glimpse of a face that showed deathly white against the swirling fog and black of the night. The face was swiftly joined by another, and then another. Then the shouting took on a new urgency, and so did I. And almost at the end of my rope, I moved crabwise over to the main soil pipe and started sliding down it with the speed of a fireman with his trousers on fire. And not a moment too soon, for a few seconds after I'd let go of the rope, it snaked down past me, and snickering impatiently it dropped twenty or thirty feet to the roof of the mews cottage below. They'd cut the rope expecting me to still be on it. They were actually trying to kill me. I could not believe it.

It was at that exact moment that my heart stopped beating. A brilliant white light engulfed me, half-blinding me, and for a moment or two I really did think I was seeing things. It was like being in a nightmare, because I thought I saw Baldy hanging in mid-air, halfway up the building. Impossible, of course, he was still out on the town somewhere. Or was he? I blinked, and blinked again, my night vision now well and truly shot to hell, but the horrible thing refused to go away. I choked back a scream; it really was Baldy in all his nasty, granite-headed malevolence, and he was just a few feet away from me, cursing and shouting like some demon enraged with piles.

He'd thrown back the heavy curtains from one of the big sets of windows and the blaze of light from the huge chandeliers inside had caught me hanging on the drainpipe like a fly stuck to fly-paper. It was a moment or two before I realised Baldy was shouting at the window catch, as well as me. It wouldn't open; it was stuck. I could've told him all about the problems you can have with those little buggers, but I didn't think it wise to stop and chat. I left him barking his head off and beating on the window frame with his fists. "You jammy sod," I shouted, "that was a bit of luck." And that was the exact moment someone started shooting at me.

The shots came from above and missed me by a mile, by which I mean several feet, but the crack of the bullets as they flew past my head was still much too close for comfort. And whatever old Winston Churchill had once said about it, he was dead wrong; there was nothing remotely exhilarating about being shot at, it was friggin' frightening.

Someone was shooting down from the roof. I wondered whether it was Flash Harry; if it was, the cunning swine must've had another pistol hidden away in his room. Bugger. Anyway, whoever was doing the shooting must've been leaning over the edge of the roof as far as he dared, and then simply firing down at random in the hope of hitting me. Other people further along the roof tried angling their torches down the side of the building, but the beams were too weak to reach me. In the fog of night and with my black balaclava helmet pulled down over my head, it would've been almost impossible for anyone to pin-point me, but that didn't seem to stop them from trying. I thanked the Lord they didn't have proper floodlights rigged up anywhere or I'd have been like a sitting duck in a shooting gallery. The bastard up on the roof must've thought he was going to hit it lucky, though, because he just kept on firing his shooter regardless, and from the sound of it, it wasn't a popgun he was using, either.

My feet had just hit the roof of the mews cottage when two things happened. I heard a crash of shattering glass, followed a moment or two later by a startled cry of fear that sirened into a long scream. Against all my better judgement I looked up, instinct winning out over training, and it seemed that in that split second it had started to rain. Yellow light glistened, hard and bright along the jagged edges of the broken glass that'd begun to splash and crash around me. And beyond the cruel rain, black shapes grew in the darkness like threatening clouds in a gathering storm. I turned my head away from whatever it was falling on me from out of the sky, and pressed myself as hard as I could into the unyielding bricks and mortar of the building's rear wall.

It was just as well I did, too, because it wasn't raining cats and dogs, it was raining dining-room chairs and dead bodies. The things thudded onto the roof just a few feet behind me, sending the broken glass flying again. It sounded just like a clap of thunder. I looked round and blinked, and ever so slowly stepped from the shadows. But I was careful not to step into the mess that confronted me; it's never a good idea to leave bloody footprints when you're creeping.

The heavy wooden chair had broken into bits, though whether from the impact of hitting the roof or from the bloke that'd fallen on top of it, I don't know. As for him, he was a right mess, his head had split open like a ripe fruit that'd fallen off a market stall and he was definitely as dead as a doornail. But I knew it was the geezer who'd been shooting at me, because the gun he'd been using was still clutched tightly in his hand. And I'd been right, it was friggin' cannon, and a Webley .455 by the look of it. He'd been shooting at me with a British Army revolver. What a dead liberty! He'd probably just overreached himself, lost his balance, and fallen from the roof. Well, serve him right, the friggin' swine. I took a closer look. It wasn't a pretty sight even in the dark, but I could see it wasn't Flash Harry Raffles; wrong sort of clothes, different kind of hair. The dead bloke had regulation short back and sides, and hair as black as a gypsy's; at least that's what it looked like, it was a bit hard to tell. I stared at him for a moment as the blood pooled around his shattered head like a growing black cloud, and the glass shards sparkled like stars trapped forever in a frozen London night.

I don't know how long I just stood there like a lemon, probably no more than a few seconds, but it could've easily been a hundred years. The truth was I was rooted to the spot, and in the end it was only the incessant clamouring of the alarm bells that'd brought me back to earth and finally got me going. Then all at once I heard Baldy barking and cursing at me from out of the big, gaping hole where only moments before there'd been a plate-glass window. And echoing all around me and about me was the sound of more and more people shouting and screaming, and the sound of more gunfire.

I blinked and shook my head to clear it, and brushed a turtle across the outside of my black canvas satchel just to make sure all the jewellery was still safely with me. Then a little voice that sounded a lot like me said in my ear, "You'd better get your arse in gear dead quick, my old son, or you'll end up as cat's meat as well." And yet for some reason, right there in the middle of the growing pandemonium, I found myself wondering whether anyone in the Embassy had heard the black-haired bloke scream, or seen him die, and whether in the end anyone would even care.

I began moving as fast as ever I'd done in my life, and even through the fog I could see that house lights were coming on down below in the mews, and up and down the street. I'd planned a number of different escape routes, but the tricky bit now was, which way down would have me home free and clear in the shortest possible time. It was like one of those stupid questions they used to set in my navigation tests when I'd been a young sea cadet. Only this time I knew my very life might very well depend on me coming up with the right answer; and quick.

I scrambled over the dark shiny slates and across the rooftops of the three adjoining mews houses like some demented spider. Then I shinned down a drainpipe, the crêpe-rubber soles of my plimsolls squealing their protest, before jumping the last ten feet to the ground. It was a dodgy thing to do, I might've twisted my ankle or something, but it was the only thing to do even if it ended up costing me one of my nine lives.

Then I hoofed it. I needed to put as much distance as possible between me and the Embassy. And I had to do it as fast as my screaming lungs could manage; because in the distance I could hear other bells starting to peel out into the night. Only they weren't your friendly burglar alarms stuck up on a wall somewhere, proclaiming to all and sundry that there was valuable stuff inside ready and waiting to be nicked. Oh, deary me, no. These bells were going like the clappers, and by the sound of them they were approaching very fast. I knew them all too well, as did every villain, tearaway, and grass in London. And they weren't the bells of St. Clement's or St. Martin's, they were the dreaded alarm bells of the Sweeney, Scotland Yard's very own, friggin' Flying Squad.

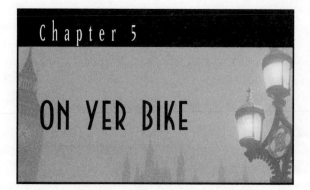

Chapter 5

ON YER BIKE

London's so full of twists and turns it's difficult enough to find your way around in daylight, but in the dark it can have you bottled up before you can get your cap on straight. So, you had to pay attention or you could quickly come a cropper, or end up with a broken leg from falling down an open coal-hole. But me, being me, I'd cased the area thoroughly and all but knew my way around blindfolded, which was just as well considering the soot-laden curtains of yellow fog that still hung down everywhere. My escape route was firmly fixed in my mind, and I'd even memorised the number of steps it took to cover the distance between streets, as well as the number of left or right turns along the way. It was my version of what London cabbies call 'the Knowledge.'

The Metropolitan Police area covers six hundred and ninety-nine square miles, and a London taxi-driver is expected to know all of it like the back of his hand. And only after he gets at least two-thirds of his answers right on his test of knowing every road and street, by name, as well as every twist and turn in between, does he get given his 'all-London' badge. It's a terrific idea, and I got the knack of it from listening to my brother-in-law, Barry, trying to practise memorising his way around town. I thought he was going to drive me barmy with it at first, but then I realised that what could work for him, could work for me. And I'm never above stealing an idea, if it's a good one.

After a few minutes' determined hoofing I'd left the Embassy and its growing fraternity of rudely awakened neighbours far enough behind to allow me to slow down and take stock. Despite the close calls, I realised I was actually enjoying myself, so maybe old Churchill had been right after all; it did feel very good to be alive. I was sorry about the dead guy, not as sorry as him, mind you, but life's got to go on, hasn't it? But within a few more streets my own troubles started to catch up with me, and I began to worry about the police throwing up a ring of road-blocks around the area. I knew that moving quickly usually went against the grain with them, but certain branches of the Metropolitan Police could come over all funny if ever politics and foreigners came into play, and by 'funny' I mean really nasty.

I was making for that tangle of back streets around Victoria Station; a good stone's throw and a full fifteen minutes' walk from Belgravia. There's always a wasteland that surrounds any major railway station: goods-yards; small factories and machine shops; garages, warehouses, and lock-ups; cheap hotels and brothels; grimy cafes and pubs. But more importantly for me, there were also lots of side streets where one more little black van in a line of parked vans and lorries would attract little or no attention. And just so long as it looked like there was nothing inside worth nicking, it was relatively safe.

I'd taken my usual precautions. The little round, buff-coloured, commercial license on the inside of the windscreen was up to date—the one that looked so much like the label on a bottle of Guinness, that in a pinch people would steam it off and use that instead. While all you could see in the back of the van was a torn oil-smeared tarp and a pile of useless rubbish covering parts of a rusty old bicycle. And even though there were always lots of light-fingered thieves about the place, I was pretty sure the van would still be where I'd left it, as I'd already removed the engine's rotor arm for safe keeping.

I forced myself to slow to a normal pace; not so much a stroll to the pub, more the purposeful walk of a man on his way to or from work. I'd removed my balaclava and stuck an old cloth cap on my head, and hung my canvas satchel over my shoulder as if it was full of sandwiches and a flask of tea. Then to complete my change from dishonest cat burglar to honest worker, I tied a dirty-white silk muffler round my neck; always a mark of the great unwashed. At first glance I could be taken for any one of London's army of night-workers; a tram-conductor, a mail-sorter, a fish-porter, even an assistant engine driver on one of the night-mail or milk trains. The only things that stood out were my plimsolls; they made no noise. And I just hoped that the darkness and the fog, and me whistling some tuneless ditty whenever I happened to pass someone would be enough to mask the missing sound.

Now that might seem an unimportant little detail, but you'd be surprised how many honest thieves have been tripped up and brought to grief by much less. One of London's legendary gentleman cat burglars, Augustus Delaney—who some say was the finest, most daring jewel thief of all time; I, of course, have my own ideas about that—was nicked by a young PC Robert Fabian. (Later to became world famous as 'Fabian of the Yard.') All because a distinctive footprint left on a balcony ledge in Mayfair led to a high-class shoemaker who identified the pattern as coming from Delaney's handmade, rubber-soled evening shoes.

It still took twenty minutes to reach my little van, so there'd been time enough for half of London's Metropolitan police force to have responded to the call to the Embassy. And as if to confirm my suspicions, I'd heard alarm bells pealing out along the main roads of the area for much of the time. It could've been one police car driving round and round in circles for all I knew, but I doubted it.

A pool of pale yellow light was doing everything it could to battle the fog and hang around the lamp-post that was giving it life. And just on the edge of the sorry circle of light sat my little van, dark and self-contained like a sleeping cat. I approached it just like any other neighbourhood tom would, very warily. I took a casual look up and down the street. I couldn't see very far, but I reckoned that if I couldn't see anything then neither could anyone else. I was just about to open the passenger-side door, when for a few seconds, I caught the red glow of a cigarette in a shop doorway a dozen or more yards up the street. I looked hard and just made out the black wing of a policeman's cape. I knew I'd padded up as silently as any cat, and I reckoned I hadn't been heard, but whatever I did then I knew it had to be quick. I ducked down behind the van as the red glow appeared again out of thin air and dropped like a spent bullet to the pavement. I heard a boot scrape the butt-end into a smeared pulp, and held my breath. An old hand, I thought. He'd had the cigarette cupped in his hand like any ranker in any army the world over. The size-twelve daisy roots stepped the well-worn pattern that always signalled the process of quietly proceeding, and I listened for the slow crunch of approaching boots. But thankfully, the footsteps moved off in the other direction, and as the night swallowed the copper, I tried to swallow some saliva back into my throat. There were two ways Dame Fortune could have gone that night, but it seemed she still didn't mind taking a step or two round the dance floor with me. "Thank you, dear lady," I said very quietly, trying not to cross myself. I never took luck for granted; in my game, you could never afford to.

The copper was another close shave, and like so much that'd happened on the creep, it was all getting a little too close for comfort. The night hadn't exactly turned out as planned, but I didn't have time to waste worrying about it, I had to make a clean get-away, and quick. My original plan had been to re-fit the van's rotor arm, and then drive off nice and easy up to my little place near Paddington Basin. But with all the goings-on around Victoria, I couldn't take any chance of getting stopped at a police road-block. So I knew I had no choice but to get on my bike; the one that at that moment just happened to be lying under the greasy tarpaulin in the back of the van. A cat burglar and jewel thief escaping on a rusty old bicycle? Never, on your life.

I'd first got the idea from a bloke I knew before the war. Him and his team did most of the big country houses round the Home Counties and the Midlands. Paddy Martin his name was, and he was a legend in some circles. He'd break into a house—he had such a lovely way with a lock—assemble everybody inside, check that everyone was wearing their turtles, then he'd point to the pieces he wanted, and all without ever saying a word. On really big jobs, he even carried a clipboard so as not to miss anything. His well-drilled team would then quickly go about their business before carting everything off in a lorry. After that, Paddy would ride off through the countryside in his tweed hacking jacket, plus-fours, and sensible shoes. He told me once he liked to hum bits of Bach as he cycled along; apparently it was the unerring, mathematical precision of the music that appealed to him. As a finishing touch he'd always have a nicely soaped riding saddle balanced across the handlebars of his well-oiled bicycle. Many was the time some young constable would wish him a 'Good morning, Major this' or 'Good evening, Colonel that.' And Paddy would always reply that indeed it was a grand day or a good night, and one that should certainly be shared by all. The truth of it is, though, as long as someone seems to fit in comfortably with their surroundings, no one ever really thinks to look any further.

Take my little Austin van, it was just like hundreds of other delivery vans that you could see on the roads all over London almost any day of the week. But I'd made one or two little changes to mine. It may have looked like it'd seen better times, and I admit the business names on the side had been repainted so many times they were illegible, but the engine was spotless, and between you and me, I'd even had it souped-up a touch. Well, if the Sweeney could do it to their Railtons and all their other motors, I didn't see why I couldn't do it with mine. I'd also fitted a hidden compartment under the entire floor in the back. It was one of my nicer pieces of work, if I say so myself. And it would've taken a very close inspection by someone for it ever to be discovered.

Trying not to make the van rock too much on its springs, I gently eased my way across into the passenger seat, and reached over and folded the driver seat forward. I pushed the ragged tarpaulin aside and pulled an old, collarless striped shirt, threadbare sweater, and moth-eaten tweed jacket from the pile of rubbish and put them on. Then I pulled the lid off the hidden compartment with a barrel key I'd made, and slid everything from the night's caper down into the open hole; my black canvas satchel and all the rest of my creeping kit, my tools, most of my screwing clothes, even my handmade turtles. Every precious piece of jewellery went in there, too, as well as my new set of twirls. It all had to go in if I wanted any chance of making a clean get-away.

I tucked my black twill trousers, now looking very much the worse for wear, into a pair of outsize Wellington boots covered in rubber patches. Then I took a small square of cardboard from the side-pocket in the door and placed it on top of the dashboard. It was a little sign I always kept handy, just in case the need ever arose. I'd used a carpenter's pencil to scrawl the words: 'Broken down, or run out of petrol? Am arranging for garage to tow away in the morning. Thank you.' The signature was indecipherable, but it somehow helped make everything look kosher. I didn't reckon the Royal Automobile Club would be popping round to help in my absence, so as far as I was concerned I'd done all I could do, and it was now all down to Dame Fortune. Again.

I peered into the darkness, checked the mirrors, and got out. I slipped round the back of the van, opened the rear doors, pushed the tarp aside, hefted the rusty bicycle out onto the road. Then, after slipping on a pair of cycle-clips I pedalled off into the soot-speckled fog—always much worse around any railway station—and what was left of the night.

I hadn't bothered to lock the van doors; there wouldn't have been much point come daybreak. For years, motor car manufacturers had very thoughtfully stamped every trunk, ignition, and door lock with a different code number on the outside, so that everyone could clearly see which key to use. How's that for ingenuity? Only one company in Britain made all the locks. So anyone who could come up with a business letterhead with the name of a garage on it, and who cared to write a polite note with a cheque or money order enclosed for the full amount, would be sent a complete set of keys, numbered one to fifty-four, through the post. I'd even done the fiddle myself a couple of times.

So locked or unlocked, it meant that any layabout with motor oil on his boots could be in and out, and off with anything worth nicking, within seconds. But the way I reckoned it, even a boatload of car thieves couldn't nick what they couldn't see. And as that sort usually didn't see much beyond the end of their noses anyway, it was a fair bet with them that out of sight would be right out of mind. And as for any chancers that might come along? Well, as with amateurs everywhere, they'd be looking for something with a bit more flash than a battered old Austin van, especially one that was broken-down, as well as empty, but for a pile of foul-smelling rubbish. (A few boiled Brussels sprouts rotting away in a biscuit tin punched full of holes work wonders, believe me.) But then as anything with four good wheels was still selling for more than it had cost before the war I was still pushing my luck, and I knew it. But beggars, like burglars, can't always be choosers, can they? So, I let the air out of one of the front tyres just for added effect.

Police cars were beginning to gong around me in all directions, so I knew I had to get myself square, and quick. The fog had settled on my clothes like dew on a privet hedge and as I moved the lamp-post's watery light caught the thousands of tiny droplets on me, and made it seem like I was covered from head to foot in poor-quality gemstones. I looked like a Cockney Pearly King trying to go up in the world.

"I could catch my death of cold, any more of this," I said to myself. I wobbled a bit at first, even though my old rubber boots were going up and down like clapped-out steam pistons. And I think I must have gone a hundred yards on the bike before I remembered to stop and switch on the two little lamps; the one on the front handlebars, and the one on the rear. You couldn't see anything by them, the light they gave out was pathetically weak, but that wasn't the point, it was the law. You had to have them lit up, so that people could see you in the dark. But even with the addition of the regulation white patch everyone had had to paint on their back mudguards for when they'd cycled through the air raid black-outs during the war, you could still hardly be seen. And you took your life into your hands anytime you set out on the highway. Anyway, in all that fog I bet that little rear red light didn't glow much brighter than a fag-end. And I ask you, how much use could that have been to anyone?

Chapter 6

RAISE THE ALARM

More often than not most burglars and thieves that got caught red-handed with stolen goods on or about their persons were given away to the police by their own fences. Alarming, but true. How else do you think most cases of robbery got solved? By good old-fashioned plodding detective work? Not in a million years; it was always due to some nerk trying to save his own skin by pointing the finger at someone else. But it wasn't only the otherwise highly esteemed fences of stolen goods that grassed on you, it could be anyone, friend as well as foe, especially if they thought you were setting up a job. That sort of information was worth a cash bonus to various interested parties down Scotland Yard.

It was a simple enough bit of police work. The nastiest detective in the squad would pay an off-the-record, out-of-hours visit to the suspected fence, and as soon as the front door was opened the boot would go in. Someone's name was going down in the arrest ledger, the only question being, whose name it was going to be; the fence's or the thief's? And guess whose name it always turned out to be?

The coppers were on a double winner every time with this approach. Because as soon as the poor unsuspecting sod who'd been fingered was in custody, it would be quietly but firmly suggested that he might like to earn himself a good word in front of the magistrate come morning by further helping the police with their enquiries. All he had to do was admit to a number of other burglaries. And for a quiet life and the promise of remission most thieves did, too, and so by turns helped clear the books of hundreds and hundreds of unsolved robberies. Which not only made the Police Commissioner very, very happy, but also made the public at large feel a lot safer. Whoever said the truth should get in the way of a good story?

No one ever knew for sure who'd done the dirty on them, but not a day went by without some nasty rumour going the rounds about some fence or other. That's why in the end so many of them had to give up the game and go straight—it was the only way they could be sure of keeping their skins in one piece. It got so bad you didn't dare trust anyone, but most burglars couldn't afford to be too choosy and so it made for some strange bedfellows in the thieving community.

Yet in all my creeping days I only ever dealt with one man, and for my money he was far and away the best fence in London, though few people ever knew of it. I trusted him as if he was my own flesh and blood, which after the death of my dad, in many ways he became. His name was Ray Karmin, and I owed almost everything to him. He schooled me in diamonds and a lot of other things besides, but mostly he taught me how to think. Later he even introduced me to the theatre and the whole art of being one thing while seeming to be another. It was from him that I got the idea of leading a double life.

Every Tuesday, Wednesday, and Thursday without fail, immaculately dressed in bespoke suit and shoes, Ray would spend his time in the Reading Room down the British Museum researching ancient history and other dusty subjects close to his heart. The BM reader's card he carried was registered in the name of Raymond L. Karmin, and to all intents and purposes he was nothing other than the gentlemanly scholar of independent means he appeared to be. However, every Friday and Saturday at the street market in Church Street, off the Edgware Road, and each Sunday in Petticoat Lane, over Aldgate way, he was known, to one and all, as 'Buggy Billy.'

Stand the two characters side by side, and you'd never think they were the same person in a month of Sundays. But as Buggy Billy, wearing his never-changing get-up of spotted bow-tie, battered bowler hat, and moth-eaten, fur-collared overcoat, he was famed from the Edgware Road to the Aldgate Pump as 'the king of bug powder.' And it was in his guise as costermonger and market trader that I'd first met him, and not surprisingly it was a diamond necklace I'd acquired in somewhat dubious circumstances that led to the meeting.

I was young, cocky, and green behind the ears, and already tired of London and tired of my lot in life. I'd chanced my arm creeping a few times, and had gotten away with it mostly, even though I'd almost been nicked twice and just missed being sent off to Borstal. It was a Saturday morning and I was nursing a mug of tea in a market cafe; dreaming of far away places I'd only ever seen down the picture house. When I heard someone talking about some stall holder who could tell real stuff from paste just by holding it in his hand and looking at it. Anyway, this little Jewish geezer had been so impressed by Buggy Billy, he'd gone on and on about it. "You would not think it, to look at him," he said, the steam from his mug of tea making his eyes glisten, "this one who looks such a shnorrer, such a tramp. But an eye for quality? Impeccable. Oy vay, such a nose. What I wouldn't give for this gift he has."

I did a bit of nosing around the market myself after that, and found out all I could about this Buggy Billy, which amounted to no more than where he'd be working the following week. I waited all that day, and as soon as I saw him breaking down his stall, I went up and asked him if I could buy him a drink. He'd looked at me hard in that funny way he has and the rest, as they say, is history. We hit it off somehow. It might've been my winning personality, but I think it was more likely the jewellery I showed him. He hardly glanced at it. "First class," he said, "for glass and paste. You should be more careful, Sonny Jim, it could still get you three years or more if you got caught. Go safe." But I was caught by a sudden burning desire to learn and I blurted out, "Show me how to see, won't you? I'll work for it."

He turned and looked at me again hard, and after what seemed like an eternity he chuckled and said, "Alright, my old cock sparrow, alright. I'll show you, but you'll start by first helping me with my bug business and then we'll see if you can work your way up. Maybe after that I'll think about it. After all, if I don't put all that cockiness of yours to work it'll probably all go to waste."

Buggy Billy was a market institution. The banner on the front of his stall said it all, words that had first been seen on balconies and washing lines round the slums of London during the old King's Jubilee celebrations years before the war: 'Lousy But Loyal.'

"Buggy Billy! Buggy Billy! Buggy Billy!" His voice would cut through all the other shouts, calls, and cries on Church Street market like a big-toothed metal file sawing through damp plywood. It began as a low growl and slid up and up in pitch till it hooked your ears and made your eyes water, but what rooted you to the spot was the sight of something held high in the air. It wriggled. It writhed. It squirmed. It was horrible. If you looked closer, over the heads of the crowd in front of you, you'd gasp along with the rest of them. For the thing waving slowly backwards and forwards and round and around was a man's arm drowning in a sea of bugs. I never missed a performance if I could help it, and neither did anyone else. I asked him once how he got all the wriggling mess of bugs to stay on. "Dead easy," he'd said, "sugar water and wallpaper paste mixed with a bit of tar. I smear it all over this long canvas bag I put my arm into, then dip the whole lot into a barrel of the bleedin' things. After a couple of dips, it comes up black and sticky with them, a bloody awful sight it is, enough to turn your stomach. I breed them on a bombsite round the back of Paddington Station. I've got enough of the buggers to start the next seven plagues of Egypt."

Tubs of his special bug powder cost him no more than tuppence to fill, plus a penny each for the cardboard tubs and the 'authentic' printed paper labels. "It works a treat, too; kills almost everything it touches. Of course, I've added some secret chemicals of my own to speed up the process, but don't ask," he'd said when I'd asked. "There's enough shit in there to strip the lead paint off an American Army truck."

On any given Saturday Buggy could make forty, fifty quid or more, but on a holiday weekend he could pull in well over a ton. And a hundred quid and more wasn't at all bad for a couple of days' work, when a cabby working normal hours earned only ten pounds a week, and a thousand a year put you in very good company. "I tell you, Jethro," he'd told me early on, "where there's muck there's brass, but where there's bugs there's cash."

He'd long since paid others to do the mixing and the tub filling for him, and to keep his bombsite bug farms buzzing along nicely. And all of it done like clockwork by his boys, as he called them. A lot of them went on to work their own pitches at markets all over London, and they did very nicely, too. He took his cut of course, but none of them begrudged it, as like me, most of them had had nothing until Buggy had given them a hand up. "It's what they've got in here," he'd always say, tapping his heart, "and in here," he'd say, tapping his head, "that's what counts. Not whether the poor buggers have got the tickets from some school some-where to say they'd be good enough to be a bleedin' draper's clerk for the rest of their lives."

I started out by looking for dippers—pickpockets—that might be work-ing the crowd, and then I worked my way up to being the number one hand-off boy; the one that handed over the tubs and took all the punters' money in return. And it was Buggy Billy that put me straight when I was up before the beak on suspicion of burglary for the third time. He gave me a right talking-to; after which, as they say, I never looked back. In fact it was after that that I made enough money to finally get me out of London, off to college and away to sea.

In the beginning Ray worked the markets simply for a living; after-wards he said he did it because it was useful; it kept his face known to the world at large and to the police in particular. Ray called it 'hiding in plain sight.' "A coster's barrow is a great window on the world," he told me, "but it's a one-way mirror. People see Buggy Billy in his tatty old clothes and look no further, they peg him as just another cheeky Cockney barrow boy, which is just the way I like it."

Mondays produced a remarkable transformation. Out went the battered bowler hat and bow tie and scraggy overcoat, and in came the bespoke three-piece suit. Even the house Buggy Billy was seen going into on a Friday, Saturday, or Sunday night was not the one Ray stepped out of on a Monday morning, or on any of the days he visited the British Museum. Both houses backed on to one another, but as far as the world at large was concerned, each one belonged to a different local character. Who, if you were ever to compare them, couldn't be more apart in terms of breed-ing or class. And even in such a close-knit community as existed between

Edgware Road and Lisson Grove, no one had twigged the deception, not even Buggy Billy's own troop of boys, and there wasn't much you could ever put over on them.

Monday was when, in my humble opinion, Ray became the best fence in London. That was when he'd meet the people with family jewels to sell that'd been recommended to him by various acquaintances from among London's émigré communities. Ray acted as the middleman between buyer and seller. His knack was knowing just who would buy the piece in question and what they'd pay for it, and arranging for the two to be brought together. Then he'd collect a small fee from both parties. He was known for his total discretion and the accuracy of his unbiased appraisal, and was hardly ever wrong in his assessment of man or stone. Which was why a scribbled note from Ray was honoured by almost every diamond dealer in Hatton Garden.

If he'd been presented with a number of fine pieces from several sources, he'd very occasionally let himself be persuaded to conduct the final transactions in person. It was the perfect cover, of course, for fencing whatever gems I brought him. At first I supplied him with pieces from round town, then later when I was working the big passenger liners, from all round the world. And he would include them in, with whatever other pieces he was showing to his very select circle of dealers. If things ever got too hot to handle he'd hold my stuff back, but if things were going well he'd simply add them to the pile. And such was the flow of merchandise that whether original and complete, and with excellent provenance, or already broken up and with no history at all, there were seldom if any complaints.

You can't beat jewels—diamonds preferably—if you've got to get your wealth out of anywhere in a hurry, and it's been that way down the centuries. To show me the truth of it, Ray once did some calculations so I could get an idea of what equalled what. I couldn't believe the number of gold bars or the amount of cash it took to match just one small packet of diamonds, but think about it for a moment. Try lugging one gold bar around let alone ten or twenty, or even try carrying a suitcase full of money and you'll see what he was getting at.

Ray's family had travelled across Europe with a tiny packet of top-quality cut and uncut stones stitched inside his father's waistcoat. And it

was those stones that they used to set up business in London. Ray's natural
talent with gems had emerged by and by, and bit by bit the word spread,
and soon more and more refugees landed up on their doorstep asking for
advice and help with a transaction. For a time the business prospered, but
Ray had a falling-out with his dad over something—I don't know about
what—and they rarely spoke to one another ever again. Ray walked away
with nothing.

He could laugh about it years later, and he said he'd only come up
with the idea of Buggy Billy because he'd had no alternative but to start
again from scratch. "From scratch, gettit? Scratch. Scratch as in scratching
bugs and lice and things." It was funny the first hundred times I heard
it, but I felt the sadness still lurking behind his cackling laugh. "No," he'd
say, "my real life's work is down the British Museum library unraveling
the Mysteries." And when I'd asked him once or twice what they were
when they were at home, he'd tried telling me, but honestly I couldn't
understand a single word he said.

A couple of Buggy Billy's boys picked up my little Austin van late that
Sunday morning and earned themselves a couple of quid each for their
trouble. They'd borrowed a breakdown lorry, gone down to Victoria, put
the hook under the front axle, and simply towed the van away, flat tyre
and all. The clever lads had taken the long way round so as to avoid any
nosy coppers still plodding about near the Embassy, and they'd ended up
at a little garage and repair shop off Maida Vale that both Ray and me
had a financial interest in. Then they'd left the van there ready for me to
pick up the following day.

I didn't go near the garage until Monday closing time, but even then
the foreman had personally escorted me to the little lock-up round the
side where the van was parked. Then with a quick nod and a wink and
a finger brushed down the side of his nose, he'd left me to it. When I saw
that the old crate was just as I'd left her, apart from the air that the lads
had pumped back into the flat front tyre, my spirits lifted as well. I made
doubly sure there was nobody hanging round the garage and re-affixed
the rotor arm. Then I pushed the front seat forward and got to work. I
did the number with my special little key and opened the hidden com-

partment and retrieved the loot. It didn't do to look at any of the stuff there, so I slipped the lot into a couple of old shopping bags and put them on the passenger seat. The rest of my creeping kit I left in the compartment. I was still deciding what to do with it all, and didn't know whether to have everything washed and ironed, or simply burned. But I soon had the engine humming away nicely, and soon after that, I realized I was, too. So, syncopating my every move to Glen Miller's "String of Pearls," I switched on the headlamps, released the handbrake, and was on my way.

"Now, Jethro, my old cock sparrow, let's have a closer look at these other little titbits you've brought me."

Ray had been purring to himself all evening like a Cheshire cat with a sparrow safely tucked away under each paw, so I knew he must've been as pleased as me about the haul. The green-shaded brass lamp on his leather-covered desk bathed everything in a promising glow, even as it cast the rest of the room into shadow. On top of the desk was a square of black baize the size of a chess-board, and the gems sparkled against the cloth with a fire that made the gold pieces alongside them look dull by comparison; golden pawns to diamond-graced royalty.

With a glass of The Glenlivet in my hand, courtesy of a very understanding bloke down a wine shop in St. James's Street, and the ormolu clock on the mantelpiece ticking away quietly in the background, I think I relaxed properly for the first time in days, perhaps even weeks. I felt a bit weary, which was only usual after pulling a job, but there were no complaints, it was all part of the game. My game, that is. The gem game was Ray's, as was every move once I'd finished a creep. His was both the second and the third act, and I was content just to leave him to it; I mean, why have a dog and bark yourself? Every piece he ever touched, whether it had once been the property of a queen or a pawnshop, he held up to the quiet scrutiny of his jeweller's loupe. As far as he was concerned every piece was potentially brilliant beyond measure; the cut and shape, very possibly the inspired crafting of genius. And until it revealed itself to be otherwise, Ray held each piece as reverently as a violinist might hold a Stradivarius or a father his new born son. His search for perfection was eternal and if in the end a piece failed to realise its initial promise, whether diamond, pearl, or gold filigree, he would sigh and gently lay it aside with a slow shake of his head and the slightest raise of an eyebrow. He said that sometimes even 'jargoons' or fake jewellery could be worthy of respect, even if they weren't worth much of anything else. It was good workmanship he admired. "It's as hard, if not harder, to make glass and paste pass muster as the real thing," he'd say to me. "After all," he'd add with the twinkle in his eye twinkling straight at me, "just look at you."

To watch him was to learn. With the glass held gently between the thumb and forefinger of one hand and the gem held delicately in the other, he saw much more than ten times the power, it was as if he saw into the very heart and soul of the stone itself. What I had for locks he had for gems, especially diamonds; his eyes always seeing beneath the obvious, his fingers and thumbs moving infinitesimally backwards and forwards as delicately as mine ever did on a combination lock. In our own ways we each became one with the very thing we searched for, and he loved gems as I did, with a cold passion. There was no more than ten or twelve years between us, but to my mind he was older and wiser in ways that could only be measured in lifetimes; he was a polished diamond, to my rough.

There were two ways to make money in gems. The way most dealers operated was to take a small profit for a quick turnover. "First money's always best," they'd always say. Our particular method of gem acquisition meant that we had to adopt the other approach, which was to control the flow of the stuff onto the market. "If it's good enough for De Beers, it's good enough for us," Ray would say. "You've just got to take the long view and be patient, that's the real key to it." Over the years his instincts had proved right time and again. And who was I to argue with success?

By the time everything had been assessed, measured, and weighed, we'd struck an agreement; it would go back in the ground until we got the full story of what had happened at the Embassy. What with the bloke who'd fallen to his death and all the shooting that had gone on, we knew that there'd be hell to pay for a time. All the Sunday papers had missed the story as they'd gone to press before I'd even begun the caper, but we were a bit surprised that the Monday-morning papers hadn't reported anything. There wasn't even a mention in any of the London evening papers, either. I told Ray I'd heard something on the radio on Sunday morning about there being reports of some disturbance outside some foreign embassy. But the newsreader had just said that an official statement was expected soon and had passed on to other news. But the incident wasn't mentioned again in later bulletins.

We also agreed that if things turned out to be diabolically bad—as in a full-scale murder investigation—then we'd simply drop all the pieces down a mine shaft and forget about them for good. Otherwise we'd leave them buried for as long as it took for things to cool down. The pieces would all have to be broken up and reset anyway, but it would still amount to a nice little haul. However, it was the matched set of twirls, the two little black leather books, and the story of the Walther pistol that really captured Ray's attention.

He reached for his glass of The Glenlivet and poured a little water into it. "A little trickle of water opens things up nicely," he said, "something women have known instinctively since the Stone Age." He took a sip, nodded appreciatively, and turned to face me. "Now these little black books of yours." He picked up the little address book with the solid gold corners. "This one's full of very important telephone numbers if the names and telephone exchanges inside are anything to go by. Try calling any one of them and you'd get a very interesting response; they'd probably call out the army, navy, and bleedin' air force, as well as all of Scotland Yard. It's been printed and bound beautifully, and the leather covers and the paper stock are of the very finest quality. There's also a serial number stamped on the inside back cover. Here, take a look. You can bet your life that some brass hat somewhere is as sick as a parrot that little thing's gone missing."

I took the book and looked at it through Ray's eyes. It was a beautiful piece, and fit for a king. I nodded and retreated back into my glass of single malt.

"But as to this other one, Jethro, the one with all the columns of numbers on every page, look closely and you'll see it's cheap rag paper. The printing isn't very good and neither is the binding, and it probably doesn't even come from this country. And as good as I am at figures, Jethro, I can't make head or tail of what these numbers mean. It's only a guess, mind, but I reckon it's a code-book of some description. There was a lot of that sort of stuff going on in the war, and I even heard whispers about there being a big house out in the country somewhere west of London where they did nothing else but try to break down all the Axis codes. If you'd come across any of this stuff anywhere else, I'd say just start a bonfire with it; we could do with the heat." He put down the code-book and picked up the black leather address book again and tapped a finger up and down on it in time with his words. "But this, this is another matter entirely. I think this is already hot enough to burst into flames all by itself."

Some people have a mean streak in them, some a streak of cowardice, but with Ray it was patriotism. He may have bent the rules from time to time, if not all the time, and he'd always been a right rascal to boot and no apologies, but he was also British through and through, and very proud of it. It seems that happened a lot with people who'd landed up in England after escaping persecution elsewhere; they adopted their new country with a passion that few Englishmen could ever match, let alone understand. In fact London's East End had been famous for its waves of immigrants and political refugees for years. Jews, French Huguenots, Italians, and Irish had all thought of it as home at one time or another, and along the way added their own flavour to the Cockney character. I know; I've got relatives that claim ancestry with all of them.

Ray claimed a different sort of heritage. "Without Winston Churchill," he'd say, "we'd have been forced to give Nazi salutes from Land's End to John o' Groats, and from Shepherd's Bush to Dalston Waste." He'd laugh then, and say he wasn't sure how well the Wehrmacht would have fared trying to march through the East End, even after all the damage the Luftwaffe had done to the place. But it was the speech that Churchill had made in America the year before that had affected Ray as deeply as anything that had happened in the war. "Adolf's final revenge," Ray had called it. And when he'd heard Winston say on the radio: "From Stettin in the Baltic to Trieste in the Adriatic, an iron curtain has descended across the continent." And then worked out what it all spelled for the future, a sense of doom had descended on him for days, and people said it was the only Saturday and Sunday markets they'd remembered him missing in years, air raids and doodlebugs notwithstanding.

"The thing is, Jethro, this Flash Harry Raffles character shouldn't have had any of this stuff at all. And I reckon it's not jewels he's after, it's other people's pearls of wisdom; blueprints, chemical formulas, metal alloys, plastics, anything at all that's useful, even dirty little secrets that can be used for blackmail. Look at it that way and he might as well be trying to nick the Crown Jewels. And you can bet your bottom dollar that the Bolsheviks are after anything at all to do with atomics. They daren't let America and Britain be the only ones to have the bomb; it threatens their whole idea of world-wide communist revolution."

He took another sip of whisky, and sighed, "That's what this new economic recovery plan for Europe is all about; the one they're calling the Marshall Plan. It's supposed to build everyone up so they can withstand the deadly embrace of Uncle Joe Stalin and his Comintern. It'll be us versus them; the white star against the red star, for years."

As if lost in thought he tapped one of the black books over and over again with a fingertip. "Anyway, this little lot you've stumbled onto calls for a word to the wise. No names and no pack-drill, but somehow they've got to find their way back to the proper authorities and as soon as possible. There's no telling how much damage this Flash Harry bloke has already done or how much he still plans to do. It wouldn't be right for us to wash our hands and walk away; I feel we have to do something. But God knows how long it would take or what would happen to us if we tried to go through official channels. I've got a feeling, though, that someone down the Reading Room will be connected with Military Intelligence in one way or another; it's just the way they seem to do things. So, I think I'd better start there."

I looked at him quizzically. "It goes right against everything you've ever taught me about always steering clear of the law," I said.

"I know, Jethro, I know, but this is that exception to the rule people always go on about. Being the son of an alien, I couldn't do much in the war, they wouldn't even have me as an air-raid warden, let alone as a volunteer in the Home Guard. You and your mates in the Merchant Navy did more than your fair shares, as did all the other boys that never came home. It's my turn to do something now. But whatever happens I'll keep you well out of it. This starts and ends with me. Okay?"

I nodded, but what else could I say?

We live and learn. Ray went down to the Reading Room at the British

Museum the following day, just as he'd done every Tuesday morning for years. Only this time he wasn't trying to solve one of his blessed Mysteries, he was trying to find a way of getting some secrets to go back behind their hidden veils and stay there. He made a wide detour around seat number G7, the one Karl Marx always used—the red-hot seat, they all called it—and quietly stepped his way to his own favored position at H17. Most of his little group of scholarly friends were already there, beavering away in silence, and each of them raised an eyebrow or a pen to acknowledge his arrival. They were all avid researchers of one kind or another, a few even held university posts, but most of them were simply self-proclaimed scholars, and over the years they'd come to accept one another as equals and a bond of sorts had grown up between them. And it was into this little pool of genteel academia that Ray intended to cast the two little black leather books. He'd decided to pretend that the address book with its distinctive gold corners was his own, and that he'd consult it occasionally, but would never proffer it to anyone to examine too closely. He would, however, hand the other book round, the one with page after page of numbers in it, in the hope that somehow, like Moses set among the bulrushes, everything would eventually end up in the right hands.

He didn't try to engage anyone right there among the semicircles of reader's desks, he broached the subject first in the tea rooms, and then later in the Museum Tavern across the road. But apparently, no one could make head or tail of what the columns of numbers meant or what they might refer to. One theory was that it was a crossword setter's notebook, another that it referred to chapters and verse in the Apocrypha, whatever that is, and another that it recorded the positions of certain star constellations at various times in history. No one claimed to know for sure, and oddly enough nobody thought to mention it might be a code book of some sort. But somebody among that little group knew exactly what was what and who should be told, yet he kept very quiet about it all the same.

After all, careless talk costs lives, doesn't it? Or at least, Ray thought it might've cost him his. Because for one awful moment it seemed that all his worst fears had come true at once, when later that week, just before six o'clock one morning, someone started breaking his front door down with an axe. But by that time, I'd had one or two little problems of my own to be getting on with. As they say, it never rains, but it pours.

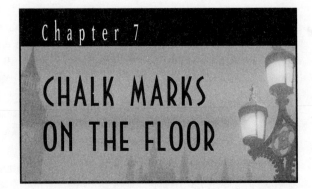

Chapter 7

CHALK MARKS ON THE FLOOR

'Ere, Jethro, there's a bloke wants to see you. Never seen him before, no one to do with the show. He says it's important, but won't give his name. Said there's a drink in it for me, the tosser. He comes on all posh and la-di-dah, but he's a shifty-looking bleeder if you ask me. Do you want me to tell him I can't find you?"

"No, thanks, Alf, I've got an idea who it might be. I'll take care of it myself. Here, have a drink on me later, I wouldn't want you going without, now would I?" I pushed a half-crown into his hand.

"Ta, Jethro, always said you were a right toff."

Alf was one of the grand old breed of stage-door keepers who knew who was who, what was what, and when to turn a blind eye. He kept things shipshape and looked out for all the girls in the show, and always had a clean handkerchief ready for them to wipe their runny mascara on. I also happen to know he was the one that told the girls who to go and see when they got themselves into trouble, if you know what I mean. Well, someone had to help, didn't they?

Alf had been at the London Palladium donkey's years and he didn't ever miss much. You wouldn't credit all the people he knew; he had autographed glossy photos of the lot of them. Gracie Fields, Vera Lynn, Flanagan and Allen, they all had time for him, even 'Big-Hearted' Arthur

Askey, who always called Alf his long-lost, little brother. Well, he would, wouldn't he? Askey was a right short-arse to begin with, and Alf being a whole inch shorter than him made him feel on top of the world.

It was good of Alf to come all the way backstage to see me, it's a big theatre, but I could tell by the look on his face that he was concerned. He probably thought someone was trying to serve papers on me as a co-respondent in a divorce case or something. I turned to the rest of the stage crew, a right bunch of malingerers. "I've got to go see a man about a dog," I said. "I'll be back in ten minutes, so keep my hand warm and the pot dry." They all grunted, but I noticed they didn't take their eyes off their wilkie bards—that's playing cards to you—for a single moment. Pathetic. If you can't trust your mates, who can you trust?

I worked as a stage-hand around town so that anyone who was inter-ested could see it was how I made my living. It was a simple enough smoke-screen, but if you let people discover something for themselves, they're far more likely to believe what they see than if you tried telling them otherwise. That's why I also tried to work a proper theatre week, which meant I had Mondays off, and it was purely coincidental that most of London's criminal classes worked the same schedule. Anyway, after all the goings-on at the Embassy it was a relief for me to get back to the madhouse at the Palladium, especially as they were fitting in a new show. The show was to include a special tribute to the Armed Forces, with one or two amateur acts thrown in for good measure, which promised to make things even more chaotic than usual. The truth was, I always found it all very relaxing as the responsibility for everything going to plan was always firmly on someone else's shoulders. Thank God.

Anyway, I worked the flies when I could, but if it needed shifting, rigging, moving, or clearing, I was your man. The fly floor, the scene dock, pulleys, grids, flats, or battens; it was all right up my street. Everything, that is, except setting up the lighting. I left all that nonsense to the sparks and they were welcome to it, I preferred the dark. I did work the limes once or twice, but I hated being stuck up there in a space no bigger than a broom cupboard; it was hotter than hell and the carbon arc lamps could burn your eyebrows off before you even looked at them. Other than that, I helped out when and where I could. As a rule, though, I tried never to stay in one house for too long. Only just enough to be taken as one of the lads, and as someone you could always rely on as being useful. I did my bit, bought a few rounds of drinks afterwards, and then went on my merry way.

I worked the big theatres, and the small. And I was as much at home in old hemp houses, such as the Saville and His Majesty's, where it always called for good old-fashioned brute force to shift anything, as I was in the more modern counterweight theatres like the Cambridge. I helped out at the Embassy up in Swiss Cottage, the Lyric over in Hammersmith, and even did a few stints with the Old Vic Company at the New Theatre. I worked the Hippodrome and sometimes even lent a hand at my local, the Metropolitan Music Hall up the Edgware Road. The Palladium—the place I was working at then and for my money the best variety theatre in the world—used both hemp and counterweight systems, as well as every other bit of stage-machinery they could get their hands on. Variety, of course, always being the spice of life for them.

As an ex-seaman I felt right at home on the fly floor, what with all the messing about with ropes, knots, billy-blocks, belaying pins, and cleats. So I have to admit that I wasn't too surprised when I was told that most of the stage-hands in Shakespeare's time had all been out-of-work sea-men. That's why it's still considered unlucky for anyone to whistle inside a theatre. Whistling was the way deck-hands used to signal to one another while working up in the ropes. So a few bars whistled offhand on stage could send up the wrong message, and you'd end up with a sandbag or worse crashing down on top of someone's head. Very nasty. But all the pulling and heaving on ropes kept me in pretty good shape. And I'd long ago learned not to whistle while I was engaged in my other line of work. So really, the fly floor helped me keep my head for heights, my eye for balance, and my hand in, for going up and down walls in unusual ways. But that was me, Jethro, the cat-burglar-cum-human-fly.

When I worked the flies I could be walking up a wall holding on to the end of a hemp rope one minute, or stepping off into pitch-darkness as a human counterweight the next. So it always paid to keep your eyes on the job or it could really be curtains. It didn't ever stop me using my ears, though, so I usually got to hear most of whatever was playing on stage even if I didn't get to see it all. But, "always get what you can, when you can," as my old dad used to say. The truth was, being one of the fly boys had a lot going for it, because nothing ever moved on stage without your say-so, and even the poshest actors knew it paid to keep on the right side of the fly floor. I tell you, it's amazing what a dropped flat could do to a soliloquy.

When it came to acting, Ralph Richardson was the Guv'nor as far as I was concerned as he never looked like he was doing any acting, and everyone reckoned him, even Olivier; and he wasn't too shabby now, was he? It was worth a month's pay to see them or John Gielgud when they were at rehearsals, and you'd always find me somewhere in the wings if I could wangle it. And watching them was about as close to envy as ever I got in my life, and I just took it all in like a sponge. But don't get me wrong, I'd watch anyone if there was something worth nicking from them. I didn't care where they came from or even if they'd already passed on, just so long as they were good at what they did and could pass on something of value to me. Variety-turn, stage actor, or film star, it made no difference; Max Miller, Robert Donat, or Leslie Howard—God rest his soul. Because when it came to pretending to be someone I wasn't, I couldn't do better than steal from the best, now could I?

So leaving behind a winning hand of poker, I set off to see my mysterious visitor. And I'd almost got to the end of the lower dressing-room corridor, when someone came tearing round the corner and nearly knocked me flying.

"Here, hold your horses, this isn't Tattenham Corner," I cried.

"Sorry, mate, I'm late and in a right hurry," he said.

"I can see that," I said, quick as a flash, "only we've won the war, or hasn't anybody bothered to tell you?"

"Look, I'm only trying to get to the rehearsals for the show," he retorted.

He was a fit lad, and he'd almost winded me, but I didn't let on, I just stood there breathing deeply, looking at him.

"You ought to be more careful, you ought," I said. "What with that bleedin' great guitar case you've got in your hand, you could do someone a right mischief."

He looked up at me and said, "Look, I said I was sorry, there's now't personal in it. Only, the tube was stopped at Edgware Road and I couldn't get a tram for love or money. But I'm here, now, I'm with the Singing Burma Boys."

"Not anymore you're not," I said. "They've been on, done their bit, and gone. Awful they were."

"What? Surely not? They couldn't have, I'm the accompanist," he said, looking right put out. "No, they wouldn't have gone on without me."

"Well, they did and they have, but don't take it out on me, my old china," I said to him. "Look, why don't you go and have a chat with that Sergeant Major-looking chappie over there, him with the clipboard, I'm sure he'll be able to put you right."

"Well, damn and blast it," he said. "If those buggers have gone on without me, I'll murder them, I will, each and every one."

The way he sounded, I knew he meant it, too. He had that sort of look in his eyes.

"Sorry I bumped into you," he said as he marched off.

"No bones broken," I said, nodding. Then I turned and made my way up the stairs and along the corridor to the stage door.

"Well, look what the cat dragged in. Why ever do you keep on bothering me? You deaf, or something? If I've told you once I've told you a thousand times, the answer's no."

It was Chalkie White, a flinty-eyed, pointy-nosed weasel, with slicked-back hair and a flashy Ronald Coleman moustache. He had a posh accent and a polished manner, but he was a right layabout despite his appearance. He was as thin as a rake and venomous as a snake, and you're right, I didn't like him one little bit. He called himself Alistair Smythe-White and told everyone he was a barrister, but I'd heard that even though he'd been called to the Bar he'd never actually completed his pupillage. Seems he was interested in back doors and short cuts even then, and had got mixed up in something too dodgy even for the wig-and-gown fraternity in Lincoln's Inn Fields to turn a blind eye to. So the gentlemen at law had quietly banded together and nipped his future career prospects in the bud. Later on, Chalkie even managed to get himself cashiered out of one of the better regiments for fiddling the mess books. It's funny, isn't it, how snakes can shed their skins a thousand times, yet always seem to end up being just as poisonous.

I just ignored him usually; he was all mouth and trousers as far as I was concerned. But there were times when even he had to be taken seriously, and I'm not just talking about the times he used his wicked little leather cosh on people once his henchmen had got them pinned up against a wall. The thing was, Chalkie acted as the posh, public school face for a certain gentleman who was downright dangerous, and whose only concern for the law was how much he had to pay to bend it, break it, or buy it outright.

I refer, of course, to the gentleman that ran all the vice, gambling, and protection rackets in the otherwise God-fearing parishes of Soho and Fitzrovia, the godforsaken Malteser himself, Mr. Darby Messima. Now the trouble with him was that he had enough muscle to furnish several boxing clubs, and still had enough left over to fill all the surrounding gymnasiums, billiard halls, and hospitals. And he would use any or all of it to fulfil his slightest whim, whether that meant nailing someone to the floor or slicing someone's face off. Messima was the stuff of nightmares and would've given Caligula sleepless nights. He was known far and wide as the Emperor of Soho, but everyone knew his influence and his reach extended much further across London than that.

But emperors need generals as well as foot soldiers to keep their empires in check, and that's where Alistair Smythe-White came in. He served as Messima's legal brief, and for some reason Messima had a blind spot where he was concerned. It might've been the old school tie Chalkie wore for meetings or the cavalry regiment cravat he affected on less formal occasions. Or maybe Messima just liked having some upper-class berk around to impress people when he invited them in for tea.

There was no reason to shake hands; we never did, we never would. He flashed his best crocodile smile, flicked his little lizard-like tongue from side to side, and made ready to speak. But he'd been pestering me for weeks and had been right smarmy about it, too, which always gave me the creeps, and I'd already had more than enough of him. And so, head down, I stepped in fast and close. It's a boxing move that usually stops people dead, as they don't know whether you're going to hit them or not. I had no intention of hitting him; I just didn't want to give him the chance of getting a word in edgewise. I pushed my face right into his so he could hear.

"Chalkie, I'll tell you just one more time. I won't do a job for you, or your boss. So, you go back and tell Mr. Messima I'm well out of it. I've been playing it straight since the end of the war, and if I weren't, I still wouldn't do a creep for anybody, and I wouldn't pull a caper with anyone, either. I never have and I never will. Nothing personal, you tell him, but these days it's just not worth it; there are too many amateurs running around in the dark bumping into one another like piss-poor blind men. Go ask Joe Stepka or Eddie Chapman if you can afford them, but as for me the answer is ... N ... O ... spelled, NO!"

My words must've passed right over his head, but they usually did with his sort. His beady eyes glinted as black as tiny winkle shells in the light of the corridor, but I knew he still thought he could talk me round. He stuck on one of his cultured smiles, but it still looked like a dirty yellow crack in an old bone china teacup.

"Jethro, Jethro, why the abuse? It's really not called for, all I've come for is a quiet word."

"No can do, Chalkie, I'm not interested."

"You're making a big mistake, Jethro. I'm offering you a chance of a lifetime."

"Not in my lifetime, you're not."

He pursed his lips, but you could see his frustration beginning to seep out. "This is getting us nowhere."

"That's what I've been trying to tell you all along, Chalkie."

He struggled to keep himself under control, but the more he tried smiling, the more the cracks widened. "Look, bucko, whatever it is you think you're putting over on people by poncing around London theatre-land, you don't pull the wool over my eyes. I know what you're really up to, you're creeping again."

"You don't say," I said, keeping my dark thoughts to myself.

"Look here," he whispered, "I've approached you in good faith. The word is you're one of the best creepers in London, and that's why I want to cut you in, it'd make for the perfect set-up."

His voice sounded like sandpaper rubbed over dead fish scales, and seemed to come from somewhere in the back of his throat. It was the worst James Mason I'd ever heard; I could do it much better.

"You just never listen, do you?" I said, shaking my head.

He went all quiet then, as if he was letting me in on some dark secret. "We're two of a kind, you and I, Jethro, we're both loners. But that's okay, we can leave it that way. We can even make it work to our advantage. We'd make a brilliant team, and no one need be any the wiser. I set up the jobs; you pull them off. We split everything fifty-fifty, then go our separate ways. And the beauty of it is, every job would be outside Darby Messima's manor, so we'd both be free and in the clear."

His last few words were lost in a staccato drumbeat that began echoing off the walls. I knew what was happening, he didn't. The two voices trilled in unison, " 'Lo, Jethro."

"Hello, Gloria. Hello Sandra."

Chalkie turned, trying to feign boredom as two of the leggiest dancers in the Palladium's chorus line clattered past on dangerously high heels, but it didn't work, he completely lost his train of thought. He even pulled off one of his gloves, twiddled with the knot of his regimental tie, and tried another one of his pointy-toothed smiles. Knowing Gloria and Sandra as I did, I couldn't blame him, they were gorgeous girls, spectacular even for the West End, and their unique assets had high-kicked many a revue and show into success. I'd had a fair bit of success with the two of them myself, so I knew how truly remarkable those assets were. He watched them hungrily as they sashayed out to give the rest of London a treat. I had to butt in then or we'd have been there all day. "You can put your tongue back in now, Chalkie. So, what was it you were telling me? Only, I've forgotten."

Chalkie blinked and we picked up where he'd left off. "You're really being very difficult, you know. This is my last time of asking."

"That's good because this is my last time of replying," I said.

Why he'd picked on me I had no idea, there had to be hundreds of creepers burgling the city blind every night, and with him working for Messima, he could've had his pick of any one of them. True, there'd always been the odd rumour floating around about me, but that was before the war, and it was only ever a whisper or two amongst a very select circle of cat burglars and jewel thieves. And since then I'd done everything I could to keep myself from popping up on anyone's horizon. Had Chalkie been earwigging some of those old stories about me? And if so, who was it, I wondered, who'd been wasting my time by repeating them all to him?

He looked at me, all milk of human kindness gone. "I'm really not getting through to you, am I, Jethro? And here I've been trying to be so very civil." He sighed theatrically, shook his head, and became all business-like and cold. "All right, then, have it your way. So let me make this abundantly clear. As far as Mr. Messima is concerned, if you're creeping anywhere on his manor, in the West End, Mayfair, Belgravia, or anywhere else in the City of Westminster, then he wants his full share of the proceeds. Nothing more, and nothing less."

I smiled my most enigmatic smile, admitting nothing, confirming nothing. It was a little too close to the truth for it to be healthy. To make things worse, he began to wave his expensive brown leather turtles backwards and forwards under my nose. The splayed fingers looked like they were giving me a bunch of V-signs.

"And as for me, Jethro, if you won't consider my offer then just remember to keep your trap good and shut about it. It never happened. And I warn you, if you ever tried making trouble for me with Messima over it, I'd make certain things got very uncomfortable for you. I'm sure you'd like to keep all your fingers on your hands. It would be such a pity for you to wake up one morning and see bits of them bobbing up and down in a bottle of vinegar on your kitchen table."

"That's very poetic, Chalkie," I said. "You been reading those Yank detective comics again? Why don't you just bugger off into that hole you slithered out of and don't ever bother coming back."

"Don't come it with me, Jethro. You just remember I can easily call up all the muscle I ever need, so just be sure and keep our little conversation to yourself or there'll be trouble. And while we're at it, let me give you one or two other little things to think about. That brother-in-law of yours, for instance, the taxi-driver, he could have a very nasty accident with a runaway lorry sometime. Or there's that pretty blonde-haired, blue-eyed sister of yours. It'd be such a shame if she couldn't keep that lovely face of hers all in one piece . . ."

But I'd already moved in, my eyes blazing, and it was no feint this time, I meant business. "Chalkie, if you so much as lay a finger on my sister or anyone I call family, you're well on your way to being dead. Got it?" His breath smelled of gin and peppermint, and his hair stank of days-old brilliantine. I was suddenly very, very sick of him.

"You're making a big mistake, no one—" He tried to finish his sentence, but as I had my hand tight around his throat I honestly couldn't make head or tail of what he was saying. I tried to slap some sense into him with my other hand in the hope he'd speak up, but I got the feeling he'd stopped trying, so I hit him again to give him some encouragement. When he'd finally got some proper colour back in his face, I banged his head against the wall a few times and let go. Then I stood back to give him some air.

He'd gone way, way over the line in threatening my sister, Joanie. I'm one thing—you could demand money or threaten me until the cows come home—but she was family, and Chalkie in threatening her or even her old man, Barry, was completely out of order. It was against all the rules and he knew it, and if he didn't, he did now. But that's always the trouble with people like Chalkie, that think they're superior to everybody else, they get ideas way, way above their station.

Chalkie slid down the cream-painted brickwork and crumpled up into a heap on the floor, his nose bleeding badly all over his posh white riding mack and blue-striped suit. After a minute or two I gave him a few gentle taps with the tip of my boot to see if he was alright, and he managed a groan that travelled all the way up from his handmade brown shoes. Then he fell silent again. But not wanting to waste any more of his or my valuable time, I leaned over and shouted, "That was personal, Chalkie, not business."

He lay there on the corridor floor as if he had all day, then his eyes blinked a few times and he slowly rolled over onto his hands and knees and he began to crawl away. Big drops of blood dripped from his nose and sploshed everywhere, and he made a right old mess. When he got to the far wall he pulled himself up and stood holding on to it for support. Then he ran a trembling hand through his lank, greasy hair and tried to straighten his tie, which was very dignified of him under the circumstances. So I kicked his briefcase across to him and he bent down to pick it up, and then he wiped the blood from his nose with the back of his hand and made for the exit. He turned back to me, his eyes as black and hard as the North Sea, and said something I couldn't quite make out. I didn't think he was trying to apologise, but I let it go. Then still holding on to the wall, he stepped very gingerly past the stage door and disappeared out into the dock-door courtyard beyond.

"Everything alright, Jethro?"

Alf had popped from right out nowhere with Mr. Wood—an old wooden truncheon—in his hand. I'm not sure how handy he'd have really been with it at his age, but I tell you, the thought that he might have had a go to try and help me almost choked me up. As I said, he was a good bloke, and there are never enough of them around.

"It is now, Alf," I said, "it is now. Thanks for asking."

Alf looked dolefully at the bloodstained wall and floor, but didn't say a word. He reached back inside his doorkeeper's lodge, returned the truncheon to its appointed hook on the wall, and with only the slightest shake of his head went off to get a mop and a pail.

"I said he was a right bleeder."

"You did, Alf, you did. But he's bleedin' gone now. And everything's back to normal."

I must admit, though, I did begin to wonder just how long that would last. Messima could afford to take the long view with me, but not for charity, mind, just business. Always practical, he'd mete out only as much pain and punishment as he thought was my due and for his reputation not to suffer. I knew I could make it up to him by agreeing to pull a caper for him sometime; and crippled or dead, I'd be of no use to him at all. So unless I was completely misreading my tea leaves, I could see I might be in for a good kicking or a striping for creeping where I shouldn't have, but not much more. At least I'd live.

But Chalkie was another matter. It seemed he'd developed ambitions of his own and now had every reason going to want to keep them quiet, which not only made him unpredictable, but doubly dangerous. He was playing a very deadly game with Messima, and I didn't want to find myself stuck in the middle of it. I also knew that after our little talk Chalkie wouldn't take things lying down; as hell hath no fury like a worm that's turned. And once he'd got his deathly pallor back, I knew he'd want to rub out the memory of me smearing up his hair and his self-esteem. He'd have to do it a bit sharpish, too, before word got round that I'd sent him packing. He'd lose too much face otherwise. And knowing him as I did, all it would take would be a dark, foggy street somewhere, and a few of his muscle-bound friends to help him wipe the slate clean. Then God help me.

Chapter 8

AND NOW ON TO BURMA

There's a bar deep down inside the bowels of the Palladium that's reserved just for the stage-hands. It sounds very thoughtful of the management, doesn't it? But it was really only to stop people like me from nipping round the corner for a quick one when we were in the middle of a show. I suppose we should've been offended the bosses thought so little of us, but we weren't, it was all part of the game. Beer and spirits were always a bit cheaper down there, so it was simply a quick way of getting our wages back off us. We didn't mind, though, the bar came in dead handy for all sorts of backstage dealings. The moral of the story being that if it seems too good to be true, it probably isn't. And that's true, only as long as you remember there are always exceptions.

Anyway, that night after the set-to with Chalkie, I didn't much fancy hanging about, so I legged it around the corner to the Handsel, the pub just a few doors down from the Palladium's front entrance in Argyll Street. I needed a telephone as far away from people's big, flapping ears as possible, and the landlord let me use the public phone at the back of the pub and didn't mind when I locked the door from the saloon bar behind me. He always thought I was talking dirty to a rich bit of skirt married to a motor dealer up in Swiss Cottage, and I never went out of my way to put him right. He was a good enough sort, but it was always the odd fan of petrol coupons that kept him turning a deaf ear.

As usual, the pub was full of people trying to drown their sorrows in watery beer—yet another brilliant idea dreamed up by His Majesty's Government to make the country's scarce resources stretch even further. But with a pint costing a whopping one and fourpence, few had money enough to succeed, though it didn't ever seem to stop them from trying. I pushed through the crowd, slipped round the back and put the pennies in the slot, dialled the exchange and asked for the number. It wasn't a long chat, but afterwards I felt a lot better about the state of things. Insurance brings its own special kind of confidence, doesn't it?

I made my way back through into the public bar, nodded my thanks to mine host, and I'd not gone six feet when someone turned around and bumped into me. Now that's a dodgy thing to have happen in any pub, but in London when you're half-expecting someone to have a go at you, it can be the first step to blood being spilt on the floor.

"What the hell . . . ?"

"Hang on, hang on, it's my fault. I'm sorry, I didn't see you . . . by bloody 'eck, it's you, isn't it?"

"What? Well, stroll on, not you again." It was the bloke from rehearsals that had bumped into me earlier. And if it wasn't for the smile on his face that seemed to say he was pleased to see me, I think I would've picked up the nearest beer bottle and smashed it round his head. Now don't get me wrong, it's just that you tend to react first and think about things later, in the pubs round our way.

"What you having?" he said. "How about a pint of Best? It seems to go down well here." He looked down at the puddle of beer on the floor with an exaggerated sigh and then laughed.

"Right comedian, you are," I said, smiling. "All right, then, very decent of you." A few minutes' chat about nothing in particular would help take my mind off things; couldn't harm, could it? So, I asked him, "You ever find out what happened with that group of yours, then?"

"You were right," he said quietly. "The pathetic buggers went on without me and didn't even leave a message in case I turned up. Well, it's their loss, you only ever walk out on me the once."

"Well, believe me, mate, they were bleedin' awful. Couldn't sing for toffee."

"Well, I sing like a friggin' lark, I do," he growled.

"I bet you do, sunshine, I bet you do," I said, laughing, but I could tell he was right choked about what had happened.

"Here, that name you called yourselves, the Singing Burma Boys, were you out there, then?"

He took a sip of his beer, narrowed his eyes and looked off somewhere into the distance, or maybe it was just the poor light in the bar. "Yeah, I was in Burma; Royal Horse Artillery. And before the war, I was a regular out in India. Joined up, as there was no work at home, and even fewer prospects. So I ran away, lied about my age, and took the King's shilling; first with the Colours, then the Reserve. Then the war started and I was sent here and there, as an instructor mostly. Ended up the war as a Sergeant-Major. You?"

"Merchant Navy. Sort of family tradition. Grandad was a stoker, dad a seaman, and I followed on, but luckily I didn't have to shovel it, as I . . . er . . . unexpectedly came into a bit of money. I went to college in South-ampton; the first ever to do so in our family. Truth was I couldn't get out of London fast enough; it was always so dark and damp, and full of disease and fog, I hated the bloody place. So I went off to sea with Cunard White Star line, saw the world, and had a high old time of it until Corporal Hitler started all his nonsense. Then when the war broke out, it was back and forth across the Atlantic more times than was good for me. And that was bad enough, but then came the Baltic, and that was bleedin' diabol-ical. What with all the ammunition, oil, and kerosene the ships were carry-ing, and everyone waiting for the next moment to be their last. I saw a lot of good mates get blown out of the water and a lot of things I don't ever want to see again. Had a ship sunk from under me once or twice, but got fished out each time; just lucky, I guess. Went in as a Fourth Officer and ended up a First, but I still jacked the whole thing in as soon as I could after VE Day."

We looked at one another and nodded, we didn't need to say more, we both knew how bad things had been before the war, and why we'd both chosen to get up and out. It was funny how easy it was to talk to him about such things, though; it was much more than I'd said to anyone else since I'd been back home. Mind you, I left out all the stuff about my night-time creeping activities, it didn't seem appropriate somehow. We were just two dogs sniffing, friendly like, finding out what lamp-posts we'd peed on in the past, but as I wasn't ever going to see him again, what did it matter what I said?

"Another?" I said, holding up my glass.

He smiled and nodded, and I got them in. And while waiting for the beers to come, I looked at him a bit more closely. I could see he was a very fit lad, and by his accent, from somewhere up North. Thick, dark, curly hair, open faced, nicely built, not too tall, about five eight, five nine, and he'd probably boxed a bit. Tough, but quiet about it, you know what I mean? Not flash, more self-contained. It struck me then just how much he resembled John Garfield, that Hollywood actor that looked like he'd fought his way up from the streets. That's probably what made me think of boxing. But this guy didn't have a mark on him and he wasn't at all banged about, so as he'd said, maybe singing really was his game.

"Cheers," I said. "Not much to sing about in India, is there?"

"Some people hated it, but I enjoyed it. Cheers." He took a sip of beer and continued. "India gets to you in ways you'd never know. Fell in love with the place if you want to know the truth. Magic it was."

He went silent. I nodded, not quite sure what to say, then I just changed the subject. "Oh, I get it now, that name, Burma Boys? Is that like we all used to write on the back of the letters we sent home?"

"That's it," he chuckled, back to his cheery self. "Well, there was now't else on our minds for most of the time, was there?"

"B-U-R-M-A." I spelled out the letters. "Be Upstairs Ready My Angel. That's something to sing about, isn't it? You got a girl, have you?"

"Yeah, back at home, she waited for me, too. I was lucky, unlike some guys whose girls went off with someone the first chance they got."

"There's just no understanding women," I said, "but I don't half love trying to find out." We both laughed at that, nothing dirty, just appreciative at the wonder of it all. But I didn't think it wise to mention that in my time I'd been one of those other guys that many of those girls had gone off with.

"Eeeh, you are awful, but you're alright with it, as well," he said, sounding just like George Formby, the ukulele-playing variety star.

"That's very good, that is, sounds just like him," I said, finishing my drink. "Here before I go, who's this then?" I turned away, pushed an eyebrow up, then looked back all cruel and sardonic, and said through clenched teeth, "You, me lady, are an elemental force full of the most human and natural passions. Yet you are forced by those same desires into crimes the result of which you can never escape."

"Blimey, that's that actor, James Mason, to the life. What picture was that from? No, I've got it. It was *The Wicked Lady*, with Margaret Lock-wood. Now, there's a lovely girl. Go on, do another one."

"Okay, just one then. Who's this?" This time I pushed both eyebrows up, sucked in my nostrils, looked down my nose, and said in a stiff-upper-lip accent, "Then we'll send Hitler a telegram saying, 'The *Torrin*'s ready, you can start your war.' All right, my boys?"

"My, but that's brilliant, that is, you even looked different. Noel Coward in *In Which We Serve*. You an actor or something?"

"No," I said, "it's just a knack I have. I work behind the scenes as a stage-hand usually, mostly up on the fly floor. But it's amazing what you can pick up from them actors just by watching."

"You're very good, you know," he said. "I'm telling you, if you're not an actor, you should be, you'd make a bloody fortune."

I already was, of course, but not quite in the way he was thinking, but anyway I was chuffed he'd liked the little bits I'd done. Well, all the world's a stage, isn't it, even a pub. And whether you're an actor or a creeper you always appreciate it when your art gets admired, and your time upon the boards—or the tiles—hasn't been entirely wasted.

"No, no, you're too kind, but say it again, anyway."

I laughed; he laughed. He was a good bloke and I was glad I'd met him, he'd helped lift my mood. "I'll be off, then," I said. "Thanks for the pint. Nice chatting with you; what was the name, again?"

"Seth," he said, raising his glass.

"I'm Jethro," I said, holding out my hand. "Well, Seth, you go easy with that bleedin' guitar case of yours, you could do someone a right mischief otherwise."

"Yes," he said, "I'll keep that in mind. You go safe, Jethro. Nice talking to you, too."

And with that, I left the bar and went out into the night.

Chapter 9

SHIPS IN THE NIGHT

I stood back from the doorway and peered out into the dank night air. There were the beginnings of a real nasty fog. It was a thick, swirling, sooty curtain even up West, where at least there were lamp-posts and theatre lights to push it back a few feet. But the bright lights were already losing the battle and turning a sickly yellow-orange in shame. The costers with their fruit barrows at the top of the street had packed it in for the night and gone off home, and the area in front of the theatre was all but deserted. And for once, even the Quality Inn cafe on the corner looked pale and uninviting. Of course, there was no sign anywhere of London's finest, stealthily flitting about in their funny helmets and capes, which was typical as there's never a copper around when you need one. A cab turned up Argyll Street and its dim headlights washed the back of Dickens and Jones opposite. There were a couple of blokes standing, smoking, in the shadow of the department store doorway, the glow from their cigarettes like two little evil eyes in the dark. Nothing sinister about that, well not much, but you get a feeling, don't you?

A well-dressed man and woman walked past the pub doorway arm in arm, just as two of the pub's noisier patrons pushed past me into the street. I stepped into line behind them all, suddenly very glad of the company. It was less than a hundred yards back round to the Palladium's stage door, but it now seemed much, much further than that. The couple—him with a bowler, she with a little black hat, grey fox stole, and antique pear-shape pendant earrings—turned left at the corner into Great Marlborough Street. Just as the two noisy blokes from the pub crossed over towards Regent Street and began to fade into the night. "That was great help," I said, quickening my pace.

Liberty's loomed up in front of me, its black-and-white half-timbering looking in the fog eerily like one of Nelson's ships passing in the night. I hunched my shoulders and turned the corner. There were a few parked cars, otherwise the street was clear. And then suddenly it wasn't. There was a bloke in a hat standing across the road next to the lamp-post at the top of the alley that led down to Foubert's Place. He caught sight of me, nodded to someone, then threw his cigarette away. It arced in the dark like a tiny tracer shell. He started across the road to intercept me, but didn't seem to be in any hurry about it. I looked up and down the street and saw why. The well-dressed couple had disappeared into the fog, and coming up fast behind me were the two blokes I'd seen standing outside Dickens and Jones. Which meant there were three of them. "Well, this could get a bit interesting," I said to myself.

The little courtyard that led down to the stage door was now only thirty yards away, but it might as well have been thirty miles. If I sprinted forward, I'd probably have ended up in a scuffle long enough for the two tearaways behind me to rush up and start giving me one. Maybe, maybe not, but at that precise moment—and directly outside the Magistrate's Court, of all places—the doors of one of the parked cars flew open and large black shapes started piling out into the street. It was a Yank motor, long nose, sweeping curves, and as big as a hearse, and I was angry with myself that I'd failed to notice it before, because I knew the car; it was one of several that belonged to Messima.

The black shapes grew hats and faces, and then hands grew razors, knuckledusters, and leather coshes. There was a whole gang of them, and they must've all sat through *Brighton Rock* a dozen times to make sure they got the look down properly. But I have to admit, it was the blood-curdling weaponry they'd brought with them that made the biggest impression. One of them had even thought to bring along a wicked-looking bayonet that gleamed in the watery light like it was ready for kit inspection. There were six of them in all, including Chalkie White, who I noticed was holding a blood-stained handkerchief up to his nose. I must've broken it earlier. I hadn't intended to, but accidents will happen, and if it really was broken then the silly sod should've gone and got it seen to. But by then it was very clear that Chalkie had decided to have me seen to instead.

Not to put too fine a point upon it, but I was well and truly buggered. I had my back to the wall and they had me surrounded on three sides. Chalkie limped his way through the assembled muscle and sneered at me. I felt chilled, but I think the damp night air was getting to me. "Chalkie, you're looking a lot better, I must say," I said jovially.

"Shut it," he honked. "You've been asking for it for a long time, Jethro, and now I'm only too happy to oblige."

"Tell me, Chalkie," I said. "Does Mr. Messima know you're out in one of his flash motors? Or are you moonlighting again?"

"You just shut it," he spat. "And get down on your knees and crawl over here and lick my shoes. You need the practice, because you're not going to be walking again for a very long time."

"No, thanks, Chalkie, my religion don't allow it," I said, my throat suddenly feeling a teeny bit dry.

"Shall I do him now, Mister Chalkie, sir?" one of them growled.

"It's Mr. Smythe-White to you, you berk. No, not yet, I want him to beg for mercy first." He stepped into the dim light of a nearby lamp-post, but stayed out of reach just in case I thought of throwing a quick punch at him. His eyes were as bright as pin-balls and there were little beads of perspiration all across his forehead. He licked his lips. "You're going to get a thorough kicking, Jethro. Then the boys are going to stripe you so bad, you're going to have more tracks across you than Charing Cross railway station."

I knew he meant it, too. I recognised one or two of the blokes he'd brought with him, and they were right hard cases. The others were strangers to me, but I did notice that the two youngest gangsters were sweating like mad and looked very jittery. Still wet behind the ears, I thought to myself. There'd be no finesse with either of them, which meant it would be very tricky second-guessing their moves.

"And once they've finished cutting you, Jethro, I'm going to slice your fingers open to the bone, so you won't be able to twirl a lock or twiddle a tit for years." Chalkie laughed. He was right into his stride now, all the smarm long gone. And, me? I was starting to shiver.

"It's not personal this isn't, Jeffro, just business." It was the other hard man. He was a big bugger. I didn't know him that well, but I'd seen him around. I nodded at him and threw a sneer at Chalkie.

"I know that, but what're you doing with this tosser?"

"Working for a couple of flims."

"Ten quid? You must work cheap, then," I said.

He didn't like that, and he immediately tucked his chin in and down; the old fighter's stance. Me and my big mouth, it'll be the death of me yet, I thought. Then he spoke to Chalkie out of the corner of his mouth, his eyes never leaving me for an instant. "We don't normally do all this larruping and stuff, guv, we usually just get in there and do 'em over good and proper."

"Yes," said the first hard man, "we do 'em, then fuck off out of it."

"I said, shut it," snapped Chalkie. He thrust his snaky little head towards me. "I want to savour every moment of this."

"You're off your rocker, you are," I shouted. And as I'd managed to get a foot pressed up against the wall behind me during all the talking, I pushed back hard and launched myself at the two young tearaways on my right. Well, you've got to have a go, haven't you?

Unfortunately the bloke in the hat was just as quick off the mark, and as I sailed past he slashed out at me with his razor, slicing through my sleeve and my forearm. But by then I'd got my hands on one of the tearaways and butted him hard in the face. And I'd just begun to swing him round to use as a shield, when the other one somehow managed to reach in and grab hold of my jacket lapels. His screech of surprise was sharp enough to cut through glass. The two packets of safety blades I'd sewn along the edges of the lapels must've cut his fingers to ribbons. I spun away and stood there, breathing hard, blood trickling down the front of my jacket. I looked at them, they looked at me, and for a moment nobody moved. Not a bad showing, I thought to myself. For someone with no hope at all of avoiding a very serious kicking. Oh well, the valiant never taste of death, but once.

My heart was thumping away in my chest like a steam hammer and I could see them all getting ready to move in for the kill. The one in the hat who'd cut me pushed aside the two young tearaways, both now a little bit the worse off for wear, and moved forward to have another go at me. My head was still ringing from the headbutt, and my left arm felt all wet and sticky, but I turned to meet him, I had no choice. Then I swear I started hearing things.

"You alright, Jethro? Are these men bothering you?"

The voice came from behind me, but I didn't know who it could be, my mind was as foggy as the night and all I could see was Chalkie and his mob taken up short. Then Seth stepped alongside me, his guitar case gently swinging backwards and forwards by his side. "Well, stroll on," I said. "It's the Royal Artillery."

"Listen. Why don't you lot just bugger off," Seth said to them in an even-tempered voice, "and I won't tell you again."

I didn't know whether to laugh or cry, and neither did they. That sort of thing just didn't happen, it's not how things were done. I mean, no one sticks their face into a load of coshes and razors on purpose, do they? The general idea is to run like hell the other way.

Well, that's all I need, I said to myself, someone else for me to have to friggin' worry about.

"Fuck this for a game of soldiers," grumbled one of the hard men, "let's just get it over with and do them both."

They started closing in again.

Seth swung his guitar case straight at the bloke in the hat and caught him smack on the wrist. The guy yelped as his hand jerked open and his razor clattered to the pavement. But Seth was already pivoting round on one leg and he kicked out with the edge of his boot and hit Hat-man in the throat. And the bloke crumpled to the ground and writhed around as if he was having a bad attack of emphysema.

Of course that set them all off then, and effing and blinding like mad one of them rushed forward to throw a punch at Seth's head. It was the ex-boxer I'd offended earlier. He had a nasty-looking set of brass knuckle-dusters on each fist, and looked like he'd had a lot of practice using them. He let go a wicked punch that would've knocked Seth right into the middle of next week if it'd landed, only it didn't. It was weird, Seth hardly seemed to move at all, he just sort of swayed slightly to one side, and the punch whistled past, the force of it pulling the big man off balance. Then suddenly out of nowhere Seth's right hand grew a hammer, and he hit the big bloke on the side of the head, just once, right behind the ear. It sounded just like a wooden mallet striking a coconut. I knew it must've done some serious damage, because the bloke stopped all his noise and fell to the pavement like a slab of Portland stone.

And suddenly it was four against two and not at all the sort of odds Chalkie liked, and he stood rooted to the spot, his mouth opening and closing like a drowning fish. Then one of the young tearaways kicked at the guitar case and sent it flying across the pavement, and the lid flew open and the guitar landed with a twang at the feet of the big bugger with the nail-studded cosh and the nasty-looking bayonet. The bloke looked down at the guitar, snorted in surprise, and then stomped up and down on it. Then he made straight for Seth.

You could tell he was out for blood, but as he charged, Seth did something I'd never seen in a fight before, he simply turned his back. Then twisting his body sideways like a spring, he bobbed up and down, pulled his left leg back with the foot held rigid, and thrust it out hard, just as the bloke ran right on top of him. Seth caught the bloke smack on the mark with his boot, stopping him cold. And he was lucky it didn't stop his heart. I think my heart stopped dead, though, because it was in my mouth, and when I bit down on it, it tasted all burnt and brown.

I'd heard stories of how the Commandos had fought in the war; down and very dirty, and over in a flash. But this was a regular street fight in London's West End, not unarmed combat on German sentries on a night raid on Dieppe. And where the bleedin' hammer had come from I had no idea, but no complaints, mind you, only a few questions.

The trouble is, just let your mind wander for a second and you land yourself in even more trouble. One of the young tearaways swung his razor towards my face; a cross-cut that would've sliced off both my cheeks had it reached me. It didn't though, thank God, because Seth jabbed the hammer handle in and stopped the kid's arm cold. But then Seth's boots slid on some bits of broken guitar on the pavement, and as he flapped air to try and keep his balance, the razor swung down, sliced deep across his arm, and came away all bloody. He rolled, taking the fall on his shoulders, then pivoting round, he swept out both his legs and caught the tearaway at calf level, and knocked him clean over. Then with another twist and lift of the legs he sent the kid flying head first into the wall. It was just like watching wrestling down the Queensway Baths. And I heard the thud and the crack from over where I was standing, so I know it must've hurt.

The other young tearaway, the one that'd cut his fingers to pieces when he'd caught hold of my lapels didn't seem to be too keen to try his hand, but he did. You had to admire him for that, it was useless and he knew it, but you never know with that kind of pluck, he might've just got lucky and ended up doing some real damage. Anyway, the kid, having seen what Seth could do, decided to have a go at me instead, and that's when the bayonet flashed into my line of sight. He'd picked the bloody thing up off the pavement, because he probably couldn't grip hold of his razor properly. But that was always the trouble with cut-throat razors, they were slippery little devils when they were covered in blood. That's why the older hands only ever slashed downwards in a fight so as to get a clean finish; the blood went over the victim then, not all over your fingers. And you had to be careful, no one wanted to slice a jugular by mistake and end up on a murder charge.

The kid ran straight at me, but it was only a feint, and at the last second he turned and went for Seth. See what I mean about being unpredictable? Anyway, as the nasty little swine lunged forward, so did I, and as he jabbed the bayonet at Seth's belly, I swung my arm down and blocked it. It's lucky most bayonets are designed like butcher's knives with a hard ridge along the top, because if it'd had a double-edged blade like my Fairbairn-Sykes, my hand would've come clean off an inch or two above my wrist. I didn't feel a thing, though, probably because my arm was throbbing like mad from the razor slashing I'd got earlier. Then that blessed hammer turned up in Seth's hand again and he smacked the kid right under the chin and knocked him cold. And it was all over.

Well, almost. Chalkie still hadn't moved a muscle. He stood all limp, his arms hanging by his side, his blood-stained hanky clutched in one hand, his wicked little leather cosh dangling forlornly from the other. And you could see from his eyes that his brain was still trying to piece it all together. So I turned towards him nice and slow, and smiled. Then I said, "Oh, what the hell," and punched him on the nose. There were a number of cracks, so it sounded like I might have really broken it that time. "I think that hooter of yours is going to need some very skilful setting,

Chalkie," I said, flexing my fingers to make sure I hadn't broken my hand. But he didn't reply, he just stood there swaying from side to side, howling, so I kicked him hard on both shins and he went down like a sack of potatoes.

"You okay, Jethro?"

"I am now, Seth, thanks to you," I said, taking a deep breath.

"Thanks for stopping that bayonet when you did, Jethro," he said quietly. "You saved my life." He narrowed his eyes at me and nodded. "I won't forget it."

"Well, I don't know about that," I said, feeling very relieved about the way it had all turned out. "But I somehow get the idea it would take a lot more than an old army bayonet to put you down."

I looked around at what was left of Chalkie and his mob, and for some reason old Winston's words on VE Day popped right into my head: "The evil-doers now lie prostrate before us." I spat at the ground and kicked the bayonet and knuckledusters into the gutter. Then I heard voices calling out in the fog and the sounds of people running towards us. Funny, isn't it? The way you always get a crowd when you don't want one. It was definitely time to go.

I turned to Seth. "Come on, Seth, let's scarper . . . what the . . . ?"

He was kneeling down beside what was left of his guitar case. "Just a second," he said, "I don't want to leave these behind."

He scooped up some folded-up sheets of paper from the wreckage of the case, letters perhaps, and stuffed them inside his jacket. He didn't seem to be too put out by his arm, but I'd begun to be really bothered by mine. I could feel blood running down my sleeve, and my hand and shirt cuff were both covered in it. A taxi-cab skidded to a stop in the middle of the road, but I was already well away, with Seth close behind me. An angry voice yelled out after us, but I wasn't waiting for any of it, there were just too many people getting interested for my liking. It was time to be good and gone. And we ran through the alley to Foubert's Place and eeled our way around the top of Carnaby Street and made for Kingly Street. It was dark and dingy and everything smelt of stale piss and beer, but then so did most of London, most of the time.

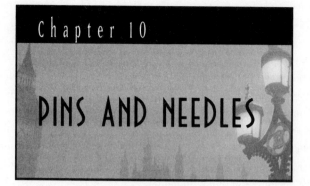

Chapter 10

PINS AND NEEDLES

It was pitch-black along those back streets, and even the fog had to think twice before going down them, but as we zigzagged down into Carnaby Street, I gave a quick nod to 'old Bill.' No, I don't mean the boys in blue from West End Central police station, I mean the boy from Stratford, the old bobby-dazzler himself, Mr. William Shakespeare.

There's a bust of him leaning out of a window in astonishment at all the goings-on down in the street below. It's one of those little sights that tickle me, London's full of them, and I often used to pop by and smile up at him when I worked the Palladium. It's got much more life to it than the memorial they've got to him in Westminster Abbey, or that statue Giovanni Fontana did of him that they put up in Leicester Square; the one that had its left hand missing for years thanks to a Luftwaffe air raid. Anyway, you can't miss him if you take the time to look. He's in a tiny recess high up in the wall over the Shakespeare's Head pub. He's there, bald head, pointed whiskers and all, just above the rusty mock-Tudor lamp, ready to light up your life all over again.

"We can nip through here and come out further down Regent Street," I yelled over my shoulder. I didn't like the thought of us going any deeper into Soho as there'd be too many prying eyes about. So we had it on our toes until I heard the tin whistles being blown, and that's when I knew it was time for us to slow down and walk. Nothing pulls a copper faster than the sight and sound of running feet; it draws them like bluebottles to a dead cat.

It was never police patrol cars you had to worry about; it was always the lone PC Plod walking his beat. A police constable quietly proceeding down the street at the regulation two miles per hour, with his sharp little eyes looking everywhere, and with him knowing who was who, and what was what, was a different matter entirely. He was a bloody nuisance. And never more so than when you were halfway up a wall hanging on to someone's slippery wet drain-pipe or you were running for your life.

"Let's just slow down and try and act normal," I shouted over my shoulder, and we slowed to a fast walk. I looked at him. He looked as cool as a cucumber and like he hadn't even broken a sweat. "Here, Seth," I said, still panting, "where on earth did that hammer come from?" He just nodded and carried on breathing in through his nose and out through his mouth. But he didn't say anything, he just nodded and smiled. So I nodded back, and we walked on in silence through the swirling smog, our footsteps echoing back at us from the sides of the high buildings that lined the dark, damp, narrow streets. I noticed a few shadows moving in doorways as we passed, but by the sound of the gruntings and moanings they all seemed to be well into what it was they were doing, and we slipped by as quietly as we could.

"Look, Seth, what you did back there, thanks a million. They were going to cut me up like a side of beef until you came along. You didn't have to stick your nose in, but you did. Why, for heaven's sake?"

"That's simple," he said quietly, "I'd already made up my mind you were a decent bloke, so when I saw you needed help I just got stuck in. I didn't know who they were and I didn't care, they just looked like a right gang of bullies. All my life, in school, the Army, or wherever, it's been the one thing I can't abide."

"But what about all that fancy footwork you did? And that hammer? That was a right turn up for the book."

"Well, as I said, I was an instructor, and sometimes it's difficult to forget all the little things they teach you in the Army."

"Well, up the British Army, is all I can say," I said.

"And this thing?" he said, producing the hammer from under his jacket. "This is what's called an 'Halifax Persuader.'"

"An 'Halifax Persuader'?" I almost choked. "What the hell's that, when it's at home?"

"It's anything heavy you can get your hands on that might turn out to be a bit useful. I always carry something like it when I go somewhere strange, and especially when I find myself down here in London. I mean, it can be a real funny place at times."

I laughed, but I knew he was being dead serious. "Well, anyway, funny peculiar or funny ha-ha, thanks for coming to my rescue."

"Don't mention it," he said. And he meant it, too. What was done was done, and it'd been no more troubling to him than lancing a nasty boil. He'd given some of the top goons in London a right seeing-to, and then put the incident right out of his mind. But I knew that once Chalkie and his mob had got themselves all bandaged up, they'd be thinking about nothing else. They'd have to stitch together some sort of believable story, and quickly, or it wouldn't just be their reputations that would suffer. Because if Messima ever found out what had really gone on outside the Palladium, and why, he'd personally exact his own pound of flesh from everybody involved. So Chalkie would have to come up with something good, or he'd get himself cut up for being totally out of order. I tell you, you'd be surprised how dangerous it could be being a villain in those days.

We padded on through the fog towards Golden Square, both of us keeping a watery eye out for anything unexpected. The blood on my hand looked black and sticky in the yellow streetlights, and my arm stung like hell, but as all my fingers still seemed to move okay, I reckoned things couldn't be too bad. But I saw that Seth's arm was covered in blood, too, and that we were both leaving trails on the pavement. It wasn't a good way for anyone to be seen round Soho.

"We'll get stopped and questioned looking like this," I panted, "so let's chance a cab, okay?"

We edged round the Square to Brewer Street, but I got the feeling we shouldn't go any deeper into Soho. "Follow your inklings," my old dad used to say, "but always keep your wits about you along the way." We hadn't gone a few yards, when a shadow stepped out of a doorway.

" 'Ere, either of you two gentlemen like a short time?"

I don't know who jumped more, Seth or me. My nerves were still on edge, but I at least should've been expecting it. The place was usually full of brasses plying their trade, and if you didn't get stopped a dozen times by prostitutes in one street, you soon would be down the next. But the old girl took our surprised stares in her stride; it was just all in a night's work to her. She looked a bit worn by it all, though, her lips weren't on too straight and she couldn't have been much more than twenty-four or twenty-five.

"You can both have it for a quid, if you like. Each, that is. But I've got a friend; redhead she is, nice with it. Speaks French. Does the frog as well. Go on, it'll do yer good, give you both a lift. How about it, boys? It's your lucky night. Well? What yer waiting for, then?"

"Not tonight, love. Thanks, but we've got some pressing business elsewhere."

" 'Ere, you two bleedin' nancy boys or something? Don't yer like pretty girls then? You tight-arsed gits. You won't get it better anywhere else, you know, even from them posh cows down Shepherds Market. Come on, dearies, you can both have me for ten bob."

We moved off, not bothering to look back, but now I had my eyes out for her pimp as well; it wasn't beyond those boys to try and roll you and steal your wallet, whether you've had your end away or not. 'Doing a Murphy' they called it, on account of it being so easy to do. So we picked up the pace and walked down the middle of the road, and I steered us back towards the lights of Regent Street.

"If anyone asks us again," I said, "just say we're the bleedin' Road Stars." Seth laughed at that. The Stars were a well-known group of buskers that entertained cinema queues round Leicester Square and Soho by tap-dancing and juggling, and taking pratfalls in the middle of the street. And with the way things had been going for us that night, being taken for a comedy turn looked to be right up our alley.

"Oh, one other thing," I said. "It'd probably be a good idea if you dropped that bloody hammer of yours down the next drain."

He nodded, and we stopped a moment by the corner of Warwick Street, and it was done. I chanced to look back over my shoulder, and off in the murky distance I saw the pale wash of headlight beams turning out of Golden Square. The motor became two little yellow cat's eyes that got bigger and bigger. Then I heard the driver gun the engine and the car accelerated, heading straight for us.

"Watch it, Seth," I shouted. I couldn't make out the shape of the thing at first, then I saw it was a black cab with its yellow 'For Hire' light switched off to show it was already carrying a fare. "No luck there then," I called out. "Just like the friggin' buses, there's never a soddin' taxi when you need one." I let my breath out, but noticed my hands were still clenched and ready for bother. I kept my eyes on the cab and for one gut-wrenching moment I thought it was trying to run us down. And we really didn't need any more trouble at that point, as Glasshouse Street police station was just round the corner, and that was the very last place we needed to end up in.

The taxi skidded to a stop in a screech of rubber tyres and tortured brakes, missing me by inches, even though I was pressed hard up against a brick wall. I yelled out angrily. And so did the bloke driving the cab.

"Jesus aitch Christ, Jeffro, what the fuck's going on? I've been driving round and round like a nutcase trying to find you in all this bleedin' fog. Why the bloody hell did you toe it when I yelled at you? Just get in sharpish, will you, before anyone eyeballs you. And you'd better bring your mate with you, if he's with you, that is, he's standing there like a right lemon."

"Wotcher, Bubs, nice to see you, too," I said, but he didn't hear.

"What the friggin' hell happened back there of the Palladium? It looked like the Blitz had started up all over again."

"Thanks for coming, Bubs," I said, pushing Seth into the taxi. "Do me a favour and just get us home a bit sharpish, will you? We've both been badly cut, and I need Joanie to help patch us up."

"Patch you up, Jeffro? I should cocoa, she'll play bloody hell with you, she will, and you know it."

Barry let out the clutch and we hurtled off with him crashing up through the gears, which was very unusual for him as he's usually such a careful driver considering it's his own cab. But it did tell me how really worked up about everything he truly was.

"So what the fuck's going on, then?" he shouted back over his shoulder. "First, there's one of Buggy's boys coming round the house with a message from him saying there's been a bit of trouble, but not to call round because he's dealing with it hisself, and he'll see you at the cafe in the morning. Then the very next thing you're on the blower telling me

I'd best get round the theatre and bring your kitbag a bit sharpish. So I repeat, what the fuck's going on?"

I blinked. The news about Buggy was very troubling, but as the message had said for me to do nothing, I put the matter aside until the morning, and tapped my fingers up and down on the leather seat pondering my own problems. But at least now I had a couple of extra life-savers to even things out should there be any more trouble. For hidden under the back seat, in my old kitbag, were my twin-barrel, side-by-side, sawn-off shotguns. Civilian sporting guns, mind you, just in case I ever got nicked by the police. The law came down like a ton of bricks if they ever found any kind of military hardware on you. So, you only ever carried a revolver if you wanted to put someone down for good; it wasn't worth the risk otherwise. Which is why I always kept my own British Army–standard-issue, officers-for-the-use-of–Webley .455 calibre pistol in a very safe and secure place. And never anywhere near Barry's cab.

A sawn-off was ideal for certain jobs, and most villains regarded it as the tool of choice for holding up banks or robbing post offices. It only ever took a single blast into the ceiling and suddenly everyone became very co-operative. I only used my sawn-offs for protection, though, and never on a job. I'd hang one on a thin leather strap under my overcoat and no one would be any the wiser. And I only used light-load cartridges, because even though they'd hurt like hell and would very definitely put the shits up somebody, the blast wouldn't kill anyone. Well, not intentionally.

I blinked again, and shouted through the sliding-glass partition loud enough for Barry to hear, "Just hold your horses a minute, Bubs. First things first. Bubs, this is Seth; Seth, this is Barry, or Bubs, as I call him. He married my sister, Joanie, which makes him my favourite brother-in-law; even though he is, in fact, my only brother-in-law."

"Hello, Barry."

"Wotcher, Seth."

"And, Bubs, a little word to the wise. Seth's what happened back there, so you just mind your p's and q's."

In the brief silence that followed while Barry digested that little lot, we went hurtling up Regent Street towards Oxford Circus. And as we rattled past Liberty's I looked down into Great Marlborough Street. The fog was still swirling about, but it looked like an ambulance or two had turned up, as well as a couple of police Railtons, their big powerful head-lamps cutting into the dark like a searchlight battery. I shook my head and faced forward, just as Barry turned round to look at me. I always hated him doing that while he was driving.

"Well?" he said, not amused.

"Chalkie White was well out of order earlier, Bubs, so I had to give him a smack. I knew he'd try to get back at me some time, only the slippery sod was a bit quick off the mark, and he rounded up some of Messima's muscle to do me over after rehearsals had finished."

I decided not to mention the bit about Chalkie threatening Joanie, otherwise Barry would've turned the taxi around right there and then and gone and given Chalkie another hiding all by himself. He'd have done it, too, no matter where Chalkie was; in a hospital bed, down the police station, in Lyons Corner House, anywhere. He's relentless when he gets worked up, and he's very protective when it comes to Joanie. "It was about to get a bit nasty for me, Bubs, when Seth here showed up out of the blue and hit them over the head with his guitar."

"What the fuck you talkin' about, Jeffro? I tell yer, there was fuckin' bodies all over the place. Have you got another shooter I don't know about or something?"

"No guns, Bubs, just the two of us. Oh, yes, and Seth's little hammer." I looked at Seth, and saw that while Barry and me had been going back and forth, he'd quietly rolled up his handkerchief and tied it around his arm to make a tourniquet. "That's using your head," I said, trying to pull a handkerchief out of my own pocket, but my arm had stiffened up and I found I couldn't manage it.

"Here," he said, taking off his tie and tying it around my arm.

"Sorry about the guitar," I said, "I'll get you another one." He nodded and smiled and went back to staring out of the cab window, and then he started humming to himself. Less than an hour before, we'd just been two ships passing in a bleak London night, and now for good or ill we were in the same boat, but where we'd land up, God only knew.

"Here you two, if you're leaking claret all over the place, do it on the blanket back there; blood's always difficult to get off the seats."

"Ta, Bubs, you always were so thoughtful for others."

"Don't you be so sarky, Jeffro, you just work out what you're going to say to Joanie when you get 'ome, that's all."

Well, that shut me up for a bit, and I just sat and stared out at the ghostly shapes of the old Langham Hotel on one side and Broadcasting House on the other. And we rattled on in silence up through Portland Place to the Marylebone Road, on past Baker Street Tube Station, and within a few minutes we'd turned up Lisson Grove, and dog-legged our way through the back streets towards Church Street and the Victory.

The Victory Cafe was managed and run by my sister, Joanie. She was part-owner of the cafe, as well, but only the two of us knew about that. I didn't want the whole street to know that it was me that owned the entire building, either, it was none of their business. They'd start asking too many questions if they knew; questions I didn't want to have to answer. So as far as everyone else was concerned, we were just lucky enough to have a very easy-going landlord. She and Barry lived in the flat above the cafe, while I lived in the flat above theirs, the top-floor flat; the one that looked out over the rooftops of London.

Joanie looked at us and didn't say a word, not one. She just went into the kitchen, put on the kettle, and got a big bottle of Dettol disinfectant out of the cupboard under the sink. Then she came back into the little hallway where we were all still standing around like pillocks. She motioned with her eyes—you know the way women do—towards the kitchen, and still not a word, nothing. But then she didn't have to; her face said it all.

"Jethro, what have you been up to now? I've been worried silly since Barry left. And who's this when he's at home?" She nodded in Seth's direction.

"Seth, this is Joan; Joanie, this is Seth. He's the only reason I'm not laying out on a slab in some hospital somewhere. He saved me from a serious kicking, and I'd never even met him before tonight."

Joanie looked Seth up and down more closely then. And when they turn their radar on, women have this way of seeing things in people that the rest of us can't. Joanie must've warmed to what she saw, because she softened and she smiled. And when Joanie smiled the sun came out. It bathed the little kitchen in its glow, and we all breathed a sigh of relief. "Come on in, love," she said to Seth, "you just sit yourself down over here. You look like your arm needs seeing to, so let's get that jacket off while we're at it. You'll be staying the night. Jethro, you get your jacket off, too. Barry, give him a hand, and then put the kettle on and make a big pot of tea. Lots of sugar."

"Thank you, that would be nice," said Seth. But notice, there were no soothing words of kindness for me. However, knowing Joanie as I did, the fact that I hadn't been given a severe tongue-lashing was welcome enough. It's only her way of showing that deep, deep down she really cares, so I tried to co-operate as best as I could by not dripping too much blood onto her kitchen lino.

Joanie sucked her breath in between her teeth when she saw the wound in Seth's arm. She simply shook her head when she saw the wound in mine. "Jesus, Jethro, you're getting too old for this." She looked from one to the other of us and shook her head again. "Right, you two, you both need stitches. Barry, put some of that hot water in a bowl and get my sewing basket. Then you'd better get out that brandy you've been hiding away for Christmas."

When she cleaned all the dried blood away from the wound on Seth's arm, it was Joan that winced. A huge scar ran from inside his wrist all the way up to beyond the crook of his arm. "Seth, you look like you've really been in the wars, luv, how on earth did you get that?"

"He probably got it instructing the Commandos," I piped in.

"Please, Jethro," she said, meaning shut it, or else.

"There's now't much to tell, Joan," he said quietly. "I had a bit of an accident, that's all. An army lorry rolled over and I went out through the windscreen, and ended up doing that to myself."

"Well, it looks like the local butcher sewed you up afterwards."

He looked up at her, his face suddenly clouded over. "I did the best I could with what I had on me, but at least I lived," he whispered.

I found I didn't want to catch his eye, so I busied myself with topping up everyone's tea with brandy; starting and finishing with me.

Joanie nodded her head and smiled, and patted him gently on the shoulder. "Well, Seth, I'll see if I can do a little better tonight. Okay?"

You never know what's going to come in handy as you march down life's highway, do you? Take Joanie. With all the clothes rationing—which went so far as to make sewing fancy lace onto a pair of woman's knickers a crime, honest I'm not making it up—Joanie had become quite an accomplished seamstress. At first, it was all part and parcel of saving material to help the war effort; after that it was to help pay for the war. And even the turn-ups on men's trousers disappeared. And why else do you think it was that all those skirt hem-lines rose as high as they did. Fashion? No, it was austerity. As I said before, though, it's an ill wind.

Anyway, with Joanie being such a dab hand with a needle, I knew she'd soon have our arms sewn up all nice and neat. But I reckoned the atmosphere in the room could do with a little lifting, so I rummaged through my mind for something appropriate. And it was the pincushion in Joanie's workbasket that gave me the idea. "Here, Seth," I said, laughing, "that time you were out in India, did you go in for any of that laying on a bed of nails lark, then? Only I can't see the point of it myself." Unbeknownst to me, though, that was the very moment Barry had chosen to start cleaning the wound in my arm. The hot water, now turned all milky-white by the disinfectant, stung like buggery and I nearly fell off the kitchen chair with the shock of it. But I was damned if I was going to start making a fuss over me, if no one else was.

"No, no bed of nails, Jethro, but I did some yoga, once or twice," he said, without paying any attention to me, or my contortions. Then for several minutes, he regaled us with some of the strange things he'd seen out in India. I listened and watched, fascinated; he didn't even seem to feel the needle going in and out of his arm. It gave me the willies, though, just looking at it, especially knowing I was next in line. Joanie dabbed on some foul-smelling Burnol cream all along the line of his new stitches, and then slapped on an Emergoplast wound dressing. Then she did some tight and tidy bandaging she'd learned with the ATS, and Seth's arm was soon looking as neat as two pins.

The very worst part as far as I was concerned was when Joanie poured neat disinfectant all along the gash on my arm just to attract my attention. But I don't remember much of the rest of it. And after a while I found I really didn't care one way or the other about the arm, as it didn't look like it belonged to me anymore, anyway. And, honestly, I don't think I fainted, I think I must've just passed out from all the brandy I'd been pouring down my throat as a way to pass the time.

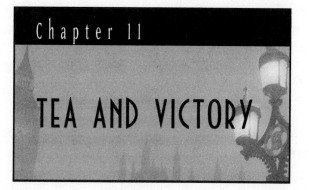

Chapter 11

TEA AND VICTORY

I lay in bed while the morning light tried to creep its way unnoticed across the cold floor and toyed with the idea of watching it go up the wall, which is what I'd been doing trying to make sense of everything. I had far too many things to itch for my liking. My arm felt like it had an army of ants crawling around under the bandaging, and my tongue felt like someone had used it to clean up a pub floor and then stuck it on a radiator to dry. I thought a cigarette might help, but they were on my dressing table on the other side of the room, and at least I was cozy where I was, so I said, "Blow it," and got on with my thinking.

I tried to remember all Chalkie had said when he'd asked me to join him in his dodgy schemes. Something had pushed him over the edge, but what? Me turning him down? Or was Messima finally on to his moonlighting? And why threaten me and my family? I was certain that neither he, nor Messima, had got wind of the Embassy job. If they had of done, Chalkie would've simply pressed down hard on that and not be bothered trying to soft-soap me. The trouble was, whichever way I reckoned it, it always led me straight back to Messima. And more trouble.

Then there was Seth. A decent sort of bloke, tough but tender-hearted, and what a blessed stroke of fortune he'd turned out to be, otherwise I might've just been waking up in a real hospital bed, or lying silently in a coffin somewhere trying to see through the pennies stuck over my eyes. All the same it was strange him coming out of the blue like that. Or maybe somebody up there really liked me.

But on top of all that, there was the news about Ray being in some sort of trouble. I had a bad feeling it was something to do with those friggin' little black books I'd nicked. And all of a sudden it seemed there was much too much going on in my little world for it all to be a coincidence. Badly craving a cigarette, I got up and out of bed without realising I'd done it and padded over to the dresser, only to find I was clean out. The black cat on the front of the red Craven "A" pack stared up at me with a smile like the Mona Lisa on its puss. "Just my luck," I said aloud, crunching up the packet. Then I dropped it on top of the ashtray, and stumbled back to bed.

It was the smell of fried food wafting up from the Victory Cafe below that finally got me up and out. I have to admit I felt right peckish, but spilling blood does that, I've noticed, especially when it's mine that's been spilt. I washed my hands and face and under my arms in cold water, and tried without much success to keep the bandaging dry. And with my arm being as it was, I decided not to shave. Shaving is its own special kind of torture, and as razors make me nervous at the best of times, giving it a miss now and then was always a bit of a treat. I just about managed to get one of my old seaman's sweaters over my head and some shoes on my feet, then with the addition of a pair of blue canvas trousers and a quick comb through my hair I was ready for the fray. And always open to a bit of practice, I slipped down the four flights of stairs as quickly and quietly as I could, hugging the wall all the way so as not to make the floor-boards creak, and that landed me out in the street, Church Street, that is.

Even at midday it was so grey and overcast that nearly all the stalls and barrows had lights up; oil lamps in some cases, but mostly electric light bulbs dotted along lengths of wire flex strung along the sides. A few stalls even had proper Christmas lights up, though it still didn't make the place look very festive. I took a deep breath and nearly choked. Even in the cold, the earthy aroma of turnips and potatoes, mixed in with the smells of honest sweat and dishonest perfume, failed to mask the underlying stench of rotting fruit and cat's piss. Add to that the drifting clouds of black smoke from meat saveloys, fish and chips, and apple fritters all being deep-fried. Throw in all the shouts and cries and calls of all the stall holders, street traders, and barrow boys. Add in the chatting and bargaining and moaning of the crowds jostling up and down the middle of the street, as well as on the pavements on both sides. And there wasn't an inch of room for doubt that all the din was the Church Street Saturday market in full swing. The noise must've been deafening, but I didn't hear it anymore. It was like the sound of the sea; once you got used to it, the only time you ever really heard it again was when you were far away from it.

Feeling right in the mood for a good nosh, I pushed open the door to the Victory Cafe. The little brass bell on top of the door clappered away like mad, and for a moment I felt like the friggin' officer of the watch. The dark blue and white paint scheme gave the Victory a faintly nautical air, but it was more the East India Docks at high tide, rather than Horatio Nelson at Trafalgar. The smell of fried bread in bacon fat caught hold of my nose and made it twitch from side to side even through all the cigarette smoke. There was the usual crowd of shoppers, and the regulars from the market, as well as one or two faces from the Metropolitan music hall round the corner. And it was 'Wotcher' or 'Gertcher' depending on who I'd lent money to, but they all waved at me with whatever they had in their hands; and knives, forks, spoons, bits of fried bread, half-empty sauce bottles, and full tea mugs all sploshed and signalled hello. In the end, there were so many things waving up and down it was enough to have made a parrot seasick.

"Morning, Vi, a mug of your best tea and a breakfast as big as they serve down the Palace; eggs, bacon, sausages, mushrooms, and kidneys, the lot." Vi was one of Joanie's regular helpers in the cafe. She was a right character. And like me, she'd lost most of her family in the war. Her mum, sister, and grandad were all killed one night when a V-2 rocket flattened a whole block of flats in Vallance Road over in the East End. It was the last rocket of the war to fall on London and it killed well over a hundred people. The real tragedy was, just two months later and the war was all over. Vi had already lost her old man at Dunkirk, so all in all it was a pretty tough war for her, but you never heard her complaining. All she had left was her little daughter, Rosie.

Vi idolised Joanie and treated her like a sister. Vi even looked a bit like her, and I think on purpose, too, but that was alright if it filled in some of the gaps in her life and helped make up for what she'd lost. Vi's blonde hair came straight out of a bottle, not that you'd ever have known it though, as she was always very particular about her roots. She'd got big blue eyes, too, just like Joanie, only Vi's seemed bigger and on account of the thick glasses she wore. She'd seen it all though, she really had, and had given as good as she'd got around the markets for years. She had a tongue on her as sharp as a tin opener and a mouth that'd make a fishwife catch her breath in admiration. She was a good old girl, especially if she'd taken you to her very ample bosom. Then woe betide anyone that ever tried to say anything bad about you; only she could do that. She was fearless with it, too, like a cat protecting her kittens, because now in her book you were family. I was very fond of her, not that I let on, mind you, you know how funny some women can be about things like that. She must've been a real looker once upon a time, and I'd have given her a pull myself if she was a good few years younger, honest I would.

"What do you think this is, you lazy bugger, the bleedin' Ritz? It's past twelve o'clock and I'm doing lunches now."

"It all comes out of the same frying pan, Vi. Not that you could ever tell with all the fag smoke and gin fumes."

"I'll give you a frying pan round the side of your head, my lad, and chalk one up on the slate if you come any more of that."

Chalk? I looked at her. Was my run-in with Chalkie round the streets already? No, couldn't be. Although you could never be sure, it was worse than jungle drums. "Come on, Vi, dish up one of your world-famous Victory specials, I'm hungry."

"Chance'ud be a fine thing, you lazy sod. You just watch it, or haven't you heard there's such a thing as rationing?"

"You watch it for me, Vi, and if you're not quick about it, I'll complain to the manageress about you harassing honest customers."

"You do that, ducks, I'm only repeating what she said herself this morning when you were still snoring away in the land of nod. There's your tea, you cheeky sod, your new friend over there's already on his third mug. And as for the other one, well, there's never any stopping him, is there? He drinks tea like a bleedin' fish, he does. Go on, I'll bring you over your plate in a minute."

"Thanks, Vi, you know I think you're a princess in disguise."

"Gertcher, you bugger, or all you'll get from me is bread and dripping, and a bunch of fives."

I peered through the smoke that was as thick as a fog at sea, and sure enough there was Seth sitting at a table in the corner. The surprise was, he looked to be in deep conversation with Ray, I mean Buggy Billy, who was sitting there holding court in his never-changing get-up of bowler hat, spotted bow tie, and fur-collared overcoat. And what was even more surprising was that the two of them were conversing about events in India.

"Morning, gents, mind if I join your table, or is this only for members of the Explorers Club?"

"Hello, Jethro."

I sat down at the table beside Seth and smiled across at Buggy.

"Wotcher, me old son," he said. "Thanks, I could do with another cup of tea, selling bug powder to London's louse-ridden populace is thirsty work, only bring over another bowl of sugar, will you, my brain keeps craving it." And with that he took my mug of tea from my hand and started drinking it. Would you credit it?

"I see you two are as thick as thieves already," I said, reaching over to the next table to nick their sugar.

"Just been talking about things in general, Jethro. You know, cabbages and kings, just cabbages and kings."

"Mr. Buggy's been telling me his thoughts on India and partition. He thinks there's going to be more trouble and that Gandhi should watch out for himself."

"Really? Old Gandhi?"

"Just you read your Shakespeare; *Julius Caesar, Titus Andronicus, Macbeth*," Buggy said, taking a breath out of the corner of his mouth as he gulped down the tea. "It's all in there; it's all happened before."

I wished he'd called it 'the Scottish play' though, it's dead unlucky otherwise. Although whether that applied to events going on around me, or what was happening out in India, is hard to say.

Seth said quietly, "I met Gandhi once when I was in India. He was a lovely man, an extraordinary man."

"What is this, the BBC's *Brains Trust*?" I said, looking at them in turn. "And what's it going to be next week, *Gardener's Question Time*?"

"Horses for courses, Jethro, horses for courses." Buggy smiled at me from under his eyebrows. "Here, Seth, forget all that 'mister' nonsense. If other people hear you, they'll think I've put on airs and graces. But be a good bloke, will you, and get me another cuppa? This lazy sod won't stir himself or his tea."

"Righto, er . . . Buggy. Can I get you anything, Jethro?"

"I'll have a mug of tea to replace the one he's just scarfed down, thanks, Seth."

Seth battled his way back through all the cigarette smoke and cooking fumes to the serving counter, and Buggy slid his gaze my way and gave me the bent eye. You never knew whose ears might be flapping around you, even in a place like the Victory.

"Listen, Jethro, while Seth's out of it for a minute. He seems a good enough sort, but almost a little too good if you ask me. I like him, don't get me wrong, but better safe than sorry. Just watch your step, that's all, and play him along for a bit and see if he's on the level. And if he's not, well, then you can sort him out later when the time comes. But for now, just count yourself lucky he came along when he did, or they might have done you for good. Your Joanie filled me in when I popped in for a cuppa early this morning. And as to my own misadventures, we'd best keep them till later. Say, sixish down The Eagle?"

"Here's your tea, Buggy. And yours, Jethro."

Ray didn't skip a beat. "Here, pass me some more sugar, will you, Seth? My brain's still craving it. Thanks, old son."

I stopped counting after his third spoonful, and found myself patting my pockets and craving a cigarette.

"Ah, now that's a lovely cup of tea," he said. "Here, did I ever tell you two about the time we were so hard up we caught some sparrows and painted them bright yellow. Stuck them in cages and sold the lot, as canaries down Club Row. Laugh. I tell you, none of the buggers would cheep. So we had to tell people they were Scottish canaries flown in special from Glasgow. Couldn't go back down the Row for a month, but it made us enough money for the week. Scottish canaries, I ask you."

We all laughed, even me, and I'd heard it a thousand times, but some people have that gift, don't they? They can make you feel like you're hearing something again for the first time.

"Well, I can't sit around here all day gabbing with you two; London's never been so lousy and someone's got to do something about it all." Ray pushed his chair back and held his hand out, "You go safe, Seth. See you around, Jethro. Get a shave, why don't you. Bye, Vi, Jethro said he'd pay for all the tea."

He went out laughing, he always does when he puts one over on me. And then Seth, still standing, nodded slowly, happy about something, and smiled. "Right then, Jethro, I'd best be going, too." He held out his hand, and I nodded, smiled, and held out mine.

"Thanks, Seth. But look, if you'll just hang on a moment while I get a cigarette, I've got something for you before you go."

He stuck his head on one side. "No, thanks, Jethro, there's no need, I'd help anyone who got themselves into a situation like that."

"I know you would, Seth, I know you would, that's what makes you so bloody unusual. But I think you'll like what I've got in mind."

Chapter 12

OPEN SESAME

It was beginning to get dark as we walked away from all the lights, the smells, and the noise of the market. We crossed the Edgware Road, and continued along the far end of Church Street, before we skirted the Children's Hospital and veered down towards Paddington Green. The police station's way over to the left, so that was no bother. But as always, I gave a little nod towards the lovely statue of Sarah Siddons, the actress, portraying the Tragic Muse; first unveiled, Ray had told me once, by none other than the great Henry Irving himself.

We nipped across the Harrow Road and slipped down towards North Wharf Road round the back of Paddington Basin and the Great Western Railway station. I kept a lock-up and workshop down there, one of several I'd managed to acquire for myself around town over the years. However, it was the first time in a very long time I'd taken anyone back there, but somehow, and despite what Ray had said earlier, I found I trusted Seth more in a day than some blokes I'd known all my life. I'd taken Ray's words to heart, but sometimes, you've also just got to trust your instincts, otherwise what's the point of having them? For his part, Seth had been quiet on the walk over, if you consider him singing and humming to himself nonstop as being quiet, that is.

"That lorry accident you said you were in," I said. "Bad, was it?"

He didn't turn his head, he just looked off in the distance. "Yeah. I lost some men under my charge. Five of them killed in a freak accident during a training exercise in the Scottish Highlands. And even though it wasn't me who was driving the lorry, I should've had them take more care. They were good lads all of them. A tragic loss. And I lost too many good mates in the war. I won't lose any more, not if I can help it."

I nodded, knowing full well what he was talking about, and walked on through the dark with my own demons. Seth began humming again, and after a little while I took comfort in it.

"Right, here we are."

We were standing by a little judas door set into two large wooden gates that to all intents and purposes fronted a small, disused machine shop. The faded lettering on the gates read 'Wolverton's Tool and Die-Casting,' a company long gone. And the battered 'For Sale or For Lease' sign had been there ever since I'd bought the building some years before. It all helped maintain the rundown feel of the place and dampen any interest people might have in it. I ignored the big, rusted padlock, and slid aside two flat bits of rusted metal plate instead. Then pulling a key from my pocket I unlocked the two special deadlocks I'd fashioned and fitted myself, and pushed the door open. It swung back without a sound.

"Open sesame," I whispered, as I motioned Seth to follow me. I closed the door behind us and reached up to pull the cord I knew was hanging in the darkness. A single flyblown light bulb sputtered into life to reveal a dark narrow corridor full of empty boxes and tea chests. To the side was a small windowless office full of mildewing cardboard box files and dusty green filing cabinets with their drawers rusted open. There was a table, but no chair, and a torn calendar on the wall that proclaimed it was still some spring month in 1937. There was nothing at all inviting about the place, not even for a rat, which was just what I'd intended. But the office and passageway made up only one small corner of the building; the rest I'd converted to my own special needs.

I felt for the wall switch, and light fell from a chipped-enamel shade hanging lopsidedly from the ceiling. It only managed to throw a few tired shadows around the room, but it was enough for me to see by. The office was exactly as I'd left it; even a pile of rubbish can have its own unseen order.

Seth didn't move, he just stood quietly wondering what the hell it was all about. But I did notice he'd at least stopped humming to himself. I stepped back into the corridor, squeezed myself past the tea chests to the battered-looking door at the far end and unlocked it.

"In here, Seth. Watch your head as you come through." He followed me inside, just as I flicked another wall switch and flooded the place with light. "Welcome to Aladdin's humble cave," I said casually. I could hear his sharp intake of breath, but then I'm sure it was all a bit unexpected. And while his mouth opened and closed like someone who's forgotten the words to a hymn, I pushed the door shut behind us, and switched off the lights in the outer office and corridor.

"Now, unless we started firing a bazooka or something in here, no one outside can hear a thing."

"Bloody hell fire," Seth said quietly. His voice barely carried in the forty-foot-by-sixty-foot space. I nodded but said nothing.

From left to right, along two walls, there was a row of well-equipped workbenches and a motley collection of safes. Not that Seth could see anything untoward, mind you, as the safes were all covered with tarpaulins. Along the third wall on the far side were two large wooden desks I'd got from a bank near Marble Arch that'd been flattened by a bomb, a draughtsman's parallel board, and a line of black-painted metal filing cabinets. There were stacks of cardboard files in neat rows on top of the desks and the cabinets, as well as large cork notice boards along the wall. The boards were covered with some of my drawings and watercolours, as well as a number of pictures I'd cut out from newspapers and magazines. It was all work in progress, so to speak. There was also a dressing table and a metal clothes rail with clothes and uniforms hanging on it, but again, Seth wouldn't have taken too much notice of them as they were all draped with dust covers.

But it wasn't my shipshape neatness that impressed Seth, it was the sleek, two-seater, T-series MG Midget in British racing green and the big black, red, and chrome Ariel Square Four motorcycle that stood reflecting the light from the double row of overhead work lamps. As he took it all in, I busied myself checking the tyres on the little, old Austin van that was standing next to a London taxi of the same make and vintage.

"It's all small garages and light machine shops around here," I said.

"And deserted nights and most weekends after Saturday midday, so it does me a treat. I wanted my own machine shop to tinker around in, as well as having somewhere private to keep all my stuff in."

"Bloody hell fire."

It was like an echo. "Yes, you said that. But you just can't be too careful these days, everybody's so hard up for something to sell that anything not bolted down or tucked away out of sight gets nicked very quickly. I just rely on the fact that most people don't look further than the end of their noses. The way something looks is as deep as most people want to go anyway. So, I find a little rust and dirt on the doors outside works wonders for my privacy."

"Lovely motorbike."

"Yes, and the MG's not too bad, neither. I use the little old Austin van to help Buggy out from time to time, and the taxicab I'm just garaging for an old friend of Barry's, but the bike, yes, it's . . ."

I've always had a knack for fishing; people or fish, just bait the hook right and they jump on it, no trouble. Seth cleared his throat. "An Ariel Square Four; in beautiful condition. Built around 1938, I should think. And with a capacity nigh on 1000cc producing, oh, about thirty-six brake horsepower, she'd be good for almost a hundred. They're heavy buggers, though, and can run a bit hot, but she'll run like a dream if you treat her right."

"Yeah, it is a nice bike, isn't it? The second one I've owned. But, well, what with my theatrical work, petrol rationing and all that, I just don't seem to get out on it as much as I once did. Shame really, it going to waste just standing there, so I was wondering if you'd consider running it around for me. You know, just to help keep it in good, working order. Sort of on a semi-permanent loan, so to speak. What do you say?"

Seth looked at the motorbike, then back at me again, then back at the Ariel.

"You're blinkin' barmy, you are," he said in that funny George Formby voice he did. It may have been the light, but there was such a twinkle in his eye, I swear he'd fallen in love with the bike at first sight.

"It's a beauty," he said, "a real beauty. The first time I ever saw or rode anything that good was when I worked on the Wall of Death with the 'Wizards of Wonder' on Blackpool Pier, back in thirty, thirty-one.

Yank bikes, they were; big Indians. Even the big BSA bikes I rode in the Army weren't in this class . . . but as to borrowing it, well . . . er, no . . . Jethro, I couldn't, really."

I'd learned by then he only ever chatted on when he was happy.

"Don't be a daft sod all your life," I said. "There's a full tank. It's got its road licence. And I'll bet that white helmet and brown leather coat and gauntlets over there will fit you a treat, too. So what do you say?"

"No, Jethro, I couldn't."

"Yes, you can, Seth, I know you can. It's easy, you stubborn Yorkshire-man, you just nod your head. It's only a loan between friends. I still feel lousy about them tearaways breaking your guitar, so this helps make up for it. It's all registered and paid for, so you don't have to worry about a thing. And I'll give you the papers as well for safe keeping."

Leaving him alone with his new love for a minute, I went over to one of the desks and pulled out a cash box. Then I had a thought, and pulled out a different one. I returned to where he was standing, and flipped open the lid. It was full of five-pound notes. I rifled through them, leaving a small pile of them on the edge of a nearby table. "Oh, wrong box," I said casually. "I must have left what I was looking for in another one. Won't be a minute." I turned round, making sure I knocked the notes onto the floor.

I went back over to the roll-top desk and opened and closed a few boxes and drawers. There was a little make-up mirror on the desk that I sometimes used as a last-minute check on my disguises. And I'm ashamed to say that I used it that time, to check up on Seth. I could see him framed behind me. And I saw him bend down and pick the money up from off the floor. I banged a drawer closed and snapped a box-lid shut, and then turned around. "Ah, found them; here they are." I walked back over, a smile stuck on my face. And by this time he had his hands all over the bike, happily humming away. The money lay on top of the box, all of it. My smile broke into a grin, and in a way I was smiling as much for me as I was for Seth.

It was only a little test, but you'd be surprised how quickly you can find out about someone when it comes down to the question of money. I put the bike's pink slip into a buff envelope, along with an official-looking identity card, and dropped in a book of commercial-use-only petrol coupons—all perfectly above board, of course—and a few five-pound notes. Then I scribbled out a telephone number on a blank postcard, and popped that in, too.

"Here you are, Seth. There's also the telephone number at Joanie's, so you can get a message to me if you ever need to. And one other thing; if anyone stops you on the bike to check up on the petrol you're using, just say you're a messenger carrying reports and stuff for the BBC. There's a bundle of unopened telegrams and sealed program files in the panniers on the bike. And you'll find a BBC identity card I borrowed from off a pal of mine in that packet of stuff I've just given you. No rules broken, or anything, just bending them a little, that's all."

He blinked, but I could see he was taking it all in. He nodded slowly, but was smart enough not to ask anything more.

"Look, I'll swing open one of the doors and you can give me a lift back up to Church Street, so we can ask Joanie to take a quick look at your arm and mine. Then after she's finished, we'll get you some of the Victory's finest black-market bacon sandwiches for your journey. And then if it won't take you too far out of your way, I wonder if you wouldn't mind dropping me back here afterwards, before you set off home."

He could barely contain his grin. "All right," he said, "you've got yourself a deal. And I won't let you ask me again."

Chapter 13

BULLY IN A CHINA SHOP

In London, a copper's reputation preceded him down every dark street and alleyway long before he ever reached the heights of Detective Chief Inspector. So even if you'd never had a run in with a particular officer yourself, there were always people around town that had a pretty good idea as to the strength of him. And his form could be discussed in much the same manner as you would a racehorse. Could he be bent or did he only run straight? Was he good for the long run or was he only reliable over short distances? Did he get spooked too easily and need fitting with an extra pair of blinders? Did he jump nicely when his help was called for? In many ways it was no different to any business where you had to play the odds, hence all the interest and all the talk, and why in some quarters the *Police Gazette* was as avidly pored over as *Sporting Life*.

Speculation swirled round some officers like flies around shit, and since the very first day he'd joined the force, there'd been as much talk in the city's spielers and billiard halls, as there'd been in police stations and canteens about one particular officer named Browno. And as he'd risen up through the ranks, people had split down the middle in their assessment of him. One lot saw him as nothing more than a villain with a warrant card, while the others regarded him as nothing less than one of the best thief-takers in London. As you might expect, Browno was a right hard man and a bull in any china shop that he was sent into, and his superiors knew it, and in fact, counted upon it.

And it just so happened that the officer in charge of the mob that smashed Ray's front door down with sledgehammers at six o'clock in the morning was none other than the selfsame, Detective Chief Inspector Robert Browno, of Scotland Yard's Flying Squad. Now it might have just been a coincidence that both Ray and me had such bad things happen to us, on that same ill-fated Friday, following the Embassy job, but I doubt it. I had the distinct feeling someone up there didn't like me.

When he heard the door crash in, Ray said he'd thought the Blitz had started up again. But as soon as he'd remembered where he was and who he was supposed to be, he'd yelled out that he was armed, and got his shotgun—a classic 'fine rose and scroll' engraved Purdey—from under his bed, and gone downstairs to investigate his missing door.

Then apparently, all Browno had said while standing amidst all the mess was, "Raymond Leopold Karmin? May we come in, sir?"

I sat nursing a pint, waiting for Ray to come. I'd got to The Eagle, spot on opening time, as I wanted to see who the regulars were, as well as find a good place for us to sit. I hummed the kids' rhyme to myself while I waited; well, you've got to, really, every time you pop in and out of The Eagle. (It's the pub they sing about in "Pop Goes the Weasel." Honest. I wouldn't make that sort of thing up, now would I?)

Once he finally arrived, Ray gave me a blow-by-blow account of what had gone on. Mind you, you wouldn't have recognised either one of us if you'd been in the pub, and more importantly neither would anyone else. Gone were Buggy Billy's bowler hat, spotted bow tie, and fur-collared coat, and instead Ray was wearing a battered brown trilby, a tartan scarf, and an oil-stained mackintosh. A simple enough makeover, but a very effective one, nevertheless, with no trace at all of Raymond Karmin, worldly scholar. In fact, he looked more like the old taxi-driver in a flat-cap that was sitting across from him at a beer-stained, marble-topped table. You could tell the old bloke was a cabby, because apart from his thick, round glasses and weather-beaten, puffy nose and cheeks, he wore his brassard pinned around his coat sleeve. But you would've had to look really hard to see it was only a copy of the real taxi license that Barry had. Otherwise, the two old codgers sitting there, minding their pints and nursing their chasers, were just like bits of the furniture.

The old cabby character was one I used for going round the city unseen; I'd tried hundreds of other ways, but it was always the best. And it was truly amazing the houses and front-door locks I'd been able to get a close look at, by simply appearing as a cab driver in search of a missing fare. It also showed what amazing things you could do to the lines and contours of your face with just a few wads of cotton wool, the only drawback ever being that it played hell with the taste of your beer.

"It's about time you got some more drinks in, Jethro, I was friggin' dying of thirst there for a minute. Now where the hell were we? Oh, yes, I tell you, that Browno's a real nasty bastard. I didn't know who the hell they all were at first, but when he gave his name and rank, and flashed his warrant card, I knew I'd heard of him somewhere before. But by then his men had started pulling the place apart, so I put on my best educated voice and yelled, "What the hell are you doing? And where the bloody hell's your search warrant?"

I shook my head and chuckled, because when he had a mind to, Ray could play the outraged gentleman as well as anyone. I'd seen him do it to great effect in the early days when I'd needed a lesson or two on how to act when nosing around a high-class jewellers or a safe manufacturer's showroom.

"I know an upper-class accent doesn't always work with these people, Jethro, but it usually gives them pause if they think they're dealing with someone that's had a proper education. But the bugger just turned to me with a blank look, and said, 'We have reason to believe that you've been in receipt of stolen property, Mr. Karmin, sir. We have a warrant here, duly signed by a magistrate, to search these premises, and we would ask for your full co-operation in the matter. And if necessary, I may ask you to accompany me later to Southampton Row police station for further questioning. Or failing that, sir, I may just smash your bleedin' face in. So, why don't you just be a nice gentleman now, and stay out of the way, and let my men get on with their work.'"

I almost spilled my beer at that, but I said nothing; I was all ears.

"Well, that was a bloody liberty, Jethro, so I shot straight back with 'There's no need to take that tone of voice with me, Inspector. I don't know what you're talking about. So, do what you must, I know by law I can't stop you, but don't you break too much or steal anything, or there'll be an official complaint to my Member of Parliament.'"

"I bet that brought the bugger up short," I muttered.

"It did, it did," Ray said, looking right put out. "But it didn't stop his bleedin' goons from pulling the whole place apart, did it?"

And it was true, they upended furniture and pulled handfuls of books and papers from off shelves. They emptied cupboards, pulled out drawers, threw up the rugs, and tapped the floors, walls, and baseboards. They looked up the chimney, behind the toilet, and inside the water tank. And found nothing. But I could've told them they'd come up empty-handed. Ray's no amateur. They would've needed one of those new X-ray machines to find anything, or taken the place apart brick by brick, but of course, they weren't to know that.

"Well, after all that nonsense, Jethro, I got browned off with it all, and threw a 'Charge me, or I'm calling my solicitor,' at the bugger. But all he said was, 'As long as you can properly account for any items we deem to be of interest, sir, there won't be any need for that.' Then if you can believe it, the fucker just picked up a bottle of The Glenlivet from off the top of the cabinet, looked at the label, and dropped it on to the floor. And then he slowly ground the broken glass into my Oriental carpet and said, 'I've got your number now, Mr. Karmin, sir, so I'm going to be looking at you very closely, and if I find anything I don't like I'm going to come down on you very hard indeed. So you just watch it.'"

I put my empty glass down very gently onto the marble tabletop, and shook my head in quiet amazement.

"Well, you know me, Jethro, that was like a red rag to a bull. So I said, 'Well, why don't you watch it for me, Inspector.' And then I asked to see his warrant card again, so I could get the spelling of his name right, and told him I'd be making a report of his wilful and malicious damage to his superiors."

Ray said you could've cut the air with a razor blade after that, but then all Browno's trilby-hatted ferrets tramped back into the room, and the moment passed. The glum look on their faces showed they hadn't found anything incriminating. Not that Ray ever had any doubts about that, as everything to do with the gem business was always well hidden away. But he was alarmed to see policemen carrying piles of notebooks and leather-bound volumes of his typed-up research notes. Another thing he noticed was they'd only taken the ones with the black covers.

"Well, I exploded at that, and shouted, 'I'll have a receipt for each one of those, they're irreplaceable. And should a single one of them end up damaged or missing, I promise you'll I'll seek redress through the courts, as well as make an official complaint to the Metropolitan Police Commissioner about you personally, Inspector.' Then I lowered my voice so that only Browno could hear, and added, 'And do remember, Inspector Browno, I've got your number, now, as well.'"

This was better than a Jimmy Cagney movie. "What happened then?" I said, my throat getting dryer by the minute.

"Well, suddenly there was spittle flying everywhere, and I had a big brown leather-gloved finger pushed right up under my nose. 'You think you're very sharp you do, Mr. Karmin, sir, so let me be perfectly blunt,' he snarled. 'Firstly, it's "Detective Chief Inspector," and don't you forget it. And secondly, don't you dare try and take me on, or you'll find yourself in a world of hurt.' You could tell he was really put out, though, because the next thing he did was put his boot through the glass-fronted cabinet where I keep all the whisky and brandy. And even I jumped; there was glass flying everywhere, it was worse than the Temperance League on a Saturday night. Then the bastard just looked at me, and said, 'Sorry about that, sir, I must've stumbled.' And then he pointed at the nearest copper with an armful of notebooks, and said, 'And you, Daisy May, better count those soddin' things and give this here gentleman a friggin' receipt for them.'"

Those notebooks were worth their weight in diamonds to Ray, so although he was putting a brave face on it, I knew the early-morning raid must've really unsettled him.

"Well, it was all over then, bar the shouting. Browno just looked down his nose, and said, 'Thank you, sir, for all your assistance and co-operation in this matter. If these items are cleared by the authorities and deemed to be of no further interest, then everything will be returned to you. If, however, examination of the contents suggests that charges might be filed against you at a later date, they may be held and used in evidence against you. Good morning.' Then he stormed out. So there wasn't much I could say after that, except, 'Goodbye, Inspector, I can't say it's been a pleasure,' but I don't think he heard me."

Part of me wished I'd been a fly on the wall, but I have to admit I felt off my beer because of the way things had turned out, and I could tell Ray felt the same way, him having just relived the events all over again.

He looked at me pensively. "I know they probably got my name, and address, and everything from my Museum reader's ticket. But the thing that niggles me is I still don't have any idea who gave me away."

I nodded, but said, "Well, it's a bit late worrying about that now, Ray. Whichever one of your Reading Room pals did it, it's brought Browno out of the woodwork, and he's bound to turn up again."

"Well," said Ray, "I thought about that and got on the phone to get the strength on him; it cost a bit, but I got his form in the end."

I leaned forward, all ears.

"There's a lot of talk about him having built up a whole army of snouts over the years."

"Well," I said, "they do say a copper's only ever as hot as his whispering grasses."

"Very true, my old cock sparrow, but by the sound of it, our Mr. Browno is a friggin' grass fire. I got it on very good authority that even the Ghost Squad eye him with something verging on respect."

That was an interesting bit of news. The Ghost Squad were a secret even to themselves, let alone the rest of London's police force. You'd never catch them wearing little trilby hats, belted raincoats, and size-twelve boots. No, they raided the wardrobe and props cupboards just like me, and for the very same reason—they wanted to disappear into plain sight, as well. The only difference being they wanted to be taken for villains so they could sink right into London's underworld and become part of it. The idea behind it all was for them to pick up whispers about upcoming jobs, and then tip off their colleagues down the Yard. They were the witch-finders to the thief-takers.

"There won't be any real villains left in London at this rate," I said, "they'll all be working for Scotland Yard."

"Well, Browno's doing very well for himself out of it all. And if the rumours are true, he and his wife manage to live far better on his pay than the Assistant Commissioner ever does on his. But whether it's all from sweeteners or not, no one seems to know for sure."

"That's why they call them sweeteners, Ray. They disappear faster than a spoonful of sugar in a cup of tea, and no one's any the wiser unless they're in for a taste as well."

"Too true, too true, but the itch I can't quite scratch is that something doesn't add up. If DCI Browno was just into sweeteners and bribes that'd be one thing, and we could all go home and have tea. But if you think about it, it should've been Special Branch doing my place over, not the Flying Squad."

"I don't get you, why wouldn't it be the Sweeney?" I asked.

"Thieving is one thing, Jethro, politics is another."

"I still don't follow," I said.

"Well, thieving is thieving, and the Sweeney trying to nick someone for receiving is all part and parcel of the game. Right?"

I nodded.

"But thieving isn't thieving when it's to do with politics, because then, my old son, it becomes something else entirely. That's when, as one old Prussian once said, it becomes war by other means."

I blinked and took a sip of whisky, and tried to keep up.

"We know the little black book with all those VIP telephone numbers had to be red-hot, so it's odds-on Browno came looking for that. And we can also be pretty sure it was our foreign chum, Flash Harry Raffles, who nicked it in the first place. Or why else would he have had all that stuff in his room? So, in my humble opinion, it must all have to do with politics and spying, and not honest-to-goodness thieving."

I took another sip and tried to pick holes in his reasoning, but I couldn't find any. "Go on," I said.

"Special Branch are attack dogs for the Foreign Office; they're the ones that deal with any foreign nonsense on British soil, not the local heavies on the Flying Squad, whose job it is to apprehend home-grown criminals. And even with the rank of DCI, Browno couldn't step that far outside his official jurisdiction; he'd be severely reprimanded or even de-moted if he did. I also got the very distinct feeling he was treating me with kid gloves. He could've wiped the floor with me if he wanted, but he didn't, and leopards like him don't ever change their spots. And so to my devious mind that says Browno's either had orders from someone very high up to be on his very best behaviour, or somebody, somewhere, has got enough dirt on him to keep him in line. So, as odd as it sounds, I reckon it's all still unofficial and that someone's pulling strings left, right, and centre to try and keep the missing black books off the record. And knowing how things work in Whitehall, it's probably some old school chum of the stupid bugger that lost the stuff in the first place."

I got in another round, two pints of best bitter and two more measures of whisky. We both looked like we needed it, I know I did.

"Cheers, Jethro." He took a long sip of his beer. "Look, I know you think it's my imagination running away with me again, but my sixth sense tells me this whole thing is a lot more dangerous than anything either you or I have come across before. And that includes Adolf Hitler, Mussolini, and the godforsaken Emperor Messima himself." He looked at me over his glasses for emphasis. "The other funny thing is, there's still been no mention in the papers or on the radio about all the shooting. Or that bloke you said fell to his death from the Embassy roof; which even forgetting all the stuff you burgled, is very unusual in itself. So, I say again, I think someone somewhere is quietly pulling strings somewhere. I don't honestly see what else it could be."

"Perhaps," I said, "it's that unknown chum of yours down the Museum Reading Room that's got all the pull."

"Could be, old son, could be, but I've been thinking. With Browno breathing down my neck, and Messima probably soon looking to breathe down yours, we better shut up shop for a while. So you and me should not be seen together until long after this thing has blown over. Agreed?"

"Whatever you say, Ray."

"That's settled then; go safe, until next." He looked at me and nodded. "Keep your nose clean and just go and disappear backstage somewhere, while I go back to just being Buggy Billy."

"Back to hiding in plain sight, is it?"

"Yes," he chuckled, "you could say that. But one thing before I go. I've had all the jewellery you nicked from the Embassy dropped down a very deep hole. It's there for a rainy day, of course, but as of now we just forget about it. Both of my houses are now cleaner than a novice's wimple. And the police wouldn't find anything now even if they came back with a set of builder's plans and a wrecking ball. And as for the little black books, I sort of dropped them down a hole, too. I cleaned off all our dabs with chemicals and had them posted to the Commissioner at Scotland Yard, with a note saying they were from a concerned citizen. And by now, the parcel will have a Manchester postmark dated last Tuesday morning; the time I was supposed to be showing the friggin' things down the Museum. It might not stand up to full forensics, but it should queer the pitch a bit."

"Nice one, Ray. You've really been busy," I said.

He cocked his head to one side. "The thing is, Jethro, looking back on it now, I know I should've just popped the bloody things in the mail in the first place. So what I want to do now is clear up all the mess. What I did was sentimental, even stupid, and I'm sorry for what I've got us both into. Just put it down to my insatiable patriotism getting the better of me, that's all."

I leaned forward across the table, mindless of the little puddles of beer. "Look, Ray, we started this together and we'll finish it the same way. There's never been any room for blame between us, and there never will be. It's just the same now as the day you first taught it to me; it's all for one and one for all, and that's all there is to it."

He went silent, and after a bit looked me in the eyes and smiled. And just for a moment he seemed more vulnerable than I think I'd ever seen him. Gone was Buggy Billy, scallywag. Gone was Ray, the finest jewellery fence in London. Gone was Raymond L. Karmin, the scholar. And there, behind all the masks, part-Russian, half-Viennese Jew, brought up a Cockney, forever a Londoner, was R. L. Karmin, Esquire, a true Englishman, from the top of his balding head to the tips of his toes.

"Thanks, old son," he said quietly, "I appreciate you saying that more than you can understand. But the thing is, we both know I'd probably do the same thing again in similar circumstances."

"No you wouldn't, Ray," I said draining my pint, "you'd do it differently. Like you've always said; you can always learn from your mistakes, just as long as you don't keep making the same ones over and over again."

He reached for his whisky. "You're getting to be a right bloody know-all, you are."

"I've had a good teacher, Ray. I've had a good teacher."

"That makes it your round again, then," he said, banging his empty whisky glass down on the table, "and mine's a double."

"It always is, Ray," I said. "It always is."

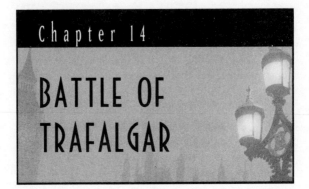

Chapter 14

BATTLE OF TRAFALGAR

The idea was for me to carry on as if nothing had happened; no Embassy caper, no death, no friggin' little black books, no Browno, no Chalkie, no Seth. But that's a lot to remember when you're trying to act normal. So I just threw myself back into my old routine. For starters I looked up one or two numbers in a little black book of my own. Then I whiled away a few hours idly musing over the respective delights of Marilyn, a leggy blonde dancer at the Club Panama, and Natalie, a tall brunette that modelled expensive dresses down Harrods. And in the end, to be fair, I took both girls out, though on different nights. But as much as I tried to enjoy myself, I felt like I was only going through the motions, and they both told me I wasn't at all my usual self.

I popped down the Palladium, but people there were still going on about the gang war that had erupted outside the stage door. And because word of my earlier set-to with Chalkie had done the rounds, quite a few people had put two and two together and a lot of tongues had been wagging my way. I didn't blame them though, sudden violence tends to upset people at the best of times, but I very definitely felt all the unasked questions behind the nervous, trying-so-hard-to-be-friendly eyes.

So not to outstay my welcome I put the word about that I was open to join a fly-team in another theatre. I hinted that it was because one of the girls in the incoming acts had dumped me in the past for a 'Sir-something-Honourable-somebody or other,' and that I had a broken heart. I choked back tears, looked off into the distance, mumbled a few words, went silent, all that malarkey. I was good, too. I even got a new pull out of it with one of the newer chorus girls who up to that point had been a bit stand-offish with me. I tell you this acting lark was right up my street.

And for a bit, life went on much as normal. And just as he'd suggested that night in The Eagle, I steered clear of Ray, though word always some-how made its way to me via the Victory that things were okay. I also got a couple of calls from Seth, who said he'd got a feeling I was in trouble and asked me did I want any help. And I told him no, but he still called back the next day to ask if I was sure, and to thank me yet again for lending him the motorbike. "It goes like the bloody wind," he said, "it's bloomin' marvellous, it is." "Well, that's bloomin' marvellous," I said back, and after several cheery 'cheerios,' he at last put the phone down. He had a knack of lifting my spirits, so I was always glad when he called. I told him I might drive down in the MG and see him and his girl sometime. And he seemed really pleased about that, and said he'd come up to town and pick me up if it was easier. Though I remember thinking he was probably only looking for an excuse to come back up to town again so he could ride the Ariel.

I got a message that Johnny Jones over at His Majesty's needed help, and as he'd come through with fly-work for me in the past, I said I'd be only too happy to help out. So, I took myself up West to go and see him. I didn't think I'd stand out too much, it was daylight after all, and the early Christmas shopping crowds would give me more than enough cover to lose myself in. I was on the look-out for trouble, of course, but I reck-oned as long as I stayed clear of Messima's clubs and spielers I'd probably be in the clear. I did take the simple precaution of adding a natty, little Errol Flynn moustache, Brylcreeming my hair back, and wearing a dark blue blazer and a striped silk cravat. Then with a pipe sticking out of my top pocket, I looked every inch the ex-squadron or ex-regimental some-thing or other. Piece of cake, I thought to myself.

I hopped on the back of a bus going down the Edgware Road and chatted up the redheaded clippie, promising to meet her for a drink the following Friday lunch-time at The Green Man pub on the corner by the

Underground station. Then I slipped down the tube and took the Circle Line all the way round to Charing Cross. I had my nose stuck in the *Daily Mirror* all the way to help pass the time. It wasn't *The Lady*, but then *The Lady* didn't have the cartoon strip *Jane* in it, did it? 'Strip,' of course, being the operative word.

My spirits lifted, I rode up the escalators and walked out to the station forecourt and stood by Charing Cross itself. I took a moment to scan the crowds by pretending to have some difficulty lighting my cigarette, and wouldn't you know it, but somebody stopped to offer me a light. Anyway, after a few puffs I lost myself in a bunch of pedestrians and crossed over the Strand to the corner of St. Martin's. I first noticed them as I stepped off the curb by South Africa House. There were two of them at first. Then four, and then six. And by then I knew I was slipping, or my sixth sense was.

I sussed it then; they must have been tailing me since I'd left the flat. I slipped into the crowd of sightseers that always seems to gather in that south side of Trafalgar Square. Meanwhile my six new friends followed me like sheepdogs, keeping me penned in on three sides, never coming too close, but always staying near enough to stop me from even thinking of toeing it. They moved parallel to me, and just as long as I moved in the direction they wanted, everything was fine. If not, the looks on their faces said they were more than ready to nip in with a snarled threat and a sharpened chiv to make sure I got the point that I was the sheep being singled out for slaughter.

They had to be Messima's mob; they were too well organised for one of Chalkie's little side jobs. And they were too well dressed to be coppers, even ones from West End Central, in Savile Row. I recognised a few of them and right bruisers they were, too, and the stripes they were wearing weren't only on their suits. I couldn't see if there were any more of them or not, but there were already more than enough to mean business. I suspected they wouldn't give a toss if I'd told them about the 1844 Trafalgar Square Act whereby it was 'forbidden to wilfully interfere with the comfort or convenience of any person in the Square,' which in this case meant me. So in the end I just kept moving.

I hurriedly joined a crowd of sightseers and started chatting to a nice lady and her kid up from Brighton for the day. She said they'd come specially to see the giant Christmas tree that Norway was sending over as a 'thank you' for everything Britain had done for them in the war. She said she'd read about it in the newspapers, and I told her not to believe all she read in the linens, and that by my reckoning they'd come up at least a week too early. I was playing for time, so to help them over their little disappointment I offered to take a picture of the two of them by the fountains with their little Box Brownie, wondering what sort of pictures they'd hoped to get on such a grey and wintry day. I stepped back, joking and laughing, tapping the little boy on the head while they stood and posed with the pigeons. And snapping away like a photo tout at the seaside, I took several shots from different angles, always managing somehow to get at least two of the tearaways that were dogging me, somewhere in the background. I didn't quite know what it would accomplish, but I know it made me feel better knowing that there would be evidence somewhere of my would-be killers if I ended up dead. I handed the camera back and smiled a Londoner's sincerest goodbye, hoping she'd remember my face if she ever saw it staring back at her from out of her morning paper.

The six heavies continued circling, their smiles signalling that there was nowhere for me to run to. But in the end, before I could make a move, it was made for me. I'd just started backing towards one of those mangy stone lions that guard Nelson's column, when they took me from behind and pinned both my arms to my sides. Notice, though, there was no signal from Lord Nelson; blind eye or no blind eye, with the view he's got, the least he could have done was shout a warning.

I was picked up bodily and given the bum's rush towards a long black saloon that had suddenly pulled out of the traffic and slid to a halt beside the kerb. I recognised it, of course. I'd seen it cruising around, impervious to petrol rationing, masses of times, as had every tearaway and copper in the West End of London. It was a big, flash American motor with white-wall tyres—since the war, the only car of choice for any villain of good standing—and it may have been a little smaller than a Sherman tank, but only just. However, it seemed to grow in size like a barrage balloon the closer I got to it. Several pairs of hands hooked hold of both my legs and I was thrown head first onto the back seat. Then someone threw a blanket over my head just before someone else coshed me senseless. It must have been a good-quality blanket, though, because I'm sure it helped soften the blow a bit. But I don't suppose they were too worried about bruising me; they would've been much more concerned about me not bleeding over the tan leather seats of Mr. Darby Messima's shiny black Chrysler Airflow DeLuxe.

"Jeffro. Jeffro, my old friend, what have they been doing to you? I don't know; you send someone out on a simple errand and look what happens. Must I do everything myself? Fingers, get him an aspirin, give him a cup of tea, give him a brandy, get him something."

Someone got the smelling salts, and the next thing I knew I was on my hands and knees wanting to heave up my breakfast, dinner, and tea. It was a nice white wool carpet, Wilton, I think, very thick and very comforting, so I decided to stay down for a bit. I did a quick mental check to see how many pieces I was in. The back of my head was thumping away like a howitzer, but there didn't seem to be any damage elsewhere. I tried to breathe in without fainting and found I could, which made me quite proud of myself. I tried for a second breath, just like any good boxer taking a rest while the referee carried on with the count, knowing full well I'd be up on one knee by eight, and back on my feet on nine.

"Get him up, will you. Can't you see he's back with us."

It was Mr. Darby Messima himself, Emperor and Lord of all he surveyed now he'd packed his brother off back home to Malta. Soho's very own answer to Nero, with every fiddle in the book, as well all the ones that weren't. He'd squeeze protection money out of someone in the morning, and firebomb the club or shop next door that same night for added emphasis. If there'd been money to be made throwing Londoners to the lions he'd have done it too, without a second's thought.

Once again, several pairs of hands picked me up and sat me down, but what shocked me the most this time was just how very comfortable the chair felt. I looked up and blinked in surprise. The room was huge and furnished like one of those ultramodern offices you'd see in that Yank magazine, *Life*; all glass and chrome and polished veneer. It wouldn't have looked out of place inside the Hoover factory out on the Great West Road, or as a Cabin-Class stateroom on the *Queen Mary*. It was so impressive, I decided to join the party.

"Water, please, water."

"Well, don't just stand there, get him some water, somebody."

I heard a few bangs and crashes behind me, but nothing serious, no one was getting killed yet, they were just the sort of sounds you'd hear coming from a cocktail bar if someone was searching for a clean glass. A tap was turned on briefly, then there was a tap on my shoulder, and a big cut-glass tumbler full of water sploshed into view.

"Well, put some ice in it, you berk."

The glass disappeared, then a few seconds and a couple of clunks and chinks later it swam back into view. Ice cubes? A refrigerator in his office? He really was going up in the world. I drank the water, thirstily, my Adam's apple going up and down like a piston, and as soon as I'd drained the glass it was taken away. I licked my lips in anticipation and hoped it would soon return, refilled. It did. But this time it was full to the brim with a golden, caramel-coloured liquid that at any other time I'd have given my eye-teeth for. Water into wine, lovely, now all I needed was resurrecting.

"You always did like a nip of single malt, didn't you now? Very cultured of you, Jeffro, very cultured, if I may say so? Mind if I join you? So how's tricks? Doing well, are you?" He spoke in questions even when he wasn't asking anything. I just grunted appreciative noises at what I thought were the appropriate places, and tried not to look too untidy or out of place. He was a stickler for neatness and social niceties.

"Ta," I said, trying not to sip and speak at the same time. Around Mr. Darby Messima, it was always wise to watch all of your p's and your q's. "A very nice drop o' Scotch, this. Thank you."

"Sorry about the bang on the head, it wasn't what I asked for at all. I only wanted them to ask you to stop by for a chit-chat. People do seem to get carried away these days, though, don't they? But times are changing and people are changing with them, so I suppose I just have to change right along with them. I blame the war, of course, it taught people to be far too independent. All this thinking-for-yourself nonsense is likely to get in the way of progress. Me? I prefer a bit of order around me, especially with business expanding as it is. So, as you can see, I've got a few new faces around me since we last met." His hand and arm swept out in an arc like a pope conferring a blessing, or a posh bit of skirt showing one of those new big-capacity refrigerators at the Ideal Home exhibition.

Soho's newest-model villains on display just for me. I was very impressed, and if I'd had enough money on me I'd have bought one for myself right there and then.

"Very impressive, Mr. Messima, very impressive." The words sounded slurred, but it might just have been the banging in my head.

"Yes. When was it we had that last chat of ours? A month? Three months? Last year? My, but doesn't time fly? Unfortunately, a couple of people have had to leave my employ permanently, so to speak, since then. I got the idea somehow that they might've been behind the gang that tried to muscle in on me. Me? The very thought of me having to go mob-handed on my own manor, would you believe it? What a diabolical liberty. Whatever is the world coming to? But then you know all about that, don't you?"

I chanced a sip of the malt. I didn't want to drink out of turn, but it was helping to revive my aching head wonderfully.

"Chalkie told me about the gang that tried to jump him and a few of the lads near the back of the Palladium while they were out taking an evening stroll over towards one of my spielers in Maddox Street. Tossers come over from south of the water, I shouldn't wonder. I tell you, sometimes I think it's as bad as darkest Africa out beyond the Elephant and Castle. Vicious they were. Bloody savages. It shouldn't be allowed."

I nearly choked. Messima, ever the perfect host, nodded sympathetically, thinking the whisky had gone down the wrong hole.

"Chalkie said you just happened to be passing at the time, and that you even had a go yourself to help him and the boys tackle the tearaways. Very public-spirited of you, Jeffro. There's not too many people out there that'd stick their necks out for anybody. So there's two hundred nicker in there for you, just to show my appreciation."

A large brown paper envelope, well used, but bulging with oncers and fivers, was stuck under my nose and dropped in my lap.

"I look after my own, I do. And I don't forget a good deed. Like another drink? What about you, Chalkie? No, you can't, can you? At least, not yet. He's a right trooper is our Chalkie, the first one out the hospital, the first one back here insisting he give a hand and help sort things out. He told me all about it. A real brick he is. Aren't you, Chalk?"

I heard a muffled 'yes' from behind me. I turned in my chair to have a look, hoping that wasn't pushing my welcome too far. Chalkie stood there in one of his second-best striped suits. He had a bandaged splint over his nose, and a big stiff leather collar keeping his chin up and his neck straight. He was beginning to sweat cobs, and if looks could kill they would've done so right there and then. He looked like he hated me with every unbroken bone in his body. But I also saw something I'd never seen in him before, the flinty-eyed madness of a cornered rat.

"Yes, old Chalkie fought like mad for me, didn't you, Chalk? And what's he got to show for it, but a broken nose, a badly bruised windpipe, and several cracked ribs. As well as a nice new, second-hand motor of his very own to drive around in, when he's all healed up and feeling better. A gift from a grateful Guv'nor. A trifle, perhaps, but one that's been well earned. Empires are built on loyalty, you know, Jeffro?"

I almost choked again listening to Messima's history lesson, but I said nothing. I didn't want to push my luck too far.

"We won't talk about them other layabouts, though, will we? Chalkie reckons it was them two young layabouts what set him up. Suffice to say they're no longer in my employ, or for that matter are now very employable. But I've already told you that, haven't I?"

He turned to me again, his loving warmth for Chalkie bathing us all in its glow. I swallowed, trying not to spill any whisky down my chin.

"I fully understand why you had to scarper afterwards, Jeffro. You wouldn't have wanted to get pulled, now would you? Not even for me? But that's sensible, that is, very sensible, and I'd have done the same myself in your shoes. I mean, I've often told Chalkie about you and your derring-do as a creeper. And how you've never ever been caught, and how very commendable I think that is." He leaned forward very slightly, and smiled. I began to sweat. "Only, I wanted to thank you in person for what you did, and also express my pleasure. That little bit of dosh in the envelope should help tide you over for a bit. You could go on holiday to one of those new Butlin's holiday camps, couldn't you? Or even buy that sister of yours a new dress, or a pair of shoes. What's her name?" He turned to the nearest goon, but didn't wait for an answer. He just looked back at me and said, "Joanie, isn't it? Nice name, that. Another drink?"

I coughed, which he took to mean 'yes.' But by then I'd had so many fingers of Scotch, you could've got your hands round my throat from the inside.

"Anyway, enough of all these niceties, as pleasant as they may be. Let's get down to business, shall we? I heard a little rumour you were back creeping the tiles again, Jeffro. And on my manor, too. No names, no pack-drill, but you know the score; people hear things and then, oddly enough, so do I. It's a bit like playing *Monopoly*. Go past 'Go' and you can get anything up to two hundred nicker depending on how closely I listen. And I tell you, you'd be surprised where some of those whispers come from. It costs me a bloody fortune sometimes to keep up with what's happening around town. Almost as much as it just cost me to keep Chalkie and the others from being brought up on a charge. They must think I'm made of money, or something. I ask you, why do they call them coppers, when it's always quids that they're after?"

He looked round at his loving band of thugs, who all laughed like drains at their boss's wit. Satisfied, he turned back to me, and said, brightly, "Did I ever tell you how *Monopoly* is my favourite game? Funny thing, Jeffro, but around here I seem to end up winning every time I play. You'd think people would learn, wouldn't you?"

The thought of Messima piling up mounds of little red and green blocks, and raking in everything bounded by Park Lane, Piccadilly, Charing Cross Road, and Oxford Street, while all the while having his hand deep in the Community Chest, would've been funny, if it hadn't been so near the truth. He might not have owned the real estate itself, but he controlled much of what went on there, and what he didn't control he had a hand in somewhere. I didn't smile, I didn't see the need. I just nodded instead, a silly look on my face that froze solid with what Messima said next.

"Now you're known as being a man of your word, Jeffro. So I'll take you at your word. Are you creeping now, or aren't you?"

The truth was at that precise moment in time I wasn't. So I told him straight. "No, I'm not creeping now, Mr. Messima. I had a fair bit of luck before the war, but once it starts to run out and you find yourself slipping, well then it's best to jack it all in and find yourself another trade." I almost added that I'd told Chalkie the very same thing the last several times I'd seen him, but I stopped myself in the nick of time. Good thing I can hold my whisky; some people can get right gabby when they've had one or two too many.

"So you're definitely not doing any creeping, at the moment?"

"No, Mr. Messima, sir, I'm definitely not creeping now, at this particular moment in time, no I'm not, no, not at all . . ."

It sounded pathetic even to me, but it seemed to satisfy him.

"Good. Have another drink. That's a nice-looking moustache you got there, by the way, had it long?"

I think I mumbled something, and desperately tried to stop my hands from flying up and touching the bloody thing just in case it came off in my hand. I turned and saw them pour my drink from the bottle. It was Glen Garioch. I thought I recognised it. Flowery and smoky, with a bit of pepper to it, and aged fifteen years if it was a day. The trouble was, I felt like I'd aged as much as that in the last fifteen minutes, and I had to cup both hands round the glass so as not to spill anything.

"This is nothing personal, Jeffro, only business. I had to ask, you understand? Just to make sure. But tell me one thing, just so as I can file it away for a rainy day."

The room went quiet and you could hear my bones creak. This was what he'd been leading up to all along. I didn't think it could be anything to do with the Embassy job, but coincidences do turn up at the funniest times. And I have to admit it, but even I was intrigued. I tried to keep a still tongue, but it was no use, I'm pathetic sometimes. "What's, er . . . that, Mr. Messima?"

"Let's just say, hypothetical speaking, Jeffro, that sometime in the future I had a nice one set up; something kosher, something real classy. Something that would need someone with just the right sort of expertise in the creeping department to help pull off successfully. Something that was a guaranteed, major earner, and was as safe as houses. So let's just say, hypothetical like, that one day you found yourself called upon for something like that, what would you say?"

I tried not to swallow my tongue, as it could've been misconstrued under the circumstances. I nodded to help get the sound out. "Mmm . . . yes. Mmm . . . hypothetical speaking. Mmm."

"Good. That's settled, then. Come on, top his drink up."

Nothing was settled, of course, but neither of us wanted to get to the word 'no,' as the consequences would've been too unpleasant to consider. Especially for me. And even going to jail without passing 'Go' was preferable to that. But at least it meant that everyone was still alive and kicking, and that we were all still in the game. Or we could all pretend that we were.

"Well, thanks for dropping by, Jeffro. The lads will see you to the door. They'll even drop you home if you like. They know where you live, I'm sure."

I stood up and put my drink down in one gulp. I had to, it would have been impolite otherwise. The brown paper envelope with the money in it slid onto the floor. "Thanks for the drink, Mr. Messima, but if it's all the same to you, I think I'd prefer to walk. The air will help clear the thump in the back of my head."

"Whatever you say, Jeffro, whatever you say. It's a free country, after all. I mean, that's what everyone fought for, wasn't it? So we should all enjoy it while we can, shouldn't we? You go safe now. I'll be seeing you." He didn't offer to shake hands, and neither did Chalkie. Actually, nobody did. But someone turned me round to show me the door they'd carried me in through, while someone else picked up the envelope with the money in it and stuffed it in my jacket pocket. The dosh was probably still wet from the printer's ink, but I didn't care, I was walking on water, I was walking on air. I was walking out of there still in one piece. And there hadn't been one word about a foreign ambassador's missing jewels or a foreign tealeaf's secret little black books.

They slammed the steel door shut behind me. I realised then I must've been out for the count much longer than I'd thought, because outside it was beginning to get dark. There was only a single, flyblown light bulb in a wire cage on the wall above the door. "How very appropriate," I sneered to the dank December air. Other than that, there was nothing, no sign, no card, no little brass plaque saying that this was the place of business of Soho's Mr. Big. The yard outside smelt of disinfectant, but it couldn't quite cover the beery smell of piss, or the ammonia-like smell of a hundred alley cats.

"Shush! Shush! Mr. Messima must be expecting company," I whispered loudly, drunk as a skunk, but the only thing that came back was the frail little echo that limped round the yard after me. The only time Messima had the courtyard washed out and scrubbed down was when he was expecting people he wanted to impress. And I didn't think for one minute that he'd gone to all that trouble for me. My only importance to Messima was that one day I might be a well-oiled cog in some daring scheme of his devising, and other than that I meant nothing to him. But I decided not to let it unduly depress me, and as I stumbled along the passage and out through the archway into the street, I refused to let the tatty-looking brasses or the tatty-coloured lights along Wardour Street and Old Compton Street get me down, either. In fact, for some reason I can't quite remember I thought they all looked really rather lovely.

I wandered up one of the streets for a bit, declining the offers of "A nice time, dearie?" every few yards. Then I stopped a cab by stepping out in front of it, which under normal circumstances, knowing how they drive, I wouldn't have dared do. But I was inside the back and yelling I'd double whatever was on the meter before the tyres or the cabby stopped screeching. I just nodded and smiled, and waved an arm that embraced the whole of London.

"I have folding money, my good man, and all I require of you this evening is my safe conveyancing to the end of Church Street, just off north London's famed thoroughfare, the Edgware Road."

I ignored the cabby rolling his eyes up to heaven. In fact, I remember laughing warmly at his antics. I was feeling flush and I didn't care who knew it. I tried to close my eyes for a moment, but there seemed to be a dance band playing a polka somewhere inside my head. After a moment or two's chat with the bandleader, when I'm pretty sure a good few quid changed hands, they slowed it down to a waltz. And all I had to do then was keep an occasional eye on the meter to see if the cabby tried taking me home the long way round. I mean, I'd said I'd pay double, but fair's fair. Because I tell you, if you don't keep your wits about you, people will not only take you for a complete mug, they'll take you for a ride.

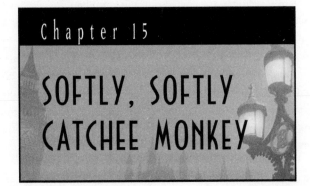

Chapter 15

SOFTLY, SOFTLY CATCHEE MONKEY

When there'd been no sign of Buggy Billy in the market for ten days, I knew something was up. It wasn't like him to vanish without telling anyone. One weekend, maybe, but two in a row, never. Some of his boys ran his stall for him, but it wasn't the same, and less than half the usual amount of bug powder got sold. So, London's fleas must've really hopped up and down with joy at that. One of the boys said they'd got a postcard from Buggy, postmarked Bournemouth, saying he was enjoying the sea air, but I knew the closest he ever got to the sea was Tubby Isaacs's cockle-and-whelk stall over Whitechapel, early each Sunday morning. I knew he could take care of himself, but I was still concerned, he was my best mate after all, and my one and only fence.

It was a sunny day, a rarity anytime, but in December a welcome gift. So like a lot of Londoners I took advantage of it and decided to walk instead of hopping a bus or a tram. I must've had a lot on my mind, because I'd crossed the Marylebone Road and meandered all round the back of Baker Street and down beyond Marylebone High Street, before I realised it. I'd just found myself in Portland Place heading down towards Oxford Circus when I heard a voice. It was so cultured, it dotted its *i*'s and crossed its *t*'s as it spoke.

"It's Jethro, isn't it? I wonder if I might possibly have a quiet word?

Not, of course, out here in the street, but I promise, it wouldn't take too much of your time. It won't take you too far out of your way, either. And I can assure you that it will definitely be to your advantage."

I blinked. Time slowed right down. And in the middle of the street, in the middle of the day, it was suddenly as if I was in the middle of a creep. The light around me became more brilliant and my senses threw away their dark glasses and white sticks, and blinked in surprise. I picked up a whiff of his cologne, and his own fresh-pressed and starched smell, and I would remember it forever. I even picked out a point on his jacket collar where the hand-stitching had begun to unravel. His tailor wouldn't be too pleased about that. I'm not sure I was too pleased, either. He'd come out of nowhere, which is especially disturbing to any creeper, and what's more he was smiling.

"Look, I know it must seem an impertinence me stopping you in the middle of the street like this, but I've got a message for you from an old friend of yours, Mr. Raymond Karmin."

"Never heard of him," I said and walked on.

"He said you'd say something like that, so perhaps I should have said the message was from Buggy Billy, instead."

I stopped dead in my tracks, executed a smart about-face, and walked right up to him. He may have looked all wet, but he didn't budge an inch. He didn't say anything, either, he just reached into an inside pocket and handed me a postcard, only this one was postmarked Brighton. I looked at it, but I studied him. The polish was impeccable, from his black and white striped tie, to the tips of his black handmade shoes. He was Eton, Balliol, the Guards and Whites; he was something in the City, or someone at the Foreign Office. He was everything Alistair Smythe-Whyte aspired to, but could never be. He was a thoroughbred, through and through, and even to Chalkie, he would have been living proof that in life it's the starting point that really matters in the end. For some, life is a moving staircase going upwards from the moment someone jams a silver spoon in their mouths. For others—and that usually means the rest of us—it's scraping a living as best you can. I offered him my hand. It took him aback, but he covered his response well, and not too many people would've noticed it, but I did. Ray used to say that when hands meet, the trumpets of pedigree soon begin.

"And you are?" I said.

When I meet someone I might want to imitate later, I try and pick up their rhythm and reflect it straight back at them. It can be their accent, a mannerism they have, even the way they walk. Hardly anybody ever catches on, they usually just think I'm being sympathetic or friendly. I've seen quite a few actors doing it, and it seems to work, so it must be one of the tricks of the trade.

"My name's Bosanquet, Simon Bosanquet. Ray's told us so much about you."

Now that did take me back, but I didn't give a toss whether he noticed or not. I looked at the postcard. It was definitely Ray's illegible hand-writing and I sussed immediately he was trying to tell me something, even if apart from my name and 'c/o Victory Cafe, Church Street, London NW8' the only words scrawled across the back were 'Pop Goes the Weasel.' That put me in mind of the last time we'd seen each other in The Eagle public house, down the City Road, but I didn't say anything, and I made sure my face didn't give anything away, either. I handed the postcard back, but he shook his head.

"No, you keep it," he said, "after all, it is addressed to you. But you might also want to take a look at this."

He showed me a warrant card. I nodded, but was lost in thought. I blinked again and looked him straight in the eye, and he looked back at me, cool, calm, and very collected. Other than the fact that he was prob-ably the best-dressed, if not the best-educated copper in London, I hadn't been able to see anything beyond what he'd wanted to reveal.

He was about my height and build. He had fairish hair, blue eyes, straight teeth, a straight nose, and a strong chin. We could have been bookends. He was about my age, even though he didn't look as well worn as me, but beneath all the polish I reckoned he might be just as hard. "Bosanquet?" I said.

"That's right," he said, "old Huguenot family; Protestants that fled France during the middle of the seventeenth century, and started all over again in the East End; well, Spitalfields, actually."

I appreciated the history lesson, but not the smoke he was blowing. "Don't try telling me you were born within the sound of Bow Bells, sun-shine, because I wouldn't believe you."

"No, it was Big Ben. I was born at St. Thomas's. I wonder what that makes me?" He smiled; a pleasant, trusting smile. He was good at it, but we both knew it was time to get on.

"It makes you a Londoner born and bred, just like me. What a bleedin' coincidence? Now, where's Ray?"

"He's okay, in fact, I think he's really rather enjoying himself. But why don't you come and see for yourself. We have a temporary place in Regent Street. We could pop down there now if you like. It's far less formal than our Millbank office, and much more convenient."

If he was trying to rock me back on my heels again, he all but succeeded. And just where the hell, I wondered, was this all leading to? I knew for sure, he hadn't been waiting in the street all by himself; there had to be others around somewhere. Like Messima's mob, most police departments tended to run in packs. I couldn't see anyone obvious, but the hairs on the back of my neck and the back of my hands were waving about like long grass on the side of a hill. And in a London street I'd known all my life, I started to feel very lonely, very lonely indeed. There were buses and cars and taxis, and scores of people, and even one or two coppers in uniform and the odd, very obvious, American tourist. But the world had suddenly turned upside down, and I felt as if I was about to follow a white rabbit down into a very dark and murky little hole.

We walked on in silence, but the strain must've got to him, because after suggesting we should wait until later to discuss Ray, he started chatting on amiably about some of the shows currently playing the West End. Funny that. I remember asking myself why on earth he'd think I'd give a toss about the theatre, but despite my misgivings I slowly found myself becoming more and more involved. I couldn't help myself, honest, he might've been a bright bugger, but I tell you he knew bugger all about the theatre. I mean, he thought Donald Wolfit was God's gift to acting. Curse more like it. Don't get me wrong, I was still guarded, but I thought, Well, two can play at this game. The little prickles were still there, running up and down my spine, but it didn't feel like I was getting my collar felt, really it didn't.

————

During one of our many chats, Ray had told me there were only ever two kinds of anything. And I'd asked him whether he was being serious, and he'd answered yes and no, but it depended. And when MI5 stepped out of the shadows and into both our lives, Ray once again proved to be dead right, because with them it was always a case of yes and no, and maybe.

There were the hard boys and the softly, softly boys; the difference being you always knew where you were with the hard cases. With them, as with backstreet fighters anywhere, you just had to learn how to ride the punches and know that if you were still alive to talk about it afterwards, the damage you suffered always looked far worse than it was. The ones you had to really keep an eye open for were the honey-tongued boys; the gentlemen with a fresh carnation in their lapels, tailor-made knuckle-dusters hidden under their immaculately brushed black bowlers, and a well-honed sword stick held safe within the folds of their perfectly rolled Swaine and Aidney umbrellas. Those blokes could have you going more ways than Sunday in a minute flat, and still knock you into the middle of next week at the drop of a hat.

Halfway down Regent Street, on the right-hand side just before the road begins its long curve down towards Piccadilly, there was a posh, export-only, crystal glass and porcelain china shop. And just beyond that, still at street level, were the double-wooden doors that led to a small wood-panelled entrance foyer for several businesses that had their offices on the floors above. I took a quick look at the business name plates painted in gold letters on a large wooden board. There were six floors in all; a distributor of this, an exporter of that, as well as firms dealing with electronics, insurance, and travel. There was even a theatrical booking agency, and my eyebrows lifted a little at finding that. There was also a commissioner in a faded uniform who did nothing more than look at us over his glasses and clean his ear with his little pinkie. He'd obviously had a really hard day.

We stood waiting for the lift, which seemed to take ages and ages. I'm sure it was made by the same people that made the buses, as there was never one around when you wanted one. Finally, we got in and I saw Bosanquet press the button for the fourth floor. It was right about then that two men in belted raincoats and wide-brim hats got into the lift behind us. They didn't talk, they hardly looked at one another, but they both proceeded to study the wood panelling as if they were international timber experts. I noticed they didn't press any buttons. It was just as well, too, because at the very last moment, just before the lift doors closed, a bloke wearing brown overalls barged in carrying a large, flat parcel. By the size of it and the way it was wrapped, it could have been a big gilt picture frame or mirror.

" 'Ere, 'old on," he said. "This is bloomin' heavy, this is. Don't want to have to carry this up all those bloomin' stairs, now do I? Thanks for holding the lift, gents. Very kind of you."

There was a little bit of shuffling and bumping before everyone got comfortable, but we all pretended not to take any notice. Someone even apologised for having his foot trodden on. All I know is, it wasn't me, and it wasn't my foot.

"Would one of you gents mind pushing the button for the fifth floor, only me hands are full. Ta. Lovely weather we're havin' for this time of year, innit? Oops, sorry, was that your foot? It's so bleedin' hard to keep your balance in these things."

Of course, the foot that time was mine. I'd half expected it, it's an old trick. Get your mind feeling out the pain in one of your extremities and you're immediately less sensitive everywhere else. They'd also worked it so I was pressed into a corner. No one spoke, but there was a good deal of coughing and throat clearing going on all of a sudden. The lift was slower than a Scotsman reaching for his purse, but we got where we were supposed to be going in the end.

"Ah, fourth floor. That must be for you gents, it's not me."

I wondered how I'd managed to get through life without helpful Charlie round my feet at all times. Bosanquet, my new friend, smiled sickly and nodded his acknowledgement of the serf without once looking at him directly. I played along with the charade. "Excuse me, excuse me, please." I was acidly polite and the raincoats duly parted in front of me like the Red Sea, but we all knew I knew I'd been given an expert going-over. Not even the dips that work the market could've done a better job. If I'd had a gun or a knife or a cosh on me it would've already been lifted. And if I'd suddenly flipped my lid and gone berserk, they'd have simply pressed and confined me into the corner with the big, flat parcel in less time than it took to blink. The lift doors closed on the bloke in the overalls going

on about something he'd only been telling his missus that morning. I
thought he was overplaying it a bit, but I appreciated the performance; a
good actor doesn't step out of his character till he's well past the sight
lines. I didn't doubt that they'd soon be reporting I was clean, and that I
presented no threat whatsoever, to whoever was in charge upstairs.

The fourth floor turned out to be the offices of Universal Insurance
Company, Limited. Bosanquet hadn't said a word since we'd entered the
building, but I didn't mind, I still had some thinking to do. So while he
talked to the receptionist, I just sat on one of the modern-looking couches
in the foyer and tried to look completely at ease.

"They won't keep us waiting more than a tick. Mind if I smoke?" His
mission almost done, he was back to his jolly old self.

"You go ahead," I said, "I've given it up for Lent."

"Really? Oh. No, no of course not, a joke." It wasn't that he was
nervous or anything, but this was the intermission before Act Two and he
was filling in the time. I wondered what they were stage-managing for me,
but why ruin the play by trying to read on ahead? If Ray was here, then
the very least I could do was wait until curtain-up.

"If you'll come this way, please."

It was a different girl from the one in reception, but they both looked
like they'd gone to all the right finishing schools. Posh skirt around an
office usually points to corridors of influence and power. I took it as
another sign that I should be on my best behaviour. She led us along a
linoleum-covered corridor, the pock-pock of her high heels echoing the
faint clack-clacking of the typewriters. Bosanquet walked behind me, still
amiable, though silent again; as silent as the shadows that moved behind
all the frosted-glass panels in the newly painted office doors.

We were led into a large windowless room. The lighting was subdued,
and the place quiet, apart from the slow, deliberate ticking of a clock. A
long mahogany table with a dozen chairs spaced at perfect intervals suggested we were in a meeting room of sorts. I noticed there were two other
doors into the room, one at each end of the opposite wall. To the left, the
far wall was completely curtained in dark green velvet. But I could see no
gilt-framed pictures, no mirrors, and no posters to remind me that 'careless
talk costs lives.' As a stage set it wasn't very original, but I supposed it
would do.

Bosanquet closed the door and quietly locked us in. So, with no quick exit, stage-left, possible through that door, and not knowing what in hell was behind the other two doors, I sat down at the table and twiddled my thumbs. And then I found myself cleaning my ear with one of my little pinkies. "It must be catching," I murmured, and I was still half-smiling when one of the doors opened and a tall, very distinguished-looking gent swept in.

"It's Jethro, isn't it? So good of you to come, it would've got us all off on the wrong foot if we'd had to arrest you. Let me introduce myself. My name's Walsingham."

He was fiftyish. Ronald Coleman played by Stewart Granger. Dapper, but physical, and perfect casting for a Guards' colonel in full dress uniform, or in the mufti he was wearing then. But even his civvies were on their best behaviour; mid-grey Savile Row suit, white Turnbull and Asser shirt, Whites' club tie. I couldn't see his shoes, but I didn't really have to, they'd have been handmade just like the rest of him. He and Bosanquet were a right pair; same model, different year.

He had a narrow, well-chiselled face lit by a pair of startlingly blue eyes and marked by a strong, uncompromising mouth. His immaculately trimmed and brushed, salt-and-pepper hair and moustache would have made George Trumper himself proud. He looked taller than me and Bosanquet, but it might've just been the way he carried himself. He moved well, but there was no stiff, parade-ground manner about him, even though he looked as if he'd been used to command for most of his life. Everything about him was designed to instil instant respect, and I must admit that even I started to come to attention. But I still didn't trust him beyond that. Fair's fair, I'd been round the block a few times myself.

"You've met Bosanquet." It was a statement not a question. "All you need to know is that he's something to do with Special Branch who's been seconded to me. And, me? I'm somebody quite high up in Military Intelligence."

I cleared my throat as if I was impressed. I was. This was double serious stuff. I'd definitely have to mind my p's and q's. He sat down and looked straight at me. And I looked straight back at him.

"Normally, Jethro, we'd play around the houses for weeks and months, even years sometimes, before we openly approached someone such as yourself. But it seems that you've popped up right in the middle of something rather sticky and caused us all a bit of a problem. I know it's unorthodox to be talking to you like this, but we have to continue to move as expeditiously as we can to find an acceptable solution."

I was content to let him rabbit on, but I kept my guard up; I mean, I didn't come across a word like 'expeditiously' very often, even in the theatre, so I was definitely intrigued. I guessed it had to be something to do with those buggerin' books I'd nicked from the Embassy. First, Browno doing Ray's place over, and now all this. What next? But I knew they'd get round to telling me as soon as they were good and ready.

"Firstly, I wonder awfully whether you'd mind signing this?"

He pushed a printed document exactly halfway across the table towards me. I looked at it and let it sit there. It might still be there if Bosanquet hadn't reached forward and placed it directly in front of me. I looked down at it. It was a copy of the Official Secrets Act.

"It's the Official Secrets Act. We have to ask you to sign it before we can proceed any further."

Bosanquet produced a fountain pen, unscrewed the top, and carefully laid it on the table in front of me. I just let it sit there. It was a nice pen, Chinese red lacquer, a Parker, and I'd have had it off him in a trice at any other time. I studied it minutely, quite ignoring the document. It was as good a time as any to try a diversionary tactic.

"Where's Ray? This Bosanquet chap said he was here, and that's the only reason that I've come. I just want to see that he's alright."

"And so you shall, my dear boy, so you shall. In fact, he's in the very next room at this moment. But, before you see him, I really must ask you to sign the document."

Walsingham turned his troops to face me and began marshalling them ready for an outflanking manoeuvre. I quickly regrouped, all the time wondering what the punishment was for robbing a foreign embassy if you threw in an accidental death for good measure.

"What if I don't sign? I mean, this is ridiculous, I don't have any secrets worth having. I'd know if I did, surely?"

Walsingham looked disappointed. I think he'd expected a more concerted counter-attack, rather than me sending out a skirmish line.

"Well, that's where you're wrong, Jethro. Wittingly or not, you are in possession of information important to the security of this country, and to the Defence of the Realm. And that's already more than enough reason for you to be here. And Mr. Karmin, as well."

I shuffled in my chair and avoided looking at either of them. It was then Walsingham brought up his first battery of big guns.

"I could, of course, throw different subsections of the Official Secrets Act at you; failure to answer questions, failure to co-operate with the proper authorities, that sort of thing. I could even use the act against you, whether you sign it or not, simply to determine whether anything that might otherwise be covered by it has already been contravened. And ignorance of the law, old chap, is no defence."

I swallowed what felt like my tongue, and he galloped on.

"Furthermore, as it also applies retroactively, if we can prove you'd met Raymond Karmin on at least two occasions since the incident at the Embassy, we could even throw a 'conspiracy to contravene the Official Secrets Act' at you. All a trifle heavy-handed I admit, but needs must."

He nodded; reassuring, reasonable, resolute, while I tried to get something out, a sound, anything, but nothing happened.

"Suffice to say, that if you don't sign the document I can assure you that you won't be seeing Mr. Karmin, or anyone else for that matter, for a very long time."

I blinked, lit the blue touch paper and fired back. But the powder was wet, and even I felt it was more flash than bang. "But that's not how English law works, is it? Whatever you charge me with, I'm presumed innocent until such time as I can be proven guilty."

Even to my ears it sounded no better than the pathetic whinings of a barracks-room lawyer. But you've got to have a go, haven't you? If I'd had any petards handy I'd have hoisted them, but I didn't, so before he could get anything in edgewise I threw up the only thing I had left.

"I've got a feeling there's a darned sight more you want from me, Mr. Walsingham, sir, than just my moniker on some dotted line. And whatever the hell it is, if you could've already swept in and snatched it up, you'd have done so."

But even then he didn't go in for the kill, he simply turned to Bosanquet and said, "Ask for tea to be sent in, will you, Simon. It looks as if we're going to be in here for a little while. And then be a good chap and signal them next door that we're ready to draw back the curtain."

He turned round to face me; open, trustworthy, calm. "I'm afraid we can't run to a single malt, Jethro, we're right out of The Glenlivet at the moment. Would a cup of tea be acceptable?"

You could've knocked me down with a feather, let alone a tea-urn; he seemed to know more about me than would be good for me. Bosanquet executed a smart about-turn and left the room by the same door Walsingham had used. Walsingham merely steepled his fingers.

"Jethro, if I tell you that Mr. Karmin has already signed the Official Secrets Act, would that make a difference?"

"It might," I said, wondering what the hell they'd threatened Ray with, "but then again, it might not."

I tell you, I'm nothing if not a terror when I'm aroused.

Chapter 16

A LOOK BEHIND THE CURTAIN

I didn't know what to expect when they drew back the veil. And I heard Ray, before I saw him. He sounded a bit tinny at first, but I knew it was him all right; once you'd heard his evil-sounding cackle it stayed with you forever. And I think it was that sound, of him laughing, that shocked me the most. I mean, the sound of a punch up the bracket or the crump of a telephone directory on top of the head was the very least of what I had in mind; the everyday stuff that comes with 'helping the police with their enquiries' from Limehouse to Scotland Yard. But it was nothing like that.

The lights dimmed and the heavy green velvet curtain swished back to reveal Ray in a room that was more like a posh sitting room or study than an office. There was a nice coal fire going in the grate, a rare enough sight in itself; old leather couches and chairs; antique side tables and lamps; walls filled with bookcases filled with books with good bindings; pictures on the walls, no Stubbs admittedly, but nothing too shabby. There was probably an Oriental carpet on the floor, I don't know, I couldn't see. But if Ray had been wearing a quilted smoking jacket and searching for tobacco in the toe of an old Persian slipper, I don't think I could've been more surprised. It put you in mind of a club down Pall Mall, and it wouldn't have been amiss in the Albany, but it certainly wasn't what you'd expect to find over a shop in Regent Street.

Ray didn't seem strained or strange, in fact, just as Bosanquet had said earlier, he seemed to be rather enjoying himself. So did the bloke with him. They looked like two professors having a good old chinwag, and that's just what it sounded like, too.

"... but Keynes's emphasis on future uncertainty applied directly to interest rates, Ray, you're being deliberately obtuse ..."

"If I was, I'd throw Kondratieff's hypothesis of long wave economics at you. No, it's Stafford Cripps and those duffers down the Board of Trade I'm on about. They officially condemn the Black Market, but it's them that created it and that now maintain it."

"But you must agree, Ray, that however stringent, any state regulation of the economy requires effective and enforceable mechanisms." The old boy had a way with words, but I'd bet a tanner to a sixpence that he hadn't come across the likes of Raymond L. Karmin in any of his lectures or tutorials. Ray turned up the gas.

"It's still like putting a lid on a kettle without a pressure valve. God's Holy trousers, you should try working a market stall for a living, you might learn something practical then. Believe me, there's no better barometer to the real state of the country. Look, whenever the supply of goods on ration exceeds the ceiling that you civil servants impose with your rationing allocations, it creates a surplus. But in turn, when the overall supply falls short, there's a scarcity. And that's when the black marketeer steps in—your entrepreneur *par excellence*. He rides the swings and the roundabouts, and provides the only balance mechanism that can relieve pressure from both sides. He uses the streets, the pubs, and the street markets to do his selling in. And given the present conditions, I tell you, it's only the Black Market that stops the whole economy from grinding to a halt."

Ray laughed again and got up from his chair, then he turned and looked straight at me. I got up and smiled, and moved closer to the glass. "Wotcher, Ray," I said, even though I knew by then it was a special two-way mirror, and he couldn't see or hear me.

"Why are you showing him to me like this? He's in there like a bleedin' monkey down Regent's Park Zoo." I didn't even bother to turn round, I knew my posh new friends could hear me well enough.

"No, it's really not like that at all," said Bosanquet.

Then Walsingham piped in. "Technically, he's not under arrest. Let's just say we've come to an arrangement whereby it's better for all concerned that he remains in protective custody for a while."

They turned off the sound from the other room and I turned to face them. I wasn't at all sure what them letting me see Ray like that was supposed to have accomplished. Walsingham put his teacup down, gently, and deliberately, but when he spoke his tone was confiding rather than confrontational.

"We won the war, Jethro, but now we must try and win the peace. The world is dividing itself more and more into two camps, and it's turning the old world order upside down and inside out. Europe is in turmoil; it's also bankrupt. And for that matter, so are we. The Soviet Union, meanwhile, is doing everything it can to extend its influence. With the result that France and Italy, and even Greece seem to be sliding irrevocably towards communism."

I stirred my tea over and over again, wordlessly grumbling to myself, waiting for the sugar to fully dissolve, and for me to finally get to whatever bitter little pill Walsingham was going to ask me to swallow.

"The American response is to rebuild a strong Germany as a buttress against further Soviet expansion, and it's in our interests to help them do it. That's why the bulk of America's aid dollars are going to Germany, and why at present, what little money we have, as well as most of our grain, is going there, too. The aim is to stop Germany from starving to death. And that's the single reason there's bread rationing here at home, even though we never once had to impose it during the war; every loaf of bread is a brick in the wall against communism."

He had no argument from me on that score, I'd much rather a wall of English bread than a wall of English dead, any day of the week. I tell you, listening to Ray or Walsingham was miles better than reading the tub-thumping nonsense that got printed in the papers, but I was buggered if I'd show just how interested I was in it all. I think that was the very first time, though, I really cottoned on to just how intertwined everything was becoming; it'd always been us versus them before, John Bull standing astride the world and taking on all comers. But now, even after the second war to end all wars, here we all were in the same boat, fighting to stay afloat, every man jack of us. What a funny old world!

"Churchill was right when he said that the Russians didn't want another war, they just wanted the fruits of war and the infinite expansion of their power and doctrines. And that's why we now have no alternative, Jethro, but to do everything in our power to stop them."

He looked across at me, but I said nothing and tried to stop from yawning, which always tends to happen when I'm listening to anyone go on for too long.

"One of the most vital aspects of this new conflict is the gathering of information. Which brings us to our interest in Raymond Karmin. For years, émigrés and refugees from all over Europe—many of them scientists and mathematicians—have searched out him or his father, because of their reputations with gemstones. Now, as well as their jewellery, people have also carried out with them stories of all the things they've witnessed. Trivialities of no real use to anyone, but nevertheless, under the present circumstances, titbits of information that could prove to be as precious to us as any jewels would be to you."

"So behind all your flannel," I sneered, "what you're really saying is that you want Ray to grass on the people he meets; you want him to become your informer?" I had to be blunt; well, someone had to be with all the beating about the bush that was going on.

He didn't bat an eyelid. "No, not an informer, Jethro, nor a grass as I believe you call it, merely a conduit for useful, possibly vital information. Nothing about the people themselves, just anything else that might strike Mr. Karmin as interesting. And if my memory serves me correctly, it was he himself that volunteered the idea."

Bosanquet murmured in the background. "That's correct, sir, Mr. Karmin suggested it at the end of our third meeting."

I admit that surprised me a bit, but after thinking about it, and knowing Ray as I did, I knew he'd probably worked out the best angle for himself. "Always drive into a skid," he'd told me, "you've got a much better chance of coming out the other end in one piece, if you do."

As if reading my thoughts, Walsingham said, "His is a different kind of loyalty than either yours or mine, Jethro. After all, his parents adopted this country, and so did he. He's a naturalised British citizen, very grateful for that privilege having been extended to him, who has been presented with a unique opportunity to render it a service."

I felt like standing up, throwing a V sign in the air, and singing "Rule,

Britannia." And if they'd unfurled a Union Jack, I'm sure I'd have saluted that on the spot, too. I knew Ray was good at pulling the wool over people's eyes, but the trouble was, this time he might've only succeeded in pulling it down tight over his own eyes. And if so, just where, I wondered, did that leave me?

I didn't have to wait long to find out. "Our interviews with Mr. Karmin concluded, we proceeded to do a little digging into your own background." It was Bosanquet the Huguenot. He had a buff-coloured folder in his hand, though where it had sprung from I had no idea; he must've been hiding it under the tea tray. He started reading his report and it was quite a surprise; his voice displayed no character, whatsoever, and there was none of the chattiness I'd experienced earlier. Someone must have paid very dearly for his education, I thought. He did name, rank, serial number, that sort of thing, and then after a bit of fidgeting on my part, he got stuck in.

"Born, Hackney, July 27th, 1916. Mother and father dead, both killed in the Blitz. One sister, Joan Eileen, lives in London. Attended Seamen's College, in Southampton. Joined the Merchant Navy in 1935, and served as a deck officer, mainly with Cunard White Star Line. At the outbreak of the war, he immediately signed a T124 agreement and was commissioned into the Royal Naval Reserve. Exemplary war service; troopships mostly. Sunk twice; the first occasion suffering minor burns; the second, almost dying from hypothermia. Awarded the British Empire medal for bravery for the latter incident. The official citation for outstanding courage and fortitude reads, that without regard of risk to himself, he was relentless in his efforts to save as many of his shipmates as was possible from perishing. He later applied for active duty with the Royal Navy, but was refused because of the Essential Services Provision. He was permitted to resign the Merchant Navy in December 1945."

Walsingham cleared his throat, but didn't say anything. It might've been a signal, I couldn't tell. But they'd been moving scenery about, and opening and closing trap doors all morning long, and now I had the distinct feeling that Act Three had finally begun.

Something was niggling me, though. If two blokes of their calibre and social standing were going through all this nonsense and palaver, conjuring up the war just to get my heart going, then I was probably up to my neck in something very nasty, indeed. I was being expertly bundled up—trussed up, more like it—in the folds of the flag, which is exactly what they do with bodies at sea. On board ship, though, they at least have the decency to wait until you're good and dead before they drop you over the side.

"Springes to catch woodcocks, my old cock sparrow," as Ray would've said, "springes to catch woodcocks." I turned back towards Ray, hoping for some kind of support, or perhaps a compass or an anchor. But he'd gone. The other room was empty, and I was left looking through the looking glass into another world. The trouble was, I couldn't tell any longer which was which, his world, theirs, or mine. And what's more, I couldn't see my way clear. Bosanquet could, though, but it sounded like he'd gone back a very long way to find it.

"Which is all very commendable, considering that as a juvenile he was twice booked on suspicion of burglary in 1930, and again in 1931. But as he was never found to be in possession of stolen goods he was never actually convicted. He was, however, given a strong caution and placed on probation instead of being sent for Borstal Training. After which, there's no record of any further misdemeanours." He paused for effect. Having learned a thing or two about the theatre myself, I let the silence hang about in the room until it died a death at the hands of a loud tick-tocking from the clock on the mantelpiece. Then Walsingham cleared his throat again, and Bosanquet sailed on.

"London was overrun with jewel thieves in the Thirties, so there's no way we could accurately define the full extent of his activities. We therefore extended our investigations to *Lloyds Maritime Registry* and examined the sailing schedules of the passenger liners he served on during the period."

The clock ticked on loudly. Someone cleared their throat, only I was surprised to find that time it'd been me.

"Once the routes, port cities, and sailing dates were established, we made discreet enquiries through our own embassies, and they in turn contacted the relevant police departments. We weren't able to get much information at all out of Shanghai or Macao, but Singapore, Hong Kong, Sydney, and New York yielded some rather interesting results. The criterion was simple; we requested reports of unsolved jewel thefts valued at ten thousand pounds or more. And despite the probability of any such correlation being almost nil, a surprisingly high number of such incidents did, in fact, match up. Our head of statistics has postulated that a match of over twenty-three per cent is far beyond the realms of coincidence. So even though we are unable to link him directly to any of these thefts, we don't believe in coincidences, either. We therefore had no choice but to probe deeper."

Probe deeper? I'd heard of butcher-surgeons that were kinder. But statisticians? Realms of coincidence? Who in hell did they think they were kidding? I swirled the tea around, but then any port in a storm, even if it does only happen to be in a teacup. I looked up and noticed the room had gone completely silent, and for a moment or two, even the clock seemed reluctant to tick on into it. It all suddenly seemed very ominous, and that was when Walsingham chimed in again.

"It's remarkable what secrets one can unlock when one has the proper key. It was the skeletons rattling around in your own cupboard, Jethro, that clued us in. The rest, like so much in our line of business, was just spadework."

Yes, and I bet it was him that had done all the digging, too, nevertheless it felt as if someone had just stepped over my grave. I brought the tea to my lips, knowing it would be stone cold. But as it was, I nearly spilled the lot when Bosanquet dropped his next little titbit.

"We then took a look into the state of his financial affairs and uncovered one or two rather interesting items. He gives his present occupation as a freelance stage-hand in theatres and music halls throughout London, and yet despite appearances to the contrary he lives anything but a hand-to-mouth existence."

He looked up from the file, but whether to reassess the quality of my tailor again, or me, I couldn't tell. Then his eyes hooded over and he really started getting down to business.

"For instance, there is every indication that he is the owner of several buildings, one of which is in Church Street, NW8. It's listed as containing a cafe called the 'Victory' on the ground floor, as well as two separate flats on the floors above. The top-floor flat is currently given as his place of residence. We have also been able to determine that he is the owner of several motor vehicles, including a Riley MPH, and a T-Series MG Midget originally earmarked for export. There's also an Austin-8 van and an Ariel motorcycle, both licensed for commercial use only."

Walsingham threw one of his looks at me at the mention of the Riley; they were as rare as hen's teeth and more than a match for the Bentley he probably owned himself, just a lot less flash. I had the car up on blocks in a garage in Finchley for when petrol rationing ended. I was heartened, though, to hear that they'd missed the Austin taxi and my BSA motorcycle combination. Bosanquet motored on regardless.

"It also appears that he has an interest in a number of businesses in and around London, the full extent of which is uncertain, but given time we believe we can establish it exactly."

I knew they'd had to dig hard to get that little lot, but there were still too many "every indications" and "it also appears" for them to have anything concrete. As far as I was concerned they could believe what they jolly well liked; I knew it was proof not suspicion that mattered in an English court of law. So it was all nothing but bluster. And I began to relax for the first time. I looked up and noticed Walsingham brushing some tiny speck of dust from off an immaculately pressed trouser leg. Then just in case I'd missed the point, Bosanquet moved in for the kill.

"Which leads us to the small matter of outstanding taxes. Should any or all of this information be forwarded to the appropriate departments within His Majesty's Inland Revenue, and Customs and Excise Services, we estimate that the tax shortfalls alone would represent well over one hundred times his currently reported yearly wage. The subsequent non-payment of which would likely translate to nothing less than ten to fifteen years spent at His Majesty's pleasure. And should our suppositions be proved beyond a reasonable doubt, then in pursuant of revenues owed the Crown, it would undoubtedly lead to the seizure of all his known assets and property. This would also apply to the assets and property of Mr. Raymond Karmin, if it was to be established that he acted as a willing accomplice throughout the period in question."

Bosanquet had missed his calling, he'd have gone down well at the Old Bailey; all he lacked was a little white horsehair wig and a black gown. I'd been led like a lamb to the slaughter, and my testicles were on the chopping block and there wasn't anything I could do about it. Of course, it was blackmail pure and simple, but played by masters of the game. The thing that nailed me was the thought of Joanie being turfed out onto the street, and Church Street at that, and perhaps Barry even losing his taxi-cab. No, I'd never allow that. And as for them nobbling Ray, well, that was completely out of the question.

Walsingham's voice drifted across the table, all matter-of-fact and let's-just-get-down-to-brass-tacks. "Let's stop beating about the bush, shall we? You are a cat burglar and jewel thief. You're also an incorrigible rogue, which is just as well, as I have particular need of you and your skills, as questionable as others undoubtedly find them. It's important to me that thus far you've managed to avoid apprehension, whatever suspicions the police might have harboured about you over the years. You have nerve, your courage isn't in question, and for the moment neither are your ethics, as bent out of shape as they undoubtedly are."

He carried on, but suddenly it wasn't like he was giving me a pasting anymore, it felt more like a theatrical review. And I have to admit, I couldn't wait to see the quotes on the playbills.

"There are any number of men such as yourself operating as jewel thieves in London, and yet you stand apart from them, Jethro. Your planning appears to be scrupulous, your methods inventive, and your ability to adopt different disguises is an interesting twist."

He looked at me and his eyes flashed into mine like a copper shining a torch into a darkened doorway.

"You work alone, and the only man you seem to trust completely is Raymond Karmin. Karmin is as clever and cunning as you, and in all probability, if it wasn't for his excess of patriotic spirit after your business at the Embassy, we would never have stumbled across either of you."

"You leave Ray out of it," I said. "He's nothing to do with whatever it is you want me for. He's just some old bloke that I've known over the years. I've enjoyed a chat and a glass of whisky with him now and again, but other than that, he's not really what I'd call a friend, at all."

Walsingham didn't even pause. "That's funny, Jethro, because that's exactly what he said about you, including your very last sentiment. And what's more, he said he'd only co-operate with us if we agreed to keep you out of this."

"I see you keep your word, then," I sneered, oddly pleased that Ray had kept faith with me, just like he always said he would.

"You're in an altogether different order of trouble, Jethro." He slowly levelled both eyes at me. "And you're in it right up to your neck. You do, however, have the opportunity to clear up Mr. Karmin's mess, as well as your own, if you agree to what I have in mind."

What he had in mind? My thoughts began running about like mad, but they came to a screeching stop, when Bosanquet piped in with, "We believe that your skills could, and should, be put to better use for the good of King and Country."

My mouth fell open and I all but choked, "King and Country?" "Skills put to better use?" My thoughts came marching back then, and in double-quick time. The two of them had gone a bloody long way round to get there, but at last we'd come to the point. Across the table a throat cleared itself again, just as another speck of dust was brushed into oblivion. I knew how it felt.

"I'll be on the square with you."

If he'd stood up and turned round three times, and then, in a puff of smoke, revealed he was blindfolded and had a dagger pointed at his chest, and that his left trouser leg was rolled up and a silken cord was draped around his neck in a hangman's noose, I wouldn't have been at all surprised. But he just sat there full of mystery and looked me straight in the eye. Walsingham was telling me in a time-honoured way that he was giving me his word as an officer and a gentleman, and a Master Mason. We hadn't spit on our hands and shook on anything yet, so it didn't count as far as I was concerned, but I felt myself becoming more and more convinced of his underlying integrity.

"We have amassed these facts simply to expedite matters, even though you may indeed look upon this whole procedure as a form of blackmail. In truth, I prefer to think of it as insurance; yours, as well as mine. I assure you, I'm not interested in handing the contents of this file over to anyone, and thus far outside this room, it doesn't exist. It's unofficial and shall remain so, if you agree to work for us."

"Well, you've got a funny way of asking for my help," I said sharply. But I did see a faint glimmer of light at the end of my tunnel.

"Quite," he replied, all matter-of-factly. "But it's imperative that I arrange for your immediate and wholehearted co-operation. That is also why Mr. Karmin will be staying as our guest, until such time as I determine your task is completed. Do you understand what I'm saying?"

I nodded; a sour taste in my mouth.

"Good. Because if you were to succumb to doubts once the operation was under way, it could very likely prove fatal for you and the mission itself. And that I will not countenance." He paused, then said, "I want you to burgle the Embassy again. There are one or two things you neglected to bring out with you on your first visit, and I'd like very much for you to go back in and get them for us."

I wasn't sure I'd heard right at first, it was too barmy for words.

"Go in again? You're off your rocker, you are, or you must think I am. I barely escaped with my skin in one piece, the last time."

"Believe me, if there was any other way of accomplishing the mission in what little time is still available to us, we would've done so, but incidentally, Jethro, thank you, for finally confirming your part in the episode at the Embassy. Admittedly, it's not a confession that would necessarily stand up in court, but it's good enough for our purposes."

Gotcha. Gotme. The tricky bastards. I could not believe it. I'd been played like a bleedin' violin.

I heard a slurping sound at my elbow, which turned out to be Bosanquet sipping his tea. It must've been stone cold and stewed rotten, but it didn't seem to bother him any. And what's more, he had a big horrible smile plastered across his face.

Walsingham uncrossed his long legs, the knife-edged creases snapping to attention, and leaned forward a fraction of an inch. His mouth smiled, but his eyes didn't.

"Now you will be a good sort and sign this, won't you? Then we can stop buggering about, and get on with the proper business of planning a burglary on behalf of His Majesty the King, and in Defence of the Realm."

He pushed the Official Secrets Act across the desk at me and Bosanquet's pen magically appeared out of thin air again, and before I knew it, I'd signed my name.

God help me, I thought. But at least I now knew the length and breadth of the high jump I'd been measured for.

It was a cream-coloured, stuccoed building in Belgravia, six stories high, including the basement. Or it was an unvarnished pine box, six feet long, not including the metalwork. And it was anybody's guess which one would fit me best in the end.

Chapter 17

ONCE MORE UNTO THE BREACH

Once more? No, thank you. I'd been to hell and back more times than ever I wanted to remember, and believe me, a day didn't go by without me feeling guilty for having survived when so many of my shipmates had perished. And my time at sea had been no different from when I was a kid growing up in the streets. The reason you fought on and on was the mates you had around you; the ones who had their eyes out for you, just as you had yours out for them. Out there in the cold and dark, all you did all the time was try and survive, and try to remember the face of the girl, the wife, or the mum you'd left back home. That's where all the bravery came from; in the end it was never for politics, it was only ever for the people you loved. I know it had to be, because it was a bottomless well, and I'd witnessed tired and desperate men drawing their strength from it time and again. No, I'd done my bit and I didn't need to do any more; let it be some other bloke's turn.

Walsingham tapped my file with the stem of his pipe, carefully placed the pipe into a large cut-glass ashtray by his side, and then slowly brought his hands together and up to his lips as if he was praying. I wondered if it was for the good of my soul or for my eternal damnation. His steely eyes lit on me like blue light through a stained-glass window, and when he spoke it sounded as if he was calling out the number of the next hymn of remembrance.

"After Bosanquet's stirring reading of the chapter and verse of your life, Jethro, I rather thought your course of action would be clear."

I thought of the consequences for Joanie and Barry, and Ray—and me—if I didn't agree to do some burgling for them. I nodded once. Walsingham clapped his hands. Bosanquet merely grinned.

"Excellent. We were hoping that you'd consider going back into the Embassy sometime in the next few days, Jethro. The night after tomorrow, if possible. *Tempus fugit*, you know."

"It does, does it? Well, so does my friggin' temper." I stared at them. "Go back into the Embassy the day after tomorrow? You're off your rockers, the pair of you. I thought you were only testing me just then, but now I know you're both as mad as hatters."

Walsingham had the nerve to chuckle. "I'll ignore the implicit insult, but yes, sometimes I think I am rather mad, at that. I certainly wouldn't be running this show if I weren't."

"Well, bully for you, but why pick on me?"

"Simple. You're what we call a 'gifted irregular.' As is your friend Karmin. You're audacious. Tenacious. And you possess skills that have placed you at the top of your profession as a cat burglar and jewel thief. You're therefore an asset of clear and immediate benefit to us."

Beware of Greeks bearing gifts and flattery from a flatfoot. I knew it was little more than the truth, but I was buggered if I'd show it by blushing, so I swallowed quietly, slowly shaking my head from side to side to cover it. But it made me think I should've swallowed those soddin' notebooks at the very start. After all, they were the real reason I was locked in the room with those two nutcases.

"I can't pay you, I can't reward you, but I can continue to look the other way and let certain sleeping dogs lie." He tapped the folder with my name on it, this time with a well-manicured fingertip. "And I can promise that I will do everything in my power to ensure that others do the same." He smiled his best thin-lipped smile. He didn't have to add, "Within reason, of course." But he did.

I nodded, he nodded, Bosanquet nodded, and for better or worse, that's when the deal was struck. If I played ball, then they would, too.

"Now all fun and games aside, Jethro, it's vital you listen, and I do not exaggerate when I say it could be a matter of life and death. It's very possible you may cross paths with someone working for the Soviets who in every respect is your equal. And that may prick at your pride, but you mustn't let it. Just do the job I send you to do, and nothing more."

The hair stood up on the back of my neck, shivers did a conga up my spine, and I sat motionless in my chair and went stone cold. And all of a sudden, I knew he had to be talking about Flash Harry Raffles. "You must mean Flash Harry Raffles," I whispered hoarsely. "I don't know his real name, but you must be talking about the flash toff that's been staying at the Embassy these last few months?"

Walsingham nodded. "The very same. He now calls himself Count Henry von Bentink, although he's gone by various other names in the past. He has a reputation of being a world-class thief, and is known to have operated in Europe and the United States, as well as in South America. He's also by all accounts a first-class bastard. He did very well out of the war, and spent most of it, peacefully, in Lisbon. He keeps his fingers in lots of pies, his feet in different camps, and always works for the highest bidder. All in all he's a nasty piece of work, and I'm deeply chagrined that we missed him here in London for as long as we did. It was one of our people literally bumping into him at some society ball that alerted us. It's surprising what a different hairstyle, a moustache, and a little tailoring can do for someone's appearance, but I'm told you're pretty good in that department yourself."

I knew he meant well, but I've never liked the idea of setting a thief to catch a thief. It goes against the grain. And as to Flash Harry having a world-class reputation as a cat burglar, well, I'd never heard of him, and neither had Ray. But as the bastard had been using different names all the time, we wouldn't have, would we? So, I might even have crossed his path before without knowing it. But it all sounded too much like a deadly game of cat and mouse for my liking, with me playing the cheese in the trap as well as the bloody mouse. I'd only managed to escape from the Embassy by the skin of my whiskers the first go-round. I knew I couldn't expect to be half so lucky a second time.

Walsingham seemed to have read my silence as contemplation not disquiet, so he pulled a soft-leather tobacco pouch from out of a pocket and gave me another bit of history to think about. "The single-minded ambition of the Soviets has always been the Marxist doctrine of world revolution, and they've never made any attempt to conceal the fact. At

best, they've only ever sought to cloak it abroad in the convoluted sim-
plicities of economic egalitarianism."

He filled his pipe, and the sweet aroma of the tobacco drifted across
the table. It was probably a blend that was specially made for him by a
little shop in St. James's, right next door to the ones who'd made his shirts
and his shoes. I tapped my foot, but not out of impatience, I was thinking
about what the hell 'economic egalitarianism' was, when it was at home.
But I soon gave that up and asked myself, Why on earth was he inviting
me to peer through the smoke?

"The Soviets believe that history is ultimately on the side of global
communist victory, and that the rest of the world will eventually succumb.
Even if it means they have to use the Red Army, their secret police, and
total terror at home and abroad to achieve it."

I nodded and swallowed, and nodded some more. And Walsingham
sped on, under a full head of steam.

"In their relentless and unending quest for world influence, we suspect
the Soviets have been quietly invading our shores, seeking out communist
sympathisers since the late Twenties and early Thirties. And it's my belief
that they've managed to infiltrate all levels of our society and, possibly,
even the government."

Well, that didn't surprise me. Fascists or communists, it was the same
difference. Before the war there'd been whispers galore about some pretty
heavy breathers in the government and the aristocracy secretly supporting
one group or the other. And it stood to reason they weren't all home
grown, they had to have had help from somewhere. Ray had got Mosley's
number very early on. But you'll never hear it from me that it was him
and a bunch of other wealthy Jewish businessmen that were behind the
young Jack Spot having a go at Mosley and his Blackshirts down Cable
Street, in the East End of London.

I looked up to find Walsingham doing things to his pipe with a solid-
silver tamping tool. I think he must've been trying to get it relit or something, so we all sat there in silence, and then waited some more for him
to successfully puff it back into life.

"Thank you for being so patient, Jethro."

I nodded, not forgetting for a moment that I didn't have any choice
in the matter. "Don't mention it," I said through all the clouds of smoke.

"These people don't go around waving red flags to attract our attention, they've dug themselves in, rather like moles in the garden. And they're here now, hiding amongst us in plain sight."

My ears jumped at that; it sounded just like Ray. Then it was Bosanquet's turn to pipe in. I tell you, he and Walsingham made a regular comedy act; Flanagan and Allen to the life.

"Registered foreign embassy, legation, or mission officials are all granted diplomatic immunity in all matters domestic, so they cannot be charged with any crime, or be unduly detained. All of which means, of course, that any thought we might have of apprehending von Bentink is made difficult, if not impossible." He looked vexed.

Then Walsingham nodded, picking up the theme. "Which is not at all a satisfactory state of affairs, considering what he's been up to. And what's more, even if we were to catch him in the act of perpetrating a crime, *in flagrante delicto*, so to speak, all we can do is request that his diplomatic status be revoked and that he be expelled."

Bosanquet nodded earnestly. "Then they would simply play tit for tat, and demand a reduction in the number of our diplomatic staff in their country. In the end it's reduced to nothing more than a game of noughts and crosses, with whoever moves first having the advantage."

I nodded to show I understood how terribly galling this must all be for them. I tried to stifle another yawn, but gave up as I thought my ears were going to pop. Then Walsingham nodded again. I tell you, we must've looked like a bunch of hobby-horses on a merry-go-round.

But then he looked at me with eyes as still as a gun sight. "I very much want you to come and help us win the game, Jethro."

I nodded, but I had an inkling about what was coming, and I felt the knots begin to tighten in my stomach.

"But you must, of course, understand that this is all unofficial, and that in any and every circumstance I would deny any or all knowledge of you. It would never do to admit we employed career criminals to steal from the embassies of our former allies. Everybody does it, of course, and always has, but no one ever admits to it. So I'm afraid that once you're inside, you'd be on your own."

I was sitting down, but I felt my legs go from under me. "Excuse me, Mr. Walsingham, sir, but that's no better than having me all stitched up and ready for the drop. I've signed your damn piece of paper, but that's as far as it goes, I've changed my mind." I was really narked at him and could feel my nostrils flaring, and that was the exact moment he pushed the hook in deeper, the swine.

"Then before we proceed, Jethro, let me remind you that thus far, there have been no official reports of any death, accidental or otherwise, at the Embassy. Though in diplomatic circles, such situations have been known to change in the blink of an eye. I do hope that's understood."

What was the use? I could huff and puff as much as I liked, but whichever way I looked, I was caught against a lee shore with no wind in my sails, and no seaman ever likes to be in that situation. I nodded.

Walsingham looked at me with all the severity of a bank manager turning down a request for a loan. "We'll have no more little outbursts then, if you please. This is not personal, Jethro, it is important business of state. So, I'll ask you again. Are you up for the game, or aren't you?"

I nodded again.

"Good. Then down to business. We have heard from the Ghost Squad that a certain foreigner has put a very high price on the recovery of various sets of jewellery and other items stolen from a house in Belgravia. There's an additional reward if their return also happens to include the name and whereabouts of the thief who stole them. We're told that it's the talk of every club and criminal dive in London. We can take it as read, then, that the person in question is von Bentink himself."

That got through to me, all right. I knew it wouldn't have taken more than two shakes of a rat's tail for someone to scurry straight to Messima with the news of the fat reward on offer. And as if to confirm my worst fears, Walsingham ventured another tasty little titbit. "Von Bentink is expending considerable effort to find you, Jethro, and so it's very probable that he'll continue on until he gets the result he's looking for. And although that may turn out to be very useful to us, it will make it particularly dangerous for you. The Ghost Squad will do their best to keep track of how things develop. And if they should hear your name being bandied about as the likely Belgravia jewel thief, which I'm certain will be the case sooner or later, I'll make sure you're immediately informed. And then you might even perhaps consider coming into protective custody yourself for a while."

I was touched, but I wondered whether that benevolence of his would really last much beyond my usefulness to him as a burglar. Even with everything they'd told me, I knew they hadn't told me the half of it yet. I really didn't fancy the idea of doing the Embassy over a second time. And even if I did, and got away with it, I knew that if Messima found out and got his hands on me afterwards, it wouldn't be single malt whisky he'd be pouring down my throat, it would be drain cleaner. But I also knew the quickest way of getting out of the whole steaming mess was for me to throw myself right back into it. I tell you, it was a very shitty way to start Christmas.

They let me go soon after that, or rather, I was dismissed. Walsingham nodded, but didn't shake hands, which was just as well as I didn't proffer him mine. Bosanquet escorted me to the lift, and with only the briefest of pauses, held out his hand; it was just as I'd remembered it, a firm, trusting handshake. Appearances can be so deceptive.

There was a different man watching over the lobby and the front door this time, but it looked to me like he was wearing the same tatty uniform, the one with the egg-stain medals on the lapels. As I walked past he yawned, put his little finger in his ear and wiggled it, but I'd had enough of that nonsense earlier and so I thrust my hands deeper into my pockets and stepped back out into Regent Street.

I looked up and down the street, but the wintry sun that'd brought some cheer to the morning a thousand years ago had disappeared, and the light had faded into a grey colour that merged street, building, and sky into one very large but badly painted stage flat. London felt irritable and cold and damp, and I just felt irritable, tired, and wrung out.

I walked down towards Piccadilly Circus, still without its bright lights because of the continuing austerity measures. And I must've still been in a bit of a daze, because I crossed Regent Street without any sense of doing so. Much, much later I realised that someone had probably been following me, but anyone in a hat and a raincoat would've stood out like a tea-leaf inside a tea chest, which is not at all. At the corner of Glasshouse Street a cabby honked loudly at me trying his hardest not to run me over. I looked up and suddenly realised where I was; it was the exact spot where

Barry had picked up Seth and me that Friday night, a million years before. But that's the funny thing about London, it's chock-a-block full of history—and oddly enough, a lot of the time it turns out to be yours.

Still drifting towards the Circus, I slipped on down Glasshouse Street, past the police station, that after the day I'd had, looked about as threatening as Hamleys toy shop. At the end of the street I stopped by a hot chestnut seller, to have a quick warm from his bright red-glowing brazier. I bought tuppence worth of chestnuts and cupped my hands round the cone of old newspaper he served them up in; the establishment didn't run to little paper bags as newly made paper was still in short supply. I stood there weighing my little bundle of nuts in my hand, wondering if that's how Walsingham had weighed me up.

Well, cobblers to the lot of them, I thought. And I busied myself with cracking open the chestnut shells and getting at the hot pulp inside. I drew cold air across my tongue and tried not to burn my mouth. The chestnuts tasted really, really good.

I walked on past an old organ-grinder, who had a little grey monkey with him. The monkey was in a leather harness and was wearing a little black-and-white chequered waistcoat and a red fez. There was a long piece of string coiled on the pavement between the two of them. The monkey had probably given up trying to run away long ago, but it still looked around nervously like it didn't know what to do or which way to turn. I knew just how it felt. I dropped a couple of coppers in the old man's hat and gave the monkey a chestnut to eat. And we all stood there listening to the music roll by and the handle going round and round, each one of us oblivious to the noise of the traffic and the incessant coughs and sneezes of the passers-by. And for a moment the music plucked me away to wander through rows of blood-red roses blooming in some far-off field in Picardy. But the monkey didn't seem to mind that I'd gone missing among the regiments of the dead, he just kept on nibbling away at his chestnut. All in all, I took it to be quite a good omen. It reminded me that at least I was still alive.

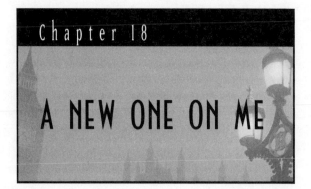

Chapter 18

A NEW ONE ON ME

Of course, MI5 insisted on the pleasure of my company the next day. And I'm sure that them letting me go home for the night was a test to see whether I'd do a runner or not. I'd declined their kind offer of sending a car to pick me up in the morning. I mean, I had appearances to think of, especially with all the nosy sods down Church Street. I just hoped that all the plain-clothes officers hanging around the place didn't get under everyone's feet too much.

Walsingham started off by softening me up again with tales of Flash Harry Raffles, I mean Count Henry von Bentink. And you'd have thought the bugger was Professor Moriarty's long-lost, younger brother, all the daring and dastardly things he was supposed to have done and got away with. In the end I began to feel quite put out about it. After all, one's also got one's own reputation to think of, even if it is only you that's looking over your shoulder.

Once Walsingham was satisfied he'd got my blood going again, he nodded, and Bosanquet dutifully opened his file and got us all down to business. "There's been a marked increase in the number of burglaries in London and the Home Counties in the last six months. As you might expect there was the usual parade of victims; City types, company directors, stockbrokers, prominent local businessmen; as well as one or two famous show-business personalities. And nothing very unusual in that, but remove them from out of the picture and a short list of a very different sort emerges, and all VIPs. A senior Government scientist involved in atomic energy at Harwell, an Oxford don and a Cambridge mathematician both specialising in subatomic particle physics, three government civil servants, one of whom is very senior indeed, and rather too close to home, someone at the War Office."

They exchanged another one of those looks, but I didn't think it proper to press for any hidden meaning. Bosanquet took a moment to consult his file. "Initially, each incident was regarded as a simple case of burglary. All the better pieces of jewellery were stolen, as were gold wrist-watches, gold sovereigns, and any cash on hand. Various fine-art pieces were also taken, but nothing major; a first edition here, a small painting or two there, a Meissen figurine; all quite exquisite, and all easily carried. And that's what put us off the track at first, we couldn't see the wood for the trees. All the VIP break-ins bore the hallmarks of a highly sophisti-cated gang operation. There were no marks, no clues, and not one tip-off, before or since, from any of Scotland Yard's legion of informers. Seemingly perfect crimes, all giving perfect cover for what we now believe was the real purpose behind the burglaries. For in each case it was later discovered that other more personal and intimate items had also been taken; address books, bank statements, notebooks, work-papers, family photographs. And while we're not suggesting that von Bentink can be blamed for all such crimes in the last six months, we do think he is at least responsible for every burglary on the VIP list."

Bosanquet paused, burrowed into his file again, and produced a set of photographs, which he fanned out on the table in front of me as expertly as any dealer down the Astor Club. Of course, I recognised the thing in the photos immediately; it was the friggin' little black book with the solid gold edges. As I felt my eyes widen, Walsingham leaned forward and flashed me his most disarming smile.

"Incidentally, we very much appreciated the safe return of that partic-ular book. The Assistant Commissioner of Scotland Yard is a personal friend, and he called me about his little parcel. We all thought Mr. Karmin's bogus date stamp a rather novel touch, and had we not been alerted to the book's original whereabouts, it might very easily have passed as genuine."

"It almost did, sir," Bosanquet piped in, with I thought, a little less tact than usual. "The item in question was stolen from an EHU. It's a highly restricted government directory issued only to extremely high-ups. It contains secret telephone exchange numbers used exclusively by members of the Royal Family, members of the Cabinet, and our most senior civil servants. It also includes contact numbers at home, office, and club for the chiefs and deputy chiefs of each branch of the armed forces, as well as the heads of the Metropolitan and City police forces. Needless to say, its loss represented an appalling breach of security."

Walsingham had the aplomb to raise an eyebrow as Bosanquet quickly gathered up the first set of photographs and replaced them with another. The second set showed the other little black book—the one with all the columns of numbers in it, the one that had caused all the fuss down the Reading Room, the one with tide tables or logarithms, or whatever it was they were, printed on every page.

Walsingham took up the baton. "The other little black book you took from the Embassy is a different kettle of fish entirely, and it's not of our making, it's something of theirs. It's what's called a 'one-time pad,' a relatively simple system for encrypting and decrypting codes that can be extremely difficult to crack quickly, or indeed, even at all. The rows of random figures on each page are substitution fields used to encrypt a message, whether in single letter ciphers or whole word codes, but for one time only. After which the whole page is discarded. However, the variables can be increased exponentially if a standard text of some sort is used in conjunction with the one-time pad. And it is this pre-agreed-upon text that then becomes the real key to everything. It's usually of book length, and very often one of the classics or a current novel, and the more innocuous it is, the better. But it could equally be something as obscure as a timetable or an annual tonnage report. Anything at all, just as long as it provides standardised page numbers and text. Sometimes, as an additional twist, the chosen key-text is restricted to a specific edition of a work. I trust I'm not losing you, Jethro?"

Losing me? I don't think I'd blinked once while he'd been talking.

Stroll on, what was the world coming to? Talk about a riddle wrapped in a mystery, inside an enigma.

"Of course not," I said, "it's fascinating. Do go on."

"So there must be a second book somewhere that is the missing key-text to the number system that's printed in here." He tapped the horrid little book once with his finger

"Don't go on," I said, "because I've got an awful feeling you're going to tell me the friggin' thing is somewhere inside the Embassy."

"Exactly," they both said as one.

The whole atmosphere in the room changed, and all of a sudden I was on the inside looking out. They even showed me what few photos they had of von Bentink that I noticed were all stamped 'Most Secret.' It was a bit like Monty keeping a picture of Field Marshal Rommel on the wall of his mobile caravan HQ in the North African desert. Know thine enemy? Not if I could help it.

They both kept on about how extremely urgent the whole thing was, and once they'd gone over it a thousand times it all seemed perfectly reasonable, if you were barmy enough to begin with, that is. But there was an added twist to the tale; it seemed there was someone inside the Embassy who wanted to defect and come over to our side. The thing was, I'd never heard the word used that way before, I thought it simply meant a failing or a mistake of some sort. And I suppose it was, if you happened to be a fully paid-up, card-carrying member for the other side. I'd heard of the terms 'deserter,' 'traitor,' and 'spy,' even 'renegade,' and 'turncoat,' but the word 'defector' was a new one on me.

And I don't know why it surprised me to find out the defector was a young woman, but it did. Apparently, she'd got word out somehow that she wanted to come across—that was the phrase Walsingham used—but as the days and weeks had gone by, she'd become increasingly terrified of being caught by her own people. And Walsingham, ever the caring soul, was afraid he might lose her, along with all the classified information she'd promised to bring out with her.

Bosanquet filled in the blanks again. "To date, we've set up two different escape attempts. We've given her the pre-arranged signals; curtains opened or closed, room lights on or off, the number of ladies' hats in a shop window; that sort of thing. But each time she's failed to follow through with either escape plan. She was one of the main reasons we'd had our eye on the Embassy; von Bentink was the other. Your burglary really set the cat among the pigeons, and the whole place has been on a heightened state of security ever since. All of which, of course, has only added to her disquiet." He paused for effect. "And to our difficulties." I nodded, hoping there were no hard feelings, and then with another barely discernible nod from Walsingham, he carried on. "All lower-level person- nel seem to travel around much as they please; mid- and senior-level, never less than in twos and threes. We try to keep an eye on them all from time to time, but we suspect that nothing is ever what it seems, and that many of the lowest-grade people are, in fact, the ones with the highest security clearances. There's always at least one security officer in any group, and they'd probably shoot someone rather than allow them to es- cape."

He paused again, but he didn't need to that time, I knew all about them shooting at people at the very slightest opportunity. I reached for my glass of water. There'd been no tea served on that second visit, they'd probably squandered the department's entire monthly allowance the first time round. At least Bosanquet waited for me to finish swallowing before he continued his briefing. "The girl is a Grade One cipher clerk, extremely bright, and privy to most of the communiqués to and from the Embassy. There have already been one or two small incidents, misplaced files, miss- ing carbons, that sort of thing, nothing that can be directly attributed to her, but enough, apparently, to earn minor reprimands for her entire de- partment."

Walsingham piped up then from behind a cloud of aromatic smoke. "The thing is, we believe the girl is close to cracking, and that's why we have to try and get her out as soon as we possibly can. The powers that be inside the Embassy believe that if they punish everybody, then every- body has an incentive to find and reveal the true culprit." He leaned forward. "It's true communism at work, the more enemies you reveal, the closer everyone is to the socialist ideal."

A look of irritation flashed across his face, but was gone in an instant. He seemed to be having difficulty drawing on his pipe. So he took out his solid-silver tamping tool again, and after a few minutes' determined poking and prodding around in the pipe bowl, in that peculiarly confident way that only the most dedicated pipe smokers ever seem to master, things got back to normal. Then through clouds of newly contented smoke he continued on. "Indoctrination and dogma, inculcated by intimidation and fear." He stopped again, for the very briefest of moments, cleared his throat, and took a deep breath. But I was hardly breathing myself by that time, I was concentrating so hard on what he was saying. "The Soviets use their Iron Curtain buffer states—East Germany, Romania, Bulgaria, Albania, and Yugoslavia—as a cover for clandestine missions particularly dirty in nature. Then, should anything blow up into a serious diplomatic incident, they can bang the table and deny any direct knowledge of the event. The GRU, Russian Military Intelligence, also use those same intermediaries to seek out and employ individuals known to be singularly adept in unpleasantry."

Walsingham placed his pipe down onto the table with a deliberate exactness that suggested he was removing some barrier between us. And I found myself leaning forward, strangely eager to entangle myself in his web. "Von Bentink is one such freelance specialist for hire. The acting head of security at the Embassy, a Major Zavis Krepstok, is another. The two have worked together a lot, apparently. Krepstok is another extremely unpleasant character, only his special delight is in causing pain. And since the end of the war he's been responsible for a number of rather nasty episodes, here and in Paris. But neither we, nor the French Deuxième Bureau, have been able to prove anything yet."

He looked down at the table for a moment, then back at me. And the look in his eyes chilled the air. And then he blinked, picked up his pipe, and carried on as if nothing had happened. "Here in London, in the last three months, there have been two separate incidents involving leading figures in the émigré and refugee communities. And in each case, we suspect the men were kidnapped and horribly tortured, before being thrown into the path of an oncoming Underground train. Cause of death was given on each occasion as electrocution and partial or complete dismemberment, but we don't believe it all occurred at the same time or in the same place. As suicide notes were found later, both cases were officially ruled as 'misadventure, while being of uncertain and unsound mind.' We suspect differently, of course."

To be honest, I didn't much like the sound of any of that. But behind all the smoke, I began to sense the ice-cold fire that smouldered within Walsingham. As cool and calm and collected as he always appeared to be, he was probably an implacable and unrelenting foe. And despite my misgivings I found myself listening ever more intently.

"There's a punishment cell somewhere inside the Embassy that they use for even the most minor of security infractions. And apparently after a few such detentions, the perpetrator is quietly shipped back home and sent off to a labour camp. If they're lucky, that is. And if not, well . . ."

Walsingham's words hung in the air again, and my imagination did the rest of his work for him, and even I saw things in my mind's eye that I found disturbing. His eyes slid up to meet Bosanquet's and then slipped back down again to look at me. I couldn't tell what had passed between them, but something had.

"The woman's name is Tanyia, Tanyia Arzhak." Even Bosanquet's voice had a little more steel in it now, and he reached inside yet another buff-coloured file and slid a photograph across the table to me. It was a large photo, an eight-by-ten, and a little bit grainy, and not at all up to show-business standards. It also looked as if it had been taken from the back seat of a moving motor car. Bosanquet leaned over and gently tapped one of the figures in the picture with his finger.

The girl, called Tanyia, was shown walking in the street alongside a much older-looking woman. She herself was in her mid-twenties, quite tall and neat-waisted. And she was wearing a dark suit that was not quite military in cut, and a cute little hat that set it all off. Somehow, it all managed to look perfectly wonderful on her, although I wouldn't have said it was anything like the new, full-skirted styles that were starting to come out of Paris that all the more fashionable women around town had been seen wearing. You could tell she'd tried her best with what she had, though, and she was even smiling at something. I found myself smiling back. And then I suddenly had a weird feeling that I'd seen her somewhere before, and then the picture in my own mind slipped into place and I could place her. And even though she wasn't wearing glasses in the photo, I was sure it was the same young woman I'd seen, or rather heard, Baldy slap round the face, that day I'd pretended to make the Harrods parcel delivery to the Embassy. I didn't tell them about that bit, but I did give them something of sorts to chew on.

"I saw that little detention room when I broke in." They both turned and looked at me expectantly, so I told them everything just as it'd happened. Of course, I omitted to mention the little leather-cased set of bones and skels that I'd taken from von Bentink's room. But I thought, Fair's fair, I had to keep one or two secrets to myself, didn't I? Knowing them, they would have only tried to pinch the lot back off me as evidence or something. And as far as I was concerned, it was a simple case of waste not, want not, and the only right and proper thing to do in such times of austerity.

Bosanquet asked me to draw a plan of the punishment cell, detailing as best I could its position in relation to the rest of the upper floor and the roof. And from the look on his face, I think that even then he had some sort of plan forming in his little, evil-scheming mind. He had the look of a choirboy, but the cunning of a born tearaway. If he'd have gone to a different school, something down our way, for instance, he might've ended up just like me. What a thought?

Bosanquet's eyes seemed to click from side to side, like one of those wooden dummies you see standing in a glass case down the penny-arcades. And then his face lit up, and he cackled like he'd hit upon the jackpot. And if a whole stream of pennies and silver tanners had emptied themselves out onto the floor from his trouser pockets, I wouldn't have been at all surprised.

"Three houses down from the Embassy is Doyle House, home of the British League and Empire Spiritualist Society. Or BLESS, for short. And I've just had the most extraordinary premonition that we'll soon be attending a very special seance there. Then you, my friend, Jethro, are going to spirit yourself away across the rooftops to make contact with a young lady who's been seeing too many ghosts under the bed."

He laughed, pleased with his own sense of humour; but I thought to myself, if that's all people like him learned at public school, then it was a right waste of time and money. The one thing everyone needed to do, right away, was get their feet firmly back on the ground. Assassins and spies and secret code books? Spooks and spirits and seances? Where the hell was it all going to end?

Chapter 19

BLESSED ARE THE MEEK

We were both dressed in bowler hats and long dark winter coats. Bosanquet looked quite dapper in his, but I looked like a right duck-egg in mine, on purpose, of course. I more resembled one of those sad-faced, eccentric characters usually portrayed by Alastair Sim. My straggly white-haired wig—one of Willy Clarkson's best-ever creations—my hollow cheeks, grey sallow skin, and heavy-lidded eyes all adding to the effect. Though it was the walk that really did the trick. All my best characters started from the feet up. And once I'd found the proper walk, the rest of it came together quite easily. It's all to do with how heavy you look and how old you're supposed to be, and how and where you place your feet. Look at that walk Orson Welles does as the ageing title character in that film *Citizen Kane;* he's brilliant. I couldn't have done it better myself. Even just wearing a bigger size pair of shoes and stuffing newspaper up the toes can be enough to turn you into someone quite different to yourself. "Break a step and meet a stranger," Ray used to say.

Bosanquet rolled around the floor laughing when he first saw me, but he was quite knocked out by how effective a few wads of rolled-up cotton wool pushed up behind the back teeth could be in producing instant, face-altering cheekbones. "That's awfully good, Jethro, old chap," he said. "It's him to the life, it really is."

"Let us just pray then, young man, that it is not also me in death," I lisped, my false teeth clacking like castanets, spittle bubbling out onto my lips like ooze from a glue pot; and even I had to laugh then.

Bosanquet was turning out to be a good bloke. As part of the overall disguise, he'd even offered to lend me two of his elegantly battered leather suitcases to pack my gear into. He must've been quite the traveller before the war, as both cases were covered in luggage labels from famous hotels and passenger liners. I recognised many of the names; I'd even pulled the odd caper in one or two of them. Happy days. All the stuff I hadn't been able to fit in the cases, I'd stowed in a steamer trunk that'd been dropped off at BLESS House earlier in the day. The Whiteley's delivery van driver and his mate—two gentlemen from MI5 in neatly pressed overalls—had even carried the trunk upstairs, which was very decent of them, as the bloody thing was heavier than hell.

The entrance hall of the British League and Empire Spiritualist Society was as busy as Waterloo Station on a Friday night. Everything in the place looked like it had been nicked at one time or another from the British Museum; it was all marble floors, Greek columns, and Roman busts. I was surprised to see large portraits of Sir Arthur Conan Doyle and Harry Houdini looking down at me from the walls because, as not unnaturally, I'm a big fan of both of them, and I made a mental note to ask Bosanquet why they were there. It was also a nice surprise to find people of all ages and classes mingling together easily, and enjoying it, too, which was a little unusual even for London. I'd seen it during the Blitz, of course, but not too often since the end of the war.

So, sherry glasses in hand, we milled about and chatted to people before everyone went off to their respective meetings. And then a charming old biddy approached us and introduced herself as the special events secretary. She handed us the keys to the top-floor meeting room without so much as batting an eyelid or a whisker, and then left us to our own devices. We carried our heavy suitcases up a huge winding staircase that got narrower and narrower, until at the top it opened onto a small landing that led to two large, metal-studded oak doors. Over the doorway was a gilded ornamental wood panel inscribed with the words: 'Blessed be all ye who enter here to voyage forth into the unknown.' That's good enough for me, I thought, and I felt my spirits begin to lift a little. But I didn't say anything, and neither did Bosanquet. We just locked the doors behind us, closed all the curtains, turned on all the lights, and began to unpack all the gear.

Bosanquet was good at planning, almost as good as me, which is saying something. Even in the short time I'd known him, I'd got the feeling he could gain access to almost anywhere in London. He seemed to know everyone worth knowing and if he didn't he very likely knew someone who did, which pretty much amounts to the same thing. It was enough to turn you green with envy; he had all the makings of a top-class creeper and he didn't even know it. Take his idea for getting onto the Embassy roof from the roof of BLESS House; it was so simple, it was brilliant. And he'd not only had someone reserve the top-floor meeting room for us, he'd also had them make a suitable donation to the society's coffers to ensure we'd be left in peace for the night. See what I mean? Planning. And planning is three-quarters of what goes into any caper. That top-floor room was key, but our real goal was the attic above it; a long, low-ceilinged box room that could only be reached through a tiny door at the far end of the meeting room. That attic was our secret way out on to the roof-tops of Belgravia—and my means of having another crack at the Embassy.

Just in case he'd had any second thoughts on the matter, I'd asked Walsingham again about what would happen if I got caught. And with only the slightest rise of an eyebrow, he'd replied, "As I said before, Jethro, I could do nothing for you. You would be entirely on your own."

The blank look on my face must've meant something, because after what seemed like only a few million years, he'd added, "However, to increase the chances of your success I will permit Bosanquet to assist you in any way he thinks fit. The only stipulation being that the entire undertaking must look as if it is solely the work of one man, and in no way can it appear to be part of a larger, officially sanctioned operation. Beyond that, all I can do is arrange some sort of smoke-screen to help cover your escape. But that's it, I'm afraid."

I hate having smoke blown up my nose at the best of times so I continued staring at him, my face still blank and unforgiving. And then he blinked slowly and pulled something from out of his briefcase. "But, then again," he said softly, "there is always this." And I knew it was a pistol of some sort, even before he unfolded the chamois leather.

"A Beretta 9mm standard Italian service pistol. And to all intents and purposes the twin of the one you said you saw in von Bentink's room; same grip, same finish, everything as you described it, even to the identification numbers being filed off."

The gun lay on the table, snub-nosed and dangerous, its dull blue sheen drawing all the surrounding light into its dark shadowy depths. I hated the idea of a shooter on a creep, the friggin' things always had a nasty habit of going off half-cocked. I still didn't say anything, but I couldn't take my eyes off of the bloody thing.

"Simon will hand you the pistol just before the start of the mission, but you should only consider using it if you or the girl are in dire peril of your lives, and it allows you to make good an escape. In that event, shoot to distract or dissuade, but if at all possible, not to kill. Then eject the magazine and drop the gun onto the Embassy roof; we can't afford the slightest risk of it being found in your possession. And if Krepstok's men do find the gun later, we think they'll assume it's one of theirs and dispose of it accordingly."

I looked at him, my eyes now as round as saucers.

"There is one last thing, Jethro. If Miss Arzhak does decide to try and escape with you, and events then go badly wrong, by which I mean her recapture seems inevitable, it is imperative that you shoot her before they can take her."

He said it so matter-of-factly I didn't believe I'd heard it right, but as I continued to peer into his face I knew I'd heard him correctly.

"What do you mean, kill her? Why on earth would you want me to do that, for God's sake? Bugger me, but you're a right piece of work you are, Mr. Walsingham, sir."

"It's to save her from certain, horrible death, Jethro. These people see torture as nothing more than a means to an end. There is no such thing as habeas corpus. And as far as they're concerned, her body already belongs to the State and they are free to do with it whatever they will, whether she be alive, or dead, or dying."

I have no idea what the look on my face must've been like at that point, but the rest of me was chilled to the bone.

"I can't order you to do it, Jethro, and in the end it can only be you that decides. I'm simply briefing you in the same way I would anyone that was about to undertake the job."

" 'Undertaker' is about bloody right, isn't it? What in hell would you have done if I hadn't come along, old man? Kill her yourself?"

"Someone always comes along, Jethro. This time it just happened to be you."

"I don't know what to believe anymore," I said, starting to shout very loudly. "It started with a creep for King and Country, and now you want to turn me into a cold-blooded killer, as well."

He was reasonability itself. "No, Jethro, that's where you're quite wrong. I can assure you, our objective is to succeed on both fronts. We very much want the girl to come out of this alive. In fact, it's imperative that she does so, she would be invaluable to us." He paused for but an instant, his blue eyes flashing their sincerity, and then he continued. "But it's also vitally important that we acquire the book she has in her posses-sion. With it, there's simply no telling what we might be able to unearth. It could help put a stop to von Bentink. It could even lead to the uncov-ering of a Soviet spy ring that I believe has embedded itself deep within the very fabric of this country."

I didn't know whether to hum "Land of Hope and Glory," or sing "Rule Britannia," I was worked up and getting very emotional, but I wasn't sure any longer what I was feeling so hot and bothered about. And through it all, Walsingham kept on talking, his voice soft and soothing, as if he was calming down an excitable horse. And if he'd stretched out his hand and offered me a lump of sugar about then, I wouldn't have been at all surprised.

"Jethro, it's my sacred duty to root out traitors and spies, and if I prove successful it will not only help save lives, it may ultimately help preserve our very way of life. So I have no choice but to grasp every opportunity that presents itself for me to confound and diminish our enemies. What-ever people here at home may think, there's still a war on, and I'm trying to fight it the best way I know how. And it's for that reason alone that I'm asking you to do whatever needs to be done at the Embassy. And so if extreme action should prove necessary, let me assure you that you would be acting strictly in Defence of the Realm, and as I've already indicated, there are provisions within my power to grant you immunity from any subsequent proceedings."

He didn't add, "providing you're still alive afterwards," but then he didn't have to, I'd got his drift. And I didn't like it. But step by step, he slowly gentled me back to cold rationality.

"The girl is too frightened to try anything herself. They randomly search people leaving the Embassy, and if she were to be caught with the book on her, it would be tantamount to an admission of espionage. So, if we can save the girl, then of course we should, and we must, and we will. But if we can't, then it's far better that we try and save her the unspeakable horror of a prolonged and agonising death."

I didn't know what to think anymore, let alone what to say. It was 'once more unto the breach, once more,' all over again, and all over me. And what's more, I was buying it. I stood there motionless while he fidgeted absent-mindedly with a heavy gold signet ring on one of his fingers. Then as if by sleight of hand, he suddenly held the ring out for me to see. It glowed dully in the room's lamplight. He pushed the ring across the table towards me. I didn't dare touch it, I think I was afraid to, God only knew what further mess it could get me into.

Walsingham's eyes shone cold and brilliant. "Show her this ring, Jethro. And she'll know you've come from me, and then she'll hand you the book."

I picked the ring up. It felt oddly heavy.

"I know it's hard for you, Jethro, but I implore you to think of the girl, Tanyia Arzhak. You have it in your power to help her. Let me also add that from what we've been able to gather it appears her reasons for defecting may be as much personal, as they are political."

I looked at him hard, and he stared back at me without batting an eyelid. A year passed. And with what I now realise was infinite cunning and patience, he let me catch up to the noose dangling in front of me, in my own time and at my own speed.

"We believe," he said, oh so very softly, "that she was recently involved in an affair with someone at the Embassy. But then apparently, once the gentleman had fully availed himself of her charms, he simply cast her aside for another. And now it seems the poor girl is somewhat distraught, and as you well know, hell hath no fury like—"

I cut in, my voice rising, "Are you talking about that bastard, von Bentink?"

"Yes, I do believe I am," he demurred.

"So you just jump in and take advantage of the poor girl's situation, so you can get what you want out of her, is that it?" I was shouting at the top of my voice now and I didn't care who heard.

"Yes," he said quietly, without a trace of irony. "That's it exactly."

"Then that makes you as big a bastard as he is," I said angrily, jumping to my feet.

But then he matched me, cold again against hot. "Of course I'm a bastard, Jethro, I have to be. And if it means I can get my hands on von Bentink and stop his evil games, then I hope to God I'm a bigger bastard than he already is or could ever hope to be."

I didn't know how to respond. I just stood there, breathing hard. It's funny, isn't it? But when someone comes right back at you with the same amount of anger, it takes the wind right out of your sails.

So I continued to glare at him for a full minute, and then I sat back down and started thinking, perhaps for the first time, about just what I'd let myself in for.

Chapter 20

ABRACADABRA

I don't think Walsingham really wanted to know how I was going to get inside the Embassy again, because that way if there was ever an official investigation into the caper he could deny all knowledge of it. Now where had I heard that before? So it seemed he wasn't above stealing a good idea if it could work for him. Anyway, it was only after he'd gone that Bosanquet first made any mention of the one or two interesting changes that had been made to the Embassy's exterior since my last visit; alterations, he assured me, of a sort not normally sanctioned by the Grosvenor Estate. Just like him to leave the good bits until last.

For starters, Krepstok and his minions had boxed up the drain-pipes at the back of the house, which was bad enough. But then up on the roof, they'd thought to erect an iron-railing fence along the raised brickwork and chimney-stacks that divided the Embassy from the houses on either side, and covered the whole lot with barbed wire. Really lovely. And then, as a finishing touch, they'd gone and added floodlights at each end that lit up the entire roof and made it look like Colditz Castle. Whoopee.

Bosanquet assured me that the Grosvenor Estate would insist on the withdrawal of the lights and the barbed wire, at the very least. But with the wheels of bureaucracy and diplomacy being what they were, it could take weeks if not months to accomplish, and time, of course, was the one thing we didn't have. I told him he'd been a great help. And he just smiled his best conspiratorial smile; Donald Wolfit to the life.

We laid everything out on the floor like a stage manager with his props table. First there was the all-important canvas-covered rope sling. Then two single-running, cast-iron blocks, and several lengths of good old British Empire, three-quarter-inch, three-ply hemp rope, all nicely set up and gasketed. Not too much out of line with the standard gun-tackle set-up used in sailing ships and theatres the world over. But to ensure that what I had in mind would work I'd also added a large wide-grooved pulley-wheel and two turnbuckles to the assembly, which meant I had three sheaves to account for in my weight calculations instead of two. The plan also called for a large black canvas punch-bag, not unlike a body in shape, a half-dozen ten-pound, cast-iron flat weights, and a length of black silk rope. The bag required its own pulley to help pull the plan off, but I reckoned a standard-sized wheel was more than sufficient for that. I looked everything over, and nodded, satisfied.

That done, I double-checked the contents of my small canvas bag; hammer, heavy-duty chisels, petercane, tin-shears, bolt-clipper, hand drill, and monkey wrench. I'd left my lovely new set of skeleton keys safe at home, as I can be as superstitious as the next man and I had the feeling that taking them back inside the Embassy would be pushing my luck. But I still had my old set of skels, bones, and twirls with me, extra lengths of black silk rope, and my ever-faithful Fairbairn-Sykes knife. So all in all, I was more than ready to do the business.

The heavy-bag was the working end of the hemp-cum-counterweight system I planned to jerry-rig out of thin air, five stories—six if you included the basement—above the pavement. I'd attached a harness around the middle of the punch-bag and sewn pouches all over it to hold the ten-pound weights, and then added canvas flaps and loops at the top and bottom to make handling easier. The lifting rig wouldn't do for a West End production of *Peter Pan*, but it would more than suffice for some amateur production playing out in the sticks.

I also had another little bit of kit I'd made up in my workshop. It was about the size of an uninflated Mae West life jacket, with every inch of it stained black. It was made of two curved thin-steel plates sandwiched between thick, saddle-leather hides, with everything held together by canvas parachute-harness straps and metal buckles, two at the top and two on each side. I didn't wear it on every creep, but it had proved a real life-saver on many occasions. If I'd said it was a breastplate, you might have got the wrong idea. It wasn't to protect me from bullets, or broadswords, or anything, although it could turn a knife blade aside, and no messing, but I'd found nothing better for getting me safely across barbed wire, or over the tops of walls studded with spikes or broken glass. Then I just unstrapped my life-saver, threw it over the offending obstacle, secured it with the canvas straps, and tripped across as quickly as I could manage. It could be easily concealed under my coat on the way to or from a creep, and wasn't really that heavy. And anyone who'd ever worn a pack on his back for King and Country would've shrugged it off as being nothing much at all.

Then, of course, there was the Beretta pistol. Neither of us had mentioned it, but when Bosanquet proffered it to me balanced on his arm like they did in duels in the olden days, he had such a grim look on his face I almost laughed. I looked down at the gun, looked at him again, and then shrugged, as if to say, 'thanks but no thanks.' But then I thought better of it, as in 'better safe than sorry,' and took the gun, silencer, and box of 9mm cartridges and put them all in a pile next to my black satchel. Then I tried to put everything out of my mind and snatch a quick rest. But it wasn't to be.

Bosanquet wanted to go over the dos and don'ts and whatifs again, and so we did. And I took the opportunity to ask him about a little something that had been nagging at me all day; which was why Krepstok wouldn't have sentries on duty or at least somebody who says, 'Who goes there?' And he'd said not to worry; that the Soviets tended to go in for high walls and barbed wire, and think more in terms of containment and confinement. "It's not so much a question of them trying to stop someone getting in, Jethro, it's more them preventing people from getting out." And I said, "I call that stupid." And he said, "Then let's just settle on it being a stroke of luck, shall we?" Then after going over everything once again, he went up the other end of the room and left me alone with my thoughts, and before I knew it, it was time for the off. Bosanquet looked at me, all serious, and said, "Break a leg, old chap." And I just nodded the once and slipped out of the window.

It's a different world up there on the roof, and your mind becomes different so as to cope with it. Even imagining is different up there, and London's roofs have their own way of dealing with space and time, just like any theatre set. There are mountains and valleys to contend with, as well as forests and plains. It has its cathedrals and its moated castles, and everywhere there are soot-covered chimneys standing like so many silent sentinels, all belching forth sulphurous smoke to engulf and overcome the unwary traveller or thief. It was a vast haunted place of pointed, elongated shadows and cruel, sharp edges that always reminded me of the old silent film *The Cabinet of Doctor Caligari*. Anyone who stepped into it was changed forever. And me? I loved every slippery, stinking inch of it.

I nosed the air. It was much the same as down below in the street, only thicker and yellower and sootier, and love or no love it was all I could do to stop myself from coughing. The roof was dark and unfriendly in the way that all roofs are dark and unfriendly until you got to know them, and in that respect they're no different from people. The first two roofs were a doddle to get across, and I took that as a very good omen, as I needed all the luck I could get. But you always do, you know, when you find yourself in the dark.

And so once again I came to the Embassy. And it was just as Bosanquet had described it, only worse. The fuckers had covered their iron-railed fence with so much barbed wire it looked as if some part of the Maginot Line had suddenly sprung up, full blown, in Belgravia. And you could tell that Krackpot, or Krepstok, or whatever his friggin' name was, was in deadly earnest because he'd even had the edges of the iron railings filed to a razor sharpness. I tell you it made my skin prickle to think of what other delights he might have in store for me, but I consoled myself with the fact that at least the floodlights weren't on. Bosanquet had said they switched them on and off at random during the night, so I felt thankful for small mercies. No creeper likes the thought of there being too much light around.

I unbuckled the steel-boned Mae West, and threw it in an easy curve up and over the top of the railings and the barbed wire, just as in my past life I'd thrown so many life-savers from the side of so many godforsaken ships and lifeboats. The two steel-boned semicircular pieces bounced on the wire and I gently pulled back on the canvas straps until the wire barbs caught and stuck in the saddle leather. Then I pulled the straps down sharply and the spiked points of the iron railings bit deep and held fast. It was like ramming a log of wood into a guard dog's mouth, and just as satisfying. And once I'd tied it all down, I had my very own pathway through the thicket of metal spikes and thorns.

The wig had gone by then, of course, as had the pale, wet-white face; I didn't need make-up anymore to achieve that effect. Instead, I had on my regular screwing kit, which was black from the top of my wool balaclava all the way to the tips of my crêpe-rubber plimsolls. I'd carried the blocks and tackle, as well as the ropes and the bag of tools myself. We'd debated whether Bosanquet should help me beyond the attic window, but in the end it was the added weight of the punch-bag that decided it. I could've carried it fireman-fashion, but it would've been stupid me giving myself a hernia. So on my final journey back and forth across the roofs, Bosanquet helped manhandle the bag through the window and over to the foot of the spiked fence. And even though the harness made carrying it a little easier, we must've still looked like Burke and Hare on a bad night.

The trickiest part was getting the bloody thing up and over the barbed-wire fence without it catching or ripping, or dropping down onto the Embassy roof with an almighty thud. That would've finished the creep even before it had begun. Luckily, though, Bosanquet was stronger than he looked and between us we managed to get the punch-bag up and over the Mae West's lovely curves, and to let it down gently onto the Embassy roof. Other than me carrying it a few feet, and lifting it up onto the parapet at the rear of the house, the black bag had little else to do but await its proper entrance into the night's play.

I nodded a goodbye and quickly got down to work. I took a piece of chalk and paced off the distances I'd be working to along the edge of the parapet, and made my marks. Then I turned round trying to cast my mind back to my earlier visit, and made for the part of the roof that I hoped was directly over the small detention room. I made four quick strokes on the tiles and then pocketed the chalk.

Getting down to the right window ledge and then getting myself back up to the roof didn't present too much of a problem. But I now had to allow for the fact that the girl might also want to escape, which meant the two of us going up the outside of the building faster than greased lightning. Climbing a ten-foot wall is a daunting enough task for most people, but doing it sixty feet up in the air and in the dead of night, they'd find all but impossible. Even if they had all the time in the world. And we didn't. And that was the reason for all the lifting gear.

Walsingham had said it was unlikely the girl would ever agree to any escape on the spur of the moment, but he'd nevertheless insisted we plan for it. He'd even asked me if I was physically up to the job, and I'd said something like, 'It's a whole lot easier than killing someone, so, yes, sure, just as long as she's a willing accomplice and not too much of a dead weight.' But I think my heavy irony was lost on him.

I carried the coils of rope, and the block-and-tackle assembly complete with its sling attachment, out along the roof's edge and set them down behind the parapet. I trailed the rope's working end—the bitter end if ever you lose your grip on it—back towards the punch-bag, picked up the big steel pulley-wheel and fed it through, and then coiled the remaining rope clockwise, 'with the sun' as we sailors used to say. I gently pulled the rope's end from out of the centre of the coil and tied it securely to the punch-bag's harness. Then from the pile of gear by the fence, I picked out two long loops of rope, each with a turnbuckle attached, and hung them from stone piers spaced behind the parapet. I suspended the big pulley-wheel next to the punch-bag, and then suspended the block-and-tackle-and-sling assembly exactly twenty feet further along the roof. I returned to the punch-bag, spliced one of the lengths of black silk rope through the loops at the top, and very gingerly trailed it back along the edge of the roof to my point of descent. Then I passed the silk rope through the small pulley and fed it over the side, to hang down alongside the block and tackle and the canvas sling. And all my reeving done, I wiped my brow.

And, 'abracadabra,' my makeshift counterweight system was all ready to go, or at least that was the theory. The idea was, that once me and the girl had our arms safely through the sling, I'd tug hard on the silk rope tied to the punch-bag and it would topple off the parapet and plummet over the edge. The downward fall of the punch-bag would then produce enough upward momentum through the pulleys, to pull the sling and its precious cargo up to the roof in two flicks of a rope's tail. Brilliant. I was sure they'd have been proud of me down the fly floor at the Metropolitan, I only hoped they didn't miss all the kit too quickly.

For a moment I stood in the swirling fog as if in a daydream. The truth of it was, I didn't like making any move before midnight, and now here I was about to barge my way into a house full of people, before everyone was safely tucked up in bed for the night. I might just as well have marched up to the front door, banged the big brass knocker and demanded entry. Every minute before midnight meant double the danger, so I knew I had to be doubly careful. "Measure twice, and cut and run once," as the old creeper's saying goes. So I measured off the distance once more for luck and found that my original chalk marks hadn't moved an inch. Then I checked my watch again and to my surprise saw that it showed it was time for the off. I quickly secured a second length of black silk rope, took a deep breath, and dropped over the edge of the roof.

I knew the layout of the Embassy pretty well from all the time I'd spent casing the building for the first caper, and I was making for the window ledge of the bathroom situated at the near end of the corridor on the top floor. By Bosanquet's reckoning and my watch, it was soon going to be time for Tanyia's bath. Everyone in the Embassy—like the rest of smelly old England—was still on a strict allowance of only five inches of water per bath, whether the water was lukewarm or ice-cold. So, most people found themselves on a bathroom rota, of some sort, with families often taking turns at using the same bath water. And, me? I was the midnight plumber come to call.

I waited, crouched on the ledge, the canvas sling hanging from the block and tackle, and the black silk rope attached to the punch-bag swaying gently a few feet off. Then I waited some more, and soon I couldn't tell where my breath ended and the fog began. I don't know how long I waited in the end, it might've been a minute, it might've been ten; I simply concentrated on holding still and, of course, holding on. Then at long last the bathroom light went on and a shadow began moving about inside. The frosted glass of the window made up for any lack of decency or discretion, however I decided to wait for the water taps to be turned on before I started tapping on the window.

I tried to recollect Tanyia's photograph and imagined her stripping down to her bare skin. It was a lovely thought. And my mouth suddenly feeling very dry, I raised my hand to knock gently on the window. Then I nearly lost my grip—a deep bass voice began singing from inside the bathroom. It sounded awful, whether it was opera or a folk song celebrating some unsuccessful peasant uprising I didn't know, or friggin' well care, but it wasn't Tanyia singing, that was for sure. And suddenly there I was with my arse hanging out in the cold, wondering what in hell to do. Meanwhile the bathroom began to steam up, and I realised if the geezer inside decided to open the window to let in some fresh night air, I was a goner for sure.

Trying to still the thumping in my heart, that I was certain could be heard all the way to Westminster, I climbed back up to the roof hand over hand, afraid even to try and get extra purchase with my toes just in case I slipped and made a noise. "What the fuck am I going to do now?" I asked myself. 'Plan B,' came the reluctant reply. It had almost been an afterthought of Bosanquet's. 'Sod's Law,' he'd called it. 'If things can go wrong, they will go wrong,' he'd said. The know-all. But he'd been right. I even wondered if he'd been blessed with second sight or something. Daft I know, because he didn't look the type, but you never can tell with some people.

I pulled myself up and over the edge of the roof, mercifully still shrouded in darkness, quickly wound my silk climbing rope around my waist, and then gingerly pulled the block-and-tackle assembly back up onto the roof. I took hold of the turnbuckle and loop of rope that the rig had been hanging from, and then pacing off the distance as best as I could, I moved everything another ten or twelve feet along the roof. I did the same with the pulley-wheel set-up. And then I hung the whole kit and caboodle over the side. So unless I was way off in my reckoning, I was now above Tanyia's bedroom window. I unwound the rope from around my waist, re-anchored it, and then slipped back over the edge. This was make or break, and I just hoped it wasn't my neck that got broken. One thing was certain, though, I knew Tanyia would be alone. It was another Bosanquet magic touch, and he—or Walsingham—must've had a very long reach to pull it off.

The two of them had been setting it up for months, long before I'd come on the scene. The woman that Tanyia shared a room with had the very posh title of senior cultural affairs officer. And somehow, our devious

Mr. Bosanquet had arranged for a group of Labour MPs to invite the woman, along with other diplomats from other foreign embassies, to travel up to Sheffield and Manchester for a cultural outing. The idea was for them all to see British industry making things by day, and then enjoy a British worker's theatre group knocking everything down again at night. And to get everyone really excited, they'd arranged one or two sherry and cheese receptions with local Labour Party members, and thrown in various music recitals. It sounded like it'd be a right old riot, but the plan had worked a treat. And the absence of Tanyia's room-mate was, of course, the reason Walsingham had been so very insistent that the Embassy creep take place when it did. Even so, he'd been concerned that they could only count on the woman being away for two or three days at most, and so to be on the safe side, they'd scheduled the burglary for the very first night she'd be away.

And so I came as a shadow to the threshold of Tanyia's bedroom, and I looked up and saw myself reflected in the dark window.

"Plan B, be damned," I whispered to the cold night air. I breathed in deeply through my nose, and very gently knocked on her bedroom windowpane.

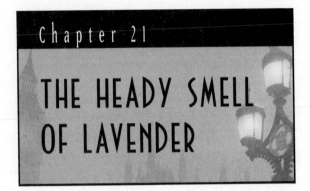

Chapter 21

THE HEADY SMELL OF LAVENDER

She pulled back the curtain and saw me, but she didn't scream. And I hung there at the end of my rope and smiled my biggest smile, and still she didn't scream. It took me a minute or two to realise my balaclava was still covering my mouth, so I hurriedly pulled it down under my chin and gave her another smile, only to feel my upper lip stubbornly sticking to my teeth. So there I was leering at her like a mad rabbit, and still she didn't scream, but she didn't smile, either. And I was running out of smiles, and time. So I waved a friendly hand, and then wiped away the sweat from my eyes. And as if by magic the window opened, and before I really knew it myself I was in and through, unfurling and stretching myself to my proper height. I stood before her and she stared right back at me, unmoving and unafraid. I was a winged messenger from the gods, or I was a dead duck, and there was only a moment or two to find out which.

I tried smiling again, ready to jump back out of the window at the first hint of any nonsense, but my upper lip was still stuck firmly to my teeth. I wiped my mouth with the back of my turtles, and over the back of my hand I caught her smiling. I felt myself begin to relax, sensing that if she was going to scream she'd have done it by now. I could feel the shadow between us slowly dissolving away, and not wanting to break the spell or to spook her in any way, I didn't move a muscle. And silently, I prayed to all the gods of good creepers everywhere that she could see I meant her no harm.

She gave a little nod, threw me a look, and then quickly slipped around behind me to shut the window and close the curtains. It was almost as if I was the outside world, and even if only for a moment, I needed to be caged. And standing there in her bedroom, I think I realised for the first time that I also stood for the one thing in the world she craved for most, her freedom.

I didn't say anything, I just very slowly removed my balaclava and tried smiling at her again. Then I slipped off my left turtle and held up the back of my hand to show her the signet ring Walsingham had given me. The ring flashed its secret message across the room. It wasn't for me to know the meaning of the cross in the triangle etched upon its face, just so long as it meant the right thing to her. I felt like Saint George anyway, come to slay her dragon. Her eyes moved from my face to the ring and back again, but she didn't smile, she simply crossed to the door, pushed a catch, turned a key and locked us in.

I couldn't take my eyes off her. She wore a periwinkle-blue dressing gown that flowed about her ankles as she walked. She was like the pale morning light over the river at Westminster Bridge, and earth hadn't anything to show, more fair. She was purple violets and lavender and blue cornflowers overflowing the wicker baskets of Covent Garden, and when she moved the swish of silk on silk was like the rustle of a thousand leaves welcoming the morning rays of the sun to St. James's Park. By God, but she was beautiful, and as well you know, beauty provoketh thieves sooner than gold.

She turned and stood looking at me, her eyes shining, and her lips enticing without even a trace of lipstick on them. The upward tilt of her chin emphasised her fine cheekbones and made the line of her neck even more impossibly graceful. She was Gene Tierney, she was Ida Lupino, she was Hedy Lamarr. Her dark auburn hair was pulled back from her face by a blue ribbon that went from the nape of her neck to a delicately tied bow on the top of her head. She pulled at the ribbon, shook her head gently from side to side, and long dark curls fell in wave after wave about her shoulders, and never for a moment did the diamond-like fire of her purple-blue eyes leave mine.

I returned her gaze, mesmerised. It felt as if I'd jumped off the top of a high building, while she looked on steady and unafraid, ready to catch my soul. I didn't know how many thousands of men had fallen for her before me, and I didn't care. I didn't mention that I'd heard she'd had a little dalliance with Flash Harry, but it wasn't discretion on my part, it was that at that precise moment there was no other thought in my mind but her. I was enchanted, in a trance, I was floating on air. I was trapped and unable to move or speak, and what passion was it, that hung weights upon my tongue?

She stepped towards me, her dressing gown falling open to reveal a simple slip, pale and pink like her skin. The silky material whispered as she walked; it caressed her knees, it kissed the slight swell of her belly, it gently cupped the perfect curve of her breasts. And it did nothing at all to hide the shadow of the triangle of hair that lay mysterious and full of promise beneath its touch.

She floated across the room like a rose petal on a trickling stream, and came and stood close to me, her hands by her side. She looked up into my face and deep into my eyes with a sort of desperation, as if she was memorising my every shape and line so that one day she might paint me in oils or sculpt me in clay. And I opened to her, and felt full and free and unbound. I could've kicked over Big Ben, lifted Tower Bridge on my shoulders, or picked up Cleopatra's Needle and twirled it round and around my head. She saw my wonder, my puzzlement, my unspoken questions, and she shushed them all to silence with the gentlest touch of her fingertips to my lips. And as expertly as any thief, she spun me first this way and then that, and silently unlocked the tumblers to my heart.

And suddenly she was real, heartachingly real; not just an idea; not just another actor in a shadow play; not just a name in some report in some buff-coloured folder. And at that moment all I wanted to do with all my heart was hold her, protect her, keep her safe, and love her. I didn't give a damn that she didn't know me from Adam, she was my Eve and this was our Eden. Time slowed and billowed around us both like a cloak of lavender-laden leaves and I breathed in deeply and caught the scent in her hair and drew her close to me.

She stood up on her tiptoes and put her arms around my neck and kissed me full on the lips. It was as shocking as falling into icy water and as intense as being licked by flame, and I felt myself stiffen. For a moment a hand fluttered across my cheek and she kissed me again. I was suddenly completely and deeply in love with her, as perhaps I'd been since the very first time I saw her in the photograph. But then I'd always had to love the woman I was with, even if only for a moment. It was only through believing that, that I'd come to learn that some moments really could be made to last for an eternity.

> *So, my darling, let us live for the moment,*
> *let us love for tonight,*
> *as there may be no tomorrows*
> *with the coming of the light.*

It was just like it had been in the war, different words perhaps, but the same old favourite tune. Just as countless lovers had sung softly to one another through all the dark desperate nights when London had been lit only by fire. I'd sung the refrain myself many times and with a whole chorus of wonderful women, but I know I never sang as sweetly as I did that night with Tanyia. And neither of us breathed a single word, not even our blessed names.

I knew for sure that we were enchanted, because from the very first moment we'd touched the house had taken us inside and made us a part of itself. Our every movement was embraced by it, our every sound covered by a whispered creaking of the floorboards or the quiet rattling of a pipe.

They say good things must always come to an end, but I tell you there's endings, and then there's endings. With us, the moment was shattered by a loud knock on the bedroom door that stopped everything dead in its tracks. My eyebrows shot up and I stiffened just as the rest of me went limp. The knocking was accompanied by a deep voice that seemed to be shouting and whispering at the same time. The only word I could make out in all the noise was 'Tanyia.' And the look on her face suggested she knew very well who was outside the door, and though it'd sounded to me like it could've turned double-dodgy in a second, she didn't look at all afraid, only a little put out. Tanyia's fingers shushed me to silence as she called out, I think, asking for a moment so she could dress herself properly.

Once again I questioned Walsingham's sense of her, to me she didn't seem to be at all on the verge of constant panic; if that was anyone it was me. She'd impressed me in the cool way she'd handled my unexpected arrival, and now here she was all cool and calm and collected, dealing effortlessly with another surprise visitor. I think she'd sussed out her situation in the Embassy very early on, and had decided to do whatever needed to be done in order to survive. If that included me, then all well and to the good. I'd have probably done no less myself if I'd been in her situation.

She went to the door pretending to be a bit sleepy, calling out something like, "Hang on a minute, comrade, I'm coming as fast as I can, you witless oaf." I noticed she'd got her foot and knee hard up against the door as she unlatched it. I was hidden behind her wardrobe by this time, my heart in my throat, my knife in my hand. The bloke said something in a voice that sounded like he'd been gargling with gravel, and a hairy arm and hand appeared on this side of the door brandishing a slightly used bar of soap. Tanyia said something, her voice soft and low, and as if by magic Gravel-breath went all soft, too. Some blokes can be right pathetic when they start sniffing around a pretty girl; I ask you, who do they think they're trying to kid? But then he started pushing the door as well as his luck, and I found I'd changed the grip on my Fairbairn-Sykes, and was up on the balls of my feet ready to pounce even before I was aware of it myself. The bloke must've been born lucky, though, because Tanyia stood her ground and pushed back against the door even harder, and all Gravel-breath ended up with was a bruised arm and his throat still in one piece. As the arm disappeared she relieved it of its bar of soap and then quickly closed the door and locked it. Then she quietly called out something, a 'thank you' probably, although she might've just been telling the bloke to bugger off, I couldn't tell.

She turned and smiled, her back against the door, and held up the soap for me to see. She whispered, "We each have our own, I left it in the bathroom by mistake. It's from Paris, my only permissible luxury, and if it didn't smell so much of lavender, the pig would have probably kept it for himself." It was the very first time I'd heard her speak. Her voice was husky like Ava Gardner's, but foreign like Marlene Dietrich's. It was one of the nicest-sounding voices I'd ever heard. And I knew that, because I found myself being enchanted by her all over again.

She smiled, went over towards a little chest of drawers, and when she turned round she held out a book. "Here, this must be what you came for."

I took it, but by the look of the cover it wasn't something in English. She smiled, came over to me and opened the book; the title inside was different from the one on the cover, for a start, it was in English. It was *Oliver Twist*, the 1935 Everyman edition. I knew I'd seen it before; a thousand years before in a room not fifty feet from where I was standing. Wheels within wheels, books within books. She took the book, wrapped it carefully in a sheet of some foreign newspaper, and handed it back to me. I don't know what I marvelled at more, the fact that her hands didn't shake once, or the smell of lavender in her hair. I put the little package in the satchel strapped across my chest. It was indeed what I'd come for, but I was leaving a far richer man.

"Mr. Burglar, I want to come with you. Now. Tonight."

She said it so quietly, so softly, as if we were sitting together in a supper club in Soho and she was whispering in my ear what she wanted to drink, that at first I wasn't sure I'd heard her right. But the sparkle in her eyes and the determined little smile on her beautiful face told me she was in earnest. It was my turn to smile then, because I'd guessed the real reason for her change of mind. I knew in my heart, it was me that had at last given her the courage to act. I didn't say anything, though. It's best not to rush things in the beginning.

"How's your head for heights?" I asked her softly. If I'd had a pack of cigarettes with me, I'd have flicked two of them out, lit them both and handed her one, then we could have spent the rest of eternity together looking at the stars.

"It's good," she said. "I am not afraid."

"Of course you're not," I said, "but you'd better get dressed, we're already late for where we're going. Put on a pair of trousers, if you have any, and a thick woolly jumper and some stout shoes. Oh, and put your hair up in a scarf while you're at it, or under a hat."

Jethro, the dresser. Life, like the theatre, was always full of little surprises. She dressed and then put her hair up, in that beautiful ballet of arms and hands that women seem to do so naturally. I watched her openly and unashamedly, and she was poetry, she was song, and her every move was music. She finished dressing, and finished me off with a little blue beret she pulled on over her hair. It was the perfect touch, and absolutely the perfect thing to wear for a quiet stroll over the tiles of London. I only wished I'd thought to bring a carnation for my lapel.

I waltzed over to the window and looked out at the night, and the gentle folds of yellow mist outside glowed as if made of gossamer. I jumped up onto the ledge, and was through the window and beckoning her on before you could say 'Fred Astaire.' I held my hand out to her and she began to climb up, and that was the second time that night, that reality tap-danced its way into our lives.

She looked at me. She looked out at the fog. She took my hand and scrambled up onto the ledge and then she leaned further out and looked down at the unfathomable darkness below, and froze. Then she gasped and pulled back. "No. I can't do it. I'm sorry, I can't. It's ... it's just too high. I ... I didn't realise."

As I said, the reality of being sixty feet up off the ground, with nothing but your hands, your fingertips, and your nerves to hold you, is instantly sobering and most people just can't hack it, even if they do happen to be angels. I often wondered why I was able to do it myself sometimes, but even in despair Tanyia didn't buckle, although I could already see the weight of her disappointment begin to etch little lines around the corners of her eyes and mouth.

"Don't worry, darling," I said, pulling myself back inside her room. "There's a plan for an instance such as this. Never you worry, we'll fly over the roof-tops like Peter Pan and Wendy tonight, or I'm not my father's son." I don't know if she understood for a minute what I was blathering on about, but she caught the determination in my voice and I saw the flame of hope rekindle in her eyes, and I knew then I'd pull everything off somehow. Or die trying.

I told her what to do, and when to do it, so that I'd have enough time to complete my side of the plan. She nodded, looked away for a moment as if she was rehearsing everything through in her mind, then she looked back at me again and smiled. Then she went up on her toes and kissed me full on the lips, and the tingle ran through every vein in my body and my heart was fit to burst.

I nodded and smiled my debonair smile, too choked with happiness to say anything else. Then I pulled back the curtain again, leapt up onto the ledge, and slipped through the window and back into the night. And Douglas Fairbanks Jr. and Errol Flynn at their dashing best couldn't have done it any better, even if I say so myself.

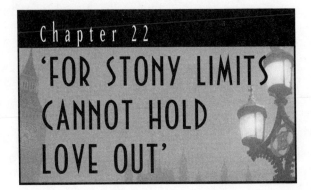

Chapter 22

'FOR STONY LIMITS CANNOT HOLD LOVE OUT'

Time, as they say, was of the essence and I had to get up the side of the building and onto the roof in seconds flat. And as I'd spent so much time preparing the flying rig, I decided to travel first class. So, I got a good grip on the sling and gave the silk rope attached to the punch-bag a good sharp tug. Then I snatched a quick breath, and braced myself for the bag up on the ledge to plummet down onto the roof of the mews below. But nothing happened.

I tugged again, and again, but still nothing happened. And cursing I reached for the other black silk rope and started up it like a sailor threatened with the cat-o'-nine-tails. And suddenly the canvas sling was going up the side of the building faster than a bleedin' rat up a drain-pipe. The rope sang through the blocks and the sling whipped back and forth, and suddenly it felt like something had caught hold of my elbow to give me a helping hand and I travelled upwards at an incredible rate of knots. I held out a hand, but before I even had time to breathe I was at the top of the building. And as the two big wooden blocks banged together, I pulled my arm free and threw myself up and onto the roof, and held on for dear life. But the tail end of the sling gave me a nasty smack on the back of my neck, and I had to shake my head to clear it.

When I could see straight again, I found that I was still in one piece with both legs on top of the parapet, and I was up and moving before I heard the punch-bag land with an almighty thump onto the roof of the mews house a million miles below. Behind me the pulley wheels whirred on and on going nowhere, and the two blocks, released at last from their heavy burden, jumped up and down for joy banging their messages of freedom in frantic Morse code against the side of the building. The cat was now out of the bag so to speak, and I didn't have any time to spare, or any lives left to lose.

I scrambled across the roof and grabbed madly at the loops of rope that the pulley wheel and block and tackle had been suspended from, and I pulled everything up and over the stone anchor piers, and just let everything drop.

"Count to twenty," I'd told her. Only I'd forgotten to say in which language; those foreign languages are much too long and complicated if you ask me, it can take years to say anything sensible in any of them. And I was just beginning to worry that she'd lost her nerve, or forgotten how to count, when I heard Tanyia scream, or I imagined I did, because suddenly, all hell broke loose. She must've been a brilliant actress, because it was as if everyone down in the Embassy started shouting and yelling at once. Then the alarm bells started up and added their tinny racket to the unholy chorus. It sounded just like old times.

Tanyia screaming her pretty little head off was supposed to give everyone the idea that a burglar was in the house somewhere still trying to escape. I wanted them to think I was clambering down the back of the building, and making for the mews just as I'd done on my first visit. While meanwhile, up on the roof, I was waiting for the floodlights to come bursting on at any minute, but it was still an almighty shock when they did. They seemed brighter than daylight, and made the rooftops along the terrace look as unreal as an Ealing Studios film set. I caught sight of my long black shadow shooting towards the edge and even though I had my back to the floods, I went blind. And I could do nothing but close my eyes and hold on. But even then, all I could see for a time were blue and purple shadows zigzagging madly against the brilliant white light trapped behind my eyelids.

I blinked and rubbed my eyes with the back of my turtles and willed them to get used to the light, but for ages it was as if I was trying to stare through fields of snow. Then my eyes cleared and as if by magic I saw I already had the hammer and chisel out of the tool bag and in my hands. I was just about to start hammering the roof tiles when I heard shouts and yells coming from directly behind me. I jumped, even as I realised it was a trick of the night, and that the noise was in fact echoing up from several storeys below me.

It took less than a second to decide, but I had to risk taking a quick look to see what was happening, as everything depended upon what von Bentink and Krepstok chose to do next. I slithered back across to the edge of the roof and peered over. Somebody was already out of one of the windows, and climbing down a rope-ladder as nimbly as a circus monkey. It had to be von Bentink, who else would've had the nerve? Then other windows started flying open, the light from inside causing an eerie glow in the fog. And I watched fascinated, as one after the other, people stuck their heads out and stabbed down into the darkness with powerful hand-torches, the harsh beams criss-crossing wildly in the night like searchlights at a Nuremberg rally.

While up on the roof nothing stirred, not even a mouse.

"Fucking hell!" I said to myself. It's such a relief when people do exactly as you planned. I turned, slipped back across the tiles, sighted in on my hastily chalked-out square, and got to work. And by then I didn't give a tinker's cuss who heard me, because I was already well past the point of no return. My only hope was that in the midst of all the riot going on down inside the Embassy, Tanyia had managed to get herself safely hidden away inside the little detention room. I hammered the chisel along the chalk lines again and again, splitting slate-tile after slate-tile, feverishly levering them up and away from their pegs, just letting everything slide or fall where it may. I used the hammer-head to smash through the wooden battens that'd held the pegs, and then picking up the tin shears I cut and tore and ripped at the tar-paper covering beneath like some demented Irish navvy. I was Jack the Ripper, I was Sweeney Todd, and I was come for revenge, or death.

And soon, through the ever-widening gash, the white plaster-thin skin between the rafters was laid bare before me like an open throat. And I slashed and slashed with the chisel in one hand and the shears in the other, until the black slashes looked like bloody wounds in the harsh light. Then I threw both tools down and took up the hammer again, two-handed this time, and bashed and bashed and bashed and bashed. And the thin wooden slats splintered and tore and fell away, and the plaster cracked and flew, and the cruel white light from the floods threw sharp jagged shadows this way and that across the roof.

Sweat ran into my eyes, stinging like mad and splitting the light into thousands of pointed shards, but I hammered on regardless until I was satisfied the hole beneath me was big enough. I scraped away the jagged edges and smoothed the sharp-splintered sides as best I could. Then I took a quick breather, wiped the sweat from my forehead with the back of my sleeve, and looked down into a hole, now fully two-foot square. And even with all the clouds of dust billowing about me, it somehow managed to look like I'd cut a hole in the night.

At first there was no movement, nothing. Then I heard the sound of coughing, and suddenly from out of the gloom below there appeared an upturned face. It caught the light, and framed by the night it caught my breath as well. It was a face full of surprise and fear and hope, and so tantalisingly close it was almost close enough for me to kiss. It was my Tanyia, and even covered in dust and plaster she was beautiful. Until that moment I hadn't realised how much I'd missed her; every second had been an hour, every minute a day.

I reached down, and grasped hold of her outstretched arms, and pulled. And she came up through the hole in the roof like a shot from a cannon, and suddenly there she was standing beside me with the alarm bells clanging and the lights blinding, and the shouting and yelling around us getting nearer and nearer.

"Time to go," I said, as if me and Errol Flynn did this sort of thing every day. And not a moment too soon, because there was a hammering from down inside the detention room as well as a rattling at several of the skylights at the rear of the house. But by then I'd half dragged and pulled Tanyia towards the narrow gap in the barbed-wire fence. I turned to her and cupped my hands to give her a leg up. She hesitated for a split second, but cottoned on quickly and then just went up and over, like a Chinese tumbler in a stage act. Which was just as well, because at that moment there was a rattling and a banging, and one of the skylights crashed open and a hand came through the hole holding a gun.

"As I said, it's time to go," I said, and took a running jump. Then the lights started to go out and everything went black, and that's when Tanyia screamed for the second time.

I'd heard a phut-pinging sound and the noise of shattering glass only moments before, but I still couldn't place the weird, little sound even when I heard it again an instant later. It was only at that point, I realised that both the floodlights had been shot out. And as I landed on the neighbouring roof, more by luck than judgement, a tiny finger of light beamed on, and then just as quickly disappeared again, but it was enough, for in that split second I'd caught sight of Tanyia being helped back along the roof towards freedom.

Behind me, howls of anger and rage were funnelling up from the open skylight, and torch beams began to rip gashes in the night. And as I didn't much fancy the idea of Tanyia's ex-comrades shooting at me in the dark, I lobbed a couple of handy smoke grenades back over the fence just to add to their confusion. After which, a few quick slashes at the canvas straps holding down the steel-boned Mae West, and 'Bob's your uncle.' I let the barbed wire spring back and dispense with the whole lot of it. I didn't want to make it too easy for anyone to follow us, I mean that wasn't part of the Great Game, was it?

There'd be no denying now that someone had paid a call on the Embassy and spirited away yet another of its prized jewels, but as to just who and how, and to what end, still had to remain a puzzle. Bosanquet had left the smoke grenades for me—a nice touch—and I'd thought at first Walsingham had only been kidding about it. Another little magic touch was the fifty-foot length of blood-stained rope that Bosanquet had left hanging down the side of the adjoining building to dangle a false trail. And if anyone bothered to look at the foot of the rope come morning, they'd find a satchel full of burglary tools, as well as a few pamphlets from various American anticommunist groups. Wheels within wheels; mysteries wrapped up in vinegar and brown paper.

I eeled my way in back through the attic window, and it was only my bloody handprint on the ledge that made me realise I must've gashed myself somewhere. I reached for a handkerchief to wipe away the blood, but when I tried to spit on it, my mouth was too dry to come up with anything. So I stuffed the thing back in my pocket, hurried across the tiny attic room, and made my way down to the meeting room below. They both turned round towards me, a thousand unspoken questions on their faces. It must've matched the look on my face perfectly.

Tanyia looked dishevelled but beautiful; Bosanquet was all business. He had a first-aid kit open, and was already tending to a nasty gash on Tanyia's leg. Her sock and shoe were red with blood and he'd ripped open her trouser leg up to her knee, but she didn't seem to mind, he might as well have been pulling a splinter out of her finger. I tore off my turtles and saw then that the blood on them hadn't been mine.

"Bad?" I said.

"Not too bad, no. She'll mend soon enough," he replied.

"Thanks for the floodlights," I said. "Air gun?"

He nodded and continued with his bandaging. "Yes, a Whittaker 177, pump-action. The .22 soft-lead slug flattens on impact. If they do find one in all the muck and debris on the roof, they'll probably mistake it for an old nail-head."

I nodded, impressed with his efficiency and forethought.

Tanyia looked from one to the other of us and laughed. Men, she probably thought, the same the world over. Then we both looked at her, then at each other, and then we all laughed. And all the tension of the last hour—and days and weeks and months—melted away until we all found ourselves shivering with cold.

"The flask," he said, "it's on top of the steamer trunk."

I went and got the flask and handed it to Tanyia and she tilted back her swan-like neck and took a long swig of whisky; and she did it smoothly and expertly, and without spilling a single drop down her exquisite chin. What poise, what grace, what fire; this was a man's woman, this was a Carole Lombard, this was a Lauren Bacall. She handed me the flask and I took it without taking my eyes off her and I smiled and nonchalantly took a swig and it was nectar, single malt of the gods, and I nodded my thanks and appreciation and smiled my admiration. She touched my arm and stroked it and said, "Thank you, Mr. Burglar, very, very much." And I said, "It was nothing." And I was ten feet tall and growing taller by the second. No creep before had ever given me such exhilaration; no jewels had ever compared to her. I was Jethro the bold. I was Jethro the conqueror. I was Jethro in love. I was Romeo, and she was my little communist Juliet.

Bosanquet nodded and smiled, and said calmly, "I'm afraid I have to ask you to go outside again. You need to find the blood trail and clean it up as best you can, and at the very minimum you'll need to do it all the way across the roof next door. It may not hold up to a full daylight search, but we have no choice. There's water in the canteen bottle and you can use these spare bandages for rags, but please go carefully and don't be seen. I'll clean up any blood in here."

The spell of the moment before broke, and the world outside invaded our cosy little nest and my midnight daydream of love vanished into thin air. There were shouts down in the street, and the gonging sounds of fast-approaching police cars. Soon there'd be lights everywhere and lots of noisy people poking their noses into the night; all of which meant I didn't have a moment to lose. Yet now the only place I wanted to be in all the world was safe and snug in that meeting room of friends, out of sight and out of mind, basking in the glow of the glory that was Tanyia and with all of my ghosts safely laid to rest.

I shook my head to clear it of its warm thoughts and made for the attic room; I had to stay sharp and cold, and the faster I was away, the faster I could be back. Just as I reached the attic door Bosanquet called out after me. I turned round, balanced, poised, cat-like, and not even Laurence Olivier at his brilliant best could've upstaged me.

"Jethro," he said, grinning. "Well done, I don't know who else in London could have pulled it off."

I acknowledged his compliment with the upward tilt of my head and the flaring of my nostrils, then I took the stairs two at a time and I was at the top before I realised it would've been the first time Tanyia had heard my name spoken.

Out on the roof the lighting was different and the backdrop wrong. It was as if I'd wandered by mistake into some other film or play, and it was as if the romantic comedy of a few moments before had by some devilry been transformed into a tragedy. The very air felt charged and threatening. Torch beams stabbed and thrust at the chill yellow curtains that hid me, and I stood stock-still and hardly breathed. I fought the urge to return again to the warmth of the room below, and I cursed the fates that had once again brought me to the point of mortal danger; hadn't I done enough already? Then I thought of Tanyia, and my heart burst and I knew why I'd been called on to give my all again. And I became as Pepper's ghost, a trick of the light, a phantom, a will-o'-the-wisp. I smiled my cruel and knowing smile, and knew I had night's cloak to hide me from their sight. And like some spirit called to do my bidding, folds of invisibility curled close around me and I slithered and crawled and moved across the tiles as nothing more than a pale shadow.

Krepstok's men shouted back and forth across the Embassy roof, and down into the lamp-lit street on one side, and down into the darkness of the mews on the other. And all of the newly arrived policemen and rudely awoken neighbours all chorused back. It was like one of those German operas, only without all the flames. But I paid them no mind, even when I heard Krepstok barking out orders like a hungry dog. After all, they had their jobs to do and I had mine. So I continued crawling out across the roof on my belly, intent on retracing the blood-speckled path that Tanyia and Bosanquet had taken earlier.

I had no light but what was in my own mind, and I imagined myself as a black crow in flight, and the rooftops became as mountains and valleys and plains, and the lines of chimneys became roads and tracks. I drew a silver thread from the point where Tanyia had fallen by the fence to the point where I'd heard her scream, and from there to the spot where, moments later, Bosanquet had used a finger of light to point the way to the attic window. And the path ran as quicksilver in my mind, and I could clearly see the line I must trace. It took me the better course of an hour to cover the path that had taken them but moments. And moving no more than an inch at a time, I used the length of my body as well as my rag-encased turtles to rub out whatever traces of blood there were, and anything else that might've marked our passing. The rooftop next to the Embassy I left to God's good graces. I'd already had more than my fair share of luck, and I doubted there'd be any more of it lying around.

I kept my ears cocked and ready for the sounds of anyone making their way over the terrace roofs. I fully expected to bump into some nosy copper trying to see his way to promotion by groping blindly across a wet roof in the dark. But whoever was in charge of London's finest that night seems to have had all his men under tight control. Either that or someone had ordered them not to be overly rigorous in their search.

Pleased with myself and the way things had gone, I was just about to fold myself back in through the attic window atop BLESS House, when from across the roof-tops I heard a voice cry out and cut the fog to tatters. And I tell you, if I hadn't already been freezing my feet off by then, it would've sent a chill right along my spine.

"You, thief of night. You, whoever you are, I shall hunt you down and kill you. That I promise. And, know this, that however long it takes, it will be done. This I swear."

The voice had to be Flash Harry von Bentink's, and I knew he meant every word. I pushed the knowing deep, deep down inside me, and responded to it the only way I knew how, even if only in a whisper. "Right, me old cock, anytime you fucking well like; guns, fists, or bleedin' knives. Because you try coming it with me and you're a dead man, on my dear old dad's memory, you are."

I slid through the opening and closed the window securely behind me. And whatever else may have gone on outside, nothing came to disturb our little tranquil idyll for the rest of the night, not even a single, solitary knock on the door. I thought it best not to mention what'd occurred up on the roof; some things are best left unsaid. And we spent the rest of the time cleaning stuff up, packing, and getting ourselves ready for morning. After that, we drank hot coffee spiked with whisky out of a Thermos flask, while Bosanquet chatted on and on to Tanyia in some foreign language. I didn't mind, though, as it sounded like it was all to do with the spying business and I'd already had enough of that to last me several lifetimes. He seemed very interested in the Charles Dickens book, and kept asking Tanyia questions and making notes about it in, of all things, a little black book.

I found myself chuckling. I'd actually gone and done it, I'd got in and got away with it, twice. "You jammy bastard," I said to myself. I shook my head. I'd never done it before, I'd never gone back in anywhere, I'd always made it a strict rule not to. And after that night's work, if I ever got the chance, I intended to stick to my principles religiously in the future. But of course I would, I was Jethro the charmer, Jethro the chancer, the bloke that always made his own luck. I smiled again, a different smile. Ray was now in the clear, and Joanie and Barry, too. It was odd, but I hadn't thought about any of them once during the caper. Not once. I suppose I'd have felt too vulnerable if I had of done, funny that. But now, we'd all be home free and clear, and me, with a right smasher by my side to enjoy it all with. I tell you, happy days were definitely here again.

Tanyia didn't say much, but she caught me looking at her from time to time, and whenever she did, she smiled at me warmly. I suppose I must've looked like a right duck egg, and I guess she must've known the truth of it even then; that I'd never be allowed to see her again after that night. But I didn't know it, I was new to the game. But that's me, Jethro; easy come, easy go. Love? Who needs it? It just churns up your insides and puts you off your food. It's either that, or it's a kick in the head and you end up senseless. Love? I was crazy about her, and if I was ever asked to do it over, I'd do it all over again in a single heartbeat. You bet my life, I would.

As capers go, the caper ended quietly enough. The straggly white wig, bowler hat, and gaunt wet-white make-up did absolutely nothing for Tanyia except render her partially invisible. I did my best, but it was difficult trying to hide all that beauty, its luminescence seemed to want to burst out and catch your throat at the slightest opportunity. In the end I used the same old trick I'd used on myself, only this time instead of wadding up the cotton wool and stuffing it in her cheeks, I pushed it down the side of her gums to give her a heavy set of jowls. Then I used a wax pencil to darken her chin, her cheeks, and that lovely little area above her adorable lips. I even laughed, so happy was I in my work. I was near, she was close, I could smell the lavender in her hair, it was wonderful, and all such a wonderful game. Then I gave her my jacket to wear under the long black coat to give added bulk to her gorgeous body, and then I finished it off by winding my scarf round and around her lovely neck. It worked to a fashion, but only just; I still thought she looked smashing and I could still see every perfect line of her silhouette through all the clothes. I still can, even in the dark.

At eight o'clock sharp the next morning, in a street still thick with cold coppers, a black cab called at BLESS House to collect the two gentlemen he'd dropped there the previous evening. Bosanquet, of course, looked his dapper self even after being up all night; I suppose that's what having a good education does for you. And that's how I remember it; the two of them standing side by side like Flanagan and Allen waiting in the wings for their cue, and Bosanquet nodding a goodbye and Tanyia flashing one last wonderful smile before she was gone out of my life. The taxi driver seemed to struggle a bit with their two suitcases, but he soon managed to stow them away in the little compartment next to the driver's cab. Then he drove off slowly, with his passengers safe and snug in the back. And if anyone did watch them go all the way to the end of the street, they'd have seen that the cab was soon swallowed up by the next wave of London's early morning traffic.

And unless they'd stayed on to watch the distant stream of buses, trams, vans, taxis, cars, and motorbikes for another ten minutes or so, they would've also missed the Whiteley's delivery van that stopped outside BLESS House. A tall, grey-haired man in neatly pressed overalls got out, and went inside the building carrying a small parcel. He was seen again some five minutes later, with a second, younger man wearing similar overalls, carefully loading a much-travelled steamer trunk into the back of the dark blue van. Then, their load safely stowed, both men got into the van and drove off, and within a very short time, it too disappeared into London's traffic. I tell you, Harry Houdini himself couldn't have done any better. In fact, from what I've heard, it's exactly how he accomplished many of his famous vanishing tricks.

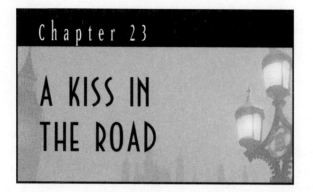

Chapter 23

A KISS IN THE ROAD

Christmas. And the goose was as fat as it was ever going to get if you could only get your hands on one. We settled for chicken, a small roast, and a bit of pork as the butcher owed us a favour, he just didn't know how big of a favour it was going to be yet. I knew he'd put something on the side for us though, once I'd bunged him a few extra petrol coupons and come up with some clothing coupons for his wife. He'd probably tap his nose for a couple of bottles of spirits as well, but that was only to be expected, it was all part of the game. But what else would you expect from someone who'd taken up butchering for a living? They're born villains the lot of them, it's in their blood.

Harry Davids wasn't too bad as butchers go, he was the one that supplied the Victory Cafe with meat and he did all right from it, too, money-wise, that is. He also got an extra helping when he came in for tea or dinner and no questions asked, even by Vi. It was one of the reasons the place was so popular; people reckoned if he ate there then there'd never be too much gristle in the stew, and whatever it was you were eating it probably wasn't horse meat. Joanie wouldn't serve it anyway and Harry couldn't stand the taste of it, but it didn't stop him from trying to off-load the whale meat the Government had been trying to push on everybody. It confused him though; what was it really, meat or fish?

The Victory was doing its best to enter into the spirit of things; there were twisted paper chains and streamers in red and green, orange and blue, and purple and yellow all tacked up around the place. There were also a few paper concertina decorations in assorted colours, all pre-war, and marked 'Empire Made,' that folded out to make the shape of a bell, a ball, or a snowman complete with a tiny top hat. There was even a sprig of mistletoe over the door, though who that was supposed to be for God only knew. Vi had a new apron for the occasion, and someone, probably Pauline, one of the girls that helped out in the cafe, had even embroidered her name with violets entwined through it, which looked quite festive. There was even some mad talk about putting Christmas pudding with homemade brandy sauce on the menu. I tell you, no expense was being spared.

Even though it seemed things everywhere were becoming more expensive by the day, Church Street market was jumping. People were at long last beginning to dig beneath the austerity measures to see if there was anything left worth having. There was still rationing on lots of things, but if you had the money—and you could say 'Harrods' without dropping your aitches—there were chocolates from Belgium, and lace blouses and perfumes from France. And shops selling Swiss watches appeared to have sprung up all over town. For the rest, there were oranges and sugared fruit from far-off sunny climes that were still out of bounds to most of us. There'd even been a rumour that bananas had been sighted down the East India docks, but no one really believed it. Next year, perhaps. But it was all starting to come back, all the tastes, all the dreams, all the cravings; like a word or a name that'd been on the tip of your tongue for so long you'd given up trying to remember.

Joanie had seen them bring me back late one evening well after dark, and she'd waited by her front door in her dressing gown until she'd seen me slowly climb the stairs up to my flat, and then she'd gone back to bed. She knew I hadn't been home at all the night before, and I knew she'd have been worried sick about me, even though I'd told her I was going to be away visiting an old friend somewhere, but she didn't say a word. And neither did I.

I felt drained. Walsingham's people had had me in a room all day asking questions about the second Embassy creep, and slowly the euphoria I'd felt earlier had seeped away like air from a slow puncture. It'd been more like a clog dance on a tin roof than a creep, but they'd insisted on me going back over everything as it had happened, again and again and again. They wanted to know in fine detail how I'd finally managed to get down to Tanyia's room, what I'd said to her, what she'd said to me, what had happened after that, and so on and so on. I hadn't told them everything of course, just the bits they'd understand; what had happened between Tanyia and me was ours alone to remember; I just hoped she felt the same way.

They'd served me tea and biscuits in the morning as well as the afternoon, and given me a potted-meat sandwich for lunch, so they must've been fairly pleased with the way things had gone. I didn't see anything of Simon Bosanquet or Tanyia, so they were probably going through the same thing in another room. And it was only at the arse-end of the day that Walsingham finally came in to shake my hand, and say how very grateful he was about everything. He told me to go safe, but I didn't think he meant it as a joke, as he also suggested it might be good if I was to lay low for a time. He said he didn't think I needed to be in protective custody yet, but that he could arrange it if I wished. And I'd smiled and said, "No, thank you very much, Mr. Walsingham, I think I can take care of myself." And he'd smiled his winning smile, and after we'd toasted His Majesty in single malt, he'd had me driven home.

Afterwards the whole world felt flat and even all the Christmas lights looked pathetic. I was listless and lethargic, and yet all my senses remained alert no matter what I did to try and calm them. I felt out of place in the flat, out of place in the Victory, and out of place wandering round the market. I didn't even trust myself going near the lock-up, because I had the funniest feeling that I'd roar off in the MG, and end up wrapping myself around a lamp-post somewhere. I was waiting for something to happen only I didn't know what, and I had no idea what to do or which way to turn. I felt like a goat tethered to a tree. One minute I was as nervous as a cat, the next as stiff and still as a dead mouse in a trap. Even the daylight began to feel odd, and I found myself missing the comfort of shadows. But the nights weren't any easier, and I usually didn't close my eyes till the dawn thundered up in its carpet slippers and rocked me off to sleep.

I'd go out to buy a packet of fags or a newspaper, and time and again I'd find myself snatching a quick peek around me to see if I was being followed. Even being in disguise gave me no relief. I tried different hats and walks, but it was half-hearted and didn't feel real; it was me just play-acting. And after a while I didn't know who I was or even who I was supposed to be hiding from. It was always wise to be on the look-out for Messima and his choirboys, especially Chalkie White, because there was never any telling what that flinty-eyed rat might get up to. But now there was von Bentink and von Baldy, DCI Browno and the Sweeney, the bleedin' Ghost Squad, and whoever else Walsingham's evil mind could come up with, including the income tax man. It wasn't that I didn't trust Walsingham, it was that I didn't not trust him, if you get my meaning. And that little lot was nothing when compared to the very dirty looks I'd been getting from some of Buggy's boys.

A couple of them had broken into his house to see if he was dead or something, but everything had been normal, and even his bed had been made. It looked like he'd simply stepped into his clothes and disappeared. I was sure they suspected I had something to do with it, and if it wasn't for the postcards signed 'Buggy Billy' they kept on getting from seaside towns around the country, I knew they'd have crowded around me with a few very pointed questions and some other sharp objects. I couldn't have given them any news anyway, I hadn't got a single card, or a letter or a phone call from Ray, and if I'd told them he was in the custody of the Secret Service they'd have beaten me up for not taking them seriously enough.

Several times I caught myself sneaking glimpses in shop windows to make sure it was really me reflected there and not somebody else. Barry told me he once saw me go back and look in the same window three times. And two days in a row, just to get out of the house, I hopped a bus up to the Odeon cinema in Kilburn High Street for the afternoon showing of *Odd Man Out*, with James Mason. Afterwards I felt like I was on the run myself, imagining eyes in doorways and in every passing lorry, bus, or car, and I'd be drenched in sweat by the time I got home.

Joanie stood for my nonsense for as long as she could. And then one morning on the stairwell, she told me straight that I needed to shake myself out of it. "You look like there's something gnawing away at you inside, Jethro, and if you didn't look so worried about it all, I'd have said you were in love. There's a lot you won't tell us, and I don't need to know any of it; all I do know, is you've got to get back to your old self, Jethro love, or you'll soon be a complete goner. I tell you, I only wish Buggy Billy was around to knock some sense into you, but where he's been hiding himself these last few weeks, God only knows."

I missed the old bugger, too. Though I didn't tell her he was still in the hands of the people that'd brought me home that night. I didn't think for a minute that the reason he still hadn't reappeared might still have anything to do with me. Shows you how dim I can be sometimes.

So that Friday, Joanie decided we could all do with a bit of an impromptu knees-up down the Duke of York. "Just the Victory staff, and a few of the regulars," she'd said, "just to get us all into the Christmas spirit." But I knew she was really worried that the cloud hanging over me might never disappear.

That night I did my best to enter into the spirit of things, and after a while, much to my surprise, I even realised I was enjoying it. Then all of a sudden it was as if the black cloud had finally passed, and I was free and clear and back home again. It felt fucking marvellous; as if a huge weight had been lifted from off my chest. I caught Joanie smiling at me, and I smiled back and pointed to myself and nodded happily. Then I looked around the bar as if seeing everybody clearly for the first time; what a grand bunch of people they all were.

Everyone was there, lifting their elbows and having a right old singsong around the pub piano; Joanie and Barry, and Vi, along with Pauline and Mavis, the two girls that helped out at the Victory. Joanie'd even arranged for Vi's little girl, Rosie, to kip round a friend's house, so Vi could loosen her stays and really enjoy herself. Harry Davids the butcher was there, never one to pass up a free drink, before he eeled his way home to his wife in their posh new house in Maida Vale. There were a couple of well-known, local costers, Eddie Stebbins and Albert Bicknell, who were always good for a laugh, a song, or some tremendous 'never-to-be-repeated-on-my-life-I'd-never-tell-you-a-lie' bargain. Both of them had had their market stalls pitched outside the Victory since long before the start of the war, although Vi was always asking them which war that'd been.

I was pleasantly surprised to see that both Tom Banbury and Stan Pipe had popped in from the Metropolitan Theatre round the corner. They were firm favourites at the Victory, and such good customers they even had their own red and brown sauce bottles at their corner table. They always left threepence under the saucer as a tip for Vi. 'Proper gentlemen,' she called them. And they left word for me, too, if they ever heard there was work going in one of the theatres round town.

On the off chance, Joanie had even telephoned Seth at the fruit and vegetable shop he was working at in Slough to see if he could pop up to town for the knees-up. He said he'd have loved to, but couldn't get away at such short notice, although he did say as she should buy me a drink, no, two drinks from him, and that he'd be up to see us as soon as he could manage it. When she told me, I thought I might just motor down and see him myself, as I knew he'd get me singing and laughing if anyone could. The MG needed a good run anyway, and if the snow only kept away, that coming Sunday might be a good time for it.

Joanie and Vi started the party off by singing their version of the Andrews Sisters' "Don't Sit Under the Apple Tree." So after that I just got right into the spirit of things, raised a few elbows, and started in on my own very special renditions of "Roll Out the Barrel" and "Ten Green Bottles." I didn't think my singing was that bad, but for some reason it soon had everybody pissing themselves with laughter. It was all great fun, though, and it did us all a power of good, especially me. And I could see that Joanie was well pleased, and that Barry was, too.

Joanie and Vi sang "I'm Dreaming of a White Christmas," and we all joined in, feeling very lucky to be alive. Then, with that sudden sense you get that the moment has run its course, we all turned as one, like a flock of London sparrows, and chatting away ten to the dozen, we got our hats and coats. And even though one or two people decided it was time they'd better get off home to their families, there were still enough of us left to continue the party back at the flat. So we sang our goodbyes to all and sundry, and off we went into the night. It had just started to snow when we got outside, so we all bundled together, and arm-in-arm we marched up the road singing "Let's All Go Down the Strand," with lots of the 'hava-banana' chorus thrown in for good measure.

We'd just about put all the lights on and taken our coats off, when we heard Vi shriek. And she came running out of the lavatory so fast, I thought she must've seen a mouse or something. But she screeched again that she'd left her handbag under her chair back at the pub and started for the stairs. I shouted that I'd go and get it for her, but she yelled back, she wasn't having any of that. Joanie at least stopped her long enough to get her to put something warm on. "Here, Vi," she said, "slip my coat and scarf on quick, love, otherwise you'll catch your death out there, you will." Then Joanie turned to me with a sideways nod and a look in her eyes that said, 'Jethro, you better go with her.' But I was already slipping my coat back on and slipping down the stairs after her.

She'd gone by the time I got down to the front door; she hadn't even closed it. But that's women for you when they're separated from their handbags, they'll let nothing stop them or get in their way. I looked up and down the street, deserted now of stalls and barrows but for a few skeletal, metal frames left standing all skew-whiff like a kid's forgotten Meccano set. There was a line of parked cars and vans, and a lorry or two, but I couldn't see much, as the lamp-posts only shed enough light to show that the snow was getting worse. The flakes big enough now for you to make out the specks of soot in them. Then I blinked and caught sight of Vi beetling along the pavement, her little legs going like the clappers. She dodged in front of a lorry and I set off after her at the run.

I heard a car motor rev up and something big and black slid past gaining speed, but I still didn't give it much thought even though it didn't have its headlamps on, only its side lights. It was cold and I'd had a few drinks inside me, and perhaps I wasn't as quick as I might have been, but something suddenly clicked and my blood ran colder, and I found I was running and yelling like a madman. It was one of Messima's Yank tanks, the big Ford V8, the same one I'd had my own run-in with that night outside the Palladium. I threw quick looks to the left and the right to see if there were any tearaways waiting in the dark to jump out at me, but the shadows didn't move, they just hung there like so many tightly closed curtains. I'd known the street for most of my life, but that night it was like nothing I'd ever felt before, it was cold and pitiless, and worse, indifferent. I blinked the snow from my eyes and balled my hands tightly into fists in a pathetic attempt to run faster.

Vi was halfway up the street, making a bee-line for the pub, her mad idea of a short cut. The car sped up, its powerful twin beams suddenly ripping back the curtain of night and spotlighting Vi in their cruel glare. Vi turned and froze, and stood there in the middle of the street as still and as stiff as a Madame Tussaud's waxwork dummy; a dead ringer for Joanie. My heart stopped and all my blood froze, and at that moment someone stepped out from behind a parked car and rushed at her, an arm swept back ready to strike. Vi screeched in terror.

"Oh, Christ," I yelled. "Oh, Jesus aitch Christ no." I tried to run faster, my shoes sticking and slipping in the heavy carpet of snow, but it was no use, it was as if everything was happening in slow motion. Vi staggered about in the middle of the road with her hands locked to her face, and just as I managed to shout her name out, the car hit her. I couldn't see it. I could only see its red brake-lights turning everything in front of me bright red as it skidded down the street. And then the world burst into a thousand shifting shards of piercing light as my blood pumped and coursed through my body forcing tears up into my eyes. "Oh, dear God no. Not Vi, not our Vi."

The car must've sent her body flying along the road, because as it sped off up the street, both its near side front and rear wheels drove over her. I heard the awful thumps and the twanging of the big suspension springs, each time the car went up and down. I can still hear them, and the ghostly echo of her attacker's running feet disappearing off into the distance, before the car screeched to a halt so he could jump onto the running board and clamber back inside.

When I got to her she was a little broken doll of a thing lying spread-eagled in the street; her blood black against the snow, her legs and arms all askew, one pathetic hand crushed to no more than bone and paste. Her face was a mess of bubbles of blood, her eyes still wide with surprise, her glasses—the big blue ones she'd worn because she'd thought they made her look like Joanie—broken and smashed. Her blonde hair, freed forever from the confines of her scarf, pulled and curled with the wind. I knelt down in the mud and the slush and the blood as the snow settled on us both like ashes, and my breath steamed in the cold night air like something newly come from hell.

They'd thrown acid in her face, an old ponce's trick, like shredding a girl's face with a razor or setting fire to her hair. Vi's glasses had saved her eyes, but it was the horrible burns to her skin and the shock of it all that would've done it, she'd probably been blinded with the hurt and staggered right into the path of the car. It's likely that they hadn't meant to knock her down, they'd probably wanted to hurt her—or their intended victim, Joanie—just enough to bring me into line. How little they knew about me; a single damaged hair on her head was enough for me to want to kill them. And that was inevitable now, Chalkie White was a dead man, and so was anyone else who'd been with him in the car.

I heard someone shouting, then someone else, then there were people crowding round and voices yelling for someone to call for an ambulance. I cradled her head. Her eyelids fluttered and her eyes opened and a dim light came on inside them like a sputtering candle on a tiny Christmas tree. "Me handbag, Jeffro, I can't lose me handbag...it's all I got in the world...for Rose's Christmas present..."

She drifted a bit, I patted her shoulder and gently rocked her back and forth, my voice as soothing as ever I'd heard it. "Don't you worry none, Vi. I'll pop in and get it back for you in a tick. We'll just hang on here until the ambulance comes; you seem to have taken a nasty fall."

"Ta, Jeffro," she whispered, "you've always been such a good boy."

"And you've always been my secret love, Vi."

Her lips tried to pull themselves into a thin little smile, but it was broken apart by a cough that started at the back of her throat and erupted in a little trickle of blood that slid like an impatient snake down her chin onto the collar of her coat.

"Gertcha, yer bugger," she said. And then she died.

I don't know how long I sat in the street cradling her head, but when the ambulance came they had to pry my hands from her. Someone made a comment about rigor mortis already having set in; I'd have thumped the shit out of him if I could've seen who it was. Barry and Joanie had arrived, I could hear them, and so had the rest of the people at the party; someone must've run up the street to tell them, bad news travels fast in our part of the world.

"Come on, Jethro, love. You done your best, they've got her now. Barry will go along to see where they take her. You just come on home now." It was Joanie, her voice warping in and out of my mind like a warning bell on a buoy in a thick sea fog. I turned slowly and drifted towards the sound, then bobbed up and down until someone thrust a glass of something into my hands. A hand helped bring it up to my lips, and brandy coursed down into me and spread like fire, searching everywhere for the chill. And then it met with the fire that'd begun to smoulder and burn inside me, and then it was as if the Blitz really was come again.

"Excuse me, sir—oh, it's you, Jethro—sorry about the old girl, she was a right character she was, a good 'un. But a few words is all, just for the accident report. The rest can wait till the morning." It was the local beat copper, PC Bob Dilley, a decent enough bloke as coppers go and liked by nearly everyone in the market; well, as much as anyone can like any copper, that is.

He touched the peak of his helmet to Joanie. "Evening, Mrs. Aitch, sorry about all this. Dreadful business, it is. Here look, why don't we all step into the warm inside the pub and you can tell me what happened."

My head cleared a bit after they sat me down, and slowly the red started to drain away from behind my eyes. PC Dilley, a steaming mug of something in his hand, did his best to speak as quietly and as gently as he could to everyone, but it still felt like an invasion. "Did you see anything, Jethro, anything at all? The make of car? Licence-plate number? Only the poor old girl's dead and it looks like she never had a chance. These hit-and-run drivers are the worst, the very worst."

I shook my head and mumbled, but mainly tried to keep from shouting out Chalkie's name and how I was going to kill the bastard for what he'd done. I couldn't really tell him what I'd seen, could I? It would've got in the way of an intended murder, and you can't have that now, can you? Good copper or bad copper, they all get a bit testy over something like that. So, in the end, I told him what I could; big black car, bloke in a black hat and trench coat, but couldn't make out his face. And nothing about them really being after Joanie. He wrote it all down in his little black book, all the time shaking his head and muttering to himself. Then he put his cape and his helmet back on, tipped his hand to its peak again, and was gone into the night. I was stone-cold sober by then, we all were, although if you'd lit a match anywhere near me I'd have gone up in flames. But it's when the fire raging inside you freezes and becomes ice that some real nasty damage can occur. And I know of what I speak.

Joanie put Vi's handbag on the kitchen table and stared at it. It looked pathetic under the ceiling lamp; it didn't even cast a shadow. And Joanie just stood there and shivered with her arms wrapped round herself as if she was holding on for dear life. She was devastated, and I went over and hugged her and let her cry it out, and after a couple of minutes she nodded and disappeared off into her bedroom. I put the kettle on and made some tea and took it in to her. When she came out later she said she couldn't spend her time feeling sorry for herself and that someone had to start thinking about what was to be done with Vi's little girl, Rosie. And she phoned Pauline and Mavis and they came over, and between all the tears they began to work something out. Rosie would be told in the morning, and then somehow she'd have to be looked after for the rest of her days.

When Barry got back from the hospital he was ashen faced, but a rock nevertheless. Once Vi had been pronounced dead, Barry had officially identified her, then she'd been wheeled away to the morgue for the mandatory post-mortem and coroner's report; all the paraphernalia of unexpected and violent death. It's funny, but it's always the quiet ones that surprise you in times of crisis, and that time it was Barry, a beacon of safety in the storm, sorting stuff out, gathering people quietly to him, settling them down and doing whatever he could to ease their pain, me included. And all the time holding his own grief in check, until later that is, when he thought he was alone and he bawled his eyes out. I saw the tears go from sorrow to rage, then to cold fury. Then he became like me; a gun, a knife, a hammer; a bullet with someone's name scratched upon it.

He looked up wiping the last tear from his eye, his lips pressed together to lock away any change of heart. He nodded and said, "Was it Joanie they were after on account of you?"

I nodded and said, "I'm sure of it, Bubs. It was Messima's motor, but it's not really his style; as evil as he is, he never likes involving members of the public if he can help it. I don't know who the bloke with the acid was, but I'm sure it was Chalkie driving the car, and I'll find them both soon enough."

"Not without me, you won't," he said flatly, and looking at his face I certainly wasn't going to argue with him. "Let's let the ladies get off to bed," he whispered hoarsely, "and then it's you and me off out."

"Right," I said, "I've already packed for the both of us."

Chapter 24

BOXING THE CLUBS

I had the Webley .455 pistol—the 'Bulldog' with the four-inch snub barrel—wrapped in a fold of chamois leather in the pocket of my overcoat, and I had my Fairbairn-Sykes strapped in a sheath across my back. My two sawn-off shotguns—oiled, loaded, and ready for business—were in the kitbag hidden under the back seat in Barry's cab. I'd even put in a couple of garden spades rolled up in a length of oilcloth; well, it's only proper to clean your mess up once you make it, if you catch my drift. There was no alternative to us carrying hardware, even though the Old Bill was coming down extra hard on anyone with a shooter since a bunch of amateur tearaways had bungled a job of robbing a jeweller's shop in Charlotte Street, early that May. A passing motorcyclist had decided to have a go at them on the spur of the moment, and they'd put a bullet in his skull. The death of Alec de Antiquis put the whole country in an uproar, and photos of the poor sod bleeding to death in the gutter were wired all round the world. The newspapers went on and on about it for weeks and questions were asked in Parliament, and the authorities used the public outcry to try and get all the guns that had flooded into Britain after the war off the streets and out of circulation. The police, never ones to miss an opportunity, simply took it as a licence to crack down hard on any villain that crossed their path.

Barry sat up front in his driver's cab and I rode in the back like a regular fare, which was good in a way, because neither one of us felt very much like talking, and we both drifted off into our own little worlds. It had turned into another bitterly cold night, and even the snow had gone off to find some place warmer. But I took no comfort in that. And as the sound of the cab's tyres cut through the slush on the roads, they kept whispering the words "slash him and slay him" in my ears, like some Greek chorus that'd got lost on their way to the Old Vic.

I shivered inside my coat and yelled for Barry to put the heater up, and he just yelled back that it was going full blast as it was. So I just shrugged, and warmed myself by gripping the 'Bulldog' even tighter and pushing myself back into the seat so I could feel the Fairbairn-Sykes between my shoulder blades. Then I thought better of it and rolled down the window and let the bitter cold air sharpen my wits. And as each breath steamed out in front of me, only to be greedily sucked out through the opening, I found I took repeated pleasure in drawing the knife-like cold back and forth across the whetstone of my lungs. And as I honed my resolve to kill Chalkie White for what he'd done to Vi, and for what he'd tried to do to Joanie, we rattled on through the night towards the harsh, glittery neon lights of Soho.

There were hundreds of clubs, catering to all fancies, tastes, and perversions in and around the square mile of London's West End. They stretched from the badly lit alley-ways of Mayfair's Shepherd's Market, up through the lights of Curzon Street and Bond Street, and across Regent Street to the rabbit warren of dark, narrow streets and even darker alleyways of Soho. And if you'd walked down Wardour Street, Greek Street, or Dean Street, almost any doorway you fell into that wasn't a pub or a restaurant would've been a club or a spieler. Most were registered, but there was always a good few that weren't, and the sumptuous stood right alongside the seedy. Some, like the Embassy Club, the 400 Club, and the Club Panama were palaces, where any night of the week you could see the champagne and orchids set at play. And along with other top spots, like Moody's, Churchill's, and La Rue's, they might look down their noses at the Shim-Sham Club, the Big Apple, or the Twilight Club, but they were all in the same business of removing a punter from his hard-earned money in the shortest possible time.

We scoured the manor from top to bottom; the dinner clubs, the drinking clubs, the gambling clubs—the spielers—and the dives. We even did the penny arcades. I did it methodically; boxing first one area, then the next, just like I'd seen the Flower-class corvettes doing time and again when they'd escorted the merchant convoys. I'd yell out the name of a place, and Barry would have us there in two flicks of a rat's tail. Then I'd jump out and drop a whisper here or a word there, a oncer here, a half-a-bar there, and always with the same question, "Have you seen Chalkie White? Only I'm looking for him."

So I spoke to doormen in smart uniforms and minders in badly pressed suits. I ear-holed barmen, bruisers, and about ten million brasses. I sidled up to hat-check girls and cocktail waitresses wearing little more than pencil heels and a smile. I also stopped by that big, posh hotel just off Piccadilly Circus, the one with the all-night tea-room down in the basement. Not that too many people knew it was also the unofficial employment exchange for all of London's out-of-work villains, but that's why it was always so crowded. The hotel management put it all down to the quality of the tea and cakes, but everyone that had to bend the rules for a living knew differently. Yet, that night, nobody there claimed to have seen Chalkie White, or had any idea of his whereabouts.

While I'd been throwing money around Soho like a drunken sailor, and getting a nasty frog in my throat from all the talking, Barry had been doing his bit as well. He'd kept the meter running whenever he'd stopped, so punters would think he was waiting on his fare and leave him be. Then whenever he saw another taxi going by, he'd flash his headlights or slap the side of his cab to flag them down, and lean out his window and give them the word on Chalkie. It was a kind of jungle drums that the brotherhood of cabbies had, and with all those extra pairs of eyes and ears roaming round the streets I'd known it to work wonders. But that night it was as if everyone had had their blinders on, and no one, nobody, had seen, or heard anything.

Most people wouldn't have told us anything anyway, even if they did have some idea where Chalkie was hiding. The rule of the street was simple. You didn't open your trap to anyone, unless you'd first squared it away with whichever villain it was had your balls in his wringer. You gave him the little titbit of news first, or got striped across your mouth for your trouble. It was like a dog carrying a dead bird back to its owner. But I didn't mind, and the truth was I was counting on the whole lot of them to grass me up. I wanted the word out everywhere, and fast. Because as any poacher or gamekeeper will tell you, sometimes the only way to bag your prey is to beat the bushes, and then just sit back quietly with a gun cradled in your arm to wait for your bird to take flight.

Our last port of call was an after-hours drinking club round the back of Charing Cross Road, not far from Seven Dials, owned by a coloured bloke called Frisco. It was known to those in the know as the No-Name Club and favoured by people on the edges of the theatre world as well as members of the criminal fraternity, always a potent mix in London. It was also just off the edge of Messima's manor, and so was widely accepted by all and sundry as the beginning of no-man's-land, which meant that tearaways and villains alike, and even the odd copper, could use it as a watering hole without having to go mob-handed.

After all the running round we'd done, I could tell Barry could do with giving his hands a rest, as he'd been twisting them back and forth on the steering wheel all night, dreaming of having them around Chalkie White's neck, I shouldn't wonder. I couldn't blame him for that, but I had to watch out for the both of us, and Barry tended to run hot and I needed him to stay sharp. After all, we had the whole night ahead of us yet, and I reckoned that the No-Name would help us kill two birds with one stone. It was the perfect place to lose ourselves in, and yet if anyone was interested, it was the proper place to find us. And even if Mr. Messima himself wanted to discuss the matter, he only had to walk down Old Compton Street. And it wouldn't have taken him more than five minutes to do it, even if he'd stopped on the way for a threepenny hot dog or tuppenny shoeshine.

I was out by a little over fifteen minutes, but he didn't come himself, he sent two of his best bruisers to talk to me instead. I clocked them as soon as they walked in, even in the dim light and even before the bald-headed barman had had time to slide his raised eyebrows in my direction. By the look on their faces they'd come to take my chestnuts out of the fire and probably feed them to me as well. I'd last seen them in Messima's office when they'd all but thrown me down the stairs and dumped me in the little yard out the back. The cold must've got to them on the walk over, because they both looked pinched and irritable, as if they'd been trying to remember exactly what their boss had told them to say—Messima being such a stickler for words. Either that, or they'd been forced to miss some riveting discussion back at the club as to whether the rumours of Al Capone's death were true or not.

They could've been twins, and they were dressed as much for the occasion as the weather. They wore nice black hats, overcoats, and lace-up shoes fresh from the shop, and both sported natty silk paisley scarves with tassels. They had that cocky pride about them that said that clothing coupons and the expense could just go hang, and it was obvious they both thought they looked really splendid. You just knew that walking past a shop window without them sneaking a peek at themselves would've been a real trial.

At any other time I might've complimented them on their tailor, he'd done a nice job hiding the bulges under their left arms, but it was best we all get down to business. I smiled, which confused them all the more, and said it was very plain that Messima was going in for a better class of help these days, and how very smart they both looked. It stopped them dead about a coffin's length from the edge of my table, and I could see by the look on their faces that they didn't quite know how to take my remark. So, I threw them another smile. And as soon as they clocked the tip of the little snub-nosed Webley barrel pointing directly up at them, from out of the folds of the *Evening News* that was laying on my lap, they got the point and began to act as smart as they looked.

"Hello, lads, nice weather we're having for this time of the year. Fancy a drink, to warm yourselves up?"

They stood, trying to think on their feet, but it was too hard for them, so to put us all out of miseries, I nodded to the barman who was doing his best, just like all the rest of the club's patrons, not to look in our direction. I tried to do the sideways thing with my raised eyebrows, not expecting any result, but it must've worked, because the barman was over with two whiskies balanced on a tin tray faster than you could spit.

"Put it on the slate," I said. "These gentlemen are old friends."

Tweedledee and Tweedledum sat down slowly, and everyone breathed a sigh of relief, because no blood or alcohol was going to get spilt yet; the clientele hated anything that got in the way of precious drinking time.

And the club gradually returned to normal, even though all eyes and ears were on full alert for trouble. Tweedledee spoke first.

"The blower's been ringing off the 'ook and Mister M. says he can't keep his mind on his business with all this palaver going on. He says it's been very aggravatin'."

"Very aggravatin'," piped in the other one in a surprisingly soft voice. He looked uncomfortable and off balance on his chair, but nothing that leaning heavily on me couldn't put right.

"So, Mister M. was thinking you should come and have a chat with him personally, seeing as it seems you've got a beef of some sort with Mister White."

"No, thanks, lads, I've business to finish tonight. No offence to Mr. Messima, but it's not convenient, I've got other plans."

They looked at one another, and then down at the 'Bulldog' sitting on my lap, and for the briefest of moments the brims of their hats hid both sets of eyes. Then everything stopped. It was like staring at the sweep hand on a watch, there's that split second when you think time itself has stopped, but of course, it never has. And neither had they, their heads slowly bobbed back up in unison, and I found myself marvelling at the precision of it; even the chorus girls at the Palladium couldn't have done any better. Their faces were expressionless, but I knew their brains were working overtime, and if there was going to be any nonsense, I knew it'd start happening soon.

"Mister M. said you might say that." It was Tweedledee again. "So, he's askin' as a favour, that you leave it out and not go round stirring things up. He's got important business going on hisself at the moment, and doesn't need the filth gonging around the place poking their noses into everything. That'd be doubly aggravatin', he says."

"Doubly aggravatin'." It was Tweedledum doing his impression of an echo.

"I can't help him, lads," I said, trying to sound as reasonable as I could. "Chalkie White was totally out of order tonight, and I'm sure Mr. Messima would understand if he knew everything that's gone down. So I've got no choice in the matter, really I haven't."

There was a slight noise off to their right and I think that was when they first clocked Barry, which was quite careless of them really. He was sitting in shadow two tables down, quietly nursing his drink, and what little light there was, had caught his face and made it look strangely un-settling. He was staring at them with a dead look in his eyes, that said, 'If I've got to do someone tonight, then it might as well be one of you.' Most tearaways learn to be a bit wary of the quiet little blokes that won't back off at the first sign of bother, because they can often turn out to be big trouble. There was also the little matter of the folded-up newspaper on the table in front of him. It must've given the two likely lads some food for thought, because seen from out of the corner of their eyes, it looked not unlike the business end of a revolver, and quite deadly. Though only Barry and I knew it contained nothing more than a short length of lead pipe, the cosh of choice amongst cabbies everywhere.

Tweedledum looked at me. "Well, we don't know nuffink about that, but Mister M. did say he heard a whisper about some sort of bother round your neck of the woods earlier this evening, and he promises to look into it. But the 'fing is, if what you say is kosher, and Mister White's gone and done anything out of order, then Mister M. will want to take care of it in his own time and in his own way."

I nodded, but I was beginning to get impatient with all the talking, and I guessed it must be wearing pretty thin on them, too. Something had to give and soon, otherwise we'd be there all night. So I gave it the nudge, while I still had the upper hand.

"Afraid I can't help you, lads, as much as I'd like to; it's family now, not business. So, finish your drinks, why don't you, and then just toddle off out of it. Please be sure to give Mr. Messima my respects."

Tweedledum began to reach into his inside coat pocket.

"I don't think so," I said, my smile sticking to my teeth. The Webley came up as quick as an erection at a blue movie, but he just shook his head and said, "No, Jeffro, nothing like that, no shooters, not here. Straight up." His voice was still all soft, but now it had a funny rasp to it, and it hit me then, he sounded just like Peter Lorre. I almost laughed, because he looked more like Sydney Greenstreet's ugly brother. I tell you, those old gangster pictures had a lot to answer for.

"Hold your horses, Jeffro, hold your horses. Mister M. said you might not go for it, so he gave us this to give to you." He held out a picture postcard of Piccadilly Circus. It had been carefully folded over in two, so as to cover over the writing on the back. As he leaned forward, his twin held up flat, empty hands for me to see how trustworthy and honest he was. I don't know if they expected me to fall for the old trick of him dropping the card, just as I was reaching for it, but the whole thing had all the hallmarks of a well-rehearsed move. I leaned back and cocked the Bulldog instead. It seemed to have the desired effect, but it must've dampened their spirits a bit, because they both suddenly looked as if I'd peed down their legs.

"Hand the postcard sideways and put it on that next table." I did the sideways-nod-of-the-head thing again, and indicated the table in front of Barry. "Then sit up straight and behave yourselves or I'll blow your fucking heads off." They each did as they were told then, but they both looked quite put out that I hadn't been prepared to trust them. Barry got up and reached forward for the postcard, his other hand still on the phantom gun hidden in the folds of his copy of *The Star*.

"It's the name of a club over towards the East End that might be of interest to you," Tweedledum whispered.

"Yeah, it's Jack Spot's place on St. Bartolph's Lane," Tweedledee added like an echo in a pub toilet.

"Bubs?"

"That's right, Jeffro, the name of the club's written on the back, and there's a big letter *M* scrawled underneath it."

"Mister M. wrote that hisself," one of them said. "He says that's where you can find Chalkie, er, excuse me, I mean Mister White."

"But he also says you never heard it from him," said the other.

"Got it?" they chorused, narrowing their eyes in perfect time with one another. I marvelled again, at what the underworld was coming to. They must've practised that act in front of the mirror for hours. I'm sure it impressed the shit out of most of the old ladies of Soho and Fitzrovia, but it was a complete waste of time on me. They were big buggers, but I was finding them about as threatening as the guardsmen clomping up and down outside Buckingham Palace.

"Got it," I said, but I'd already forgotten Messima's two toy soldiers, because my eyes were suddenly pulled towards a disturbance in the curtain by the door. The whole place clenched its collective sphincter again, and for good reason. Two large shapes in overcoats and hats appeared out of the gloom. If it was a deputation of faces from one of the other London gangs, then things were about to get interesting. One of the Tweedles looked round, while the other kept his eyes fixed firmly on me. Though a quick word out of the corner of his partner's mouth soon worked wonders for his demeanour. And suddenly, he was all smiles.

"Well, nice chatting to you, old cock, but we really must be going," he said brightly.

They stood up, downed their whiskies in one, then as nonchalantly as they could, they both banged their glasses down onto the table. I felt almost moved to tears; if they could dance even half as well together, they had a definite future on the stage.

I looked towards the door where one of the newly arrived shapes stood doing a passable impersonation of the Rock of Gibraltar. Then, as I and everyone else in the place watched, fascinated, it detached itself from the shadows and headed straight towards us.

"You two scumbags piss off out of it." A big, brown leather-clad thumb jerked back towards the entrance-way and then a forefinger the size of a Polish sausage shot forward and pointed directly at me, just as I was in the process of getting to my feet. "And you just sit it and shut it, I've got business with you." He didn't raise his voice, he didn't need to; even though it had the rasp of a rusty razor, it cut right through all the noise and smoke, and stilled the club to silence.

"We were just leavin'," one of the Tweedles ventured; quite bravely, I thought, under the circumstances.

"Now isn't soon enough," the big man in the big brown hat said without even looking at them. And the twins slowly edged past him, pressing themselves hard against walls, tables, and chairs. You could almost see them deflating like a pair of punctured barrage balloons.

I knew who the bugger was the moment his shadow fell across me, and so had Messima's two goons. He sat down, but didn't remove his hat. He sniffed at a mug of something that was put down very carefully on the table in front of him. I hadn't signalled for anything, so I guessed he must've ordered it when he'd come in. It was the on-duty copper's favourite nightcap; steaming coffee with something stronger swirling round inside it. Well, it was cold outside, so I couldn't fault him for that, in a way it almost made the bastard seem human.

I'd already slipped the Webley—still wrapped in the *Evening News*—down between my legs and onto the floor, and kicked the whole lot behind me as I'd scraped back my chair and pretended to get to my feet. I just crossed my fingers and hoped the gun had slid out of sight under one of the other tables. I nodded dumbly, stuck a bored look on my face, and chanced a quick glance in Barry's direction. He was still sitting a few tables away, minding his own business, and looking as if he didn't have a care in the world. I noticed his paper had also disappeared from off the table. With the very slightest wrinkling of his nose, he reached for his glass, and that was when he caught the copper's eye.

"Oi, you, hop it." Barry looked up to see the leather-gloved finger pointing at him, but knowing his face meant nothing at all to the copper, he played it as well as Johnny Gielgud ever could have done, and with the merest raise of an eyebrow he stood up and shuffled off the stage. I watched him go, but continued looking round so as not to give anything away. Everyone had the same nonchalant look stuck on their faces, and everyone seemed to be doing everything they could not to notice me or my new visitor. It also looked as if most of the regulars were busy finishing their drinks, having suddenly all remembered they had urgent appointments elsewhere. The bloke was already doing awful things to the night's takings. I hated to think what he had in mind for me. I didn't have to wait long to find out.

"Browno, Detective Chief Inspector, Scotland Yard."

So this was official. I had wondered, because I had heard those things about him doing extra work outside office hours. He flashed his warrant card, but it could've been his membership credentials for the West Ham branch of the Communist Party for all I could tell.

"A quiet word with you, sunshine. But first things first. Are you carrying, only I heard you were going around all tooled up like a tart with a brick in her handbag?"

"No," I said, spreading my arms out wide, but I think the symbolism was lost on him. "You can search me if you want."

He just stared. "Shut it, smart arse, and wipe that look off your face. You better not be carrying, now or ever, or I'll have your balls locked up so fast there won't be time enough for your eyes to water."

I could tell it was going to be one of those one-way conversations, so

I got all my yes-sirs, no-sirs, and three-bags-full-sirs in order, and tried to get a handle on what was going on. Browno was busy snorting and stomping the ground looking for all the world as if he was getting ready to charge, but just as had happened when Browno had turned Ray's place over, I got the strangest feeling he was really only going through the motions. It was flattering in a way, him going on like he was, even if it was only for the sake of the other customers. But if he felt it necessary to put on a play for all of the No-Name's regular villains, faces, narks, grasses, and Ghost Squad coppers in disguise, then who was I to argue. It was already very obvious to me, having met the bloke, that if he'd wanted to beat me up, fit me up, run me in, or kill me, he would've done and could've done without so much as batting an eyelid.

"Listen, scumbag, I've been hearing things about you running round looking to top someone. I don't know if that's true or not, but I tell you, that's definitely not on, not now, not ever. But you've popped up on my radar now and that means you're a marked man. The whisper is you're a right villain, even if no one can prove it yet. But personally I don't give a tinker's cuss how clean your record is, I just know you're dodgy, and you need watching. And there's nothing better I'd like to do than run your arse inside now and throw the fucking keys in the river."

After that stunning opening speech he quietened down so only I could hear. "But as I've got a red card on you, so you're to be left alone for the time being. Now I don't know why that is, or who's involved, and it's not my job to know so I don't fucking care. But what I do know is this, if you even fart out of tune in anyone's direction I'll smell it, and then I'll ram a truncheon up your arse so hard, your nose will bleed."

Browno had such a colourful way with words it took me a minute or two to get the hidden message. The shock was in realising it wasn't a warning he was delivering, it was my third-party life insurance policy. So Ray had been right all along, someone was pulling Browno's strings, and that someone with all the pull just had to be Walsingham. I mean, who else could it be? And a red card? I didn't know what that was when it was at home, but fuck me, if it meant I was to be handled with kid gloves, I was all for it. I really didn't know whether to laugh or cry, or look relieved. I think I just about managed to keep a straight face. But don't get me wrong, I didn't think for one moment that Browno wasn't deadly dangerous, he still had the word 'lethal' stamped all over him like postmarks on a parcel.

After a bit more theatrical bellowing that would've done Donald Wolfit proud, Browno pushed his finger in my face and gave me a very loud, final warning. Then he finished off the rest of his drink in one gulp and stood up, deliberately knocking over his chair. I heard something splinter and was just glad it wasn't me. Browno didn't bother to pick up the chair, he just stormed off through the club and threw aside the heavy curtain at the door with an irritated flourish. Then he stepped out into the night, his Detective Sergeant following silently in his wake. Browno didn't reappear to give a final curtain speech, but it was such a dramatic exit he really didn't need to.

I sat there not moving for a moment, and calmly finished my drink; well, if it was theatre that was called for, two could play at that game, and me, I'd learnt from the best. I stood up and made a show of looking for my overcoat. I turned this way and that, loudly scraped a few chairs and tables back and forth, and then slowly and deliberately picked up the coat and buttoned it up, the Webley now safely tucked away in one of the pockets.

"What a bleedin' liberty," I said loudly to no one in particular, "you come in for a quiet drink and all you get is some bleeder from that thievin' lot down the Yard, coming round and asking for a donation. It's getting so you can't get drunk in peace and quiet anymore. Well, sod it, I've had enough of this, I'm off home."

As I left, I gave a nod to the bald-headed geezer behind the bar, and he breathed a sigh of relief and rolled his eyes in reply. And Barry had the cab well on the way to the East End before I'd realised I hadn't paid for any of the drinks. Though knowing Frisco as I did, once he'd heard about what had gone on in his club, everything would go down on my slate anyway, even the cost of a new, second-hand chair.

I looked out the window at the cold, hard streets sliding by, and settled back into the seat and tried to get myself warm.

Chapter 25

A COLD NIGHT IN HELL

East is east and west is west, but the one place you could meet without too much of the wrong blood being spilt was the Saint Bartolph's Club. A gambling club owned by a well-respected villain by the name of Jack Spot, it was hidden away in a lane of the same name just beyond the far edge of the City and the start of the East End proper. Jack's usual manor was over by where I lived, the Edgware Road, Paddington, and Marble Arch area, but he carried a lot of clout almost everywhere in London, north of the river. (More about Jack later.)

With Messima's postcard held tightly between my turtles we'd winged our way eastwards, sailing through every traffic light as if the gods themselves had had a hand in it all. It was Barry really, he'd taken one of those so-called blue-light routes that all the ambulance, fire-engine, and police-car drivers are taught to use, so they can avoid as many potential traffic bottlenecks as possible. Cabbies learn the routes when they do the Knowledge. Anyway, that night it seemed as if something was giving me the green light, because I could feel the old magic cloak of time-slowing-down settling around my shoulders, even as the cold, dark, and deserted city streets flew by. I was fire. I was ice. I was a flaming arrow of retribution. I was Jethro the Terrible.

I could taste it, I really could. The plan was to lift Chalkie and take him out to Hackney Marshes and bury him; whether he'd still be alive when I shovelled the earth on top of him was a moot point. It depended on what condition he was in once he'd finished digging his own grave.

I wanted to make a quick getaway once I'd dragged Chalkie out of the club with my pistol pressed hard against his kidneys, so I left Barry sitting in his cab with one of the sawn-offs down by his side. And if there was to be any trouble, I reckoned Barry and me approaching it from two directions at once could get it sorted out, dead quick. We'd both already crossed the line anyway, there was no room for remorse or second thoughts; the only thing that remained to be done now was the deed itself. And if any of the club's workmen, or any other tearaways that were hanging around, wanted to accompany Chalkie on his trip to hell, then they could get themselves buried right alongside him and I'd be only too happy to oblige. I had the 'Bulldog' in my pocket and my sawn-off hanging down on a rope lanyard inside my overcoat. The side-by-side felt cold to the touch even through my turtles, but I was nevertheless nicely warmed by its presence. I sniffed the night air.

The club didn't need to advertise its whereabouts, you either knew about it or you didn't. It was on the first floor over a parade of shops, most of them long since boarded up, and the big laugh was that at one time the place had been headquarters for the local temperance society. The light from the street lamps was pitiful, but I could see a few cars parked along the street, as well as one or two three-ton Bedford lorries in a nearby side-street. Most of them had a crust of snow on top, but there were a few, newly parked ones, that didn't. If it hadn't been such a bitterly cold night, there would've been someone standing sentry outside. But as it was, I was free to push open the outer door and make my way up the short flight of stairs to the entrance proper; a little vestibule where they checked your membership card and took your hat and coat and gun before they took all your money.

Red-painted light bulbs and walls seemed to be someone's idea of the very latest thing in decor, but I didn't reckon it myself, it was too much like being in the middle of someone else's nightmare.

"Hello, Jeffro. I heard you were tooling around up West. Long time no see, but all the same I'm a bit surprised to see you out this far east. What can I do for you, sunshine?"

It was Tommy Nutkins, an old friend from way back. He was by himself. I'd heard he was working as one of Jack Spot's minders, but our paths hadn't crossed in some time. Even done up in a sharp suit and tie he looked like he was ready to go ten rounds with all comers.

"Wotcher, Tommy," I said, "fancy seeing you here. I want inside, is all."

"Sorry, old son, can't let you in; boss's orders. But, look'it, Jeffro, Chalkie White's not inside. We 'aint seen hide nor hair of him, neither."

I don't know what the hell we both must've looked like bathed in all that red light in that little hallway, but I remember thinking that at least they wouldn't have too much trouble dealing with all the blood stains afterwards. I think Tommy saw the flat look in my eyes, because he stepped from behind a black-painted table and moved towards me with a grim smile on his face. "Look'it, Jeffro, we don't need no trouble you and me, Chalkie's not worth it. He 'aint been seen round here in the last couple a weeks, and the last we heard of him he'd had a bit of a barney with some mob from south of the water." His face cracked open then; he always had a grand smile, did Tommy. "At least that's what we heard, but straight up, Jeffro, he's not in here. Pity, really, because he throws his money round like a legless sailor, if he's got people wiv' him he's trying to impress."

He was a big bloke and I knew he could be fast on his feet, but he stood there, unmoving. I blinked very slowly. Behind him were double doors into the club, and behind me the flight of stairs down to the street. Not exactly the best place for a no-holds-barred punch-up. Or a point-blank shoot-out. But it was all there was, and suddenly I didn't feel that choosy about when and where I was going to die.

We stood there like a couple of bad guys in one of those Hollywood cowboy pictures, him at one end of the street, and me at the other. I knew he had to be carrying, and he'd been told I was. He was an old friend, but my business with Chalkie was family business, and that put everyone else on the other side of the line, no exceptions. But there was Tommy standing large as life in front of me. Fuck it. Fuck it. I stood there and the red all around me just got redder, and all I could see was the image of Vi's head pooled in blood and all I could hear was the blood coursing through my ears like a mill race. For the second time that night it could all go off at any moment, and time was running out like blood from a slit throat. Vi spoke, but it was with Tommy's voice, and then I saw and heard it was really Tommy that was speaking, and then Vi faded away and was gone into the blood-red shadows on the wall.

" 'Ere, Jeffro, who told you he was here anyway? 'Cos I reckon you've been stitched up, my old son, and that doesn't sound too much like you, does it?"

And then it was happening again, his voice warping like a warning bell adrift in a thick sea fog, only all I could see was sea and waves as big as houses and everything was blood-red and it was cold and I was burning, I was burning. And there was Tommy, barely afloat, barely alive, the oil and the blood running in black rivers down and around his head each time he came back up for air.

"Jeffro, Jeffro, my old son. Come on, mate, we don't need any of this. Jeffro, look at me, it's Tommy. I'm here, you're here, we're both here, we made it and hundreds and thousands of other poor buggers didn't. I'll bell you, Jeffro, if I hear anything, I promise I will. But leave it out for tonight, old son, it 'aint worth the candle, whatever it's for. It's not me you want to top, that's for certain, and I sure as hell don't want to top you. Jeffro? Jeffro?"

Time had stopped. Not at all like the slowing down it did when I was on a caper, it just stopped dead. Perhaps it was for no more than two or three ticks of a clock, but it stopped all the same. Fuck it. Fuck it. A war was going on inside me and I didn't know who was winning, or which side I was on. Fuck it. In the arse-end of the city, in the arse-end of the night, my past had come back to warn me, reason with me, and it was there now standing in front of me like Marley's Ghost, all done up and ready for the funeral parlour.

Tommy had been a dead 'un once, a goner, and I'd saved him. His time was up, and I'd squeezed and pumped the fuel-oil-scummed water from out of his lungs and kept him coughing, kept him living. Did that now give me the right to chuck it all back and leave him dying in a pool of blood on some poxy club floor, in the depths of the night? Or did it mean he was free to kill me and put the tally of the dead back to rights?

As I said, Tommy and me went way back. I'd known him on the boats before the war, and later we'd even been on some of the same troopships working the Atlantic convoys. We'd both been dead lucky and come through again and again until the hell that someone named 'Bomb Alley.' Tommy had been one of the blokes I'd fished out of the sea, and pulled onto the Butterfield raft that'd bobbed up against me only a few moments, and a thousand lifetimes, before. There'd been dozens of red life-jackets bobbing up and down like discarded corks amidst cruel, knife-edged waves. With everything lit by the oil's flaming red glare and the steely-grey light from the flurries of Snowflakes rockets. A cold and dreadful sea, bound only by the ever-fainter cries of the dying and the eternal silence of the dead, as one by one they were sucked down forever into the murk and dark of the depths.

No, I hadn't gone soft, I'd just lost it for a moment, and then all the pain and anger slipped away from me and slid beneath the wall of blood-red waves that seemed to be all around me. It was as if somewhere deep inside me I knew there'd been too much killing, too much sad and un-necessary death. The cold you feel when you set out to kill a man is the same cold you feel when you're trying to save one. You're not there with them somehow; you're hovering nearby just watching your body going through all the motions.

I blinked, and blinked again, and white light broke over me like the wash from a wave. Like I said, it only took seconds, but it was my lifetime spread before me, nevertheless. What a turn-up for the books, Tommy Nutkins; Big Tom, one of Manchester's finest. But I knew he'd tell me the truth, even if it meant we might fall out over it. The funny thing was, if he had to go all the way he'd die trying, too, and not just because it was his job, but because that was the way he was made. And I was the same, or at least I thought I was, but I'd lost one old friend that night, and with each heartbeat I knew I couldn't afford to lose another.

"Oh, fuck it, Tommy, of all the gin joints in all the friggin' world, you had to—"

"You had to walk into mine. Yeah, and you don't even look a bit like him, you Cockney layabout." Tommy laughed, but his eyes still didn't give an inch. "I owe you one, Jeffro, but it 'aint worth either of us cashing it in tonight." His voice was surprisingly tender for such an ugly fucker.

"Here's my hand on it, Jeffro. Chalkie's not here, straight up. And wherever he is, he'll keep till tomorrow if you still feel like doing him in. But why don't you just call it a night now, and just slip off home?"

I nodded. I felt cold; I mean I was freezing. I nodded again and turned round and slowly went down the stairs. Way off in the distance I heard two women shrieking and laughing. They must've pushed open the club doors on their way to the lavatory or something, because suddenly the noise from inside the club got louder and louder. But then I heard Tommy say something and the laughter stopped dead as if he'd cut it with an axe, and whoever the women were, they went back inside without making another sound. I got to the foot of the stairs and pushed the metal door open, and stared out at the cold, dark world outside.

"You go safe, Jeffro," Tommy said. And I knew without looking back he'd still have his eyes glued on me.

"Yeah, Tommy," I said, my breath already clouding into steam. "You look after yourself, 'an all."

What a friendship! What a fucking, beautiful friendship!

Chapter 26

THIEF OF HEARTS

I climbed the stairs to the flat, reflecting on all the unfairness of life, when suddenly everything in me went on full alert. It was as if someone had switched on a light, and I knew the place was out of joint even before I saw that anything was out of the ordinary. That's what comes from learning to trust your senses, trust them once and they work all the harder for you the next time, and mine had started sending urgent Morse code signals the moment I'd unlocked the front door.

I stood stock-still and willed myself to slow down. I breathed in deep, taking everything in, and with the in-breath time slowed, and on the out-breath I sent my senses faster than thought, out through the flat to search each room in turn. And the sounds of the day diminished and the cloak of silence settled upon me, and in the flat light of day I began to do a creep in my own drum. At first I was disoriented; there was too much light and too many things coming at me from all directions. It was like being in a fog, only this time, the fog was me. I stopped and blinked again, almost sleepily. "Softly-softly-catchee-monkey," I whispered. I searched inside me for the silence between heartbeats, found it, settled myself and closed my eyes. And when I opened them again I found I could see through the curtains of my life, and clearly see all the things that familiarity had numbed me to only moments before.

Apart from a faint smell of tobacco, nothing much jumped out at me at first. On the surface everything seemed normal, but here and there I began to notice that little things had been moved. Never more than a hair's breadth or a fraction of an inch, but enough to break a line of things set in a row, or to disturb the symmetry of a seemingly random grouping of objects. One thing out of place, I could ignore; two, I could live with; three meant something was rotten in Church Street; four meant someone had been inside the flat.

Then I caught a slight whiff of something, the very faintest trace of soap or hair cream that wasn't me or mine. It smelt expensive, more Jermyn Street than Praed Street, more gentlemen's hairdresser by-appointment-only than the local barbershop. Which, incidentally, was why I only ever used plain soap, and why I never Brylcreemed my hair before a creep; the pong of that stuff alone was enough to start most alarm bells going like the clappers.

After that it was like pulling and unravelling a thread on an old pull-over and not believing your eyes as the time-worn, familiar shape starts to unravel in front of you. I knew it hadn't been Joanie. She popped in from time to time, but only if I'd asked her to do a favour or something, and Barry never would, it would've been too much of a liberty. They liked their privacy, and respected mine. And I knew it wasn't Mrs. Mac, the old girl who charred for me once a week. She dusted and cleaned, and took stuff of mine home to wash and to iron, and she even cooked the odd pot of stew for me when I could get her a good piece of meat on the side. But she knew better than to disturb anything or ever to come round unannounced. Anyway, she'd already been at the beginning of the week, so I knew it wasn't her. But someone had definitely been in the flat, I was dead certain of that.

After all my time at sea I couldn't abide a messy place, which was why I always tried to keep my flat spick and span, and shipshape. Joanie said it was like an illness with me, and Barry was always kidding that the men in white coats had been round asking about me again. And I had to admit I was neat to a fault. I folded everything properly; my clothes, the towels, even the newspapers, once I'd finished reading them. And I'm not brag-ging when I tell you the boots and shoes at the bottom of my wardrobe would've passed any kit inspection going. My gramophone records were stacked in a neat pile, and all my books, arranged by subject, were on bookshelves along one side of the room. Even the pictures and drawings of mine I'd framed, all lined up with each other on the wall. And I had photographs in serried ranks along the mantelpiece and on top of the sideboard. The rest I kept in photo albums in the bureau, along with all the picture postcards I'd collected from around the world when I'd been in the Merch. I always sent myself a postcard from whatever port or city I'd landed in; places like New York, Hong Kong, and Sydney. There was never any message, just the time and date and place printed in neat capital letters on the back. Even what little food there was in the flat, was stacked in the pantry as neatly as the stacks and shelves in the food hall at Harrods or Fortnum and Mason's. Everything had its proper place and everything should have been in it, only it wasn't, it'd been deliberately pushed out of line, and like Queen Victoria had once said about something or other, I was not amused.

A book of Jack Frost's sketches on London that I'd bought off a bloke down the Caledonian Road, was jutting out of line, and on another shelf a number of orange-spined Penguins had been pushed in a little too far. I had a sudden thought and looked along the shelf to where I kept an old, leather-bound set of Charles Dickens, and I saw *David Copperfield* had changed places with *Oliver Twist*. I looked on the sideboard and noticed that the pewter mug that'd been presented to me by some old shipmates, had been picked up and put down, smudging its containing ring of dust. Then I noticed the silver buttons from my dress uniform, that I kept in a glass ashtray I'd nicked from the Starlight Club, on Broadway, were no longer all facing up as I'd originally arranged them. Don't get me wrong, it's not that I'm funny about things like that, it's just that once I've thought about something and found the right place for it, I don't have to waste time thinking about it ever again.

After finding so many little things out of place, I wondered if it had all been done on purpose to test me, rile me, and piss me off, because if it had, it'd succeeded. But he was good, whoever he was, and he knew it and was bloody cocky about it, too. Every drawer in the house had been opened and closed again, as had every cupboard, suitcase, and box. And even though I could tell he'd rifled through everything, everything was more or less still in order, which showed he'd taken his own sweet time to do his creep. He was taunting me, telling me he hadn't had to give a moment's thought about being caught. The bastard couldn't have known that I'd be out, preparing for Vi's funeral. Or could he? That little thought set up its own little flurry of worry.

I stood in the middle of the living room and turned round slowly, but I still couldn't see anything missing. And the very moment I had that thought, things began to jump out and hit me left, right, and centre. There were several photographs missing for a start; some from atop the mantelpiece, some from off the sideboard. I got an itchy feeling and crossed over to the bureau and pulled down the fall front to reveal the desk behind. I reached for one of the photo albums I kept there and quickly leafed through it. There were more photographs missing. He hadn't taken every one, just enough to make a life. Me as a schoolboy, me in the market standing in front of Buggy Billy's stall, me in uniform as a cadet and then as Fourth officer on my first ship, and so on. Blank spaces that had been friends and family from home, and mates from the sea. Now, dead and gone. I pulled out another album, the one with all my picture postcards in, and it was the same story, a lot of the cards were missing. Times, dates, and places, all gone.

I knew I'd been done over by Flash Harry friggin' Raffles von bloody Bentink himself, and I'd known it from the very first moment I'd come through the door. I just hadn't wanted to admit it, that's all. What was his game? Had he hoped to find me in? Probably not, that would've only ended up with one of us being dead. No. He'd wanted something back badly enough for him to come and beard me in my own den. I knew it couldn't be the jewels, because he'd have known I'd have had them fenced away immediately.

I wondered if it was really the matched set of twirls he was after. But I had the lovely things locked away in my lock-up down Paddington Basin and no one outside my immediate family knew about that place; so tough luck there, sunshine. But I suppose I'd have missed them, too, if someone had nicked them from me. I could see him being pissed off about it all, but not enough for him to want to come and search me out. No, he must have wanted to put the wind up me; and he'd succeeded in doing that in spades. Yet there still had to be more to it than that, surely. Maybe he'd thought I was magpie enough to have kept back some little trinket for myself. Bugger. I ran into my bedroom and looked on top of the dresser drawers. And of course, the big, gold Rolex I'd nicked from him, the one with the inscription on the back in Bulgarian or Russian or Albanian or whatever it was, had gone. The bastard had nicked it back.

He'd been right, I hadn't wanted to give it up, even when I'd handed everything else I'd nicked, including the gold cigarette lighter, over to Ray. I didn't even know myself why I'd kept the friggin' thing. A trophy? A medal I'd awarded myself for a creep well done? A prized spoil of war? Maybe. It was possible. A creeper could be dead funny about his time-piece, what with time and timing being so important. I fingered my wrist for my own watch and was strangely relieved to find it was still there. If I'd found he'd nicked that as well, I honestly think I would've jacked in creeping for good, right there and then.

I'd been such a stupid berk, I was almost tempted to, anyway. But how was I to have known that the damn Rolex of his would damn me? It was the only thing in the flat that could. And now von Bentink knew for sure, I was the one that'd done the Embassy the first time, and it was odds-on he'd put me in the frame for the second job, too. Nicking the jewels might've been put down to a reckless London cat burglar, but lightning striking twice, that was different. And me coming back a second time and nicking Tanyia, well, that went way beyond regular thieving, that was akin to waging war.

So now I knew why, but the burning question still remained, who'd given me away? And who'd told the bastard where I lived? Christ, he'd come and shit in my backyard and climbed over Church Street roofs to do it, too. The daring fucker. Creepers weren't supposed to do that to one another, it was an unwritten law. If a villain couldn't feel safe and secure in his home, and think of it as his castle, then he might just as well have stayed out marauding and pillaging. And that would never do. Coppers breaking your door down at all hours of the day and night was one thing, that was to be expected, but being done by another villain, and a foreign one at that, that was something else entirely.

I moved to the window, but there were no marks. Of course, I hadn't fixed up any sort of alarm, I'd never thought I'd ever need one; honour among thieves and all that. I went to the window in the bathroom and there they were, a scratch, a scrape, a scuff mark, the almost invisible, tell-tale signs that another creeper can read as easily as a road map.

Then for some reason I remembered the smell of carbolic, and I put two and two together and came up with twenty-two. And I knew for sure then that it was Messima that had sold me down the river. Von Bentink and Baldy must've been the very important business that the Tweedle brothers had been going on about. Even so, Messima would still have had to be guessing to put me in the frame. Although knowing him as I did, he could have easily set up three runners in a three-horse race and bet blind on at least one of them winning. He couldn't lose. I wondered who else von Bentink had burgled before he'd got to me. My past form was still good enough to put me in the frame with London's other top creepers. I had no idea, though, where I'd be on that very short list. Mind you, if I wasn't number one or two, I wondered what Eddie or Don would've made of their foreign gentleman caller. I knew that Eddie still fancied himself as a dead shot with a Luger, and Don, well, Don could've had you in stitches before you even knew you'd been visited with a knife.

I definitely owed Messima one now. And I knew I'd have to find some way of getting back at the little Maltese bastard, as dangerous as that could be for me. And what with sorting him out, and Chalkie, and von Bentink, too, I could see I had a very busy Christmas and New Year ahead of me. Von Bentink must've paid Messima a very pretty penny for him to throw me to the wolves, like that. I'd counted on my mumbled promise of helping him with his next big jewel caper as my insurance. But obviously that wasn't the case. And everything now depended on what happened next. Could I expect another visit from von Bentink? It was doubtful, but I couldn't be sure one way or another. Perhaps Messima would come looking for me himself, now that he had proof I'd been creeping, and worse, that I'd lied about it to him, too. Fuck it, I knew I should've just stayed on the fly-floor.

I decided to get my side-by-sides out from their hiding place inside the settee and keep them under my bed for a few nights. I knew I should also get in touch with Walsingham. I had MI5's secret telephone number safe in my head, and all I had to say when I called was that I wanted to make a donation to BLESS, which was the code for anything to do with von Bentink. If the threat came from Messima, I had to say I had tickets for an exhibition boxing-match at a sporting club down Marble Arch, and ask if they wanted to come. Though the silly sods hadn't thought to give me a code for if von Bentink and Messima were both looking to kill me together. It was all too much cloak and dagger for my liking, but what say did I have in the matter? None, that's what.

And what was really beginning to burn, was the idea that perhaps von Bentink really was in a class by himself and that at long last I'd met my match, and that didn't sit too well. The flash foreign bastard was creeping his way up and down the country with nobody at all to stop him. And in his wake, people were either being blackmailed or were ending up very dead, which in my book meant he was getting away with blue bloody murder. And that not only put him in a different league from me, it put him in a completely different game.

To try and stop from getting too worked up about it all, I poured myself a large glass of single malt and sat down. Something else was niggling me, and it wasn't just that I was down to my last bottle of The Glenlivet. Let me explain. There's thieving and there's thieving. There's the time-honoured purloining of everyday things, or the redistribution of wealth as it's called in the creeping business. Because a thing is only something that someone once made that was sold on to somebody else. And things like that can always be replaced, which is the only reason there are places such as jewellery shops, insurance companies, and banks.

So, it was only ever the well-off and well-insured that I went after; the ones who put their wealth on show for the rest of us to admire; the ones with money to burn. I robbed the rich because they could afford it and gave the money to the people who really deserved it. But don't think for a moment I'm talking about any of that Robin Hood nonsense, because on every occasion the deserving poor turned out to be me and mine. A far worse thing is when something truly irreplaceable gets stolen. For the only real value that something has, is the sentiment that gets attached to it. And it's the loss of that, that hurts people the most. Which is why I never stole a woman's wedding ring or engagement ring. Of course, as some upper-crust tarts made an entire career out of marrying different blokes, I did make exceptions. But this whole thing with von Bentink was different. It broke all the rules. Although he hadn't stolen anything of real worth, he'd stolen something from me that I now realised I valued even more than diamonds. My life, and my history. Because when that's gone, I ask you, what else is there?

I'd fought my way up from the streets. I'd hated the Smoke and all its soot and shit and grime. I'd hated all the poverty and the squalor, even though as a kid I'd never known any different or how different life could be for people with money. London was just like a huge Newgate Prison; cold, grey, hard, and pitiless; a stinking, horrible place you could never escape from. And I dreamed of the far-away places that I only ever saw in picture books at school or down the public library, and I was determined to get out somehow, or die trying. And I'd worked when I'd needed to, and stolen when I'd had to, and I'd finally got away to sea and gone round the world. Then I'd done my bit in the war and somehow managed to survive it all. But I'd lost both my mum and my dad to the Blitz, and an awful lot of mates along the way. And the question I still couldn't answer, was whether anything had really been worth the price we'd all paid. And as much as I tried to add it up, the bloody awful truth was, with things as they still were in the world, none of it made much sense and none of it added up to even half of what it had cost.

I really didn't give a tinker's cuss about von Bentink nicking his gold watch back, and in the end, I didn't even feel that upset about him breaking into the flat. After all was said and done, it was all part of the game, wasn't it? He'd done the unexpected and I hadn't expected it, so more fool, me. But I'd learn from it and move on. No, what really got me was all those photos of my family and friends, and all the postcards of my life that he'd thieved. None of that could ever be replaced.

I took a drink and stared at the wall. He'd gone round the country stealing people's memories and trinkets and he hadn't given a toss about any of it. It meant nothing to him; it was just someone else to be caught and imprisoned between the covers of some secret file somewhere. And now he'd stolen me and mine, and I couldn't ever forgive him for that. I looked round the room. It was as if I didn't know who lived there anymore, I felt like a stranger in my own drum. I took another drink.

What a very shitty day. First Vi's funeral and then this. But I wasn't dead yet, was I? And the game's not over until the ref blows the final whistle, isn't that so? The ball was still in play then, and it was my turn to have a go at goal. And I would too just as soon as I'd had another drink or two. I reached for the whisky bottle again.

Chapter 27

PURE AS THE DRIVEN SNOW

Snow's a bit like life. In the beginning it looks so clean and pristine, so full of promise, that people rush to the windows and press their noses against the glass in excitement. A few minutes later and they're complaining about how cold it is, grumbling about the inconvenience of it all, and they walk over it without a second's thought.

Snow's a bit like people, too. It shows all the marks and the abuse that gets heaped upon it, and then it turns to dirty grey slush before your eyes, just before it fades away forever. I've known a lot of people whose lives have gone like that; men, women, young kids, old codgers. They start out all bright-eyed and bushy-tailed, full of the joys of spring, and life goes along nicely for a while until some bastard comes along and puts the boot in. And somehow, the perfect bastard always seems to be lurking somewhere in the wings, ready to kick them to pieces and all their promise down the drain. But that's life, isn't it?

My old mum used to say, "It's a grand life, if you don't weaken." And Ray often quoted some German bloke that had come up with: "What doesn't kill you, only makes you stronger." All I can say is, it would take a bleedin' Jerry to say that, now wouldn't it?

We had the wake on the Friday night, following the funeral in the afternoon. I hadn't realised that Vi had been part-Irish, but it was a good enough reason to send her on her way with a drink and a song. It'd started in the York pub. Had it really only been a week since we'd all been there, having a knees-up together? And then a few of us had gone back to Joanie's. The coroner had returned a verdict of death by misadventure. A tragic accident, but an open-and-shut case. An open-and-shut coffin more like it, because I knew it'd been no accident and so did half of London. And me? I was simply biding my time until Chalkie resurfaced from whatever rat hole he was skulking in.

The funeral had been quite well attended and a few of the local names had either come themselves or sent flowers. Joanie and Barry were there, of course, as were most of the regulars from the Victory. Even Harry Davids, the butcher, had come, leaving his wife in charge of the shop. And there were quite a few others from the market, even though Fridays were usually a very busy day for everyone. So that in itself said how much Vi had been liked.

Stan and Tom arrived with a wreath of yellow flowers in the shape of a threepenny-bit, and a brown paper envelope with almost twenty quid in it. They'd had a whip round at the Metropolitan and all the lads had chipped in, including—much to everyone's surprise—Mr. Vasco, the tight-arsed manager. The same went for most of the boys in blue down Paddington Green police station, and they also sent some money along with a bunch of flowers, which was very decent of them, considering. And the crowd at the Duke of York had done themselves proud by filling a big glass jar in the saloon bar almost to the brim with tanners, shillings, half-crowns, ten-bob and one-pound notes, and even the odd fiver. And all of it for Vi's little girl, Rosie, who'd looked very smart in a new pair of shoes, and new coat and hat that her uncle Jethro had come up with the clothing coupons and money to buy for her.

The morning after started for me well past noon, but that didn't stop the thumping great big headache I had from thumping on and on. Barry had taken Saturday off from his cabbing so as to keep an eye on me. I'd heard him and Joanie talking about it the night before while I was in my drunken stupor, and so I knew how very worried they both still were about me. Barry gave me some cock and bull later about him having a bad cold and not feeling well enough to work, but I knew different. And I'd even seen his nose twitch once or twice with the cooking smells that kept wafting up from the cafe.

I looked up from the newspapers I'd been trying to read. " 'Ere, Bubs, where's that whisky you've got hidden away? Only I fancy some hair of the dog. Come on, don't be a Scrooge all your life, it's almost Christmas, and it's high time we had some more cheer for Tiny Tim."

Barry turned round in his chair, stared at me hard, and then wrinkled his mouth, which is quite hard to do if you think about it.

"What the friggin' hell you on about, Jeffro? You murdered that off last night, as well as all the other bleedin' bottles I'd had hidden away for Christmas. Or don't you remember that "Knees-Up, Mother Brown" you did on top of the table, and then you singing "Roll Out the Barrel" and the "Twelve Days of Christmas" at the top of your lungs out the bleedin' window at two o'clock this morning?"

"I don't remember too much about anything, Bubs," I said.

Barry slowly shook his head from side to side like a vicar who'd seen too many sins. "Maybe that's just as well then, innit? All I know is, it was a bleedin' wonder you managed to get yourself back up those stairs after-wards, without falling flat on your face." Muttering, he went back to pick-ing the winning dogs running down Harringay.

"I'm Jethro, the fly-man, Bubs. I can climb up and down walls."

He peered over his newspaper. "Yeah, that's what you said when you tried swinging yourself from the top of the landing all the way down to the street without your feet once touching the bleedin' stairs."

"It's only my theatrical nature, Bubs; a touch of the Errol Flynns, is all."

He put his paper down with the rustle and crack of tortured newsprint, and gave me the bent eye. "More like a touch of the bleedin' Vera Lynns, if you ask me," he said.

"You saying I mixed in a few gins with all that whisky and beer?"

"A few Veras doesn't even begin to cover it, Jeffro. I know it only happens once in a blue moon that you decide to get totally rat-faced. But let me tell you, sunshine, last night was as blue as ever I've seen you."

He paused, as if he was considering whether he should continue or not. I arched my eyebrows at him through the silence. He nodded and said quietly, "We've all been worried sick about you, we have, Jeffro, what with you going round for days looking like you were stuck under a black cloud and afraid of your own bleedin' shadow. First, there was the whole friggin' business with Chalkie. And then what happened with poor old Vi. I tell you, we thought you was bad a week ago, but these last few days leading up to the funeral you've been like a dog with its balls cut off. So, anyway, last night when it all started to come out of you, Joanie gave it the nod, and we all just stood back and left you to it."

It was the longest speech I'd ever heard my brother-in-law make without him 'effing and blinding every other word, and I knew him well enough to know that it meant he was still really choked up about everything that'd happened. I know I was. And I slumped back in the chair and let my guard down. I stopped fighting then, and let everything in, all the events of the past weeks, the good, and the bad, and the diabolical, and just let it all crash over me in one big black wave.

It was true. I'd pushed it all away and tried to blank everything out. The break-in had upset me. And I was still pissed with myself for not having found Chalkie. But deep down it was feeling responsible for Vi's death that was really eating me up. I kept saying to myself, if only I'd done this, or if only I'd done that, but in my heart of hearts I knew the accusing voices would still be haunting me long after I'd put Chalkie down for good and finished my dealings with Messima and von Bentink. That's why I'd wanted to drink myself completely senseless, and for one night, at least, it seemed as if I'd succeeded.

I looked at Barry, and said softly, "Thanks, Bubs, for you and Joanie sticking with me through all of this, I won't forget it, ever. It's very, very good having you as family."

He looked at me and I think he let go of something inside, too, because in a voice hardly above a whisper, he said, "The road goes both ways, Jeffro. The road goes both ways."

"Yeah, well what do you say we always remember to walk down it together, then," I said gently. Then something just popped in my head, and for a moment it was as if I was alone in the room, and I said aloud:

> *Golden lads and girls all must,*
> *as chimney-sweepers, come to dust.*

"What's that you say, Jeffro?"

"Oh, nothing, just something I heard someone say in some play, that just sort of stuck in my head. You know what, Bubs? I miss our Vi, I really do. Pure as the driven snow she was."

"We all miss her, Jeffro, she was a queen, she was, a bleedin' queen. You, me, Joanie, everybody, we all felt it. All this nonsense, it wound us up something chronic, and we all had to let the grief out somehow. It just so happened Vi's wake was the proper night for it."

"Bubs," I said, "when you hit the nail, you hit it right smack on the head." And I let his words slowly sink in. I found it helped.

He leaned forward, his elbows on his knees. He looked sad. It might've just been a trick of the light, but I think it was the shadow that continued to walk over his grave, every time he started thinking about what he'd have done if Chalkie had succeeded in killing our Joanie.

"You okay, Jeffro?" he said, his voice hoarse.

"Yeah, thanks, my old china, right as rain, never been better." I got up, patted him on the shoulder, and went to the door. "Look, why don't I pop over the Duke of York's later on and get us a bottle or two. I need to clear up the slate there anyway, and until then, I've got one or two things I can be getting on with upstairs. I'll poke my head round the door before I go to see if there's anything else you want."

He looked at me as if I had a dozen rabbits up my sleeve, but he nodded, and said, "Okay, Jeffro, see you in a bit."

So, just after opening time I slipped back downstairs and knocked on the door. Joanie had already been in and gone out again, by then, as she and a few of the women had decided to get together to see what they could do for Vi's little daughter over Christmas and the New Year. Little Rosie may have lost her mum, but I tell you, the good old girls of Church Street would see she never lacked for a welcoming smile or the milk of human kindness.

But I'd already decided Rosie would never want for anything as long as there was breath in my body. And I even had one or two ideas knocking about in the back of my head on how best to care for her future. For starters, there was this headmistress of a very posh school for girls down on the coast that still owed me a big favour. And I knew that when the time was right, she'd come through for me and Rosie. And then, when

Rosie was older, I'd have put a little money by for her, so she could set herself up in whatever it was she wanted to do. Under the circumstances, that was the very least I could do.

I knew that whatever I did, I'd always feel funny about what had happened with Chalkie. If he hadn't been after me in the first place, then he'd never have gone after Joanie. And then things would've turned out . . . well, you know. As I said, there's always some bastard waiting in the wings somewhere, and it didn't help me sleep nights to think that the person tapped to play the role this time might well have been me.

Barry appeared at the door scowling. "Hello, hello, hello," I said. "It's that the man, again. Fancy that drink I was talking about?"

He let me in, and I saw the evening paper was already folded up on the pile by the fireplace. So I knew straightaway that he'd been out to the newspaper shop across the road and that he hadn't had any luck on his dogs, his horses, or his football pools. But I didn't say anything, I just put on my best winning smile.

" 'Ere, Bubs, what do you say we start the evening off by lifting a few elbows with our old friends Mr. Johnny Walker and Mr. Haig. Then once we've drunk ourselves sober, you can put whatever's left over in the back of your wardrobe, and keep it hidden for Christmas."

The surprised look on his face told me that really was where he'd been hiding all his Christmas booze. I might have known. I laughed and said, "I won't be long. Is there anything else you want?"

"Well, as you're asking," he said. "A packet of Senior Service or Navy Cut wouldn't go amiss. Oh, yes, there was something else. What was it, now? I'm sorry, I can't remember."

"That's okay," I said, "it'll come to you later. Anyway, look, I'll—"

"Oh, yes, I got it. Joanie said to tell you that your friend Seth telephoned the cafe for you, earlier."

"Any message, was there?"

"Yeah, there was. What was it, now? She did say, Jeffro, but for the life of me, I can't remember, I had my head in the evening paper."

"Well, never mind," I said, "she can tell me later. If it'd been anything urgent, she would've knocked my door and told me herself."

Barry nodded, still trying to remember what it was he'd been told. He stared at me, the puzzled look still on his face, then said hurriedly, "Here, slip my coat on over your jacket, it's bloody cold out there."

I smiled and did as I was told. He was genuinely concerned. And it seemed I'd never want for human warmth, either. Lucky me.

I felt along the edge of the fat fold of fivers in my pocket. There was more than enough flims there to cover both the cost of whatever had been added to the slate from the night before, as well as a few extra bottles of spirits from the Duke of York's secret Christmas Club stock. Only the good stuff, mind you, the stuff that Reg, the landlord, kept hidden away in the double-padlocked cupboard in his little back room. I slipped down the stairs, pulled Barry's coat collar up round my ears, and stepped out into the dark and the slush that was Church Street.

The cold weather hadn't deterred the Christmas shoppers. A lot of people came up to town specially for the markets, and with Paddington railway station being so close, Church Street was a regular favourite with punters from as far away as Slough and Maidenhead. Everyone was on the look-out for a bargain, and sometimes they got one, too. But more often than not when they got back home, the set of cutlery they'd bought would turn green the first time they spilled vinegar on it. Or the cups and saucers wouldn't match the plates in the rest of the set. Or the quality of the fruit on top wasn't the same as the stuff at the bottom of the bag. Though now, at the arse-end of the day, there weren't too many punters still hanging round looking for last-minute bargains, and who could blame them? It looked like it was getting ready to snow again. And the market, ever sensitive to prevailing winds, was already packing up and disappearing faster than money back into a Scotsman's pocket. Up and down the street the lights were going off one by one and the barrows were being wheeled away, and whatever had been left on the stalls was being packed into cardboard boxes and tea-chests ready for another day.

The York was already full when I got there, so it must've been a good day for some. Reg took me round the back, and I got myself three bottles of Johnny Walker whisky and two bottles of Gordon's Gin, with all the proper export labels and seals intact, and two bottles of French brandy. Reg swore blind they were all kosher, which meant he'd probably seen them fall off the back of the lorry himself. He asked me if I knew whether

Joanie was in the market for any tea, only he'd just happened to come by two tea-chests full of the stuff, from a friend of his brother-in-law, who knew someone that worked down one of the docks. I said I didn't, but I'd ask, and that he'd better put one aside just in case. And I thanked him for giving me the nod. Then I topped my order up with a couple of bottles of sweet sherry for Joanie, some tonic waters and ginger ales, and a couple of big bars of American chocolate from some KPX somewhere. All good, under-the-counter stuff, of course. And Reg, ever the sensitive soul, not wanting to offend his other regular customers, who were probably drinking watered-down God knows what, wrapped everything up in old newspaper like so many portions of fish and chips and stuck it all in a carrier-bag. I felt myself lucky to get away with paying only an average working man's monthly wage for the lot. And what with that lot, and the monies I owed the pub for what had been chalked up on my slate, Reg must've thought Christmas had come early. And seeing him stuff my fivers into his back pocket with the expert flourish of all fixers everywhere, I suppose it had. And a very merry white Christmas to us all, I thought to myself, courtesy of a very black market.

I yelled a cheery 'cheerio' through all the smoke and the chatter, and the tuneless singing that was going on round the old piano, but I didn't stop for a pint, even though several people waved their glasses at me, indicating that I should stay and have one with them. Though, knowing that lot, they would've all probably expected me to pay for the pleasure as well, the scrounging buggers.

The snow had picked up a bit by then, and it whipped against my face as I pushed through the pub door and crossed the street. The world was all black-and-white just like in a photograph. I stood for a moment and lit a cigarette with my natty, wind-defying Zippo lighter; clever buggers those Yanks. In the flickering flame I caught sight of the jolly jack tar on the Player's Navy Cut packet, and I blinked and shook away the dark memories that started bobbing up and down in my mind. And I screwed up the empty packet and threw it in the gutter.

I started to trudge back down the street towards the Victory clutching my carrier-bag full of Christmas cheer, but I hadn't gone more than a dozen steps when there was a sloshing sound of tyres behind me. I half-turned, expecting the worse, not sure yet whether to run for it, or whether to just drop the bottles against the running board and throw the flaming Zippo at the mess.

It was a big black sedan, of course; what else would it be? They must sell the buggers by the dozen, I thought. The big round headlights flashed off and on again. I blinked, and heard windows being wound down as the motor purred up alongside me. I gave it a stare. From the two blokes sitting up front, it looked like it could have been some of Walsingham's people again, all dapper and debonair and deadly.

"God's holy trousers, not you lot again. Haven't you got any real villains to chase? But look, now you're here, I was just about to give—"

"Park it, Jethro, show just a little respect, there's a good lad."

I knew the voice, it wasn't Bosanquet or Walsingham, but it was one you didn't forget in a hurry. And even though it wasn't entirely cultured, it wasn't for lack of trying. I turned, ignoring the two nattily dressed heavies in the front, even though the one sitting kerb-side deliberately tapped his bulging overcoat just where his heart would have been if he'd had one. It was obvious he was carrying something, and it probably wasn't just an extra packet of twenty cigarettes. So still holding the carrier-bag in front of me, I peered into the darkness that was the back of the sedan. The voice curled out again from inside the back of the car and caught me in its reasonableness.

"This isn't a business call, Jethro, it's purely pleasure. Just a few words in your shell-like ear is all."

"Didn't see you there at first, Jack. It's getting so you can't tell one big flash Yank motor from another these days."

"That's alright," chuckled Jack Spot, "everyone's entitled to at least one mistake, even you. Hop in."

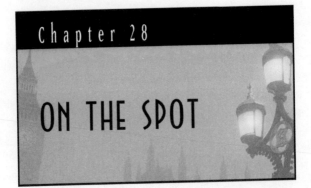

Chapter 28

ON THE SPOT

Jack Spot, Guv'nor of the Manor, everywhere but Soho. From Queensgate in the west to the Aldgate Pump in the east, all the way down to the water, he was in control of, or had his hand in, everything but the vice rackets. "A right villain, I may be," he'd say, "but I'm no ponce." Charming, stylish, and sometimes deadly, he was always dressed in a beautifully cut brown suit, snap-brim brown fedora, and handmade shoes. His silk ties came from Sulka in Bond Street, his shirts from a 'by-appointment-only' gentleman's outfitters, complete with Royal warrants, in Jermyn Street. Every morning after a visit to the barbers in Edgware Road Underground station, where they'd shave him to immaculate perfection, he would walk, sharp as a newly honed razor, down towards the Cumberland Hotel, near Marble Arch. And ever gracious, he'd nod a good morning, or wave a regal wave to anyone who happened to catch his eye, the aromatic wisps from his imported cigar and his patchouli after-shave trailing him all the way down the street.

Then he'd sit in the hotel's Bear Garden until noon, dispensing justice and advice to all who came to pay him court. If you had a problem you took it to Jack, and more often than not he'd take care of it on the spot. If not, with or without the prescription of some future damage needing to be visited upon some person or other, his promise to make good was as good as the deed already having been done. Very seldom was anything asked for in return, but somehow all debts came to be handsomely repaid over the course of time.

His real name was Jacob Comacho, then he'd become Jack Comer, but what's in a name when an X cut across a guilty cheekbone marked the spot so much more effectively? But don't get me wrong, Jack wasn't all flash and slash, he was someone you could respect, and even get to like. A Jewish lad, from Whitechapel, the son of immigrants from Poland, he'd spent his life fighting his way up from the bottom. But he'd never made any apology about it, he'd always just got on with the business in hand. I'm not saying he was a Robin Hood, either, but as a lad, back in the Thirties, it was Jack who'd headed up the gang of tearaways that'd torn apart Sir Oswald Mosley's blackshirted British Union of Fascists, when they'd tried to march through the East End. And it was Jack that had later taken on the race-track gangs controlled by the Sabinis, and had won because of the lengths he was prepared to go to. He didn't stand for liberties being taken then, and he certainly wouldn't stand for any being taken now.

"Step lively, Jethro, we'll freeze our balls off if we keep this car door open any longer."

"Right, Jack, that's very kind of you, I only live a little way up the street."

"I thought we'd just go for a little ride around the block first. Won't keep you long."

I climbed in the back. I noticed that the courtesy light didn't go on when the door opened, or closed. Jack leaned forward and motioned me to one of the jump seats. A glass partition separated the two heavies in the front from the compartment in the back, which made for some sort of privacy. You always had to be careful; careless talk could cost you your livelihood. I must admit though with the heater going, it was really quite cozy in the back. The car moved off smoothly. Jack drank from a solid silver hip flask and didn't spill a drop. I knew it was really full of lemonade, as he didn't drink anything else in case it ever interfered with business. But that was never a problem for any friends of his who were serious drinkers, as he always had a second silver flask on hand that contained twelve-year-old Scotch. He passed it to the bloke sitting next to him in the dark. Nothing if not a natural stage director was our Jack, every movement for economy or effect.

"You know Billy Hill." It was no question, just a simple statement of fact.

"Certainly do, Jack. Wotcher, Billy."

" 'Lo, Jethro. Long time."

The yellow light from the passing parade of shop windows and lamp-posts reached into the back of the car and caught the side of Billy Hill's face in a play of splintered shadows, which only served to emphasise his pointed features and the angular set of his jaw. His eyes were small, flat, and black, like burnt cork on a kid's papier-mâché mask. Always quiet, self-contained, and conservatively dressed, Billy Hill was never one to stand out in a crowd or a police line-up, and he was never one to use three words when one would do. Even though his voice was thin and raspy, it was a voice that didn't ever have to shout to be heard, or obeyed.

"Alright, you two pen pals. To get right down to it, Jethro. It's been whispered about that you've been having a bit of on-going bother with our old chum Messima. It all started with a serious barney back of the Palladium, so we heard. A handy team of out-of-town tearaways versus Chalkie and his band of choirboys. We heard that you were involved in it, but no one can say exactly how, but it's not your style to go round mob-handed is it, Jethro? You've always been a bit of a loner. Anyway, it seems that Messima got so steamed about it all, he sent his boys clattering and banging around the streets for days afterwards to give any strange team they came across a right seeing-to, but they couldn't find anyone, apparently. Not a bleedin' soul. Seems Messima was right put out about it, and all. Drink?"

"Er, no, thanks, Jack."

"Get it down you, you silly bugger, it's brass-monkey weather outside; you don't want to freeze your balls off. Anyway, it'll save you having to break open what you've got hidden in your carrier-bag."

He must've heard the bottles clinking together. Either that or he could see right through several layers of newspaper. Knowing Jack as I did, it was probably the latter. I raised the flask. "Right, cheers then, Jack. Cheers, Billy."

"That's better. Cheers. We're all friends here. Where was I?"

"Them all chasing round looking for the other team."

"Yes, ta, Billy. Anyway, Jethro, the way we heard it, Chalkie White then got it into his head to get at you by going after your sister, Joanie, but instead he ended up doing . . . er, what's her name?"

"Violet Vickers," Billy Hill whispered. "She was married to old Harry Vickers, who got topped early on in the war."

"Yes, that's it, yes, Violet Vickers. Chalkie done for old Vi Vickers after he mistook her for your sister. Don't hold with acid, though; much too messy, gets where it shouldn't. And then the sod went and run her over with his motor. Very nasty business. I knew Harry Vickers years ago, when his family kept a stall down Petticoat Lane. From round Whitechapel they were. Good people, too, always cheery. Harry's dad clipped my ear once when he caught me nicking things off his stall, he said it was to teach me not to get caught the next time."

Spottsy seemed to be having such a nice time walking down memory lane with Billy Hill, I didn't think it polite to interrupt them. So clutching my precious carrier-bag to me like a life buoy, I tried to look as though I was holding on to their every word, which for obvious health reasons I was; nodding first at the one, and then the other. And as the big sedan turned a corner and rolled on its springs I noticed my reflection in one of the darkened windows. My lips looked as if they'd stuck to my teeth again. I tried to think of something to do that wouldn't draw undue attention to myself, and so I tried licking my lips. But then I remembered that that was what Billy Hill was famous for doing when he had a razor in his hand, so I just swallowed hard instead and hoped for the best. Then I heard my name being mentioned, and my mind rushed me back for the start of the second act.

"Yeah, I remember Harry Vickers and his dad very well, indeed. Luvvly folks. But now all dead and gone. And now poor Vi, too. Nasty way to go. Anyway, it got us both to thinking, Jethro, about why Chalkie should have got so steamed up about you and yours. It had to be something personal, so you must've put his nose out of joint somehow. Turning down a special job close to his heart or something, probably. Or perhaps Chalkie just thought himself sly enough to be able to lay one of his nasty little fiddles at your door, so you'd end up carrying the can if Messima ever sussed him. Who knows? Another drink?"

"No, thanks, Jack."

"The thing is, Jethro, it always pays for us to know what's going on in the Smoke; all the ins and outs and whats and whens. And what Messima does with you is your business, Jethro, but what you do to mess him up is definitely ours. And we thought you should know that. You see, the thing is, we can't stand the bleeder. Isn't that right, Billy?"

"Certainly is, Jack. He's a ponce. Don't like ponces."

"There you have it, Jethro. Messima's a ponce on a grand scale. And apart from that, he's got too many bloody foreigners running things for our liking. Those Malts don't even think of themselves as being British, they call themselves Europeans, whatever the soddin' hell that's supposed to mean. What's more, they don't even run the spielers or the drinking clubs right. There's a lot more money to be made from punters pulling their wallets out their pockets for a whole night's drinking and gambling, than there is from them just pulling their willies out their trousers for a quick one."

He cleared his throat; I think he was coming to a point.

"There's very serious money to be made in Soho if everything were to be run right. As it is, Messima's boys lay it on thick and fast with anybody that shows his face. It's getting so bad, you can't go down Soho for a quiet night out, without going mob-handed."

He cleared his throat again and took another swig of lemonade. If his throat was drying out that quickly, I knew he had to be sore about something. I only hoped it wasn't me he was mad at, and I cleared my own throat to show him I was still listening.

"Soho needs controlling, and it needs controlling properly. It's far too big for one mob to have to itself anyway. And there's just too much fuss and bother with Messima running the show. Shooters are bad enough, but striping tarts' faces and then throwing them out of the bleedin' window for not working hard enough is bad for everybody. The coppers down Savile Row have got to go stomping about like elephants then, so they can say in the linens, they're doing their job and cleaning things up. And no one can make a decent living with all that going on day in, day out, not us, not them, not nobody. Isn't that right, Billy?"

"Certainly is, Jack. Soho needs a good cleaning."

"What we're saying, Jethro, is Messima will get his dose of worm powder soon enough. And when we're good and ready, we'll be the ones that give it to him. But until the proper time comes for us to fix him, what we wanted to say was, whatever you do to fuck him up has our full blessing. And we just thought you should know that, didn't we, Billy?"

"Certainly did, Jack. Our full blessing."

"Anyway, Jethro, we just wanted to drop that in your ear ourselves, just in case you might have worried about it unnecessarily. Oh, yes, and there's this."

He reached inside his beautifully tailored overcoat; the rustle of his silk neck-scarf sounding as loud as a crackle from a radio set. And as if on cue, Billy Hill did the same. I swallowed hard, it could've signalled anything. And then both of them pulled out fat brown paper envelopes.

"We had a collection for Vi's little girl, what's her name, Billy?"

"Rosie, little Rosie Vickers."

"Yes, that's it, Rosie. So, you'll find a monkey in there for her, we thought it might help the little girl more than a teddy bear." He chuckled, took Billy Hill's envelope as well as his own, and dropped them both into the carrier-bag.

"The truth is, Jethro, no one round the Smoke really likes Messima that much. And that goes double for that flash little bastard, Chalkie White. But Billy and me being betting men, we're betting we won't be seeing much of Chalkie anymore. Not unless we got our buckets and spades out, and drove over to Hackney Marshes and started digging around, that is." He made a noise at the back of his throat that might've been him chuckling. "Anyway, from what we heard, Messima himself went and had Chalkie rubbed out. There was even a whisper that some young tearaway who fancied himself as a bit of a cat burglar got buried right alongside him. Though what the silly bugger was doing getting mixed up with the likes of Chalkie White, God only knows. Pity really, the kid had a lot of promise otherwise, and he'd been coming along nicely. It's all just a rumor, though. And the funny thing is, Jethro, given all the circumstances, and knowing you as I do, it could so easily have been you that done for them both. Isn't that right, Billy?"

"Certainly could look that way, Jack."

"Anyway, let it rest. But there is just one other little thing we're both thinking about betting on . . ."

So, Chalkie had been rubbed out and some young tearaway with him. Whether the kid had been the one that'd thrown the acid or driven the car didn't matter much anymore. They'd both gone to meet their maker in exactly the way I'd planned for it to happen. Funny that. God certainly did move in mysterious ways when he put his mind to it. I felt my spirits begin to lift, and then I heard someone clearing their throat to attract my attention.

"Er . . . um, what's that, Jack?" I thought I should say something, just to prove I'd been listening all along.

"Ta, I thought I'd lost you there for a minute. So tell me, sunshine, just how long is it going to be before you ring down the curtain on this theatre lark and get back into the game, proper like?"

"I'm out of it for good now, Jack." I turned to look at the other face still hidden in shadow. "That's the God's honest truth that is, Billy. That's what I told Chalkie. That's what I told Messima. That's even what I told that bastard, DCI Browno of the Sweeney, when he pulled me over the coals recently in the No-Name Club."

"Yeah, we heard he'd paid you a visit."

I looked at them, my face a mask of sincerity. "The war really finished it for me, it did, and I've gone straight ever since."

Billy Hill snorted at that. Jack merely chuckled. "Of course you have, Jethro, of course you have. So I'm sure the fancy foreign git that's put up a ton of money to get his jewels back, along with the name of the tealeaf concerned, has nothing whatsoever to do with you, either?"

"I don't know what you're talking about, Jack."

"Funny, that's exactly what Eddie Chapman and Don Machin said, when we asked them. But whatever Mr. Messima, or Mr. Browno and his fearsome Flying Squad choose to believe, we're not them and we know better. And so do you. We're all Londoners born and bred, Jethro, and none of us has had any choice but to use our wits to survive and that just doesn't ever wash out. Not once the Smoke gets in your lungs, it doesn't, there's never any getting rid of it. It's like the lettering in a stick of Brighton rock; it goes from end to end and all the way through, all throughout your life. Isn't that right, Billy?"

"Certainly is, Jack, all the way through."

"We'll take your word for now, Jethro, because it's Christmas and we're both in a good mood. But we also know that if sometime in the future we had a special creeping job that needed doing properly, well, you'd make an exception for us, wouldn't you now? As from what we've heard, that sort of arrangement is right up your street."

I wasn't expected to answer, it was a statement of fact. However did they get to hear so much? They had bigger ears than Browno. And if you ask me, they must've been paying straighteners in every police station from Leytonstone to Ealing Broadway. Or perhaps they were just pulling my chain to test the waters. I couldn't know for sure, so I just continued to deny everything. It was safer.

"I don't know what you're talking about, Jack."

"Of course you don't, Jethro, of course you fucking don't. Can we drop you somewhere?"

As if by chance, we'd arrived back outside the Duke of York pub. They let me out.

"Nice seeing you, Jethro. Wish your sister Joanie and her old man Barry a merry Christmas from me, will you?"

"Of course, Jack. And a merry Christmas to you, too." I was nodding my head backwards and forwards like a nun with a collection plate. "And a merry Christmas to you and all, Billy. See you ... er ... um ... both around sometime."

"Not if we see you first, Jethro. Not if we see you first."

I got out clutching my carrier-bag and blinked the snowflakes from off my eyelids. The cold didn't hit me too badly, I was already shivering so much inside. And all I heard as the car door closed behind me was the sound of the two of them laughing their heads off. The big motor gunned into life and sped away up Church Street. "The bleeders could've dropped me off a little closer to home," I said to the street lamp. Then I thought better of it, they could've done much worse, they could've dropped me for good. At least I was still in one piece, so maybe it was going to turn out to be a merry Christmas after all.

It's amazing how your spirits can lift when you least expect them to; like the moment you realise a double-decker bus has just whistled past and missed you by inches. It sort of gives you a whole new outlook on

life. I picked up my pace and trudged back towards the Victory. Along
the way, I think I might've even started whistling a Christmas carol or
something.

I shook out Barry's overcoat, hung it up, and went into the kitchen.
"It's more than a bit nippy out there," I said, shivering. "It's friggin' freezing, it is. I swear my nose is so raw, I could double as Rudolph the Red-
nosed Reindeer in a kids' panto."

"What the bleedin' hell happened to you, then? You stay for another
knees-up or something?"

"Not without you, Bubs, it wouldn't be no fun otherwise."

I turned to the bulging carrier-bag on the kitchen table, picked one
of the newspaper packages out without looking, and unwrapped it to reveal a bottle of Johnny Walker. Lucky guess. "Here, Bubs, break the seal
on that, will you, while I get us some clean glasses."

"Luvvly stuff," he said. "I thought for a moment you'd gone and got
fish and chips instead. Can't smell a thing with this cold."

"No, of course you can't." I smiled and played along with his little
white lie. "I did the business with Reg, but then got taken for a bit of a
ride. The funny thing was, for a few awful moments, I thought I'd really
had my chips, too."

"Reg don't have the bottle to put one over on you, Jeffro."

"No, Bubs, it wasn't him, it was Jack Spot and Billy Hill."

He looked me up and down. "Blimey. Royalty. That's a turn-up for
the books. You alright, are you?" he said, sounding worried.

"Yeah, they said they just wanted a word or two in my ear."

Barry looked at me from over his glasses. "If that's all they wanted,
then you just be thankful for small mercies, my old son. The thought of
dealing with either Spottsy or Billy Hill is enough to get most people's
knickers in a right old twist. Gawd, the two of them together could put
nutcrackers out of business."

I poured two generous glasses. We nodded, and said, "Cheers."

"Well, I tell you, Bubs, between the two of them, they've already
squeezed out five hundred quid or more from somewhere, and all in used
ones and fivers, and all for little Rosie Vickers. It's all there in the carrier-
bag with the bottles and things. They'd heard about Chalkie, Vi, everything. Oh, and talking of the devil, Spottsy told me that Messima has

finally done for Chalkie, and that Mr. Smythe-White is now resting in pieces in Hackney Marshes somewhere, which is dead funny, because that's where we were going to bury the bastard."

Barry sighed, a long-drawn-out sigh, sniffed and nodded, sniffed some more, and then seemed to put the whole sorry mess behind him. I looked at him and wished I could do it like that. He raised his glass. "Cheers to that, then. And may the bastard rot in hell."

"He very probably will, too, but I'll tell you something else, as well. Just as they let me out of the motor, Spottsy wished you and Joanie a very merry Christmas."

"Bleedin' hell, that's like having your name in the linens. I think I'll have one of those fags now, Jethro, if you don't mind, it's made me come over all funny."

"Help yourself," I said, "I could do murder for a 'Harry Rag' myself, where are they?"

He looked at me over his glasses again, like a schoolteacher. "I thought you were going to bring some back, so I had the last two while you were gone. I don't know; send a boy to do a man's job."

"And you can pack that in right now, you cheeky sod," I said. I patted my pockets and felt behind each ear. "I'm right out, Bubs. I had my last fag coming out the pub. So, there's nothing for it, I'll have to go out into the bleedin' cold again." I looked at him, sitting all nice and cozy in his armchair. "I tell you, it's all right for some."

"No," he said, making as if to get up, "I'll go, Jeffro, you've only just got back in."

"Yes, and you with a cold, and in your slippers and cardigan; Joanie would play merry hell with me if I let you catch your death. No, I'll go, Bubs, it'll be quicker. I wouldn't even think of standing around waiting for a bleedin' taxi driver in this weather, anyway."

"Gertcher, yer bugger."

"Yes," I said, "and a merry Christmas to you and all."

I ignored all the voices in the pub yelling, "It's that man again," and "Can I do yer now, sir?" The old lines from everyone's favourite radio show, *Itma*. Turned a deaf ear to the muttered, "Didn't think it was like you to pass up a drink, Jeffro," and pushed through to the bar. Reg was wiping a glass with a clean bar-towel, which was a sure sign he was cel-

ebrating something, it might've even been Christmas. He looked nervous
when he saw me, probably thinking I'd had second thoughts about how
much he'd charged me for all the booze. He nodded his head sideways,
and we found ourselves a quiet spot at the far end of the bar.

"Two packets of twenty please, Reg. Twenty Senior Service, and twenty
Navy Cut. Only, I forgot them before." He nodded with his eyes and
reached down under the bar. Then covering them with his hand, like a
nervous card dealer, he slid them across the counter top to me.

"Right you are, then, Jethro. Only, for one minute, I thought that
perhaps you'd come back to ... er ... um ..." He raised his eyebrows, as
if he wasn't really sure whether he was going to be given some extra food
coupons or a poke in the eye with a blunt stick, but I just smiled my best
Cheshire-cat smile and gave him the bent eye instead.

"That's alright, Reg," I said, pocketing the fags, "that's alright. Just
put it all on the slate again, why don't you. Good night."

He nodded, and I was outside and cutting a swath up the street before
you could've whispered the words 'Sweeney Todd.' And as I felt the snowflakes swirling around my collar once again, I said to myself, I've been
here before. I knew there was a word for when you got a funny feeling
like that, but for the life of me I couldn't think what it was. It's odd the
way your memory plays tricks sometimes. I shrugged and put the tickle
on the back of my neck down to the empty street.

Church Street's different when it's not bursting to the brim with people. At night, when it's deserted, it can feel like a dog with its fur shaved
off. And that's just what it felt like that night, the street didn't quite know
where to put itself. And in the gathering gloom, the soiled white carpet
under my feet only added to my growing sense of unease.

I felt for the Zippo in my pocket and was just thinking about lighting
up, when I heard the swish of car tyres slowly wheeling their way through
the slush and the muck of Church Street. And as the big black sedan
whispered up beside me, I wondered what on earth it was that the likely
lads had forgotten to tell me. Only this time, the motor drove on a little
way ahead and I think I blinked in surprise as its big, red brake-lights
went on just as the rear passenger door swung open. I remember noticing
that the courtesy light in the back of the car had also come on, just as

someone came up behind me and knocked me right into the middle of next week.

All that bit about you seeing stars isn't true. When I was tapped on the head, all the lights upstairs went out immediately and I dropped straight down into a coal-hole blacker than the black hole of Calcutta. And then a whole lorry-load of coal sacks were dropped on me from above and I was pushed deeper and deeper into a bottomless hole that was already full to the brim with blackness.

Chapter 29

'YOUR GOOSE IS COOKED, SIR'

I was sitting in a straight-backed chair, trussed up like a friggin' Christmas turkey. They'd blindfolded and gagged me, but I was still alive, so I suppose that counted for something. Tilting my head back, I took a peek under the bottom of the blindfold and saw they'd tied me to the chair with electrical flex, which they'd then wound around me like I was a friggin' bollard or something. Fucking hell, I thought, this is a bit serious. I tried to wriggle, but it was of no use, I couldn't move an inch. I took it to mean I wasn't supposed to be going anywhere soon.

I closed my eyes and tried to take stock, but then my brain tapped me on the shoulder to tell me I was freezing to death, and I began shivering uncontrollably. I'd been wearing Barry's coat and a jacket once upon a time, but fuck knows what'd happened to them. I took another peek, and that's when I noticed they'd ripped my shirt and pullover to shreds. Messima must've really lost his temper. There were hardly enough tatters left hanging on me, for me to know it was me I was looking at. And there was no sound of ice cubes clinking in a glass of single malt, this time; all I could hear was the chattering of my teeth.

I tried tilting my head back farther, and what I saw nearly made me jump right out of my friggin' skin. It wasn't my legs being stark naked that made me break into a cold sweat, it was seeing that whole lengths of the flex they'd bound me with had been stripped to expose the bare copper wire. And worse, they'd gone and wound the bare flex around my upper thighs and, Jesus, even around my family jewels. Fair's fair, but that was a bit much even for Messima, I mean that's why they're called privates in the first place, isn't it?

"He's awake."

The voice came from behind, although I wasn't too sure at first, as somewhere in the back of my mind I was all but screaming my head off.

"Wet him down."

I'd once been told that if you brace yourself for a shock it helps reduce the impact. Well, you be careful who you listen to. Always expect the unexpected, right? I did. I do. But what happened next was diabolical. At first I couldn't make out what had hit me, I only knew that my chest had exploded. The cold-hearted bastards had thrown buckets of icy cold water all over me from two sides at once. I tell you, they couldn't have done any worse damage if they'd used a pair of sawn-offs.

"Take it off."

They tore off the blindfold and the gag, and light exploded behind my eyes, and it was as if I'd been buried headfirst in snow. I heaved for air, but all my lungs did, was cough and wheeze like clapped-out accordions. And then I spluttered and gasped, and just started bellowing my head off, yelling every vile and nasty thing I could think of, turning the air around me crimson with the bluest, blackest swearing I'd heard in a long while. And, I tell you, the things that I called Messima, well, even old Vi, God bless her, would've been proud of me.

The curtain of water running down my face reduced itself to a trickle, and I blinked the water away from my eyes and took a quick look around me. I was inside a machine shop. It was too small to be a factory, but I knew it was something to do with engineering, as I could see metal lathes and various bits and pieces of welding equipment. Out of the corner of my eye, I saw big, double-wooden doors, which together with a very strong smell of paint, paraffin, and motor oil meant I was probably in a garage workshop of some kind. The workbenches were littered with tools, and piles of rusted tins of this and pots of that, and I saw a line of ten-gallon oil drums, all shiny black and new, that'd probably fallen off the back of some khaki-coloured lorry.

I was wet through and cold beyond freezing, but I could feel warmth coming from somewhere. Then I heard the unmistakable sound of a shovel scraping against a fire-grate. It must've been a little pot-bellied stove or something, because my nose began to twitch with the licks of smoke from the burning coal. And I remember thinking that they couldn't have had a very understanding coalman, as there wasn't enough heat to dry a drowned rat, let alone me.

I struggled against the chair for a bit, and yelled some more, but after getting no response from anyone, I calmed down. And after all the racket that I'd been making, it seemed almost peaceful.

Then a voice said, "Hit him. Hard."

Then some bugger hit me hard behind the ear, and I couldn't hear myself yell for all the bells that were clanging in my head. Then the man with the fists moved in closer and got down to work, his leather turtles smashing into me again and again. It was like being hit by a pair of steam-hammers. And I tried to keep my chin down, but it didn't seem to break his rhythm any, he just hit me with an uppercut and carried on.

I had to swallow it and keep myself focused, or it was all over for me there and then. So over and over in my mind, I said, "Whoever you are, Puncher, you shit-head, you better enjoy it while you can, because once I get out of this you're a dead man." Anyway, after he took the first five rounds, I just left him to it. I felt one eye begin to close under the weight of the blows, and then the other one closed out of sympathy. And I was blind again, but it didn't matter much, I really didn't feel like seeing anyone.

"Enough. I think that's helped put us all in the proper mood."

Puncher stopped rearranging my face, but that still left the voice of the bloke in charge ringing in my ears, like a bell signalling 'seconds out.' It definitely wasn't Messima, and it wasn't one of the Tweedle brothers. It sounded all stuck up and very la-di-dah and I knew I'd heard it some-where before. But what with my head thumping so much, I just couldn't place it. I ask you, what on earth's the good of having a memory if it doesn't work when you need it to?

"It's, Jethro, isn't it? The infamous burglar and jewel thief? No, please don't answer yet, all I want you to do for now is listen. You've put me to a great deal of trouble and expense, you know, Mr. Jethro? And the question is, whether you've been a very lucky amateur, or whether someone has been helping you. Because if you really are as good as people say you are, then I can't quite believe that you would have been so stupid as to burgle the same place, twice. Unless, that is, you had no other choice but to do so."

It felt odd having the voice come echoing out at me, from out of nowhere, it was a bit like listening to God speak. I thought it best that I should stay stumm.

"So why not be a good fellow, and tell me who you are working for, right now. And then perhaps we can avoid all this unpleasantness."

The only sounds apart from the coal settling in the stove was the lick of the flames and my teeth chattering ten to the dozen. Then I heard someone give an exaggerated sigh worthy of Donald Wolfit himself.

"You can play dumb, if you so choose, Mr. Jethro. But it will only serve to make things that much more difficult for you as we go along. Though, in the spirit of fair play, I should perhaps warn you that you will talk in the end, everyone always does."

I still didn't think he expected a reply yet, whoever he was, so I kept my thoughts to myself. Funny thing, though, he didn't sound like he'd be working for Messima. The way he spoke sounded much too educated and cultured. But then, Chalkie Smythe-White had gone off to the big Inns of Court in the sky, hadn't he, so perhaps Messima had hired himself a very posh, new legal brain to do his threatening for him.

"Tell me who you were working for. Was it British Intelligence?"

When I didn't say anything, Puncher hit me again.

And then so did the voice. "Let's make it a little easier for you then, shall we? Just nod your head once for yes. The word 'no' needn't concern you. Were you perhaps working for somebody in MI5?"

When I was hit again, my head fell onto my chest and I just let it stay there, which I think they took as a sign of me not co-operating fully. So they started hitting me again. Then it came to me in a flash, or it might've been another punch to the head, but I knew the voice. It was von Bentink. I tell you, I could be right thick sometimes. So I was in his hands then, was I, and not in the clutches of my old friend Messima.

It was his questions about British Intelligence that'd given the game away; the only spying Messima ever got involved with was in the canteen of West End Central police station, or in the pubs around Scotland Yard. I never thought in all my life I'd ever miss Messima, but I did at that moment, and that told me just what a bloody awful mess I must've dropped myself into. Meanwhile, in between telling me how very irritated he'd been by the theft of those two little black books, and his posh little set of skeleton keys, Herr von Bentink kept on throwing questions at me about the British Secret Service, and how much, if anything, they knew about him. He also asked me whether I read Charles Dickens or not, which I thought was a very odd question; didn't everybody? Puncher hit me every now and then, just to add all the proper points of emphasis and punctuation.

I must've blacked out or something, because all of a sudden it seemed like I was walking down a long white corridor, going towards some place nice and warm and peaceful. And as it looked as if the corridor went on forever, I whiled away the time thinking about how everything had come to pass.

The truth was, I had no one to blame but myself. I'd had all those itchy feelings about being watched and followed, hadn't I? And it'd got so bad at times, that it'd felt like I was coming down with the chicken-pox. And I think it was all that going on inside me, that had dulled my senses, long before I ever thought of reaching for the whisky bottle.

The eyes in the back of my head were always on the look-out for Messima and his gang of layabouts, which was only natural. It was all part of living in London, like avoiding the tallyman or dodging the taxman. But since that time Messima had had me in to speak to him, all the usual faces around London had seemed that much more suspicious, dark, and threatening. And it had given me the willies, and no mistake. Watching out for yourself every moment on a rooftop at midnight is one thing, but having to also do it in the middle of a crowded street and in broad daylight is quite another. It wears you down.

Of course, I'd had itches on my itches after that second Embassy break-in. And at first I'd thought it was the Ghost Squad, or DCI Browno, or even some of Bosanquet's Special Branch friends that had been stirring London's muddy pond to see what turned up. And just maybe, I'd been cocky enough to want to let them do it, too, hoping that if ever von Bentink came out of the fog looking for me, I could at least scratch one of my itches and test myself against him. But I really never thought he'd ever come after me. Messima maybe, but not Flash von Bentink. No. He was just a picture in a society magazine, the smell of Turkish tobacco in an empty room, a photo in Walsingham's file, or a ghostly voice in the night. He was a story to frighten children and me with, nothing more. He wasn't really real. And then the brazen fucker had gone and broken into my flat in broad daylight and turned my neat little world upside down. And I should've had Walsingham spirit me away to safety the moment it happened. But I didn't. And now it was too late. I'd still been feeling so very guilty over Vi's death. And then I'd wallowed in my misery like a little schoolboy, and gone and got myself stinking, steaming drunk. Clever me.

I'd been warned that Messima would probably give my name up to von Bentink. And I'd thought that if it ever happened, I'd be able to eel my way out of it, just like I always did. But I'd well and truly gone and fucked myself, now, and no mistake. Yet I was left with the itchy feeling that I'd been set up right from the start. And that all I'd had to do was show up and not bump into any of the furniture, while everybody else just sat back and waited for everything to play itself out. And now here I was heading for the final curtain and in the hands of the real villains of the piece, the international cat burglar and spy Count Henry von Bentink, and his evil henchman, Major Zavis Krepstok.

"Fascinating. Was your mind wandering? Please don't think of leaving us yet, Mr. Jethro. We have so much more to talk about."

I had a sharp pain in my head, like someone had stuck a pitchfork up my nose. And I gasped for air and got a strong whiff of ammonia, and I put it all down to me having been sick, or something, and I very noisily got on with my shivering. But I could still hear von Bentink clearly, as the sound of his voice floated round the garage like some story before bedtime I was listening to on the radio.

"The first time you burgled the Embassy, Mr. Jethro, I must admit, I was a little irritated, but also somewhat intrigued by what I regarded as your reckless daring. The Ambassador's wife and daughter, however, were very, very angry with you for stealing their jewellery. The Ambassador, too, for you having tarnished his diplomatic standing. And because you'd stained their honour, and with me being their guest, mine also, a bounty was placed on your head throughout the London underworld. Set a thief to catch a thief, as I believe you English say."

He paused for a moment, as somebody stoked the fire in the stove, and then we all got comfortable again and settled back for more.

"I know that you will have already sold all the jewellery, Mr. Jethro, and at the moment that is really of no concern to me. However, there is something, or should I say someone, that concerns me very much, indeed. So let me ask you, again, did the British Secret Service mastermind the escape of the woman called Tanyia Arzhak? Or was it the Americans? The Anti-Communist League, perhaps? Only we found leaflets, but no, no, that was probably just a clever ruse, wasn't it?"

I shuddered at the sound of Tanyia's name on his lips, but given the condition I was in, I don't think anyone noticed. My mind began to wander again, but I still didn't think I was expected to say anything sensible yet. Then I heard noises-off and got a very bad feeling that we'd come to Act Two in the proceedings. But stories, or questions, or no, I felt so knackered that I really didn't care much what he said or did, anymore, and I think I showed my disinterest by dribbling blood and spit down my chin. Though with all the talk about things that'd gone missing from the Embassy, I did wonder why he hadn't yet thought to mention the bloke who'd died that first night. The two of them must've been really close.

"You know, Mr. Jethro, all of this blood on the floor concerns me. We can't have you shuffling off this mortal coil quite yet, can we? So, let's just clean you up, before we move on to something a little more sophisticated. No, don't get up, we'll come over to you."

The noises-off stepped centre-stage. And then the voice was directly behind me, and I shuddered in fear.

"Mr. Jethro, are you listening to me? Good, because I want you to concentrate fully now. You work a lot with your hands, don't you? And that's very good, it simplifies things enormously. We're going to start by pulling your fingernails out, one by one. Then, as I see we have all the proper instruments here, I think we'll crush each one of your knuckles, and then follow that up later by breaking both of your wrists."

I didn't think I'd heard him right at first, he might just as well have been ordering dinner in a restaurant up the West End. The trouble was, this time it sounded as if he was going to make a five-shilling, three-course meal out of me, instead, and I didn't fancy that at all. I started sweating then, even in the cold.

"Good, I can see I'm beginning to get through to you at last. I want you to clearly understand what we're going to do to you, as I've observed in the past that the anticipation of pain is almost as effective as the pain itself. The history of torture has so much to teach us, if only we take the time to learn. Isn't that so, Herr Major?"

Krepstok must've been wearing new jack-boots, because when he clicked his heels together it sounded just like Puncher's fists hitting my face. I think, of the two, I'd have preferred taking another beating; at least I'd grown up with stuff like that. Even getting striped with a chiv was routine where I came from, and you just learned to live with it. But all this talk about torture wasn't natural and it was starting to get to me. I shuddered again, and got on with the rest of my sweating and shivering.

Krepstok barked an order, and someone loomed over me and bathed my face with what felt like a chamois-leather filled with grit. Water dribbled down my swollen cheeks and stung like blazes. Then I felt someone's fingers clumsily trying to pull my eyelids apart, and I yelled blue bloody murder at that. Although whoever had their digits in my mince pies probably didn't hear anything but a few tired groans.

Then I heard more scraping noises and without warning I went up in the air and the world spun round, and I think I was so confused I shouted out in terror. I didn't know what to think at first, but all they'd done was pick up the chair and turn me round to face everybody. By which I mean my judge, my jury, and my executioners. It was quite a shock, but nothing compared to what was to come.

I tried to see through puffy, swollen eyes, but it was impossible. I tried again. I squinted and blinked, and blinked again, and very slowly details began to emerge. There were five of them; big, bulky, black shapes tinged with red. I tried not to shiver, but shivered anyway, and all of a sudden my eyes clicked into focus. They were all standing round an open stove, wearing warm overcoats, and hats, and gloves, and scarves. And they were all smoking away like chimneys, so somebody must've been handing around the fags like it was Christmas or something. One of them, who was wearing a short, bum-freezer jacket, stood wiping something from off his leather gloves. The dark stains on the rag he was using, could've been motor oil, but I just knew, somehow, that it was my blood. I shook my head and tried to gather what wits I had left. So, that was Puncher. He had a face like a fist and I tried to fix it firmly in my mind, and I promised myself again that I'd kill him if I ever got the chance. Next to him were two blokes that looked to be made of solid muscle from the neck up and the neck down. And from the bored looks on their faces, I could tell I might just as well have been a piece of meat hanging in a cold-storage locker somewhere.

Then the big, black unmistakable shape of Major Krepstok turned and slowly walked towards me. It was still a shock to see him in the flesh. He creaked as he walked, and I think it took me a moment or two to realise it was the long black leather trench coat he was wearing that was making all the noise. I tried to sneer at him, but all I did was make the cuts and bruises on my face bleed all the more.

His beady little eyes looked at me with dull disinterest. He'd probably seen people in my state a thousand times before, because I noticed he didn't even flinch when he came closer to inspect the damage. He leaned in, his breath smelling of something awful, but he didn't say a word and didn't even grunt, so I'm not sure whether I impressed him or not. Looking back on it now, I think he must've been trying to work out how much more pain they could inflict upon me, before me and my carcass gave up the ghost for good. Either that, or he was already measuring me for a pine box, the friggin' swine.

Then suddenly from out of the shadows stepped the tall, elegant figure of Count Flash Harry Raffles von Bentink, himself. It was so nice to finally put a face to the voice. He was wearing a beautifully cut, camel-hair overcoat, and was sporting a red spotted silk scarf. It's funny the little things you notice sometimes. He looked every inch the perfect gentleman, but I felt his slate-grey eyes and wolfish grin tearing into me all the same, and I started shivering all over again. I peered up at him through the narrow slit of my eyes and knew his cold-hearted smile for what it was; the look of a man that's decided to kill you, and who doesn't give a fuck that you know it.

"Mr. Jethro. It's so good that at last we meet, face to face. I had once hoped that we'd meet on a rooftop somewhere in the dead of night, in a fight to death just like Sherlock Holmes and Moriarty at the Reichenbach Falls. But I'm afraid that would have been so terribly melodramatic and foolhardy. For who knows, even though I am superior to you in this strange nocturnal art that we both practice, in a fight, you might have just got lucky and killed me. And that was a risk I was not prepared to take. I could have waited for you and killed you that time I burgled your home, but I didn't. I first wanted to take from you what you'd stolen from me, the sanctuary of my place of retreat, and then to relieve you of a few precious little mementoes. For as you well know, nothing provokes a burglar more than the thought of being burgled. But enough, enough of my talk, Mr. Jethro, for you still have a schedule to keep."

I stared blankly, while he shot a shirt cuff at me. Then he flashed his big, gold Rolex; the one I'd nicked from him, the one he'd taken back from me. "This was given me by a very great man, who was very grateful for the service I'd given him. And I would have killed you for stealing this, if for nothing else." I blinked slowly and tried to look all nonchalant, but he didn't seem to notice. He just reached inside his coat, and like someone producing a rabbit out of a hat, pulled out another watch and dangled it in front of me. And what with me being tied to the chair so tightly, and not being able to feel a bleedin' thing, let alone whether my old Breitling had gone from off my wrist, or not, it was still a bit of a shock seeing it there hanging from his hand.

"I'm afraid, Mr. Jethro, your wrist-watch doesn't appear to be working." He turned, dropped the watch onto one of the benches, and did his best to smash it to pieces with a big claw-hammer. I mean, I know creepers can be funny about their timepieces, but I ask you, how pathetic was that? Don't get me wrong, I wasn't that put out about it, I mean, I had a whole drawer full of the bloody things back in my lock-up, but you've got to keep things in proper perspective, haven't you?

Even so, it made me feel quite queasy watching him do it, but I'd be buggered if I was going to let him see how upset I was, so I just sat there, looking unmoved by it all. But then things got worse. The fucker reached for a cardboard folder lying on the workbench beside him and pulled out some of the photographs and postcards he'd nicked from my flat. He picked out a couple at random, and held them up for me to see, and even from over where I was sitting I could tell that one of them was me, in my dress uniform, that last year at Southampton; peaked cap, silver buttons and all.

He cocked his head at me. "You really shouldn't have come back a second time. The first burglary was an irritation; but the second, a gross insult." Out of the blue, a gold cigarette lighter appeared in his hand, and he slowly set fire to the corners of the photographs. And as he held them up and turned their faces into the licks of flame, I squinted and saw the photos crisp and turn brown, and then finally blacken and burn with a brief intensity into nothing. Then what had been me so many years ago became little curls of ash floating for a moment on the air, until they too were gone. And I was gone with them. He smiled, all friendly-like, his teeth looking impossibly pointed and white. "And there was no way in the world that I'd ever let that go unanswered." Then he turned and said quietly, "Show him what we've been keeping warm for him."

One of his men bent down and pulled something from out of the mouth of the stove. The thing scraped along the iron grate for what seemed like ages and I didn't like the sound of it at all. I couldn't make out what it was at first, but it glowed fiercely and didn't seem to be of this world. Then, whatever it was, it came closer and closer, and it was warm, then hot, then friggin' scalding, and then I swear it even began to throb. And as the thing waved in the air inches from my face, my skin did its best to crawl away from my body. And God knows how, but I managed to keep my eyes focused on it and saw that it was a pair of long-handled pincers, the jaws glowing white-hot. I didn't even breathe, I couldn't, I was hypnotised by the friggin' thing. I blinked, which is hard to do when your eyelids are the size of pigeon eggs, and that's when I saw the bloke holding the glowing tongs was wearing a pair of thick padded, leather gloves. So straight away I could tell I was in the hands of professionals.

"Enough, I think."

I relaxed and let my breath out. Then I went straight to hell.

It went beyond me screaming. I couldn't have heard anything anyway, because every bone in me was rattling, and every sinew, nerve, and vein was shrieking and hollering in rage at the blood that was boiling, and the body that was smoking and burning and about to burst apart. Then I died. There was blackness and I was without pain or memory of it. Then there was light and I was born again into a world of hurt, that hurt so much I didn't even bother to breathe, there didn't seem to be much point.

After an eternity, that may have been no more than a minute or two, or an hour, I couldn't tell, my mind got to work searching out the bad news. It wasn't good. They'd electrocuted me, of that I was sure. How strong the current had been I didn't know or care, I'd never had much of a head for science, but I did know I'd forgotten about those bare wires wound all around me. Clumsy. It wasn't like me to forget anything as important as that. In my mind's eye I could see Krepstok's face, and the hint of a smile that'd started to play across it, just moments before they'd fried me. He'd had his hand on something that looked like a clock face, and then he'd slowly turned the big pointer on it from one side to the other. It must've been what he'd used to control the amount of electric current he'd put through me. Probably a rheostat they'd pulled off some machine, which they'd then wired up to me, and to a plug in the wall. Crude, but very, very effective.

A full two-forty volts would've stopped my heart cold, but it was still banging away inside me like the clappers so I knew I wasn't dead yet. But my body felt like one big, open, suppurating wound. I whimpered. And that's when I first noticed the wisps of smoke coming from down around my privates. It felt like someone had kicked me in the balls, only a hundred million times worse, and I was sick down myself. I chanced a breath and smelled something burning. I think it was me.

Then they dropped me straight through a hole in the floor and I began another descent into hell. The breath that I'd taken came out in one long drawn-out scream. It was the North Atlantic again, and convoy HX229 or SC122, or it was the Baltic or Murmansk or Kiev, it really didn't matter which or where, Hell had so many names and numbers to go by in the War. It was black and cold below, and there was light and fire above, but no hope. The sea was ice. The waves were like mountains and craters, and the water as dark and as foreboding as the moon in a storm, and no man could survive there long, even with his Mae West for company. The sea was afire, the slick surface alight with burning oil and heavy with the stench of burning rubber and flesh. I'd forgotten about the smell and the smoke of burning flesh, and the screams of drowning men bobbing up and down, up and down, caught for eternity between the ice and the fire.

I'd erased it all from my mind and even my darkest nightmares, but these were new and awful depths of pain I was being plunged into, and I yearned for oblivion.

And gracefully the dark lady came, and she had all the voices and all of the faces of every woman I'd ever loved or that had ever loved me. And she was my sweet mother, and my dear sister, and my sweetest love. And I reached and reached for her as she embraced me in all the blackness, and she was saying softly, oh so softly, "Jethro, what have they done to you, my love? Come, rest beside me, and be with me."

I would've cried then, only I'm sure my tears would've turned to steam. And then the cruel air came back into my blackened, tattered lungs and someone wiped my face again, but I felt nothing. When you're dead and burned and cold, your flesh doesn't belong to you and you feel no pain. And the truth of it is, whatever else you may think you are, you're not just your body, that's for sure. I know. I've been to the sea of lost souls, and I know for certain it's true.

I tried to see through my tears, and my bruised and swollen eyes. Then von Bentink got straight to work on me with his voice, again, and the softer it sounded, the harder it stung.

"Now we're beginning to get somewhere, Mr. Jethro. I do believe I can start to take whatever you say a little more seriously now. I've learnt never to be too trusting until all hope is abandoned. So, let's just settle down to a nice, little fireside chat, shall we? And then you can tell me everything I want to know. Otherwise . . . well . . . ?"

He let the word linger just long enough for me to breathe out, then they gave me a short sharp shock that rattled my teeth. I should have expected it, but I didn't, I can be right pathetic sometimes. I know I wept again, but this time they were tears of joy. I think it was from realising that I still had all of my teeth in my head.

"We have a few hours, yet, before we must return to London, Mr. Jethro. But I want you to understand, very clearly, that from this point on, the more you make me wait, the more pain I will inflict upon you."

I tried to arch away from the chair, but it was useless, we were bound together until death us do part. I had to keep on trying, though, even if it was the last thing I ever did. But my choice was now more and more limited to whether I went out with a bang or a whimper.

"No, not yet, Mr. Jethro. I decide; not you. This has to hurt you much more than all the pain and irritation you've caused me. And part of my pleasure is knowing just when you shall experience pain."

He and Chalkie were a right pair; all their talk of taking pleasure in someone else's pain was a very nasty characteristic. Then I wondered if I was already too far gone to even care. I mean, I was sinking fast. And even though it may seem odd, deep down inside, despite all the pain I must've been in, it all seemed quiet, even peaceful. I took refuge there, and tried to take longer, slower breaths. "Steady boy, steady," I said to myself, "you've seen Seth do it, a child could do it, so you just do it. Easy, now. *Nil desperandum.*" Now where in hell did something like that come from? The mind can be such a funny thing sometimes, can't it?

I'd just begun to lose myself in my desperate little reverie, when that harsh, metallic-grating sound reached in and found me again, and shattered it to pieces. My heart flew into panic as my eyes fluttered open, and I nearly shrieked. Von Bentink had his face no more than a few feet from mine, and behind him off to one side and getting closer was the bloke with the glowing, white-hot pincers in his gloved hands.

"Who were you working for? Tell me, Mr. Jethro, I know that you want to. Tell me, now. And save yourself all this needless pain and suffering."

As the eerie glow grew and grew before my eyes, I found that all my resolve dissolved into a puddle. I can't remember now if I pissed myself or not, I don't think I did, I don't think I had anything left in me. But suddenly, the only thing I wanted to do in all the world was tell Count Henry von Bentink everything, anything, something. And I tried to, I did. Honest. My mouth opened and closed, and opened and closed, but none of the words would come out right, they'd only come out as more tears. Stupid tears.

"That's quite all right, Mr. Jethro. I know you want to tell me everything now. Let me give you a moment to collect your thoughts."

That's when they turned the current back on. I began to scream then, long and hard, and quite unashamedly. And let me tell you, all that 'stiff-upper-lip' stuff people go on about is nonsense. When someone's got your balls in a wringer, and they fancy having a fry-up with them, there's nothing stiff about you anywhere.

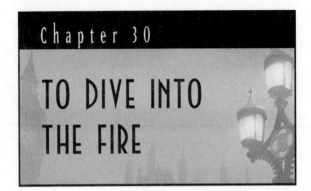

Chapter 30

TO DIVE INTO THE FIRE

It was just as well that I was making such a horrible racket, because it helped mask what was happening outside. It began as a whining noise a long way off in the distance, and then grew louder and louder until it erupted into a full-throated, howling roar. Then there was an almighty crash, followed by the sounds of all hell breaking loose. Wood cracked and snapped, and tortured metal screeched, and there was a strange hissing noise like a railway engine venting steam from one of its valves. Stuff was flying about all over the place, and bits and pieces of God knows what struck the back and sides of my chair. Not that I could feel much, anyway, as I was still too busy whimpering in gratitude that the electric current had been switched off. I swallowed, and gingerly felt round my mouth with my tongue, but it tasted metallic and bloody, just like chopped liver. And as for my heart, it was banging away like mad and short of stopping dead, it seemed desperately intent on getting out of my body in any way it could.

All the screaming and shouting centred around whatever had come crashing into the garage. I didn't know what the heck it was, and I couldn't see much of anything, as there were clouds of dust and smoke swirling about. And yet, bit by bit and against all reason, my mind trying to make sense of it all, I began to feel hope. The throbbing sound seemed oddly familiar, and I felt that whatever new danger it might represent, it meant no harm to me. It was definitely an engine of some kind and a big one, and then all of a sudden I realised it was a motorbike. Then the sounds began to separate, one from the other, and I knew for sure the bike was laying on its side with the throttle jammed, because I could hear the drive-wheel going round and round, and going nowhere fast. There was something else, too, a soft pinging sound that I couldn't place. And so I focused on the drumbeat of the engine. I knew that I knew it, but it was like an old tune running through my head that I just couldn't catch hold of. Then all of a sudden, I knew it was the big Ariel Square Four that I'd given Seth. By God. Seth. It had to be Seth. And if it was, the gods had truly smiled on me again and there was a slim chance of me coming out of this thing alive.

I turned to face the storm and was met with another wave of shouting and screaming. There was also the ugly smell of roasting flesh. I was pretty sure it wasn't me that was burning this time and that cheered me up no end. I forced my head round to look. There'd been five of them to start with, but now only three of the bastards were left standing. And Seth, popped right out of nowhere, friggin' marvellous. But how in heaven's name had he managed it? I think if I'd had any spit left in my throat, I would've swallowed it in excitement.

Krepstok stood shaking his head, blood trickling in little streams down his big, blunt forehead. But the guy who'd waved the white-hot pincers in my face was having a far worse time of it. His coat and trousers were smouldering badly, and his flesh was sizzling like black-pudding in a frying pan. The clumsy lad must've dropped the blessed things onto himself, and he just sat there in disbelief trying to remember what his legs once looked like. His screams were no match for my earlier attempts, but I knew he'd get there in the end if he kept at it.

Then I saw the big motorbike on its side, its front wheel jammed underneath one of the workbenches, its back wheel spinning round like mad. And across it, spread-eagled face down with arms out like a crucifix, was old Raffles von Bentink himself, or what was left of him. The bike, having crashed through the big, double doors, must've careened across the workshop floor and hit him square on. Well, what else would you expect with an Ariel Square Four? The force of it must've broken his legs or crushed his ankles at the very least, because it had literally knocked him right off his feet. Very nasty, but it seemed there was yet worse in store for the once elegant Herr von Bentink.

By the look of it, the bike had swept him along the floor until one of the workbenches had stopped him short and snapped his spine. It was a wonder it hadn't cut him in half, but in a way his end was just as bad. The underside of the bench had driven his body back across the bike, and pushed his head down into the spinning back wheel; the steel spokes shredding his face to pieces as efficiently as any bacon-slicer down the butchers. And from the smell of it, the exhaust pipe wasn't doing too bad a job cooking his flesh. But that was always the one trouble with those 'Squariels' as we used to call them, the rear cylinders always tended to overheat a bit. But it was a great machine, nevertheless, very responsive, and heavy enough to smash down doors if necessary. And to this day, I think of it fondly as being one of Seth's best ever 'Halifax Persuaders.'

All Flash Harry's smarm and polish had come to a very sudden and sticky end. "Shuffle off this mortal coil, eh? Where be your jibes, now? Fucking chopfallen, if you ask me, you flash foreign git," I said, almost choking. It must've come as quite a shock to him; in charge one minute, discharged the next. And I think, for one brief moment, I almost felt sorry for him. Then I thought better of it; the cold-hearted bastard was going to fry me without mercy, so what was left of him could go roast in hell.

This was all happening in seconds and eternities between breaths, mind you. Meanwhile, Puncher, trying to save the wear and tear on his hands, had picked up a length of metal pipe and was wielding it over his head like an old-fashioned cavalry sword. He swung at the white dome that was Seth's crash helmet and when I heard it connect my heart jumped into my mouth for safety. But mercifully, the pipe just clipped the side of it, before it slid off, knocking his goggles askew. Dead lucky.

Seth shook his head and moved in fast, his arm swinging out, his fist unballing to a blade, and he caught Puncher with a chop to the side of the neck. Then he pivoted on one foot, the nail-heads in his boots screeching on the concrete, and drove a knee deep into Puncher's kidney. It must've ruptured something, because the bloke's whole body arched backwards, nicely offering up his throat. A sharp downward chop brought Puncher's boxing career to a close and he crumpled to the floor, the steel pipe clattering noisily beside him. Seth swung round to face the others, the tattered skirts of his leather coat billowing out around him.

I blinked. Krepstok was struggling with the pistol in his shoulder holster, hampered only by his heavy leather coat. The real heart-stopper, though, was seeing the big bugger next to him, swinging a double-barrelled shotgun round to level at Seth; the stiff-spring clicks of those hammers being cocked, the very worst sounds I'd ever heard in all my life. "Shooters!" I yelled. Though the only thing I heard was a croaking noise that I couldn't recognise as being me.

But Seth had already darted forward, and with an outstretched arm, he swept up a pile of work-tools from off one of the workbenches and sent the whole lot flying at the shotgun.

Time stopped dead as those spanners and hammers and metal files somersaulted and spun through the air to clatter and clang and snick against the sides of the evil-looking, blue-black shotgun barrels. And though there was no more force behind them than a bunch of pebbles thrown against a window pane, they were enough to deflect the blast, even if only by a fraction, and I felt the shock wave pass me even before I heard the shot screaming through the air. I uttered the shortest prayer I knew, "God help us." But I'd already been blessed, I was at the edge of it all; the wider blast-pattern from a sawn-off would have seen me off for sure and no messing. Some of the pellets hit the chair and I felt a few stings to the side of my head and my legs, but the flex around my body must've shielded me from anything worse, and I found myself in one very ragged, but still-breathing piece. It's an ill wind, isn't it?

The sound of the blast was still banging away inside my ears, when I heard an agonised scream. Though I can honestly say, without any sense of shame, that as soon as I realised it wasn't me screaming, I felt my eyes welling up again with tears of gratitude. But it was no time to celebrate, so I blinked them away for later and squeezed my eyes back into focus. The massed shot from the blast had peppered and cleansed Pincer's upper body of much of its flesh, and I saw that what was left of his torso was still tumbling backwards and spreading in a gleaming, steaming bloody mess across the cold concrete floor. It wasn't a pretty sight, but at least he didn't have to worry about his burns any longer.

I blinked again and looked up to see Seth forcing Shooter back into

Krepstok with a flurry of combination punches. It was the fine art of boxing being visited upon a street brawler and just as well, too, because it looked like Krepstok had finally succeeded in getting his revolver clear of his leather overcoat. Seth lunged forward, with a growl, grabbed hold of Shooter and brought his knee up hard, pushing Shooter's balls up into his chest. The bloke's high-pitched screams would've done justice to a new set of bagpipes, but his noise was cut short by the sharp crack of a pistol echoing round the workshop. Once, twice, three times. I flinched in shock with each shot, and waited for the bullets to tear into me, but none did, so with my heart back in my mouth, I twisted my head round again to see what'd happened.

And for the very briefest of moments nobody moved. It was just like the girls down the Windmill Theatre presenting one of their famous nude tableaux. Shooter and Krepstok were pressed so close together they might as well have been Siamese twins in a stage act, and I read the play in a trice. The pistol was still stuck down between them, and Krepstok unable to control his itchy trigger finger had fired, with very dire consequences for Mr. Shooter. The first shot had hit the floor and ricocheted off somewhere, but the poor lad must've still been shuddering from the impact of Seth's knee to his privates, when the other two shots had blown apart his leg and shattered one of his ankles. See what I mean now about ill winds?

Then everybody moved at once. And as Shooter drew breath to scream again, Seth butted him hard in the face, stopping his noise dead. The poor bloke must've bitten right through his tongue, too, because suddenly there was blood everywhere. But Seth, his arms going back and forth like pistons, just kept on pushing Shooter's convulsing body back into Krepstok, keeping the bald-headed bastard off balance, and his arm and pistol well and truly trapped.

But as Shooter finally dropped to the floor with the sobbing sound of air escaping a ruptured inner tube, he almost buggered everything up by taking Seth down with him. And as Seth's boots slipped and scraped on the blood- and oil-slicked floor, Krepstok scrambled backwards, his arms windmilling like mad. I tried to swallow, hoping that he'd fall as well, but somehow the bastard managed to stay upright, and he swung his arm up and fired. The bullet missed me, though, and I said a quick 'Hail Mary' for yet another deliverance.

Seth lunged at Krepstok, but one of his boots caught in Shooter's crumpled overcoat and he fell headlong. He grabbed for the edge of Krepstok's long leather coat, and even though his grip didn't hold, it at least made the granite-headed bastard slip. And as Krepstok threw his hands out to break his fall, the pistol clattered to the floor and fired again. I think we all blinked at that, but luckily for Seth and me, the bullet went straight out through what was left of the wooden doors. I said two more 'Hail Marys' and counted five shots. I tried to think of how many rounds those friggin' Lugers could hold, but gave up. I knew there was still more than enough bullets left yet to kill us all.

Krepstok was down in a heap, but so was Seth, and Krepstok rolled over and started kicking out at him wildly. One of his black leather jackboots struck Seth on top of his helmet and I saw his head jolt back from the force of it. Then like a dirty black smear, Krepstok scrambled sideways and struggled to his feet, his leather coat cracking and creaking, like a jumping-jacks firework. I didn't dare breathe. Seth was still down on his hands and knees, shaking his head, and I sat there, suddenly deflated and dejected, waiting for it all to be over. But then, instead of rushing at Seth and finishing it, Krepstok turned and started searching for his fallen pistol.

Some people never learn, do they? And thank God for that, because it gave Seth the second or two he needed to get to his feet. And at the sound of Seth planting his boots firmly on the concrete, Krepstok spun round and growled, although whether from frustration or fear I couldn't tell.

It wasn't a question of guns or knives or hammers anymore, it was just bare hands and feet and teeth, and no mercy given or expected. It probably wasn't the way Krepstok liked to fight, but he hadn't got where he had by arranging flowers, had he? And as I strained against my bindings, they rushed at one another, arms straight out in front of them, like two old-fashioned fairground wrestlers. The crash sounded like a clap of thunder, the staccato slaps of leather glove on leather coat like big fat raindrops hitting a tin roof. They struggled to get a grip on each other, but after a minute of grunting, muscle-straining effort they broke apart as cleanly as if a referee had shouted for them to do so. And they stepped back a few paces, drew breath into their heaving lungs, and took another moment to size each other up.

Then Seth took another step back, slowly unfastened the leather strap from under his chin, removed his white crash helmet and set it aside on top of one of the workbenches. Then very calmly, he removed his leather gauntlets and dropped them, one by one, into the still-wobbling, upturned helmet. Krepstok seemed transfixed by it all; I know I was. I swallowed, my mouth suddenly as dry as old bone.

"Pack it in now for your own sake and we'll let the proper authorities deal with you." Seth's voice was hoarse, but I think more from exertion than emotion. He took another step back then, as if to give Krepstok more room to think. But instead of giving up the game, the fucker lunged for the shotgun lying on the floor at his feet.

Seth still didn't move a muscle. "It's empty," he said quietly. "Give it up now. And I won't tell you again."

But Krepstok wasn't listening. He had the gun by the barrels, and now with his makeshift club held tight in both hands, you could see he thought he'd regained the advantage. I shook my head. He might've been a right tearaway at one time, but however tough he looked now, it must've all gone to fat in his head.

Krepstok rushed at Seth swinging the gun above his head. But Seth, every inch the old boxing pro, stepped back and to one side, and the polished wooden gun-stock slid off the padded shoulder of his leather coat. Then Seth darted in quickly, pushing the shotgun down and away with a sweep of his arm. And as Krepstok's own momentum brought him round, Seth pulled back his elbow and drove the point down hard. I'd seen him do that to one of the tearaways round the back of the Palladium, and just as had happened then, Krepstok's hand jerked open and the shotgun went flying. It must hit a nerve or something. It looked like a neat trick, though, and I promised I'd try it myself sometime, if I ever got the chance.

Krepstok stumbled back against a workbench and shook his head, and I think that was the first time he saw what had happened to his old pal, von Bentink. Krepstok probably didn't give two monkeys for any of his men, but now he got his first real look at his future prospects all going up in smoke. It was also probably the first time he'd got a whiff of Raffles being roasted; a very nasty smell, indeed. And it must've really got to him, because I heard the growl in his throat, even above the throb of the Ariel's engine. He spun round enraged, a claw-hammer in one hand and a big, sharp-pointed metal file in the other. He snorted, wiped the blood from his nose with his sleeve, and began moving crabwise around the workshop.

Seth, his eyes narrowed, his curly black hair plastered across his forehead, matched Krepstok's every move, and slowly the two of them inched their way round towards me until all three of us were in a line. And as if that was the moment he'd been waiting for, Krepstok rushed forward. But even as the claw-hammer swung down towards Seth's now unprotected head, he dodged to one side, and bobbing and weaving like mad, he stepped in close and the hammer whistled past over his shoulder. It looked to me as if Seth had completely ignored the hammer and focused on the big metal file that Krepstok was trying to skewer him with. Which was an interesting move, but still a very dodgy one.

Seth hooked his arm over Krepstok's hammer arm and pulled hard, forcing the bigger man off balance. It was only a matter of fractions, but the thrust of the metal file was altered, and Seth swept his free arm up in an arc and blocked the file inches from his stomach. He pushed it down and away to one side, then gripping hold of the file, he slid his hand up the length of its jagged face until it caught up against Krepstok's thumb. He pushed hard and even I heard the heavy click of dislocating bone. But this time Seth didn't stop, and twisting his body like a man using a scythe, he hit Krepstok across the face with his forearm and swung back and hit him again on the side of the jaw with his elbow.

The claw-hammer thudded to the floor and so did the big metal file. And as Krepstok fell backwards, Seth hit him again square on the jaw with the heel of his hand. Krepstok's teeth banged together like a big steamer trunk slamming shut, and he toppled back, banging his big granite head into the metalled edge of one of the workbenches with such force, that I swear you could hear every one of the bones in his neck snap. I swallowed. And suddenly it was all over.

From my throne I squinted round me at all the vanquished lying in pools of blood and oil and shit, and I didn't feel a thing, not a thing. I peered up at Seth, but I still don't think I was seeing straight, as my eyes were all watery.

"Jethro, it's me, Seth. Are you all right, my old pal?"

I tried to murmur something, but I was suddenly very, very tired, and the only thing that came out sounded like a cat mewing.

"Easy now, I'm going to cut all this stuff off you. By bloody hell, what were those bastards trying to do to you? Hold on."

Somewhere, on the other side of the world, I heard the sound of scissors or shears, cutting and snipping, and I tried not to shiver with fright. The throbbing of the engine had stopped, and I could quite clearly hear the sound of my teeth chattering. There were other noises, too; the groans and creaks of things settling back into silence after violence has run its course.

"Easy now, Jethro, easy now. Just a few more snips, then we'll get you off to hospital and get you all fixed up."

He picked me up, but I didn't scream, as the body he had hold of didn't seem to be mine. I think I must've groaned a fair bit, though.

"Easy now, my old friend. Just let me lay you down for a moment and get a blanket over you. Easy, Jethro, it's over. I don't think any of them will be harming anyone else for a long time. You're safe now, you're safe."

Seth's voice was as sweet as music to my ears, and for a moment I almost felt like humming along until I remembered all I really wanted to do was sleep. Just sleep. Then I'd slip off this burned and blackened mortal coil of mine, and wave 'cheerio' to the flights of angels singing me to my rest. I wanted nothing else but to float away on the tide forever. And yet something held me back, like an anchor holding a boat fast against the clutching currents of the pulling tide. What was it? I was damned if I knew. I was shivering with cold, or shock, or something, or it might've even been the joy of knowing I'd never have to suffer anything ever again, I don't know. All I knew was, I was floating, gently bobbing up and down, and the water was warm and Seth was talking to me again. I followed the sound of the voice and drifted up against something, and I remember holding on to it and climbing hand over hand very slowly up an anchor chain. And it was cold, so very cold, and my hands were numb, and I wondered where on earth my turtles were.

"Just you keep warm, Jethro. I'll be back in a minute. I'm going to see if I can get one of their motors started. There must be some car keys round here somewhere. If not, I'll try wiring one of the buggers to get it started, then we'll get you to hospital."

I yelled up at him, but the silly sod didn't seem to hear a word. What was wrong with him? I yelled, even louder. I knew I was out of the game, and probably for good, but I was still thinking things out, playing the odds. But that's me, isn't it, always trying to think beyond the next step. And what I realised was that it would be much better all round if Seth just got the hell off out of it. He could call for an ambulance or a doctor or an undertaker or whatever it was he thought I needed, from a telephone box somewhere. And the sooner the better, unless he wanted to end up inside. I knew they'd pin manslaughter or murder on him, otherwise. And if that happened on account of me, I think Joanie would've killed me all over again herself, even before Seth's little wife, Dilys, could get her tiny Welsh hands on me. So I had to try and get him to see sense, didn't I? But from all the response I was getting from him, you'd have thought I was barely whispering or something.

"What's that, Jethro? What are you trying to say? Don't try moving any, I'll come closer. Take your time, take your time."

What the hell was he going on about? Was he deaf? I was yelling at the top of my voice. He leaned closer.

"Here, sip some water."

Water? Here I was about to go down for the third time, and here he was giving me water. Was he daft? I thought I'd best humour him, though, just play along . . . but it tasted good, it did, the water, it tasted bloody marvellous, and I think I even tried shouting for more.

"Yes, please. Thank you, thank you." I lapped the water as fast as I could, but with every trickle of it down my dry, cracked throat, I could feel the tide turning and I knew there wasn't much time, even if he didn't. Seth swam closer and I suddenly felt much warmer.

"I'm putting another blanket on you, Jethro. Try not to move."

I tried to tell him one last time. "Go on, Seth, scarper. They don't know about you. It's better for you. Me. Ray. Joanie. Dilys. Much better if you just leave. Go on. Leave me. Just leave me sleep."

"Don't you fret, Jethro, you have a little kip. Be back in a minute."

What was the use? You try your best, even though it doesn't always get you anywhere, but you can't give up, can you? You've got to keep on trying or else what else is there? My old dad said, "Never say die," the day he died, and he'd always told me I took after him.

And I'd tried, I really had. But I felt so tired. I'd try again in a bit. I closed my eyes and drifted off, but then started wide awake. I could hear bells. Bells? Someone was having a bloody church service somewhere; mine, probably. But what did I want with a church, even though London was full of the blessed things thanks to the likes of Wren and Hawksmoor; and every one of them glorious, wonderful, and inspiring.

But when had any of that ever mattered to me? I was always going to be buried at sea. Then I felt the tide pulling again, and suddenly I was impatient to get it all over with, so I quietly slipped off the anchor chain, slid back into the warm water, crossed my arms, closed my eyes for good, and slept the sleep of the dead.

Chapter 31

IN REMEMBRANCE OF THE DEAD

Hell is a parade ground full of barking-mad sergeant-majors, and squads of soldiers square-bashing forever in their hob-nailed boots. I know, because I've been there and seen and heard it all for myself. And I tell you, the bloody racket they were making with their blasted left-right-lefting and about-turn-quick-marching was enough to wake the dead. I know, because it awoke me.

I didn't know where I was at first, or for some time afterwards, everything just kept floating in and out on the tide, with me boiling hot one minute and friggin' freezing the next. And when I finally managed to stay awake for any length of time, my head hurt, my back hurt, my ribs hurt, my privates hurt, my legs hurt, in fact, I bloody well hurt all over. Most of the time, the pain was like some distant memory; it was there, but I was elsewhere, if you get my drift. And all due, no doubt, to the ruddy great big needle full of morphine or something that some old cow in a uniform kept stabbing into me when I wasn't looking. "There, there, whist now, hush your fuss, you terrible man," she'd say. "This will help the pain and let you get some sleep." But I didn't believe a word of it, and I cried out in shock and shame whenever I saw her approaching in the dark. I tell you, Hell's got nothing on a senior ward sister that once must've trained with the Commandos.

It was a hospital, I'd worked that bit out, but I was in a room all on my tod, which was unusual. They usually stuffed the sick inside a ward with dozens of other people coughing and groaning and farting in your face at all hours of the day and night. But there I was in a top-floor room, all by myself, and why else would that be, I wondered, unless I'd been brought there to die.

All alone, that is, apart from the old copper outside my room, who kept looking in to see whether I'd woken up, or not. I played dead every time he poked his big nose in, and even with me bandaged from head to foot and with my arm in a sling, it was a doddle. But after the first hundred years of playing hide-and-seek with my eyelids, I just went back to sleep again, it was all too much like hard work. The thing that got me, though, was that whenever the old bugger stuck his head round the door to look in on me, he'd slowly shake his head, and 'tut-tut' sympathetically in my direction. Then he'd mutter something under his breath that I could never quite make out, and go back to sitting outside in the corridor with his mug of tea, his fags, and his newspaper. The way he kept going on, you'd have thought I was in a bad way or something. Old coppers? I wouldn't give you tuppence for them, or your old watch and chain.

The odd thing, though, was that sometimes the copper had a nurse's hat on, or his face was old or young, and he was a blonde or a brunette. And I swear that once he even looked like Tanyia, and had a look of such sadness on his face, her face, that my heart seemed fit to burst, and I cried out in anguish and pain. Then it went dark again. And then there was a dark, curly-haired bloke that I knew I knew, but whose name I just couldn't place. Then the copper had Joanie's face and then Barry's face. Then it was him, again, only with a different nurse's hat on. And then all of a sudden the dark went away and the light stayed on, and my throat was parched and I dreamt of water, to drink or drown in, I didn't care, I just needed about a million gallons of the stuff.

Then it was dark again and time passed, and the days and nights all ran together, but it didn't matter much, as there was always fog, fog, and more bloody fog and nothing else to see. Then it was bitter cold and I was freezing, and it was snowing so hard everything was white, and then the snowflakes broke apart and dissolved into black coals. And then the coals were all glowing blood-red, and white-hot pincers were burning and tearing at my skin, and I was screaming and screaming. Then the banging and the crashing and the throbbing filled my head again. And then there was only the smell of roasting flesh, and the swelling chorus of men's cries, and the tolling of the bells. Then I was deathly cold and drifting slowly out to sea to die a seaman's death.

Then one day it was different. I was awoken by horrible tortured sounds, worse than if someone was stabbing a dozen cats caught in a potato sack. I sat bolt upright. "What on earth? What in hell's name?" I shut my eyes and shook my head to shut my ears, but that didn't work. So I tried shaking my head up and down and from side to side, but it only made things worse. And still there were those sounds, those bloody awful caterwauling sounds, and I couldn't get them out of my head. And I thought I'd finally gone mad. Was this how it was all going to end, then? Well, bugger that, I thought. Time to go out like a lion, so I took a deep breath and prepared to face all my demons, whatever they were.

"Fuck off!" I shouted at the top of my lungs. And things began to clear. And through the white mist I could see shadows turning into shapes and shapes into colours, and then the shapes were moving from left to right and left-right, left-right, they were marching up and down to ... the banshee wailing of the friggin' bagpipes. I tell you, I didn't know whether to laugh or cry or shit myself, and I think I probably did a bit of all three, just to celebrate, I mean I was back from the dead, wasn't I?

And at that precise moment the old copper stuck his head around the door and said, "Are you alright?"

"Where am I?" I whispered hoarsely.

"King Edward the Seventh hospital in the Royal Borough of Windsor, that's where you are, matey. Right opposite the Guards barracks. And it's the Scots Guards guarding the King and Queen, at Windsor Castle, this year, I think."

"Well, that friggin' well explains everything," I said, staring madly around the room. And then I promptly fell back asleep again.

They seemed quite pleased that I was awake and talking. I still had to be fed and watered, and have my burns attended to. Then there were the inevitable bedpans, and the sponge baths where they rolled you back and forth so violently it was enough to make you seasick. And, of course, whenever I wasn't looking there was that bloody cow of a ward sister again, with her ruddy great big needle, and me yelping and cursing and complaining until I fell back once more into the pit of sleep. And even that took a different turn from before, because it wasn't me sweating through a nightmare, anymore, it was me, all warm and cozy, just drifting backwards and forwards with the tide. I had a few little turns for the worse, but very gradually I got better.

Then they started letting me have proper visitors. Joanie and Barry came first, and they both fussed over me like a couple of hens. Joanie was the worst, picking holes in this, poking holes in that, and just being generally dissatisfied with the standard of nursing I was getting. I think she secretly blamed herself for not having been on hand to sort out the filthy swines that had tortured me. And at one point she even went off to find the ward sister to complain about something or other, and came face to face with her in the corridor, and before you could say boo to a goose they were both chatting away ten to the dozen. I don't know what was said, but all of a sudden I heard these peals of laughter come drifting back from outside, and after that the two of them were as thick as thieves. And the needles kept on coming my way, so whatever she'd said to the old cow didn't do me much good in the end.

Anyway, after about another couple of hundred years of being up one minute and down the next, I was propped up against the pillows feeling well and truly knackered and a bit depressed by it all when I fell into a restless sleep and began drifting off somewhere. But then someone started gently calling me back. It sounded like someone I knew, but I couldn't put a name to the voice, and then all of a sudden I knew it was Seth. I tried to open my eyes, but his face just kept on rippling on the waves and looking like one of those Picasso paintings you see sometimes in the art galleries down Bond Street. An eye here, an ear, and another eye over there, the mouth sideways, and the other ear down where the chin should be. Not exactly my cup of tea, I know, but I could still see it was Seth.

"Hello, Jethro, my old pal. Is there anything you want? Shall I sing you a song? Do you want me to tell you a joke?"

I could hear him plain as day, at least I could if those Scots gits, or whoever it was, that was making such a bleedin' racket in my head, ever decided to pack it in. I tried to say something, but nothing happened.

"It's no good, Dil, he can't hear me, so we better leave him in peace. We'll come back again, tomorrow."

"Seth?" I heard a croaking sound that might've been me. "Seth, is that you?" It was me.

"Hello, my old pal. Yes, it's me, Seth. Dilys, look, he's awake. Yes, Jethro, it's me and my wife, Dilys. She's come to see you, too."

" 'Lo, Seth." My mouth was as dry as a sack of seed. "Water?"

He reached for the pitcher by the side of my bed and poured water into a glass, it was one of the sweetest sounds in all the world.

"Here you are, old pal, sip this." So I sipped and sipped, and he said soothingly, "This is just how I left you, but you're safe now." And that's when I started screaming, but no one heard me but me, and water spilled down my chin and I couldn't breathe and there was Seth again holding my head up above the waves helping me back towards dry land.

"Water," I said. "More water."

"Take it steady, now," he whispered. "Just sip it, sip it gently. There's plenty more where that came from."

I sipped, slowly, and then hurriedly, and tasted the sweetness of life again, and swam slowly back from the depths of the dead, and felt more alive than I'd done in years.

It was Seth, better for me than all the pills and needles in China. The first thing I noticed was the brilliant white bandage that covered his left hand, but he didn't seem to be paying it too much attention, so I let it go and didn't mention it. He looked resplendent in his dark brown, chalk-stripe demob suit, and his red tie and white pocket-handkerchief. And everything all nicely set off by the little white rose in his lapel, and the big smile on his face. I tell you, Savile Row couldn't have turned out anyone smarter, and looking at him, just knowing he was there, I even started feeling better myself.

He had a smashing-looking girl with him. A tiny little number in a navy blue suit with big, hazel-green eyes and dark brown wavy hair, and I knew at once that it was his wife, Dilys.

I tried talking again. "Good to see you, Seth," I said. Then I tried smiling, and said hello to Dilys. And she smiled back, and said hello to me, and then we were all off to the races. "What the hell happened back there?" I said. "I can't remember a bloody thing." Not knowing, of course, whether I was ready to hear all about it or not.

Seth nodded to Dilys, and she came over and put down a little brown paper bag full of fruit on my bedside table and smiled at me. "My Seth says you're a good man, so you just get yourself better, Jethro, and then you come down and see us. Okay?" She squeezed my hand. "I'll leave the two of you to talk, while I go off and find myself a nice cup of tea in the canteen. Ta-ra." She turned, stroked Seth's good arm as she went by, then quietly slipped out the door. The old copper stuck his head back in to make sure everything was all right, and I just smiled and nodded, and he left us alone, all looks of sympathy now gone.

Seth had a quick look to make sure the door was fully closed, and then he came over, pulled up a chair, and sat down by the side of the bed. "What our Dil doesn't know won't hurt her, and I think it's best we keep it that way. It got very bad back there for a time." I nodded, he was right of course. "Shall I start from the beginning?" he said.

"Yeah, and don't leave anything to my imagination, it's bad enough as it is."

"Well, my old pal, it was like this."

And he told me of how it had all started for him the day that he'd rung up Joanie, to ask if he could speak to me. And she'd told him about how badly Vi's funeral had affected me, and how worried she was about me. Then, of course, that was it, he told her straightaway that he was coming up, and no messing. And so he'd come up to London the very next day on the Ariel, to see me and to bring all our Christmas presents.

"I hadn't been able to make your little get-together the week before, and I didn't know about that lady's death, or her funeral, or I'd have been up earlier," he said, biting his lip. "But maybe just as well, and all, the way things turned out."

And, of course, then I remembered that message that Barry had forgotten to remember. I wondered if it would've made any difference if he had. Probably not. But then again, if I'd known Seth was coming up to London, I might've called him back and stopped him because of the bad weather. Which would've had me all alone, tied to that chair again, but with no one around to save me. I shuddered, and tried to smile.

He'd got to Church Street, parked in a space in between two empty market stalls, and put the motorbike up on its stand. Then he'd just taken off his gauntlets, goggles, and helmet, and bent down to get the Christmas presents out of the saddle bags, when he'd heard a car screech to a halt in the street, followed by the sounds of a scuffle. And he'd looked up and seen what he thought was me being bundled into the back of a big black sedan. So he'd ducked back down again as the car went past, but was already putting his gear back on to follow me. And even before the car had reached the end of Church Street and turned left into the Edgware Road, he'd kick-started the bike and was giving chase.

"It was a touch and go at first, Jethro, with me weaving in and out of the traffic, but I soon got them in my sights and got into the rhythm of their driving, then I just settled back and let them set the pace. I wasn't part of Phantom for nothing, you know, I did many journeys in the dark with no more than a narrow slit of light for a head-lamp."

I felt my mouth go dry again, but Seth gave me another sip of water, and this time I managed to drink from the cup all by myself. "Go on," I said, sipping hungrily.

"Well, after going along Bayswater Road to Notting Hill and Shepherds Bush, they headed for Hammersmith and the Great West Road. Then it was straight on to Slough before they turned off down towards Eton and Windsor. They kept on going through Old Windsor towards Ascot, and then just a few miles beyond, they pulled off the road into an old coach-builder's yard. It was easy enough to see, there was another motor car waiting for them, and they both had their headlights blazing. They milled about outside for a bit, and then carried you inside and closed the doors. So I hid the bike behind some trees, and crawled my way back up to the building. The windows were filthy dirty, but I found a corner of one I could see in through. Everyone was standing around a little pot-bellied stove and there were shadows all round the walls. I couldn't see you at first, but then I saw them lift you up, pull your trousers down, and tie you to the chair."

Listening to him was almost more than I could stand. A tingling started down in a place I hadn't been able to feel anything in for weeks and I'd have scratched myself if I'd had a free hand. I swallowed instead, my mouth as dry as the bottom of a parrot's cage. "Go on," I croaked.

"Well, there's not much to tell after that. I waited almost until it got light, and that's when you finally came round on your own. They'd tried slapping your face, smelling salts, the lot, but they hadn't been able to get much of anything out of you. But once you'd surfaced they really started in on you. Then when I saw the big bloke pull the red-hot pincers out of the stove, I knew I had to do something fast, so I scrambled back to the bike as quick as I could. I don't know what they did to you, but I could hear your screams half a mile away. So I bum-started the motorbike and roared up the track towards the garage. I put the bike down into a skid, set it straight at the wooden doors, and it sent the whole bloody lot flying. Then I slid in behind it on my backside, sounding just like the milk train arriving at Paddington Station. That leather coat you loaned me is a bit the worse for wear, but I tell you, it certainly saved my hide. But the bike, well, er . . . sorry about that, Jethro, it was . . . it's a write-off. And I had to leave it there."

I shook my head. "No need to be sorry about that, Seth, that's the least of my worries, I'm only glad you found it useful. So what the hell happened, then?"

"Well, not too much. I sort of told them 'I wouldn't tell them again,' if you get my meaning. After that I cut away the wire flex they'd tied you up with. But you were in a pretty bad way by then, my old friend, and I'm only sorry I wasn't there sooner. Honest to God, I am."

I swallowed again at the thought he might not have got there at all. "Don't you ever be sorry about that, sunshine, or anything else, not ever. I wouldn't be here now if it wasn't for you. I owe you a beer for that. No, make that two beers." He laughed, but he sounded as choked as me about it all. "Go on," I said.

He cleared his throat. "Well, I managed to get some water down your throat, but then I heard alarm bells ringing in the distance, and that's when you said it was best I scarper. And you got quite shirty about it. So I left you bundled up as best as I could, made myself scarce, and hid inside an old, broken-down van that'd been left in one of the fields nearby. Then suddenly the place was teeming with police cars, and there were coppers in uniform and plain clothes swarming over everything in sight. But what was interesting, Jethro, was that they all came fully armed, and by that I mean every man jack of them was carrying a rifle, a revolver, or an automatic pistol. Then a tall, distinguished-looking bloke in civvies got out of one of the cars; clipped moustache, grey hair and all, officer written all over him, you know the type. Anyway, he took charge and everyone got down to business. He had a younger, fair-haired bloke with him who looked a bit like you, oddly enough. The only reason I mention it, is that they both seemed quite concerned about you being so poorly."

I pondered that for a bit. It had to be Walsingham and Bosanquet he was talking about. And armed, too. I didn't know they cared enough about me to turn up out of the blue like that, especially as they couldn't have known it was me inside the garage. Unless . . . unless. And they had got there so very quickly after the shooting started, hadn't they? "Go on, Seth," I said, my mind suddenly as clear as a bell and whirring away like well-oiled clockwork.

"Well, then several ambulances arrived, and after a couple of the attendants tended to your wounds, they had you on the first stretcher out of there. Everyone wanted to give a hand; they were treating you like royalty. Then the tall grey-haired gent went off with you in the back of the ambulance, leaving the younger bloke in charge. And that's when they started carrying the other bodies out. I think two of them were dead for sure, and one probably won't walk again, I can't say about the other two, but they weren't moving too much when I left them."

He'd told them that 'he wouldn't tell them again.' I could've told them what that meant, but they'd never have believed me. I mean, who would? Two dead, maybe three. And suddenly it hit me how far things had gone. I hadn't been in any position to worry about it before, but now I had no choice, I had to think and quick. I only hoped Seth would be alright with it, after all, he'd only done what he'd been forced to do, but killing someone, even when they deserve it, carries its own special can of worms. I know.

"Are you all right about all this, Seth, only I . . . I . . ." I stammered.

And suddenly he was serious, and the still waters ran very deep. "Look, Jethro, I didn't fight the Jerries and the Japs halfway around the world to be pushed around by bullies like that. Or to stand by and see people torturing a friend. They were mad dogs and they got what they deserved. And that's an end to it."

And it was. Neither of us ever mentioned it again. "Amen, to that," I said.

He continued on, all matter-of-fact. "So, then I just scarpered across the field and made myself scarce. I used the cover of a nearby wood for about a mile and a half, and then walked along the main road until I got a lift back into Windsor from a lorry driver. And after that, I managed to hop on a bus that took me all the way home to the Farnham Road."

I shook my head in amazement; he'd seen off the best gang the Soviets and their stooges had been able to muster, and then gone off home by bus. Only in Merry Old England.

Chapter 32

TWO TURTLE-DOVES

Dilys popped her head round the door then. "We'd better get off, Seth, love, we've got a bus to catch."

I don't think she ever realised why I started laughing my head off, but before long we were all at it. It hurt like hell, but I tell you, it was worth every rib-tickling shake and shudder.

Seth grinned. "It's bloody good to see you on the mend, Jethro, my old pal. We'll pop in again and see you soon, won't we, Dil?"

"Yes, love," she said. And then she produced a buff-coloured envelope out of her handbag and handed it to Seth, which, without any palaver, he handed straight to me.

"I thought you'd probably like these, Jethro, seeing as they must all belong to you anyway."

And suddenly all—well, nearly all—of the photographs and postcards that von Bentink had nicked from the flat fluttered out onto the blanket like a flock of pigeons come home to roost. I didn't know what to say, but I think the tears that welled up in my eyes must've spoken volumes. Someone once said there's no one more sentimental than a villain, and I wouldn't have argued just then. I blew my nose into a clean handkerchief that Joanie had given me during her last visit, remembering in the nick of time not to finish up by wiping it on my sleeve. Well, I had company, didn't I?

Something just popped into my mind then, a question I'd always meant to ask, but had not remembered until that very moment. I smiled at the two of them, but my question was for Seth. " 'Ere, Seth. That night outside the Palladium, what were all those bits of paper you went back for? Only, I've always meant to ask."

He chuckled and reached inside his jacket and showed them to me right there and then. "It's a list of my favourite tunes," he said, "just in case anybody ever asks me to sing them a song."

And as Dilys, standing beside him, rolled her eyes and smiled, even I had to have a laugh.

"Well, my old china," I said, "when I finally get out of this place, we'll have more than a song or two out of you, we'll all of us go out on the town and have a right old knees-up."

Then grinning that big, shy grin of his, he said, "Here, Jethro, we brought these for you, too. Merry Christmas, from us both."

And a nicely wrapped Christmas parcel dropped out of nowhere, and I unwrapped it quickly, tearing at the patterned paper with theatrical gestures and gay abandon. I was suddenly doing everyday normal things that friends do with friends come Christmas time, and I must admit, it felt so very good to be back in the land of the living. The present turned out to be a pair of black leather turtles that were just my size.

"Thanks, you two wonderful people, they're terrific, just what I need to get myself out of here," I said, really pleased.

"They're not the ones we had made up for you by your friend Morrie Templeton, as they sort of went missing, but—"

"Morrie? How in heaven's name do you know Morrie?" I said, genuinely surprised.

"Your Joanie told me," Seth said. "She said you had all your gloves specially made by him. So we sent him a postal order and had him run you up a pair. He knew your hand size and everything."

"That's right, good old Morrie; best turtles man in London. Gee, thanks, you two, you shouldn't have done, but I'm very glad you did. Knowing you went to all that trouble gets me right here." I touched the place over my heart. "These, these are wonderful. Ta, very much." I held up the turtles and waved them slowly back and forward like royalty, and gave them my biggest smile. "And thanks for coming to see me, too. I feel so much better now, I really do."

They were just leaving, when the door opened again, and of all the people, it was Walsingham and Bosanquet; all bowler hats, rolled umbrellas, and knife-creased mufti.

"Aaaghm." Somebody, somewhere cleared their throat. "I'm sorry, I do hope we're not bothering you, we can come back later."

"No, that's all right, love," said Dilys. "We were just leaving." And with that she took Seth's good arm and they made for the door.

"Bye, Jethro," they said, with their best butter-wouldn't-melt-in-my-mouth looks plastered all over their faces.

"Bye," I said, mentioning no names; giving no pack-drill. I tell you, I might've been as weak as a kitten, but there were no flies on me.

They left. The door closed shut. And I caught a quizzical look on Walsingham's face, and the very slightest answering shake of the head from Bosanquet. Good. If they still hadn't put Seth in the frame with me yet, then they probably never would. I decided to take the initiative and suddenly I began to feel a whole lot better.

"Hello, you two. Very nice of you to take the time to pop in, you being so very busy 'Defending the Realm' and all. I suppose I have you both to thank for all this?" I waved an arm vaguely at the room.

"Yes, it was the very least we could do in the circumstances." It was Bosanquet, filling in the background as usual.

"Think nothing of it," I said. "What's me being nearly beaten to a bloody pulp and then tortured to death, between us friends?" I hadn't realised how pissed off and angry I was about everything, but the pennies had started to drop into place. The two of them had to have known that von Bentink and Krepstok would kidnap me.

"Look, you're not feeling well. So, perhaps we should come back another time?" Walsingham said, smiling his 'I'm really so awfully concerned about you' smile; as ever, as smooth as silk; as supple as a fox.

"Oh, no you don't," I said. "And don't you dare try flannelling your way out of this one, either. I risked life and limb for you, so give."

It was Bosanquet that stepped in to pour oil on troubled waters, but then who else would it have been?

"The problem was simple, Jethro. The Ghost Squad informed us that the reward for the Embassy burglar had been increased to two thousand pounds, and that your name was already being bandied about in connection with it. So it's odds on that you would have been abducted sooner or later, and von Bentink would have had you in his hands, and we wouldn't have been any the wiser. And so we couldn't take the risk of you being kidnapped, and us not knowing."

Blimey, two thousand quid, on my head? I'd have given myself away for that much. You could buy yourself a very nice house for that.

Bosanquet chatted on. "So we had no choice but to put the finger on you ourselves, so to speak. To protect you."

The words sort of hung there in the room. The sun tried to shine. The clouds scudded, the birds chirped, the soldiers marched. There was no clock to tick, but my heart filled in the empty space, and I could hear the sound of it beating loudly in my ears. I blinked. And blinked again.

"What? You . . . you gave me up to them yourselves? You? You did? You swines." The pennies I'd had in my mind hadn't dropped that far. I suddenly didn't have enough energy to shout, "You fucking lousy, double-crossing, good-for-nothing, bull-shitting bastards!" at the top of my lungs, so it came out sounding pathetic, and more like, "What . . . what the bleedin' hell did you go and do that for?"

It was Walsingham that spoke. "As Simon said, Jethro, it was done simply to protect you. We had to bring things to a head. Otherwise there was absolutely no way of knowing when they would take you. With word of that kind of money on the street, someone would have put it all together sooner or later. So I chose to act first and I gave the order. And I'm terribly sorry, old man, about what happened to you."

It was as near an apology as I was ever going to get, but like I said before, I didn't know that then. He cleared his throat, and continued.

"Simon got the word out through contacts of DCI Browno's, so we were confident the information would quickly find its way to Messima, and then via him, to von Bentink. We expected our foreign friends to be quick off the mark, and were fully prepared for the event. We had teams of men watching you twenty-four hours a day, ready to protect you and apprehend them. You were supposed to be perfectly safe."

"Well, that all went to cock, then, didn't it, Mr. Walsingham, sir? Or did I miss something?" I was doubly pissed off, and I tend to forget my manners sometimes when I get that way. And worse, I almost missed the bit about him confirming his link to Browno.

"Well, yes, it was a bit of a cock-up. It was a change-over between two of the watching teams. Apparently, they thought that you were safely tucked up for the night and didn't expect you to go out again. I've had Simon remonstrate with them at length over the incident."

"Well, that makes me feel so much better, I must say," I said, my heavy irony thudding to the floor all around me. "So, I suppose that none of your wonderful teams of watchers noticed the bastard burgling my flat the day before then, either, did they?"

"Good God, man," he said, looking surprised. "You should have called the number I gave you, the moment you discovered you'd been burgled. I'd have brought you into protective custody, had I known."

"Yes," I said, glaring at him fiercely, "but would that have been before, or after, von Bentink's men had lifted me?"

He looked out the window at all the marching soldiers. Then he turned to face me, ramrod straight, his face set. "Perhaps you did deserve better, Jethro. But let's all just be grateful it's over and done with now, shall we? But do be assured that His Majesty's Government does greatly thank you for your services in 'Defence of the Realm.' As, indeed, do I."

Then Bosanquet gently stepped in. "I'm sorry, Jethro, but we really had no other choice in the matter. Von Bentink had to be stopped. And even though things didn't go quite as smoothly as they should have done, it did all come out right in the end, thanks to you."

He sounded contrite, but simple thanks weren't enough, and I just glared back at him, too. But, as always, he sallied on regardless.

"We really worked hard to keep very close tabs on you at all times. And once our people saw that you'd been abducted from Church Street, they set off in immediate pursuit of the car and the Embassy man who was riding your motorcycle. Unfortunately, they lost sight of both vehicles around Marble Arch. So they radioed in, and we put out an all-points bulletin on you. Then about an hour later, both the car and motorcycle were spotted going through Eton High Street. And then not too long afterwards, they were seen again out on the Ascot Road, just beyond Windsor. We immediately put up a cordon of road-blocks in and around the area. After which it was a question of closing the net until we finally managed to locate their car in the coach-builder's yard."

It all sounded so well planned and scientific, but that hadn't helped me one bit, had it? I'd almost died. What did they think they were playing at, toy soldiers?

"One thing, Jethro." Bosanquet's voice changed in tone, just enough to alert me. "What did happen inside the garage? Did they fall out among themselves? Was that it? Because we found the motorbike all smashed up, and everyone else either dead or in a very bad way."

They'd made a right meal of it, and now all of a sudden they wanted me to feed it to them on a plate. Well, bugger that, I thought, they're not getting another thing out of me.

"Yes, that's exactly what happened," I said. "They started arguing among themselves as to who should have the honour of doing me in first; the bloke with the white-hot pincers or the bugger with his big, ham-shaped fists. And then Krapsick, or whatever the bleedin' hell his name was, got very grumpy, because he'd brought along his electric train set and wanted to run over some of the finer points of it with me. So then everyone started joining in, even Flash Harry von Bentink. And then they started arguing with shooters, and God knows what else. How the fuck do I know what went on? I was spark out of it for most of the time, wasn't I? For all I know, it could've been some of Messima's goons impatient for their money. I couldn't see their faces clearly, but it definitely seemed like they had some right villains in there with them."

I hoped my little outburst would satisfy them, especially that last bit about Messima, as I don't think any of his men had been at the garage. I was still very annoyed with Walsingham and Bosanquet for stitching me up, so it felt really good blowing some smoke up their arses for a change. The main thing was, though, I didn't want them putting two and two together and coming up with Seth.

"Yes, yes, of course, that must've been what happened, or something very much like it. How else could it have resulted as it did?" Bosanquet was doing very well, convincing himself, so I thought it best to leave him to it. But Walsingham was another matter.

"Von Bentink died a nasty death, as perhaps befitted a man of his unsavoury nature and reputation. Herr Krepstok still lies in a coma. One of his men was all but cut in half by a shotgun. And of the two fortunate enough to be left alive, I think one may walk again with the aid of sticks, but the other probably never will. Whatever happened inside the garage made for one hell of a bloody mess, both literally and figuratively. And the entire affair is still under a 'D-notice,' while diplomats from both sides deliberate upon the matter and ready their reports on the incident for official consumption."

I must've made some sort of farting noise or something, because Walsingham turned, chin to his chest, and looked at me from beneath his eyebrows. "But all in all, I can't say I'm too displeased with the outcome."

I returned his stare, blank look for blank look, and tried my best not to swallow, but he didn't even blink as he moved in for his kill.

"There may well have been no honour among thieves, and von Bentink may indeed have had a falling-out with members of Messima's gang, but there are still one or two little loose ends that need tidying up." He paused. "The thing is," he said, "we can't account for these."

It suddenly started raining Christmas wrapping paper again, the exact same sort that I'd seen only minutes before, and that even at that moment was lying in torn pieces on the floor under my bed. And then two lovely turtles dropped from out of the sky onto the red bed-blanket. Morrie Templeton's best; real works of art, leather like butter and all the seams hand-stitched on top, so as to leave the finger pads and finger sides without any unseemly encumbrance from other dutifully working digits. Things of beauty they were, even lying there on top of the blanket; they were all black and slippery and slithery; they were poetry in motion. As Ray would've said, they were turtles par excellence.

"Nice gloves, are these for me? You shouldn't have," I said.

Bosanquet was in then, as fast as a rat up a drain-pipe. "Yes, they are for you, but the message on the wrapping paper says they're to you from a couple, with the names of Seth and Dilys. Friends of yours?"

I just as quickly put two and two together. "Oh, yeah, old, old friends of the family, from way back when. They gave me the presents weeks ago, in case they didn't see us all again before Christmas. Stupid me, I must've left them in one of the saddle-bags on the motorbike."

Bosanquet looked at me as if he hadn't believed a word I'd said. So I threw something else in for luck. "I think there were some stuff in there all wrapped up for my sister, Joanie, and her husband, Barry. You didn't happen to come across them as well, did you?"

It rained presents again, and Seth and Dilys's Christmas gifts to Joanie and Barry sailed through the air and landed next to the turtles. By the look of it, it was probably a scarf and a pair of socks. I chanced it. "It's a lady's scarf, a bottle of *4711* perfume, and some socks, I think, they said it was. And very nice, too, in all this weather we're having."

"Very well, then. I think that helps bring things to a closure." It was Walsingham. "For the time being, we'll disregard the other items we found that were supposedly destined for the BBC. They were a little out of date, anyway." I held my breath, but he carried on. "Simon, work up a couple of official releases along these lines, will you? One. 'That the bodies of two foreign diplomats, recently reported as missing, have been discovered, the apparent victims of a tragic road accident. Police believe the men were involved in a collision with a motorcycle that must have gone out of control due to extremely hazardous conditions. And that the resulting crash appears to have been the cause of their unfortunate and untimely deaths.' Got that? Good. And, two. 'That after extensive investigations, authorities believe that rumours of certain secret dealings between an international diamond smuggling operation and members of London's gangland appear to be totally unfounded, despite unconfirmed reports of a number of a recent deaths having been formerly linked to such an association.' That sort of thing."

I half-smiled. He was good at covering tracks; he'd really given them the old one-two. "Yeah, that sounds about right, Mr. Walsingham, sir. Funny lot, those foreigners. Because when all's said and done, you never know what's going to get them going off their heads, do you, especially when there's a Malt, er . . . I mean someone like Messima in the middle of it all."

They looked at one another. I couldn't tell whether they were amused or pissed off. Then Walsingham nodded.

"And Simon, you'd better have DCI Browno bring in Mr. Messima for questioning about his dealings with Herr von Bentink. He deserves having his knuckles rapped until he learns we take a very dim view of British villains secretly consorting with foreign powers. Have them pressure him and keep him in custody for as long as possible. Release him only after his legal brief starts yelling 'habeas corpus.' And then have them re-arrest him on a new charge the moment he's released. Harass him hard for a week or two, he'll soon get the message. Further, have someone in the press come up with some unseemly stuff about Messima being Soho's 'Emperor of vice' and London's biggest call-girl racketeer, that sort of thing. That young reporter fellow you've had your eye on for a while, what was his name?"

"Duncan Webb, sir, of the *People*."

"Yes, Simon, I think he should do nicely for a start. Then have someone else on one of the rival Sunday papers come up with something on the current outbreak of gangland feuds and rivalries."

"Yes, sir, it'll be a pleasure."

Seeing how tickled they were getting with themselves, I jumped into the breach then, with both feet. "What about Tanyia, how's she doing? Is her leg healed? Is it possible for me to see her sometime? Or better still, perhaps she could even come and see me for a visit?"

They both really looked pained then. I started to tidy up all the things on my bed, I mean I had appearances to keep up.

Bosanquet even sounded quite apologetic about it. "Well, Jethro, I don't think that's really going to be possible, you see—"

But Walsingham, as was his wont, put the boot right in. "Jethro, I want to thank you for bringing both the girl and the 'missing' book out safely. The two code-books have already proven themselves to be of inconsiderable value. And as for Miss Arzhak, well, let us just say that she is safe, on the mend, and being well looked after. She sends her heartfelt thanks to her 'Mr. Burglar.' As, indeed, do we all." Then he cleared his throat and that was that, subject closed.

I blinked, but I'm not sure whether I had something in my eye, or whether I was just thinking about what he'd said. Because then he threw in, "And as to your close friend, and confidant, Mr. Raymond Karmin, let us just say that now that everything has reached what I deem to be a very satisfactory conclusion, he'll be free to rejoin you, shortly."

Then without missing a beat, it was, "Simon, it's time we were leaving. Jethro, you need to get your rest. After all, you've got to get yourself back fighting fit, you never know when you might need all your strength." Then he added, as if it was almost an afterthought. "It's odd, but I have the distinct feeling, our paths might well cross again somewhere." I didn't find the thought of that at all funny, but the bastard just smiled, stepped back, set his bowler on his head and saluted me with his tightly furled umbrella. "Belated Christmas wishes, Jethro, old chap, and do and be sure to have a happy and prosperous New Year." And with that he executed a perfect about-turn, and quick-waltzed out the room.

Bosanquet only stopped long enough to nod his agreement, and do his own version of an officially concerned smile. "I'm truly sorry, Jethro, that you had to go through what you went through and that you had to suffer the beating, as well as all those burns. But, however you managed it, I'm awfully glad you survived in one piece." Then he smiled a real honest-to-goodness smile. "All in all, old chap, you're quite a bloody wonder. See you around, sometime. Cheerio."

And with that he disappeared off into the corridor in a puff of smoke. And there I was, left twiddling my thumbs. I looked down. Well, at least those thumbs of mine now had two new pairs of turtles to play around in. "Two turtledoves, and a partridge in a friggin' pear tree to you and all," I sang to the room.

Then a worm of an idea wriggled its way into the back of my mind, and I smiled my best Fu Manchu smile. Once I was back on my feet, I'd get even with Mr. Walsingham. I'd visit him with a special little creep of my own. I'd ruffle his feathers a bit, take the furl out of his umbrella, blunt a few creases, and see how he liked it. What a hoot that would be. Nothing taken, of course, just one or two little things rearranged and pushed out of line. Well, I mean, if a good idea isn't worth stealing, what is? Psychological warfare, I think it's called.

Suddenly feeling a lot better, I looked round the hospital room, the lord of all I surveyed. It wasn't much, but for the moment it was as safe a harbour as I was ever likely to get. So I twiddled my thumbs some more, and wondered where all the doctors and nurses were; down the canteen swigging tea, and scoffing a black-market tin of chocolate-covered digestive biscuits, probably, the greedy so-and-sos.

I tried humming a Christmas carol to myself, but it started sounding too much like the bagpipes, so I gave it a rest.

Then I remembered that Walsingham had said that it was almost New

Year. I'd missed Christmas, and silly, sentimental bugger that I am, I found I was really quite sad about it.

Oh, well, I thought, it would soon be time for some "Auld Lang Syne," or whatever the hell that was, when it was at home. But then I thought of all the noise the Jocks would make, celebrating that Robbie Burns character, and piping in their haggis for Hogmanay. "God give me strength," I sighed, "and some cloth ears as well."

I felt disgruntled again, and as so often happens, like goes to like and bad goes to worse, and Messima slithered and slid into my mind. After Browno had finished with him, Messima would be like a bear with a sore arse for weeks afterwards. And until he'd worked off his temper, people round Soho would find themselves getting striped for no reason at all. I knew he'd be mightily pissed off at missing out on his two thousand quid, but then again, maybe he'd already got his hands on his money, in which case everything would be just fine and dandy. I felt my mood begin to brighten.

But before I even got halfway to a smile, I had another thought. If he hadn't actually got his money there'd be hell to pay, and I'd probably be the one who ended up doing the paying. I suddenly began to feel very unwell again. And worse, there'd still be the little matter of him hearing that I'd been on the creep again, when I'd told him on my word of honour I'd given it up for good. I'd have to do a special job for him, just to make amends. He could never walk away from an offer like that, could he? I tell you, there's never any rest for the wicked, is there?

Then, out of nowhere, I had a bright idea. I'd let Messima find out through a snout or two, that it was really Billy Hill and Jack Spot that'd set me up for the Embassy creep. That'd put the kibosh on him, he'd have to take up the matter with them then, and he wouldn't want to do that now, would he? Problem solved. I began to feel better. But then, I thought, if word of that got round the manor, there'd be the little problem of having to square it away with Jack and Billy themselves, and that'd mean I'd have to do a job for them. Or maybe even two, or three, or four. My headache returned with a double thump.

I tried to get my head down, but all I could think about then was that ward sister from the Commandos and her soddin' great big needle. See what I mean? From bad to bleedin' worse. I tossed and turned for a bit, and I may even have managed to doze off for a minute or two, because the next thing I knew the old copper had stuck his head round the door for the final time. "Here you are, matey," he said, cheerily, "someone left this outside for you, and I thought I'd best bring it in."

It was a big basket of fruit, and right in the middle of it all was a bunch of bananas. I couldn't believe it. And neither could the copper.

"Someone must like you an awful lot, we 'aint seen hide nor hair of bananas like them, since before the war."

"Yes," I said, reaching for the card that was stuck to the basket with a pin. It said, 'Keep your pecker up, old son. And don't let the buggers get you down. And if anyone tries it on, you just pop their weasel.'

The copper was trying to read upside down so I handed the card to him, but he still couldn't make head or tail of it, so he just put it back down on the bed beside the fruit.

"Only I'll be off, now. I've been told to pack it in outside. That means the top brass all think you're as safe as houses now, and no one's going to be bothering you."

Safe as houses? That didn't give me much cheer, but I knew he meant well. "Here," I said, "you have the bananas for you and yours. I know it's a bit late, but merry Christmas."

He didn't quite know what to do, but his hands began to reach for the lovely, long-fingered, green-edged, yellow fruit anyway.

"Well, only if you're sure then. Ta. Thanks very much from me and the missus, and the kids as well. Only they've never seen one for real like, other than in their school books or in *Picture Post*."

I smiled and said, "Well, I hope they enjoy them all, then."

And then his voice suddenly turned hoarse, and he stepped out from behind his uniform, and he looked straight at me and said, "So, look, I still don't know who you are, or what you did to get yourself stuck in here. But the word is, you did us all some real good somewhere, and it cost you. So, even though you make this old copper's nose of mine twitch like mad, you take care of yourself, you thievin' bugger. And I mean that, whether you're a real bloody tealeaf or not. Any road, all the best to you. And cheers."

And with that he took his bunch of bananas and left. And I was alone, and for the first time in weeks it felt like I wasn't being watched all the time.

"Yes, we have no bananas," I sang, "we have no bananas to—" I stopped short. Inside the basket of fruit where the bananas had once been there was an envelope. It was marked 'Private' and it had my name in block-capital letters on the front. I reached for it, and felt there were several hard, round things inside, about the size of a shilling. I ripped the envelope open and the gold-foil seals from off the tops of five bottles of The Glenlivet fell out onto the bed. I unfolded the letter, and immediately recognising Ray's hardly legible scrawl, I read it hungrily:

> 'You silly sod, you should have been more careful. But I have been assured you're well on road to recovery. Good. Am still down by the sea, courtesy of an old BM Reading Room chum. (A close friend of Mr. W.'s!) Was told it was for my own health, but think it was more to keep you in line.
>
> Called BB's Church Street Irregulars. Told them BB will be back with his bugs in New Year. Cheered them up no end.
>
> People here all returning to London and other duties. House will be empty, but for cook and gardener. Food's good. Also there are still 7 bottles left of your favourite single malt as of time of writing. Come down, pop your weasel, and stick your beakle in Mr. W.'s treacle. We'll eat, drink, and be merry. And then talk of cabbages and kings until you're ready to go home. Mr. B. says transportation is all arranged.
> Cheers.

There was no date, no signature, and no address. There never was with Ray, you either knew it was from him or you didn't.

So, my reward for it all was going to be a nice, New Year's holiday down by the sea, no doubt with the rain pelting down in buckets and the wind blowing a ten-force gale. I only hoped that the snow would have gone off on holiday somewhere by the time I got there. But with food for mind and body, and single malt as spirit for the soul, yes, it definitely had its appeal. I could do with some fresh sea air, too. I'd pop down and visit when I got a bit stronger. A couple more days should do it, and then I'd definitely get my skates on and go.

I sighed, and realised how much I missed . . . missed everybody. I missed my old mum and dad. God bless 'em. And dear old Vi, too. God bless her, too. I missed Joanie and Barry. And my old friend Ray.

I missed all the lads that worked the theatres and the halls, the pubs and the market stalls. And I missed Marilyn, and Natalie, and Gloria, and Sandra, and all the other girls I knew and loved around town. (And I promised myself that when I got home, I'd take each girl out, in turn, and tell her just how much I really, really loved her.)

But I suppose, the real truth of it was, I realised just how much I missed London itself. All the bustle and the noise, and the fog, and the smoke, somehow seemed full of warmth and charm to me now.

Spottsy had been right, the Smoke never leaves you, it goes all the way through, and for ever. It was my home, and always was. And it always would be.

When I was a young tearaway I'd hated the place with a passion, and I hadn't been able to think of the city as anything but a cold-hearted prison. And just like Ernie Mott, that Cockney character Cary Grant played so well in that film of his, *None But the Lonely Heart,* I'd wanted with every bone and breath in my body to get out and away from London, for good, and for ever. And never once look back.

And now here I was, and I couldn't wait to get back to the godforsaken, stinking, horrible, lovely, wonderful, blessed mess of a place. Funny, isn't it, what you start to miss, once you realise it could have all so easily been gone for good?

I scooped up the five gold-foil seals and dropped them one by one into the basket, and put the whole lot down onto the floor beside the bed. Then I lay back, closed my eyes, and snuggled up under the blanket like I used to do when I was a kid. And then I just let myself drift off.

It didn't seem too long, though, before I started to feel a bit peckish. And so I sat up again, and looked round for the paper bag of fruit that Dilys had popped on the bedside table, and it jumped right into my hands and no messing.

I peered inside. Apples and pears, just the things to climb your way back to health with. I took out a pear and began to eat it, feeling happy for no other reason at all, than the lovely sweetness of the fruit.